BOOK FOUR OF THE LIFE & DEATH CYCLE

THE SEEDS OF VERMILLION

E.S. BARRISON

Dedicated to Grandma Rhoda & Grandpa David

You taught me that our past holds the key to the future.

I hope you see that in this book as well.

To Kainan
Knoll
Hutch's Creek
Newbi
Ar
To Heims Norte
The Capitol
Maedee's Outlook
Ab Aeterno
Grover's Marsh
Opal's Canyon
Stilette
To Rosada
To Heims Sur
To Volfium
To Proveni

Graycott
To Spinoza
To Evylain
To Delilah
Errat
To Yilk

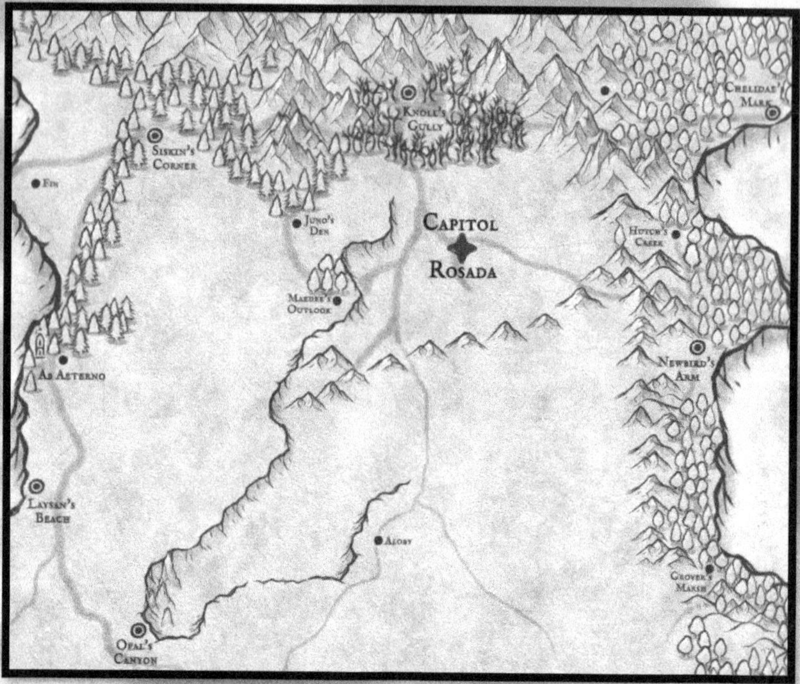

Siskin's Corner
Fen
Knoll's Gully
Chelidae' Mark
Juno's Den
Capitol
Rosada
Hutch's Creek
Maedre's Outlook
Ab Aeterno
Newbird's Arm
Laysan's Beach
Aloby
Opal's Canyon
Grover's Marsh

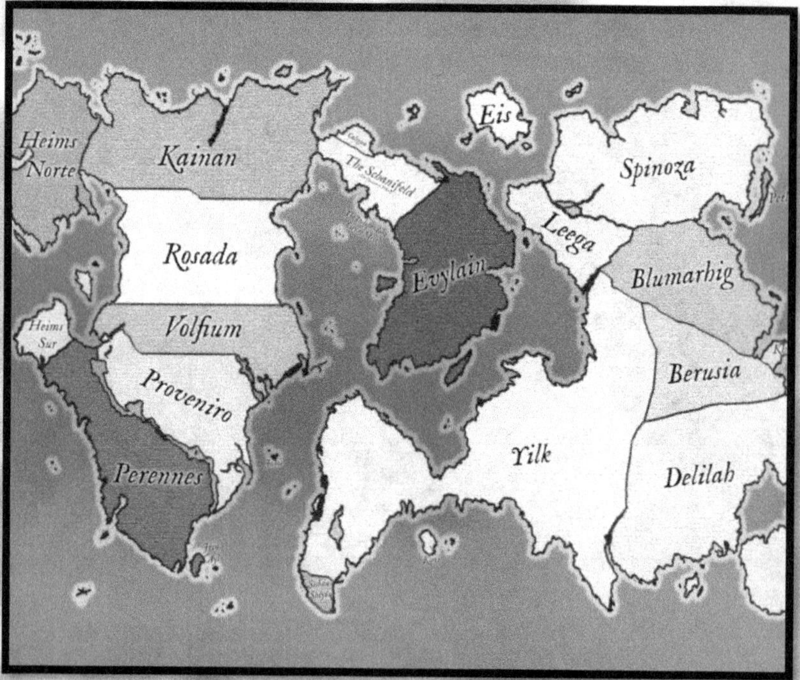

Heims Norte
Kainan
Eis
Spinoza
The Schanifeld
Rosada
Evylain
Leega
Volfium
Heims Sur
Blumarhig
Proveniro
Berusia
Perennes
Yilk
Delilah

THE COUNCIL OF MIST KEEPERS

NINGURSU
The God of Death

AELIA
The Healer

TOMAS
The Peacemaker

JULIETTA
The Painter

JIANG
Null

MALAIKA
The Cartographer

ALOJZY
The Architect

CAROLINE
The Illusionist

BRENT
The Story Collector

THE TOWERS IN THE MIST

The tower moved across the landscape in a cloud of mist and dust. Christof clenched the windowsill, eyes locked on the horizon as the Capital emerged from the smoke. *Soon.* That word hung in the air with every passing moment. Soon he would leave this nameless tower, abandon the façade of a nameless guard, and once again be the loyal son of a captain and guard of importance.

Well, he wasn't a son of a captain anymore.

Whenever he closed his eyes, death returned to him with the crashing of glass. His father's body and lain before him, strewn out over the pews in the destroyed

Tower of Ab Aeterno. Beneath the broken Year Glass, his father had fallen.

All because of *that girl.*

Christof clung to that memory. Everything that had gone wrong in the past couple of years could be traced to *her.* Briannabella Smidt, the girl he had fawned after for all those years; he never imagined that she would pulsate with magic so repulsive that it left his stomach knotted and head turning. Every way of her fingers gave birth to destruction.

With those delicate hands of hers, she killed his father.

And the Tower of Ab Aeterno fell.

Now, for almost two months, Christof had been trapped in an indistinct tower, circumnavigating the nation of Rosada. He held no rank in this tower, a mere cadet after years of service. Outcast. Alone. He hadn't trained with any of these guards. The captain only ever called him "cadet" and nothing more. *Nothing.* That was the word, wasn't it?

At least soon, he would be back with Jemma, the pious sister of the Order who had locked Christof in a prayer of enticement. He crawled into her chambers and worshipped her like the Effluvium itself. Yet, he hadn't heard from her in two months, leaving him floundering alone in a tower with no rank.

He grunted, squeezing the windowsill so tight, his knuckles turned white. This was what he got for saving Jemma's life. No honor. No rank. Just a nameless position in a nameless tower. Why did he bother? Sure, Jemma enticed him with her blessing, but was it worth not avenging his father's death? If he had killed Briannabella Smidt, the little terrorist with a knack for plants, wouldn't that have given him a true honor? He'd have ended the life of the girl who had ruined his country, tainted his beliefs, and left him empty.

But no. That wasn't the path he took.

And now, the uncertainty hung in the air: did Briannabella Smidt live?

If she did, and he saw her again, would he have the heart to kill?

"Cadet!"

Christof straightened his back and turned. "Captain Rivers."

The towering Captain Rivers stood in the doorway, his body casting a long hulking shadow over Christof. He did not smile as he spoke. "Stop daydreaming, Cadet. We'll be arriving shortly."

Christof glanced back towards the window. The Capital still waited in the distance, flickering in and out of the deepest crevasses of the mist.

"Cadet? Are you listening?"

"Yes, sir. Coming, sir."

"Hmph." Captain Rivers left, removing a flask from his hip as he left.

Christof narrowed his eyes as the captain disappeared. Something about the captain made him uneasy. Captain Rivers did not hail from Rosada; with insurmountable height, unusually long hair, and a constant hankering for alcohol, it left Christof wondering why the Guard put this *foreigner* in charge of a squadron. Did he even believe in the Effluvium? Would he defend Rosada to his grave?

Christof restrained his doubt and followed Captain Rivers down the tower. Other members of the Guard joined him in his descent, and with each slowing groan of the tower, they swayed in unison.

One step, two steps; polished and poised.

That was the way of the Guard. Everyone blended, everyone behaved, all for the Effluvium and for Rosada.

He followed in step behind the other cadets. As the tower slowed, they gathered in the lower bunker, still like a statue, waiting as the different lieutenants readied the doorway. Each lieutenant bore that same determination except for one who briefly caught Christof's attention. Amongst the ranks, he looked out of place, his uniform slightly too big and face heavy.

But Christof's attention returned only to the door, perfectly still, ready to hold to his duty and protect his vows.

For order.

For Rosada.

For the Effluvium.

A beat passed.

The gear on the outside of the bunker door churned. With each creak, the loitering, obnoxious scent of gasoline and smoke tore through the air. As the door fell open, mist entered, wrapping around the Guard and pulling them forward, one step at a time. Step by step, one by one, in unison, they strode forward, out into the crunching grass.

Christof peered over the heads of his fellow cadets. At first, nothing appeared on the empty plains. Why did they stop here? There was nothing more than the Effluvium, locking them tight in prayer.

But as they gathered, a uniform entity, more towers emerged from the mist, gathering for miles, their gaze dominating. All the same. All unified.

For order.

For the Effluvium.

Christof stiffened as he took his place amongst the droves of guards. Again, the same as everyone. Nothing more.

A nameless cadet in the crowd.

Only the scar tissue on his face set him apart, a constant reminder of the destruction of his home. He'd escaped with his father and Senator Cordova after Bria Smidt ignited the vagrants.

His thoughts always came back to her. Why? She kept a hold over him, an obsession lingering on his lips like a kiss. Even now, after everything she did, he thought of her more than Jemma, about the life he could have had with her.

If it wasn't for her attraction to that buffoon and vagrant, Brenton Harley. If she had accepted his marriage proposal all those years ago and let Brent Harley rot in the Pit, would they be standing amidst this smog waiting for war?

Christof did not flinch at the thoughts. They were constantly there, his intrusive companions. And with them, he would honor the death of his father.

No. Avenge it.

As more guards gathered and Christof took his position beside other members of his squadron, the entire plain grew silent. Everyone waited. Why had they been told to stop so close to the Capital?

That was the question, wasn't it? Why?

Why?

Why had the vagrants rebelled? Why had magic reemerged from the shadows?

Already, Christof could feel the silent stories being shared amongst the guards; those illegal stories hid in the shadows, and even at night, he heard guards pass these stories like common hobnobbing. Didn't they understand stories were illegal? Didn't they understand stories dismantled the entire premise of the Effluvium?

That was why they fought; that was why they were here.

Right?

The silence deafened Christof as he stood amongst the guards. Waiting.

Watching.

Unmoving.

Even as a light drizzle fell.

But, as the rain fell, the mist opened like a curtain. Guards gathered farther than Christof could see, filling the space between over thirty towers circumnavigating the empty plains. In the center of it all, like a beacon, stood a smaller tower constructed out of a hodgepodge of different architectural fixtures. Combined with a misshapen Year Glass, a tall radio transmitter, and a tremendous spyglass, it looked more like an invention by some obnoxious engineer than a tower.

But Christof couldn't take his eyes away from it as a few people climbed to the platform at the top of the tower. Even from a distance, Christof recognized the stout older man. Beside him waited a woman in a blue robe, her red hair falling to her shoulders like a plague of fire.

Senator Cordova stood beside Jemma Reds, his commanding presence like the gaze of the sun. Christof could barely make out as Senator Cordova removed something off the radio transmitter and held it over his mouth.

Static buzzed, bouncing from tower to tower, until his voice followed.

"Thank you for joining us here. Today marks the change we have been expecting for months now," Senator Cordova boomed.

Silence.

"As you are all aware, the region of Knoll's Gully fell to the hands of vagrants eight weeks ago. We have not been able to reclaim the region. The Necrowood has become unnavigable. And the magic that was hiding in Knoll has grown beyond our wildest imaginations."

Still silent, Christof maintained his composure, eyes locked on Jemma as she stood beside the Senator.

Poised.

Calm.

Loyal.

The Senator continued, "We have gathered as many squadrons here today as a promise, above all else: Rosada will not fall. We are more powerful than some reckless Magii. We are stronger than the stories they have exchanged throughout the country. And we will protect the Effluvium, just as we have for a thousand years."

Stillness.

Silence.

A beat.

"We have been fortunate enough to form a couple of alliances over the past few weeks that will help us reclaim our great nation. Kainan in the north has volunteered to send reinforcements. In addition, we have obtained multiple experts from across the world who will help us defy these hideous Magii. Over the next few months, there will be changes, but ones that are necessary for the security of Rosada."

So that's what's up with Captain Rivers, then, huh? Christof scanned the area for his captain but could not find him, refocusing on the Senator.

"There is a saying though, that sometimes, to defeat your enemy... you must become them," the Senator continued. "And while it is regrettable, we have harnessed magic to our own accord."

Murmurs filled the crowd. Christof's stomach churned, but he didn't move.

"Do not fret, for I promise, we did it under the guise and supervision of the Effluvium. Our very own Elder An Drew helped us prepare this abnormality, so it may behave just as we need and end magic once and for all." Senator Cordova raised his hand. "I understand the concerns. I understand the worries. But this is all for the best of the Effluvium. And today, we will show you exactly why. Sister Jey Ma, if you may?"

Jemma stepped forward, looking like a regal goddess in her royal blue robes. She stared out across the droves of soldiers before glancing back once at Senator Cordova.

Christof held his breath. What was Jemma doing?

She held out her hands. Around her, the mist gathered.

Then, exploded into an array of a thousand colors.

For one moment, everything froze.

And the Effluvium wrapped itself around the towers and the Guard, locking them each in a prayer of awe and fear.

CHAPTER TWO

THE WOMAN IN THE FOREST

Yaz loved the forest.

Especially now that it was green.

It provided her a blanket of comfort, despite the gnawing migraine working its way through her head. Ever since she'd escaped the Council of Mist Keepers, the headaches became her constant companion. Only in the forest did she find solace, away from the bustling city of Knoll and the constant bickering of her new friends Chander and Anandi.

Even at night, sleep provided no relief. Most nights, Yaz lay awake on her makeshift cot, unable to fight the nightmares rippling across her brain. Despite escaping the grasp of the Council of Mist Keepers, heralded by an evil skull named Ningursu, almost two months earlier, she couldn't stop dreaming of them. Everything had happened so fast. Ningursu lured her away from the only home she ever knew with a promise of greatness. Despite only knowing the makeshift tower that her guardians, Ms. Kai and Mr. Nasr, used to travel the landscape, she couldn't escape the allure of adventure and family.

Really, they only wanted her as a mere weapon. With the help of strange elixirs and an abundance of mist, she learned to control monsters made of nightmares.

Or maybe they really controlled her.

Either way, the pernicious Mist Keepers didn't care if it caused her to lose her life.

At least until a kind Mist Keeper, who told stories with a nice smile, saved her. He called himself Brent, but before she could learn more, he disappeared with the rest of the Mist Keepers in the middle of the forest. Yaz remained alone with two women in the heart of a battle.

One woman became a tree, and with her transformation, brought the forest to life with a promise of protection.

And in the city of Knoll, people whispered that the Forest Queen had returned with a fury of life, bringing color back to the bonelike forest called the Necrowood.

And amid that newfound greenery, Yaz found peace.

Not that she wasn't thankful for everything the other woman who she'd met months earlier did for her. That woman, who called herself Lana, brought Yaz back to her home in the shanty part of the city called the Pit. She gave Yaz a warm cot and a place to stay in the Pit. Since then, Yaz rarely saw Lana and instead meandered the streets of the Pit alone.

At least until she met Chander and his sister, Anandi.

She met them a week after being brought to this shanty town while gathered in the square to get food. Chander was a quiet boy a few years older than her, with contemplative gray eyes and a large personal space bubble. If Yaz sat too close, he inched away at once, scowling whenever someone brushed up against him. He only let his sister Anandi into that space. If he was darkness, she was light, always bubbling with ideas and adventures. Yaz clung to her joy, following Anandi into the flourishing Necrowood and even to meet the smoke-like dragon perched on the hill overlooking the city.

But even Anandi's friendship did little to quell her nerves. Only in the Necrowood did she breathe without fear. There, she knew, no bad person would find her.

Not the Mist Keepers.

Not the monsters.

No one.

Well, except for Chander and Anandi.

"Yaz! There you are!" Anandi shouted from the trees. She bounded to Yaz, her long black hair flowing behind her. She wasn't much shorter than Yaz, despite being two years younger. With a pep in her step, she approached, smile wide. "What're you doing here all alone?"

Yaz adjusted her glasses and shrugged. "I like it here."

"Well, you wanna come exploring with us?" Anandi bounced on the soles of her feet. "Please! You know how to get to the good spot!"

"Anandi, it's late. We shouldn't be out here. We can go there tomorrow," Chander mumbled as he fumbled with a smoke. He lit it with a single match, then stomped the flame out on the ground.

Anandi glowered at her brother. "I thought you weren't going to smoke anymore! What would Grandpa say?"

"Grandpa is dead..." Chander continued, shifting the dirt with his foot.

"But he wouldn't like it!"

"If you don't like what I do, then why don't you hang out with the other kids? There's plenty of them, and you can leave me alone." Chander took a swig of his smoke.

Yaz wrinkled her nose and turned her attention back to the forest. Her glasses fogged up beneath the summer humidity. While many children loitered in Knoll now, free from the grips of the pernicious towers rising above the city like skeletons, she had yet to mingle with most of them. Back when she traveled the world with Ms. Kai and Mr. Nasr, she never interacted with many other children.

Anandi continued arguing with her brother beside Yaz, "I wanna stay in the forest, though! It just smells when you smoke!"

"Well, deal with it." Chander snapped.

Yaz said nothing, instead climbing to her feet and following behind the two siblings. She never had siblings of her own or really knew any of her family. Years ago, for whatever reason, they gave her to Ms. Kai and Mr. Nasr. She only held quiet recollections deep in her heart, distant stories that might have been nothing more than whispers.

Did her parents even remember her?

Did Ms. Kai and Mr. Nasr?

Her thoughts wandered as the siblings bickered alongside her. Yaz didn't have any destination in mind, following the quiet path in the forest to the deepest greens and brightest colors. Perhaps if she followed far enough down this path, they'd stop arguing. After all, it'd been so much quieter when they weren't there.

Not that Yaz would ever say that.

As Yaz led them deeper along the path, the siblings' argument diminished to a few quiet whispers. Yaz knew exactly where they wanted to go; it was where everyone went, deep in the forest, past the drizzling silver streams and winding roots. Brambles surrounded the clearing that called them the one that held all the secrets.

Here, the forest breathed of mist and colors.

And the Forest Queen slept.

"How do you always know where she is? Whenever I tried to find her on my own, I get lost for hours!" Anandi asked.

"I just memorized it." Yaz pushed the brambles away, wincing as the thorns cut into her hands.

"Think you'd be smart enough to bring a knife by now," Chander remarked.

"I don't want to hurt her," Yaz whispered.

"Yeah! Think about it, Chander!" Anandi pushed in front of Yaz to get a better look.

In the moonlight, the Forest Queen lay amongst the foliage. She lay there, with roots clawing over her body, her arms spread out, weaving their way into the earth. From her body, white flowers bloomed. They interwove with the roots that grew from her skin, traversing the clearing, giving life to the trees and heart to the world.

To Yaz's surprise, no one else waited in the clearing. Usually, Lana, the older woman who'd helped Yaz after she escaped the Mist Keepers, stood watch over the Forest Queen, keeping so-called "hooligans" away from the clearing. This time, the clearing held only the Forest

Queen, breathing in and out with the pulse of the forest. Where was Lana, though? Surely, she couldn't be far. Even with Yaz's curiosity begging her forward, she refused to budge past the wall of thorns. This clearing belonged to the queen and no one else. It would be wrong to invade it.

Anandi pressed her face into the brambles, unphased by the thorns. "You think she'll ever wake up?"

"What does it matter?" Chander grunted, pushing aside a few more of the branches.

"She saved us! Don't you remember the tower?"

"Then why don't you try waking her?"

"'Cause that wouldn't be nice either!"

Chander rolled his eyes and took another puff of his smoke. Yaz didn't ask what they meant about the tower. Everyone had their own stories, riddled with their own demons and darkness.

Just like her.

"Ugh! Can you stop smoking while we're here at least?" Anandi complained to her brother.

"I said if you don't like it, then go away," Chander grunted.

"No! Stop!" Anandi snatched the smoke from Chander's mouth and threw it over her shoulder, her glower stitched across her face.

Time froze as the smoke toppled through the air. Yaz's mouth dropped open. The voices of her friends drifted into the background.

The smoke toppled.

Then landed on the body of the forest queen.

Its burnt edges caught the surrounding leaves

And gasped with an uproar of flames.

Yaz cried out in fear. With a single blink, she traveled back to yellow. Once again, she was a monster, starving for magic, begging for a meal. Her mouth watered.

Become the fire. Eat the magic. Roast. Eat. Survive.

"Oh no!" Anandi screamed.

Yaz blinked, pulled back to the present with a sudden gasp.

"Shit!" Chander cursed, "C'mon! We gotta get outta here!"

Yaz protested, "But—"

"Now! Before Lana sees us!"

"Shouldn't we—"

"Yaz! Don't be dumb!" Chander tugged at her arm.

Yaz glanced back into the clearing, where the fire glimmered. Lana had risen from her spot, but the smoke suffocated out the scene.

Her stomach groaned with hunger.

But she didn't fight Chander as he dragged her and Anandi away, back into the arms of the greenery and out of the yellow.

CHAPTER THREE

GREEN

Everything was green.

So much green.

All she could see was green.

Flickering in out of the green, sleep became her companion.

For how long? She didn't know.

But then, like a gasp of air, it became yellow.

And orange.

And red.

It burned.

Everything. Everywhere.

She flailed. How could she escape it?

How could she stop the burning?

Rain.

She opened her eyes with a gasp. Fire rose in embers around her.

But so did her magic.

It came naturally, all at once. With a single gasp of will, she sent a whisper to the clouds, with tears staining her cheek. They obeyed with a thunderous clap, and in the darkness of the forest, it began to rain.

The fire died.

And Bria rose from the ashes.

Her entire body creaked like the trees in the wind as she rose to her feet. As she stood, her knees quivered as if they hadn't been used in weeks. She swayed once, only to be stabilized by the roots clinging to her skin. Her right arm, composed of nothing more than branches and roots after an unfortunate amputation, remained latched into the dirt. She tugged once to free it, but her entire body screeched in protest.

"Fuck…" Bria muttered as she sunk back into the ground. Tears stung her face as she blinked, taking in the clearing. Trees blossomed with greenery and flowers. A thick humidity, drenched with life and lacking smoke, cradled her.

And with another gasp, everything rushed back to her. She had led an attack on Knoll's Gully. She had destroyed the Tower of Ab Aeterno, and then… it all grew hazy. What happened after she fell from the top of the tower?

She remembered the pain, she remembered the mist, and she remembered people shouting her name.

Bria…

Bria…

"Bria!?"

She had heard no one approach. With energy fleeting, she didn't even bother to raise her head as they knelt beside her.

"Bria!? You're awake!"

She squinted, taking a moment to let her vision stabilize. Her voice cracked, "Lana?"

Angelana Gonzo knelt beside her.

Sweat matted her brow, trickling down her face. It caused the hourglass-shaped brand on her cheek to glisten. A legend herself, Lana bore a story that Bria knew too well. At birth, Bria entered the world with a camellia growing from her head. In a fit of psychosis and fear, Lana buried Bria — her daughter — alive in the garden.

Bria survived with a blessing of magic.

She became the queen of the legends: Rhodana.

All the while, Lana, lost and confused, rotted in Knoll's Pit.

"I can't believe you're awake! What did those damn kids do to you!?"

"What're you talking about?"

"I saw some kids running away from the clearing. I went to chase after them, but then you spoke."

"I... I don't know what happened..." Bria glanced around the clearing. "There was fire... and I woke... and I'm... I'm..." Bria winced. The surrounding rain had reduced to a mere drizzle, but she still recalled the burning.

"Fire..." Lana recited as she eyed the surrounding area. "Damn kids. Guess your magic is still strong enough to fight a bit of flame."

Bria nodded. Exhaustion had already returned, pushing her closer to the ground.

"Eh eh, no sleeping. Here, you're probably parched!" Lana removed a canteen from her hip. "Drink."

Bria fumbled with the canteen, but with Lana's help, she brought it to her lips. She inhaled the water as if she hadn't tasted it in months. How long had it been? What happened after Knoll fell?

Lana placed a gentle hand on Bria's back, keeping her upright. Her warmth comforted Bria. It was an odd comfort. Months ago, Bria never thought she would meet her mother again. Then, this mysterious woman in red from Knoll's Gully took an interest in her.

This woman, by chance of fate, turned out to be her own mother. The one they called a witch and the one who tried to kill her as a baby.

But those stories distorted the facts.

Even with those facts, Bria doubted that she would ever call Lana her mother.

They didn't speak as Bria finished the canteen. In the light of the moon, she took in the forest buzzing around her. It pulsed with green and prosperity. Life reigned. The world beat.

"This is the Necrowood..." Bria whispered. It didn't look like the Necrowood. When she arrived in Knoll, the bonelike forest greeted her as the natural border of Knoll. Knitted together by streams of silver, no life survived its maze-like pathways. Only the towers, glowering from above the canopy, could navigate it.

But now, everything was green.

Lana eyed Bria. She said nothing.

Bria glanced at her branched arm again. It remained laced into the ground. Taproots, stems, flowers, moss, and leaves decorated her skin. Upon raising her good hand to her hair, she found her hair knotted with weeds.

"I did this... didn't I?" she asked.

Lana spoke without looking at her. "You healed yourself and the Necrowood."

"How long did it take?"

"That doesn't matter."

"Lana! How long was I out?" Bria's throat tightened with the question.

Lana sighed, "Eight weeks."

"Eight weeks!?" She lunged forward at the revelation. The roots and vines tore from her skin as she pulled away from the ground. Blood gathered at the wounds, but she brushed it off like drops of rain. Even her arm snapped, causing her little branch to wither behind her ear.

"Bria! Wait!"

Lana's words didn't stop her. Nothing mattered. The world spun. Every part of her told her to run, to find a way back in time, and to forget this horrible forest. She continued wandering with looking back, wiping her eyes as she walked, trying to keep her emotions in tow. Moss coated her good hand. On her face, flower buds dotted her skin like acne, while sap masked the area beneath her nose. She felt more like a tree than a human.

More like Rhodana the Forest Queen than Bria Smidt. Perhaps they were the same.

It took all her strength to continue forward, ordering the trees to keep Lana away from her. As she hurried forward, her heart landed on one destination: Brent Harley.

She didn't know where he was, or why he didn't wait for her in the forest, but she had to find him. Surely, he had just gone back to the Pit, perhaps to tell stories to the children. That would make sense, right?

Once she found him, she'd be at peace again. He would tell her the truth and whisper comfort into her skin. His laughter would warm her. And his smile would be her waking dream.

Once she found him...

He had to be here.

She couldn't ignore it.

But something felt wrong. Deep in her core.

Her stomach flipped as she stumbled along the path.

He has to be here.

Focus.

Bria dug her fingers into a nearby tree. Pain shot through every part of her body. And with each step, the trees pulled from her energy, feasting on her.

Or perhaps she was giving her life to them.

She arrived at the edge of the forest. The tower ruins greeted her, hanging over the city of Knoll like a constant omen. But despite the destruction, not a single guard occupied the streets, leaving a kind of peace hanging in the air. Even in the heightened darkness of the evening, it was like walking into a fairy tale. The streets glowed with gas lanterns. Festivities filled the plazas. All the while, people bustled along the paths, talking and laughing. Some bore the black stamp, others with silver eyes, and others just... *people*... undeterred by the strange walks of life.

But as she walked, the earth followed. Moss grew in the cobblestone, and flowers sprouted in the dusty planters. Behind her, the Necrowood continued to sing, following her every movement and carrying with it a chance at life.

How much more would the earth have come alive if the fire didn't wake her?

And where did her magic end?

It doesn't matter. He'll be here. I'll find him. We'll be together soon.

Bria continued to move forward in a bubble. People spoke, but she didn't listen. Every step belonged to the earth; she belonged to the earth.

Would she ever be human again?

She didn't quite know where she was going or where she had been. All the buildings blended. Faces resembled nothing more than monsters.

Was she a monster?

Was everything else turning green?

Would it ever stop?

Where is he?

Where am I?

"Bria! Wait!"

Lana caught up with her. The woman looked more worn than she did in the forest. Perhaps the life of the forest gave her a newfound glow. But out in Knoll, her short black hair hung with grease while burn marks scorched her forehead beneath the sun's summer rays.

Bria turned away to lock her gaze on the city of Knoll. A few people stopped to stare at her, with a child pointing in her direction. She still couldn't hear them, as the world spun with such ferocity, all while crying her name.

She didn't flinch as Lana placed a hand on her shoulder.

"Bria."

She said nothing.

Lana's voice quavered. "We need to get you some true rest. You're still not fully healed. Please... I... we cannot lose you to the forest again. We need you."

Bria glanced at Lana. A new question formed in her throat at the single statement: *We need you.*

"Where's Brent? Is he back in the Pit? I need him." Bria asked, her voice shaking.

Lana didn't make eye contact. "Later."

"Lana! What happened? Where is he?" Once again, the tears flowed. Bria inhaled once. She couldn't be a victim to her emotions, not when her magic reacted to every single movement. Her voice cracked as she reiterated the question, "Please... tell me."

Lana sighed, then glanced back towards the Necrowood. "I don't know."

MR. PINEAPPLE MAN

Brent snuck into the galley, shifting in and out of the mist as he took each step. He rubbed his hands together, wincing at the hunger pangs mounting in his stomach as he searched along the cabinets for food. He had to act fast. The Library might have been its own city, but one wrong move and Ningursu would discover his hiding spot.

How Brent managed this over the last few weeks eluded him. He spent every day shifting through the mist, riding on the wings of stories, and suffocating in their clutches. The monster in his head mocked him. He had destroyed the Diabolo over a year and a half earlier, but it remained, clinging to him with a constant gasp of yellow nightmares. Without the medication that the immortal doctor, Kek, gave him, the Diabolo bounded back in force. Some days, he meandered the Library as nothing more than a story, reenacting movements of the other Mist Keepers, before collapsing on the floor in a fit of laughter. The mist served as his safeguard, and every time someone approached, he vanished back into the twisting maze of bookshelves and rooms.

He couldn't leave the Library, though. It'd become his prison, and when he came out of his psychosis, he recited his name and constant like a prayer. *My name is Brent Harley. My constant is Bria Smidt. And I am the Story Collector.* He raised his hand to his lips. With countless marks on his right arm, a tattoo artist created a beautiful tattoo reminiscent of tree roots. They pulsed around the black stamp on his wrist, interweaving with the veins of his hand. It had shrunken and grown over the past few weeks, but the tattoo's magic told him one thing: Bria had survived.

His memory of her kept bringing him back; the last time he saw her, she lay on the forest floor, breathing heavily, attention fleeting. What was she doing now? Had she fully recovered? With no one exiting or leaving the Library, the stories were lacking. Even the silver pools scattered throughout the Library did not shimmer with a portal to other parts of the world. If any did, well, Brent could only assume Ningursu kept watch.

He always kept watch. That damn skull never took his eyes off his Council. It had to frustrate him beyond measure that Brent fell outside his purview. But Brent had escaped Ningursu's attempt at destruction, disappearing in the mist. Now, Brent understood the mist... or at least, it came to understand him. While he still struggled to control it, with his body fluctuating between solid and gas, he could somewhat use it to his advantage. The mist became a shield within the Library, allowing him to sleep, hide, and eat.

He glanced around the galley. One of the few rooms that appeared unscathed from the events over the last year, its marble floors glistened with each step. He didn't dare steal food from the counter or the icebox, slipping deep into the confines of the pantry. His fingers danced along the shelves, searching along the different breads, vegetables, and fruits. He stuffed a loaf in his coat pocket, as well as a couple apples, a lemon, and a bag of raw potatoes. As he hoisted it over his shoulder, he paused, coming face-to-face with his worst nightmare.

"What do you want?" Brent hissed at the pineapple, staring at him from the shelf. "I'm not gonna take you, a'ight? It's not happening. You're a vile demon fruit, and you're not going anywhere near my tongue...a'ight?"

The pineapple continued to stare at him.

"Don't be like that. You should be happy. I'm not going to eat you. I mean, you'll get to live for another day."

Was the pineapple crying? No—it had to be in his head, right?

"I'm sorry, but it's a no."

Brent's head pounded as he watched the pineapple. When did it grow eyes? Or a mouth? Was it about to start talking?

He swore it opened its mouth as if to cry.

"No! Stop!" He lifted the pineapple up with his free hand. "No, no, no... no crying. I'll... I'll take you with me, but I'm not eating you. A'ight? A'ight. Good."

With the pineapple in his arms, he stepped backward, and, as if reading his thoughts, the mist engulfed him.

Stories dominated the mist. As Brent moved out of the galley, he saw everything that had happened over not just the past few months but over thousands of years. He saw Ningursu, a literal melted skull, carried on a pillow by his now-faded brother, Nedo. The head of the Council, Ningursu, bore command over his subordinates. Brent broke that chain.

And that scared Ningursu above all else.

Nedo's stories, laced deep in Brent's mind, helped him put together all the other tales bouncing around the Library. Brent helped Nedo abandon the intermediary between Life and Death. With it, he received Nedo's story: of living thousands of years, of protecting those he cared for, and of being Ningursu's slave. So as the stories wove around Brent throughout his hiding, he put the story together as a mental almanac, like a guide to the stars.

He soon learned about all the Mist Keepers in more depth than he initially understood.

Aelia, the Second Mist Keeper, bore healing abilities. But Brent had seen more in the course of his time; she healed with the mist but also knew of alchemy. She trained for centuries and thus could even heal death. Her apprentice, Tomás, had vanished from the Library after Brent helped Nedo pass through the mist. But his story, one of broken hearts and peacemaking minds, still reverberated through the Library. He wanted peace, he sacrificed his love for peace, but it was all for naught.

Tomás left the Library with Julietta, the kind Mist Keeper who forgot her history. She painted memories with the mist yet could never remember her own. Though her story lived etched in the walls of the Library, Brent could only hope he would collect enough of it to help her see again.

Then there was Jiang, the one who refused magic, whose talents lay only in his guile and strength. He fought magic as a warrior after his own family got led to slaughter, using only wit in his time as a Mist Keeper to release souls. Well, and brew his own alcohol and potions.

His apprentice, Malaika, had the weakest story. She never returned to the Library, often lost in her maps. It was amazing she trained Alojzy, the architect of the Library. Alojzy had spent little time in the Library in recent weeks, his stories often cloaked in robes from the Order of the Effluvium. He worked his hands through the world, molding it in Ningursu's image.

He tried to mold his apprentice, Caroline. But Caroline, despite everything, only wanted to be loved. She would never admit it, but everything she did was to be the best—to impress those stronger than her. The few times Brent caught a glimpse of her in the Library, shame seemed to lurch over her body; in her mind, Brent was sure she thought she had failed.

After all, Brent was the bane of the Council—the rogue apprentice, the pure Mist Keeper left untamed.

Whatever that meant.

The stories overwhelmed him. Brent struggled to put them together, to understand their truths. As he landed in an empty room, mist pulsing around him, they escaped him like a gasp of air. At his core, he held the history of the Council and a base knowledge of each member. But it was like a dream. What did it all mean? How could he use it to escape?

Brent placed the pineapple on a dusty shelf and glowered at it. The pineapple stared at him, laughing at him even.

"Stop it," he hissed, "if you saw it all at once, your head would hurt too."

The pineapple stared.

"I mean it, Mr. Pineapple Man. Don't appreciate your mocking or anything."

Despite the pineapple's relentless mocking, Brent returned to the corner of the room, emptying his pockets of food. The breads, potatoes, and fruits clunked on the floor. It didn't matter how old they were. His stomach roared loud enough, and slowly, he picked away at the food.

The pineapple might be fresh, but I'm not hungry enough to eat it.

Brent paced the room, picking away at a stale piece of bread while mumbling his constants to himself. He couldn't stay long. He could never stay long. Ningursu always watched. Even in this empty room, with blank paint canvases leaning against the wall, he would not be safe. One wrong move...

One wrong noise...

A single gasp would take away his freedom.

Wouldn't it be easier to accept imprisonment? His Diabolo chided in his head. He had tried for such a long time to swallow it down, but without his medication, it came back reeling.

Or was it the pineapple taunting him?

Brent focused on the blank canvas in front of him. It begged to be filled. Would writing the countless stories help his head stay on his shoulders? It wouldn't be hard to recall everything he'd learned.

His attention fell on a piece of charcoal lying on the floor. With a trembling hand, he picked it off the ground and began writing:

Stories. That's what everything has always been.

Creaking pulled his attention from the canvas. He glanced around once at the pineapple, then back at the canvas. He then wrote:

That's what it always shall be.

Another footstep. No. This wasn't the pineapple.

Brent dropped the charcoal and approached the fruit. He lifted it up to eye level. "What are you doing now?"

This time, the pineapple responded in a shrill voice. "Well, I am not a pineapple if that is what you are implying."

"Shite!" Brent threw the pineapple across the room.

Only for a set of slender hands to catch it.

Before him stood none other than his old teacher, Caroline Walsh. Her hair hung from her face in strings, her cloak hung loose on her body, and her skin hung like wet clothes on a line. Across her face, pale and chapped, she wore a blindfold.

But she caught the pineapple, nonetheless.

"Caroline..." Brent stepped backward, nearly knocking over the canvases. His voice ached at her name. As far as he could remember, outside of his new pineapple friend, he hadn't spoken to *anyone* in weeks. What if he made a mistake? What if he said something... ridiculous?

Too late for that.

Brent shook his head, pushing the Diabolo back in his mind. He wrapped the mist around his fingers. Could he trust Caroline? Would she tell Ningursu?

"Do you want your pineapple back?" Caroline asked, holding it out to him. She didn't move from her spot, blindfold in place, stance poised.

"How do I know you're not going to bring me to Ningursu?" Brent asked.

"I blindfolded myself, so he cannot see you. Once I caught your mop of hair and hideous stench, I decided it was better safe than sorry."

"Do I really smell that bad?" Brent sniffed his pits and scowled. "Ah, yeah. Sorry. Hard to bathe when hiding."

"But you have time to rummage through Julietta's canvases?"

Brent glanced around the room. He hadn't noticed Julietta's story. But there it was, a story of a woman meandering through the canvases, painting to her heart's desire. In some tales, Caroline joined her, smiling in a way Brent had never witnessed.

"Oh, uh...sorry."

"No, it is fine. It...only got my hopes up that she had returned." Caroline sighed, dropping the pineapple on the floor.

Brent raced over as the pineapple hit the ground and rolled over on its side. He exhaled with relief upon seeing no blemishes on its skin.

"Brent...did you just sigh in relief over a pineapple?" Caroline chuckled.

"Uh..."

"You have been alone far too long."

"It's not like I can escape the Library."

"No one can. They've locked the doors tight. I think only Alojzy can let people in and out." Caroline twiddled her thumbs. "I will not stay here much longer. I would hate for Ningursu to discover you."

"Wait! Caroline!" Brent reached for her arm. As his fingers grazed her skin, he froze. There, in that moment, he saw her story; her heartbreak, her loneliness, and her years of wandering. She'd known loneliness just like him; she had worn it on her soul, sailing across the sea in search of a cure for her disillusioned life.

Brent pulled his fingers back and inhaled, whispering his constants under his breath.

"What is it, Brent?" Caroline asked, still calm and focused.

"I...I don't know what to do. I've been causing problems for two months...but I don't know how much longer I can last. Ningursu is bound to find me, and then...then I don't know what will happen. Please...help me." He let the pineapple fall from his hands and to the floor. "Please..."

Caroline shifted her head slightly as if checking to see if anyone was watching. Her eyes remained covered. "All I can recommend is this: you have a way to obtain knowledge beyond anyone else here. Use that knowledge, and you can find your way to freedom."

"If you mean the stories... you don't... I mean... it's hard to understand everything when your head is always spinning."

"You are the storyteller, Brent. Not me. I do not understand your magic. But perhaps, if you can dissect them enough, you might unlock secrets that even I do not know. And trust me, I know very little." She smiled, then her shoulders fell. "I promise, Brent...I will seek out answers for you if I can. Ningursu is letting no one leave this Library, but know that I am on your side if you will trust me."

Brent stared hard at Caroline, cradling his pineapple close as he took in her stories. She showed no deception, no lies; her stories bore honesty as she spoke, calm and without fear.

After all, the stories never lied.

"A'ight. I'll trust you."

"Very good. I will see you again soon, but I shall not seek you out. Be safe, Brent."

"You too."

Caroline smiled one last time, then turned away in a swirl of black smoke. Behind her, she left a trail of silence. Even the stories in the room did not fill the void.

Brent carried the pineapple back over to the canvases and placed it amongst the other food. *Dissect the stories...* he squinted at the blank canvas where his scratchy handwriting stared back at him.

Like you'll be able to do that. The Diabolo mocked.

I'm a storyteller. That's what I do. Brent knelt before the canvas. He wouldn't be able to remain here forever, but at least he could begin his record.

Perhaps, like any storyteller, he needed to put the tale in writing.

He picked up the piece of charcoal and marked the number "1" on the bottom right corner of the canvas.

Then, with the stories close to his chest, he continued to write:

They say to understand who we are, who we shall be, we need to understand our tales.

I understand that more than anyone.

CHAPTER FIVE

SISTER JEY MA

Christof greased the hinge of the tower, glowering out at the smoke-riddled plains. Already, a few of the towers had left, receiving their orders from Senator Cordova and his brigade. But Christof's tower had yet to leave, left to scrummage about, waiting for new orders to be handed to them.

Yet Christof's attention fell far from his orders. Instead, he loitered in his thoughts, greasing the same hinge over and over again. What happened to Jemma in those last few weeks? She stepped out, poised as ever, only to erupt into a whirlwind of magic. She controlled the mist, and with that mere wave of her hand, everyone succumbed to her demands. Even Christof watched in awe as the mist bowed and twisted. How much more was she hiding?

And would her powers truly save the Effluvium?

Christof's stomach churned at the thought. Jemma's movements might as well have belonged to any other Magii. It didn't matter if it was for the greater good of the Effluvium. Magic was outlawed for a reason. It was unnatural, disruptive, and full of corruption. They outlawed stories for the same reason.

How could Jemma abandon those beliefs? Did she even believe them in the first place?

He gripped the hinge, digging the cloth deeper into its surface.

His father ingrained in him since childhood the horrors of magic. Christof had seen the same disarray.

How could Jemma take magic so willingly? And what did Senator Cordova do to convince her to accept its grotesque hand?

He glowered at the obscure tower loitering in the distance. What were they doing now?

"I think it is clean enough, Cadet."

Christof turned. A lieutenant approached, a smirk on his lips. Yet, despite the smile, an emptiness haunted the lieutenant's eyes.

"Sorry, Lieutenant..." Christof eyed the name on the uniform. "Drayton."

Most superiors would have flogged Christof then, but to his surprise Lieutenant Drayton merely shrugged, his attention seeming to follow Christof towards the obscure tower in the distance. It didn't move like the others, with no clear path in front of it. Each leg stepped forward, its rickety structure teetering on the edge of success and collapse.

The lieutenant spoke again, "You're Cadet Carver, correct?"

"Yes, sir," Christof said without looking at him.

"I was asked to bring you to the Curio Tower."

"The what tower?"

"The one we're looking at. The young sister there, Jey Ma... She requested your presence."

"Jemma..." Christof murmured.

"Yeah, lucky you. You must feel special, hm?"

Christof knew better than to respond, and with the lieutenant ushering him forward, he followed in step, his focus set on the tower. His stomach churned. No excitement slithered into his thoughts. Jemma had enlightened him, but now, his beliefs sat at odds. Every time he closed his eyes, he saw the Effluvium bending to her will. It reminded him of the nightmarish yellow smoke that captured his home of Newbird's Arm, that captured the entire town in a well of terrors. But this time, rather than Brent Harley or Bria Smidt or one of those other vagrants, it was the woman he said enlightened him.

He shook the image from his mind as they approached the tower. Lieutenant Drayton hadn't spoken a word since they started their trek across the field, and every other guard seemed to watch with either envy or mockery. What did they think? Were they laughing at the twenty-three-year-old cadet still not promoted after nine years? Christof knew they whispered about him. He didn't hear it, but it was common knowledge at this point. The young guards back home, led by his deceased *friend* Chet Lawry, would laugh whenever his father berated him.

He shook the judgment from his shoulders, focusing on the hymn his mother used to sing from the *One Scripture* when he was a child:

Open your arms,
Breath in once,
Do you taste its life?
It is with you,
Every step,
Every bite,
Inhale once,
Inhale twice,
It knows you in truth,
It knows you right,
So say it again,

"I am part of its soul...so it knows," Christof muttered to himself.

"What was that, Cadet?" The lieutenant slowed his pace near the tower.

"Sorry, sir. Just praying."

"Hmph. Wish I had that resolve." The lieutenant eyed the tower. "I don't have much faith anymore, but I do what I gotta do."

Christof nodded without speaking.

But the lieutenant continued as they reached the doors. "Cadet, listen, this order comes from the top. If there is anything unusual in there, please report it to me."

"Unusual how, sir?" Christof asked.

The lieutenant furrowed his brow, choosing each word with care. "Per Captain Rivers, it is already known that the Curio Tower will have some oddities. But we want to make sure every element of that tower is...in compliance with how the guard conducts itself. Senator Cordova might be...a senator...but if he is doing things that do not sit well with the guard or the country, it needs to be known."

"Like what, sir? We already know of magic."

"You'll know, Cadet. You'll know."

Christof held his breath as the iron doors of the Curio Tower slid open. He coughed as dust gathered around him, welcoming him to a shop decorated with tchotchkes and odd relics. The items made his skin crawl. These didn't belong here; they reeked of magic and demons. Even worse, the man sitting at the counter, with his haunting red eyes, held the same horrendous nature.

The man hardly acknowledged Christof as he entered. "Sister Jey Ma is waiting for you on the overlook."

Christof grunted, then turned his attention to the narrow stairwell. Unlike the stairwell in the guard tower, this one twisted and turned, stopping at different small landings leading into closed doors. His footsteps did not echo, and his breaths remained silent; he moved like a warrior, and if the walls watched, they could report no wrongdoing.

He passed the bridge of the ship, where a woman sat in the chair, looking over the range of gears and lights. Christof paused, taking in her striking beauty. Her long black hair, olive skin, and chisel jawline reminded him more of a statue than a living person. His stomach dropped as she turned to face him. Each eye shone a different color, baring into his soul.

The woman smirked, then returned to her console.

Christof snapped out of her hold and returned to his trek up the stairs.

At the top of the stairwell, a small doorway opened to the light. Smoke poured through, capturing Christof and pulling him onto the deck.

There, she waited, her red hair pinned in a bun on her head like a halo. Her blue robe bellowed behind her while smoke rose and fell at her feet.

"Christof…" She turned as he arrived. "I have missed you dearly."

"Jemma—"

"Sister Jey Ma now. I have embraced my role with the Effluvium and have hence let it cut apart my name."

"To make room for the Effluvium in your heart?"

"And in my life."

"I see."

"But…" She placed a hand on his chest. "That does not change where you sit in my life, Cadet Carver. I find you as enlightening as ever, and I want you by my side as we win this battle for the Effluvium. Magic must be controlled. Any story whispered in the shadows must be suffocated. I need someone I can trust by my side to do this."

"And what would you have me do?"

"Be my loyal guard."

"As I promised you," Christof recited.

"But more than that, Christof. Senator Cordova has shown me what is happening. Storytellers are weaving tales about a hero across our country. They have painted Bria Smidt as a hero! That cannot go on, nor can we let them speak about the beauties of magic. It has always been in the shadows. We never stamped it out. It was all a ploy that the government spewed, but they never cared." Sister Jey Ma exhaled once, closing her eyes as she continued. "According to Senator Cordova, soon we will go to the Capital. I want you here because while I take the Effluvium by its hand, you can be my eyes and ears."

"You mean...stories?"

"You and your father were always the first ones to find Brent Harley telling tales. Even other kids, you would find. But Brent especially would hide in those narrow alleyways, and you would always pull him out. I saw. Even when we were betrothed, I noticed." Sister Jey fiddled with his name tag. "You could lead this charge against the hidden rebellion that surely lingers in the streets. This could be your charge."

"My charge..." Back in Newbird's Arm, Christof had his cohort; here, he was alone. But now, he could see it clearly in his mind. He would find those whispering fallacies in the street and bring them to their knees. Tales would crumble. The Effluvium would thrive.

"And with that, if you are successful, comes that promotion I know you long for, Cadet Carver. You've been training for far too long. I want to see you become an officer. How does Private Carver sound? Or better yet, Lieutenant Carver?"

"Yes," he breathed. Every worry he had escaped him with that thought. Finally, he could taste the promotion. Sister Jey Ma had Senator Cordova's ear; no matter what they were doing, at least it was with cause. What could Lieutenant Drayton have meant by something weird other than magic? Everything else appeared...well, sound.

And a promotion. At last.

"Then you will be by my side, Christof?"

"Of course."

"Good." She leaned forward on her toes, lips grazing his mouth. His whole body warmed at her touch. "Then come with me."

He did not stray from her touch as she led him down the stairwell again. His head spun with the possibility of his future. No more sitting in a grimy tower; no more acting with no motive. Now, he had a place again. Not in Newbird's Arm. Not in Knoll's Gully.

But in the Capital.

And the prospect followed him down the stairs.

Lassoed by desire, he almost missed Senator Cordova as he slipped into a room off the stairwell.

And he almost didn't notice the red-eyed little boy on the senator's hip.

But as Sister Jey Ma led him into her room, he forgot about everything and fell into the embrace of the Effluvium.

CHAPTER SIX

THE TASTE OF IMMORTALITY

Bria lay in bed, blanket pulled up to her chin, with her dog Nix sleeping against her side. The dog had bounded towards her the minute she entered the Pit, tail wagging like a whip as she leapt into Bria's arms. The tears came at once, and with the dog at her side, she returned to her room in the tenement hall that she had shared with Brent.

Since returning, she only left her room to use the bathroom. Otherwise, she lay in bed, barely touching the food that Lana brought and refusing to answer any knocking on her door otherwise. People wanted to see her; she was already a whisper on their lips, with a story passing through the air. Every day, she heard the song.

She winced every time they spoke those words. They told a story about her like she was a queen, but really... was she nothing more than a terrorist? A heathen? A murderer?

Every time she closed her eyes, another memory assaulted her: the tower crumbling, a man's screams, and mist...

So much mist.

Her only solace came with the tattoo on her wrist, flourishing with flowers. The magic given to it by the artist Hortense told her one thing for certain: Brent Harley lived.

In what state, in what mentality, she hadn't a clue.

But he lived.

"We're going to find him," Bria whispered to Nix as she sat up in bed, taking a glance at herself in the mirror. Her hair was still matted on one side. Despite all the work she and Lana had put into brushing it out, the knots remained stubborn and angry, wrapped with branches and leaves. She brought her fingers to the side of her head. The coarse hair felt more like the ground than anything else.

Bria couldn't bring herself to cut it, instead bringing the brush to her head and continuing her slow routine without leaving her bed.

Lana and Hue, the doctor, checked on her regularly, clearing the weeds from her skin and making sure she did not slip away again. Yet, some nights, Bria could feel her body begging for the earth. Every touch spawned her magic; she could hear the floorboards, taste the air, and even smell the mold growing one floor below her. Back before the attack on Knoll, she had grown more in tune with her magic than ever before, sensing every element.

Now, her entire body remained in a heightened sense of magic. She could not shake it. One wrong move, and she might destroy the building.

Or worse.

She ran her good fingers through a few strands of hair and tugged them apart. Her branched hand still hadn't reformed in its entirety, grappling towards different parts of the room whenever Bria tried to reform it. Oh, how she missed having two working hands. At least then, they were in her control.

But no, slowly, she was becoming more plant than human in some regard.

Would the earth swallow her whole again?

She glanced back at the window and sighed. On her way back to the tenement hall a few days earlier, she had checked countless entrances to the tunnels. Lana seemed unphased whenever Bria kicked at a root. The only time Lana reacted was when Bria tried to create a sinkhole, but even that did not bring her to the tunnels.

No, the Council had locked her out of the tunnels she used to call home.

Perhaps the Council was right. They never belonged to her.

The door to her room opened as she continued unraveling her hair while lost in thought. Nix raised her head, but neither the dog nor Bria budged.

"So, this is the *noble* forest queen?"

Bria turned. Lana stood in the doorway, but she was not the one speaking. Rather, someone else stood there. Someone that made Bria's stomach churn.

"Edith..." Bria rose to her feet, trembling. This woman, with her curly red hair and wide-mouth smirk, left Bria's stomach in knots. Bria had tried to rid Edith from her mind, but every time the woman appeared, her sins returned in full force. That woman had tormented Brent in the magical city of Mert, carving the word 'reaper' into his skin. She acted without resolve and morality, wearing her immortality like armor on her chest, just as she manipulated metal to her will.

And with that resolve, she slaughtered Madame Owiti.

It had happened so fast; Brent had seen it and told Bria after the fact. Madame Owiti, Bria's friend from Mert, helped her connect with the Palaver of Immortals and Seers, led by the ancient alchemist Kek. But now she was gone.

Dead.

Her magic and sight gone, left to bleed into the silver pool that decorated the world, Madame Owiti's story faded.

Another seer lost. Another death.

Gone.

"What are you doing here?" Bria asked, her body stiff as she stared at Edith. "Why aren't you in prison? You killed Madame Owiti! You—you--"

Lana stepped forward and held her hand out. "Bria. Relax."

"Relax!? Edith killed Madame Owiti!"

"Bria, it's fine. We have given her freedom."

"Freedom!?" Bria's branched hand extended, blossoming with camellias in a single gasp. She shook her hand once, letting the flowers flutter to the floor and lace into the wood.

Edith chided, "Things aren't so black and white, girl. Ever thought I might be in the right for once?"

"In the right? You killed Madame Owiti and... and..." Bria winced. Pain shot through her side, and a gasp escaped her lips. It was too much so soon after waking. The world spun. If Brent were here, he'd be able to see the truth.

If Brent were here, would she feel so alone?

"Lie down, Bria." Lana raced to help her back onto the bed, but Bria stopped her.

"No, I'm fine." She brushed Lana's hand away and continued to glower at Edith. "You are not in the right. You only think about yourself and no one else, you bloodthirsty... ugh."

"I only think about the greater good."

"The greater good for you."

"What benefit did I gain by killing that pathetic old woman?"

Bria placed a hand against the wall, letting the wood pool around her fingertips. "You're a monster. It gives you pride."

"That's where you're wrong, girl. I spill every drop of blood with purpose."

"What about Brent!?" Bria nearly shouted, "You tortured him and—"

"He deserved it."

"Bullshit."

"Oh, and here I thought you were nice and poised. Turns out the little queen has a mouth, doesn't she?"

"Oh, fuck off." Bria waved her hand. From the floorboards, much to Bria's surprise, branches emerged from the growth-rings in the wood. They reached for Edith's ankles.

Edith bounced away from them, taking a small razor from her pocket and ordering it to extend. The metallurgist formed a sword from the swatch of metal, a mere extension of herself, and sliced through the branches in a single movement.

"You know, girl, I came here to be nice...but perhaps that is too difficult for you to accept." Edith swayed towards Bria. "Pity, really."

"You don't scare me."

"I should. I could slice you like any lumberjack in the forest. Trees bow to blades."

"This tree won't." Bria hissed.

Lana interjected, sharper than any of Edith's knives. "Oh, stop it. Both of you are acting like ridiculous children."

Bria paused and glanced in Lana's direction. She'd almost forgotten Lana was there.

Edith stepped back once but kept her blade outstretched.

"Thank you," Lana said. "If you are both done acting inappropriate, we came here for a reason."

"Oh? Really?" Bria laughed to herself and crossed her good arm over her chest. Her bad arm remained hanging at her side. "You couldn't have said to me, 'Hey Bria, just to let you know we freed a murderer'? That would have been an important piece of information!"

"You were recovering. You still are," Lana replied.

"I would appreciate it if people did not hide information from me!" Bria inhaled once, pulling back on her anger. If she let it get away from her, who knew how her magic might act?

"We wanted to wait until it was the right time."

"Basically, Lana wanted to make sure you didn't throw a fit," Edith chuckled.

"You shut up too. You're behaving just as badly."

Bria sank back onto the bed and clutched the blanket. She inhaled again, then whispered, trying her best to ignore Edith's haunting stare, "I'm sorry. It's a lot. Please...just tell me what is going on, Lana."

Lana answered without delay, "Edith is the reason you're alive."

"What are you talking about?"

"If it weren't for Edith, you wouldn't be alive. When we found you, you'd fallen from a great height. Under normal circumstances, you would have survived."

"But I have my magic."

"It's not like your magic lets you fly." Lana glanced at Edith, then back at Bria. "You were dying when I found you. Once we left the tower, I poured some water from the silver river into your mouth. Thought it was just water with how dark it was getting, but it wasn't. Turns out it was—"

"Part of the silver pool," Bria finished.

"Or, as Edith put it, magic water."

"But the pool only acts as a window or door unless an alchemist manipulates it," Bria recited to herself. While she had traveled through the strange silver pools and visited different parts of the world, she never manipulated it into other forms. That fell into the hands of the alchemists, such as Kek. What did it matter if she drank that water if Kek wasn't here to manipulate it?

"But there is one standing potion that exists within the pool that Kek established many years ago, before I was even here." Edith leaned forward, tilting on her toes. "I know you know the story, right? You know why Kek, me, Varden, and all of us are good and alive?"

Bria licked her lip. She had learned the story in the Library a few months earlier when Brent discovered the truth about Ningursu's brother, Nedo; in a pure reflection of that history, they saw the way Kek slaughtered a seer named Merta, thus granting him immortality for many years. Other seers died so Kek could keep on living.

"You killed Madame Owiti to add to the immortality elixir," Bria said slowly.

"Exactly. At death, their magic escapes their body. If they are by the pool, their magic fuels life."

"So her death gave the pool power…" Bria glanced at Lana. "And you gave me a drink from the silver water that comes from that pool?"

Lana nodded, her attention locked on the floor.

She turned back to Edith. "But how would you know to do that?"

Bria tried to wrap her brain around the subject at hand. Of course, Edith didn't need reason; murder coursed through her veins without a second thought.

"Because the old lady told me to kill her."

"What?"

"The old lady. She waded into the river and said to kill her. Said it was to save the world. I didn't question much of it, but she probably saw you taking a tumble. You should have died. The elixir saved you." Edith spun her knife in her hand. "So I think you owe me an apology."

"She…sacrificed herself…for…me?" The room spun around her. "No, she couldn't have. No one should do that."

"Oh, don't be so full of yourself. She did it for the world. You're just the key."

"No one should give their lives for me," she repeated. "I don't understand why she would..." Bria stared at her fingers. "No..."

"Never seen someone so upset to discover they've been given a second chance."

"Second chance? She died! And I... This elixir...does it mean that I'm...immortal?" The word burned her tongue.

"Don't know, honestly. You were so messed up that it's hard to tell. Not sure if it focused on healing you or solidifying your magic and everything."

"What about others who drink from the river?" Bria's mind continued to race. "It's not just for me. Will everyone become immortal?"

Edith picked at her nails as she responded, "Probably not. Has to do with magic, but I don't know. Not my wheelhouse. And frankly, I don't care."

Bria stared. Her mind raced with possibilities while her heart sank deeper into her stomach. The mere thought that someone sacrificed themselves for her didn't sit right. She never wanted anyone to do such a thing. *I'm just a gardener.* She flexed her branched fingers. *But people want a queen.*

"I couldn't rationalize leaving her in the cell after she told me," Lana spoke finally.

Bria didn't respond.

"She has a lot of knowledge about...well, everything. She's been a huge help in rebuilding Knoll, and she says she can help with your magic." Lana reached out to place a hand on Bria's shoulder but retreated before touching her. "I think it would be beneficial to you."

"Whatever you think is best."

Bria climbed to her feet and slipped on a pair of shoes. Her mind continued to spin. All of this was far too much to take in at once. Did she ask for this immortality? Did she deserve someone sacrificing their life?

She didn't look at Edith or Lana as she pulled on her shoes and opened the door. Nix bounded after her.

"What are you doing?" Lana asked.

"Going for a walk. I need time to process all of this."

"Oh. Right. Just...remain calm and relax. You're recovering."

"I'll try." Bria glanced once more at Lana. The wall appeared between them again; any time emotion bubbled, neither of them dared act on it for too long. Bria didn't think she could ever call Lana her mother. They'd forever walk a tightrope between friendship and disdain.

It was for the best.

Edith cackled again as Bria shut the door. One step at a time, Bria headed down the stairs. Those who waited in the hallway paused as she passed, and even as Bria stepped outside, the groups of people gathering in the street paused.

They all stared at her.

They all waited.

Then, they cheered.

Bria slinked back, bowing her head as more people joined the applause and praise. The slowly forming crowd suffocated her with questions and their calls rocking the air. She shied away from heroism, yearning for silence and peace.

Part of her still clung to the idea she and Brent used to share of a little house in a forest tucked away from everything. Now, she could only turn her back on the crowd and race toward the trees before panic attached itself to her heart.

She let the trees embrace her. Their branches wrapped around her waist and hoisted her into the canopy, carrying her away from the commotion and into the silence of the forest.

There, she could pretend she was back in Newbird's Arm, watching the clouds from a tree in the garden.

There, she could believe this had all been a nightmare.

There, she was home.

CHAPTER SEVEN

TAP-CODE

Bria stayed hidden in the forest for hours, leaning against the trees, camouflaged by the surrounding branches and leaves. Once the trees placed her back on the ground, Nix joined her, and they huddled in the silence of the now-green forest.

She didn't want to think about what had happened. With no consent, a new magic riddled her body. Neither Edith nor Madame Owiti had asked for her permission; rather, they'd taken her life and manipulated it.

Just like everyone else.

Wasn't that what Lana did the moment after Bria was born? Or what Kek had done when they had discovered Bria's powers? Or what about the Council attempting to control her every movement?

No more. She dug her hands into the ground. Despite all her focus, she could not hear the tunnels beneath the earth. More than anything, she yearned to find Brent, then run away, far away, where no one could ever find them.

But with Ningursu watching every corner of the globe and magic pushed further back into the shadows with each passing day, it was not possible.

But how could she stop all of this? She still didn't have the strength to travel far from her home. Even after a few days, she hadn't been able to reform her arm. Every element called to her, reached for her; one wrong move and everything would collapse.

Lana had given her a book months earlier, *The Rules of the Apothecary*, that had details about every element, but Bria didn't have the time. That knowledge took years to master. With an unknown amount of time until the next altercation, everything she didn't know taunted her.

Bria missed those days when it had all been simple. The plants bent to her whims, but she was nothing more but a gardener with a few tricks. Adventure had been within reach, and without care, she could see the world. She always knew it would get more complicated.

Little did she expect that Brent Harley would be the catalyst.

She pressed her head to the tree. When she shut her eyes, she saw Brent smiling at her and fumbling with each step. Not once did she blame him, but there was no denying how he affected her future. If he hadn't entered the tunnels by accident, he never would have met the Council. He never would have seen her in the hideaway. He might have never learned of her magic.

But then what? Would Brent have married Jemma Reds as his betrothal agreement entailed? Would Bria still be in Newbird's Arm, or would she have fled?

Would there even be this uprising?

And even with all the sweat and pain and tears, wasn't this chance at freedom for the best?

But at what cost?

Bria hugged her knees close, letting her branched arm wrap around her skin. As the sun teetered in the sky, she still didn't move, letting the late summer air dance over her skin in pools of gentle sweat. Birds tweeted, the wind sang, and Nix snored beside her.

It almost seemed peaceful.

At least until a monstrous horn blew.

Bwaaamp.

Bria shot to her feet, the noise echoing. *A tower? Here?* She didn't wait for any other sounds, immediately taking to the trees to get a better view. Nix barked along the base of the tree.

"Shh!" she hissed as she peered through the trees.

Her nerves broke with a sigh.

The tower was none other than the one she'd led to Knoll all those weeks ago. She recognized its dismantled flag and vine-laced body in an instant. With that tower, she had carried a barrage of blood.

At the bottom of the tower, a few people worked, led by none other than Bria's childhood friend, Micca Fein.

She hopped through the trees before letting the branches carry her to the forest floor. Nix greeted her with a bark, then bounded towards the tower.

Part of Bria wanted to stay away from the tower, to hide in the trees and never announce her presence. But with Nix running forward, she could not hide.

"Ah, Nix!" Micca exclaimed, "Been wondering where you were at. And look at that here—it's Beebelle!"

Bria peeked out from the trees and waved at Micca. She'd known Micca for as long as she'd known Brent. When she first moved to Newbird's Arm with her father, Micca welcomed her into his entourage at once. There, she met Brent...and really, without Micca, she might have never gotten close to Brent in the first place.

In their adolescence, he was shy, quiet, and a bit of a troublemaker. At first, Bria avoided him, not wanting to get her magic interlocked with a storyteller. But Micca pushed them together, always knowing how to make her smile.

"Ah, get over here, Beebelle! Stop your hiding!" Micca rushed towards her. In one movement, he pulled her into a bear hug.

"Micca..." She choked. Tears bubbled in her throat as she sank into his arms. Micca had this way of giving hugs that reminded her of a heavy blanket; warm and kind, it was like the warmth of her grandmama's house on a cold winter day. But she didn't have that anymore.

At least she had Micca.

He patted her shoulders as he stepped back from her. "I thought I heard you woke up but wasn't too sure. Makes sense that Nix ran off to find you. Glad you're not a forest anymore. Didn't really suit you much, you know?"

Bria glanced at her feet and whispered, "I'm glad I'm not a forest anymore, too."

"What was that like? Being a forest? Did you get to do foresty things?"

"I honestly don't remember. It's like a dream. I just re-member...green." Bria ran her finger over a nearby branch. She'd lost almost two months of her life to the forest...but Brent had lost more to the Diabolo. She couldn't bring herself to feel sad over her own loss when he had given up so much of his life. And despite all that, he kept his head high.

She only hoped he remained himself, wherever he was, whatever was happening.

"Ah, damn. Wish you actually had foresty things to talk about. I wanna know if these trees are plotting something." Micca tapped a nearby pine tree.

"They're not plotting against you."

"But you said you didn't do foresty things!"

"But I know the trees. They speak to me!"

"You speak tree?"

"No! It's like a sensation."

"Beebelle, I'm not gonna judge you if you speak tree."

Bria stared up at a nearby tree. The branches waved to her, thanking her for a sacrifice she never intended to take. She sometimes forgot how much it impressed people. This was just her life, her existence—talking to trees, controlling the earth. It wasn't everyone else's reality.

Just her. Alone.

Lana had some of her magic, of course, but not to the extent Bria did. As far as Bria could tell, Lana could control some flowers and branches, but otherwise, her magic fell flat. Perhaps in a different life, Bria's magic might have behaved the same way.

She turned her attention back to Micca, redirecting the conversation. "What are you doing out here with the tower?"

"I see what you're doing, Beebelle. Don't think I'm dropping this conversation yet." Micca winked, then glanced up at the tower. "Lana wants us prepping this beauty for travel. This war is only just beginning, and even with magic, it doesn't mean we're stronger than those Order pricks. Lot of us don't got no clue about the magic or nothing."

"What've you done with it so far?"

"Not much. Took us a bit to get it back into the forest. Was ruined after the attack a few weeks back. But Marisol and I have been busy getting it good. C'mon, I'll show you."

Before Bria could protest, Micca took her hand and led her into the tower. As the entrance engulfed her, her arm brushed its stones, and Bria winced. She had last passed through this door with confidence. Now, she shrank in defeat.

Inside, vines still coated the interior, a flag to the forest queen in a way. Engineers and other workers hurried along the interior, some fixing different pieces of machinery while others cleaned the floor or trimmed the branches. They'd turned it into more than just a weapon, but a home and flagship for their mission.

Micca motioned as they walked. "We've been trying to make this all more homely. If we're gonna be transporting kids and such, we don't want it to be too much of a mess. Your vines give a nice, pretty feel to it and all. Don't want to frighten no one."

Bria dragged her fingers along a branch, allowing a few flowers to bloom. "How many kids did they find in the towers?"

"Honestly, don't know. A lot, though. We've already gotten some back to their parents here in Knoll, but we gotta get some of the kids south, and they're not gonna be comfortable unless this thing is nice and friendly." Micca scowled. "Poor kids. They were not doing all that well. I'm sure there's more in other parts of Rosada. Timothée and I have kind of adopted a couple to watch after who don't got any homes or anything."

"Do they all have magic?" Bria asked.

"Not sure, to be honest. Some definitely do, but others...I don't know. The kids I got, two of them have magic for sure. Kinda creepy if you ask me, but I dunno. This magic shite is over my head. Even Timothée's magic doesn't make any bit of sense."

Bria said nothing. She didn't know Timothée all that well. He had gotten her in trouble with the guard a few months back in Aeterno Village, but she had long forgiven him. Micca was smitten, though. He'd jumped into a full commitment with the man, enchanted by his ability to cast different colors through the air in a mere few days. Bria was never one to judge her friend for his expedited decisions, though. Micca lived his life as he wished, and that, she could respect.

"Ah! And there's Marisol!" Micca said as he led Bria into one of the control rooms. "Mari! Look who I found!"

Marisol spun, her long black hair pulled back in a ponytail like a whip. "Ah! You're awake!"

Bria didn't have time to react. Marisol raced over and pulled Bria into a hug. Bria stiffened. She'd only known Marisol for a few months after they were locked into a prison tower together. With the ability to get anyone to speak the truth, she both scared Bria and placed her in a bubble of awe.

Marisol released Bria with a smile. "Sorry. We've all been worried about you."

"Yeah, I know." Bria glanced around the control room, eyeing the strange wiring. On the table, an array of objects, each with a knob and a lever attached to them, waited. Behind them, a stylus sat above a long strip of paper. Every few moments, the machine would beep, spitting out a list of dashes and dots.

"What's going on in here?" Bria asked.

Marisol grinned. "Tap-code. Lana wants us learning it. At least a lot of us."

"Tap-code?"

Micca huffed. "Don't get why it's so important. We could come up with such a better code."

"Oh, shush." Marisol rolled her eyes, then turned back to Bria. "Lana said about fifty years ago or so, the guard used to use it all the time. She found these old machines in one of the towers. Said it'd be a good idea to communicate with it again. They don't really train the guards to understand it or anything now, with all their fancy radios and such."

"And Lana knows tap-code?" It wouldn't surprise Bria if she did, in all honesty. Lana had a list of knowledge pulled from her travels and adventures long before Bria was ever born.

"Yeah, she got us a book and is having us all learn it each day. That's what I'm working on right now. But let me tell you, it's a headache trying to understand each one of these dashes and dots. I have no clue how anyone used to do this regularly." Marisol pressed down on the knob on a machine. "See, when I press this, it makes a noise. Then it can get transmitted to another tap-code machine somewhere. Kind of cool if you ask me."

"It is..." Bria approached one of the machines. She tapped the knob once. *Technology... That's one thing my magic can't touch.* She released the knob, then repeated it again, watching as the receiver on the other side of the room produced a list of dots and dashes on the paper.

"Sorry, this isn't all that interesting or anything," Micca said. "We're just prepping. For what? I don't go a clue, really. But at least we'll be ready."

"No, it's fine…" Bria pressed on the transmitter again.

"Nah, just admit you're bored, Beebelle. Really. I'm bored just looking at these things!"

"No, I'm not. Actually…" Bria made eye contact with Marisol. "Can I learn with you? I think it'd be important for me to know…right?"

Marisol's eyes lit with excitement. "I doubt Lana would have a problem with that. Plus, learning together is so much more entertaining!"

"Seriously, you're interested in this shite?" Micca asked.

"Shush, Micca. You're the boring one," Marisol said, then motioned Bria further into the room. "C'mon! I can show you the basics if you want."

Despite Micca's griping, Bria joined Marisol. If nothing else, this would provide the distraction she needed.

If nothing else, this would help her grow.

CHAPTER EIGHT

THE FOREST QUEEN'S PROMISE

Yaz hid in the trees, watching the tower breathe in the forest. She escaped Chander and Anandi, once again allowing herself the silence she needed. The two siblings hadn't stopped bickering since they set the forest woman ablaze, and the last thing Yaz needed was to listen to their incessant arguing. She didn't need to be reminded that they set the Forest Queen on fire.

Chander and Anandi never followed Yaz to the tower. While Yaz marveled at each gear, remembering her days in Ms. Kai and Mr. Nasr's tower, her friends feared it. When she asked Anandi once, she merely said, "Bad things happened there."

Yaz knew better than to ask what bad things; she had her own bad things. If they found the tunnels that led to the Library of Mist Keepers, would she want to show them to her friends?

Probably not.

But it didn't stop Yaz from watching people as they worked on the tower. She always waited each morning as the smoky dragon that lived above the forest descended from the sky. Upon it, each day, an engineer with patchy overalls and a wide smile hopped off its back. He would kiss the dragon rider, then bounce off to do his work. He reminded Yaz of an excited mouse or a hyperactive squirrel.

Ms. Kai told Yaz to not ponder stories, but she could help but wonder if the engineer was a rodent in another life. Or maybe even a kitten or puppy filled with a bucket of energy. She giggled, imagining not only that engineer but all of them as different animals. What would that be like if all animals behaved like people? It seemed ridiculous—and it would cause Ms. Kai to lecture her—but she didn't care. Besides, she no longer had to listen to Ms. Kai.

Did she even have to listen to anyone? She had no mother, no father, and no guardians.

She was free to be herself with no one else.

In her head, she could be anyone: she could be the engineers working on the tower, a dragon soaring through the sky, or a woman made of plants sleeping in the forest.

She glanced back at the sky. Over the past few weeks, she had all the opportunity to be anyone. More than once, Chander and Anandi invited her up the mountain to visit the dragon. She retreated to the forest each time. The dragon, as it soared through the sky, pulsed with mist. Gentle mist. Pure mist.

But mist, nonetheless.

What if it started to bleed yellow?

Would the monsters return, bringing Ningursu and his Council behind them in full force?

What would she do? Would that man from the forest save her again? Was he even alive anymore?

She jumped at the sound of the tower doors opening. A few engineers exited, blabbering amongst themselves. They didn't take notice of Yaz hiding in the bushes, returning to their homes like any other day of work. It was strange to think only a few weeks earlier, buildings stood in shambles, and smoke destroyed the landscape. Now, the city almost looked normal, like any place Yaz had traveled with Ms. Kai and Mr. Nasr. Towers scraped the sky while the pathways danced with cobblestones.

Like the forest, the city was reborn.

How did things change so fast? In one blink, the world transformed from disarray to beauty. Why did it all have to change so fast? Couldn't someone just stop to tell her what was happening? Instead, she sat here, with only the demons and ghosts as her secret friends, whispering in her ears at night. Sure, Chander and Anandi were her friends, but they knew just as much as her.

What good were fun and games when the world kept changing?

She turned her attention back to the tower. As a few more engineers exited, her heart leapt. Out of the tower, with an overstuffed bag over her shoulder, walked none other than the Forest Queen.

Yaz recognized her at once. She bore a dismembered arm constructed of roots that blended in with the forest. Her thick hair lay in a twisted braid on her shoulder. And even her eyes reminded Yaz of the oak trees. She was more glorious alive and walking than asleep in the forest. Something about her screamed 'power.' Yaz couldn't describe it, but she followed in awe as the Forest Queen walked away from the group of engineers and back through the forest.

Despite the little voice in her head telling her to stop, Yaz followed behind the Forest Queen. She walked alone, and as she disappeared further and further into the trees, her body shrunk in on itself. Even when a misty dog joined her side, she didn't perk up, placing her hand on the dog's head with a sigh.

Yaz stumbled behind the Forest Queen. Twice, she thought the Forest Queen heard her, pausing for a second before continuing along the path. As the queen walked, flowers trickled behind her.

Yaz approached the edge of the path where a white flower bloomed. She placed her fingers around it and plucked it from the ground.

The Forest Queen's dog turned its head and barked.

Yaz's stomach fell.

Beside the dog, the Forest Queen turned her head.

And smiled.

"Oh, hello. What're you doing out here?" The Forest Queen asked as she approached, her dog at her side.

Yaz shrank as the dog neared her, tail wagging.

"Nix, back." The Forest Queen motioned the dog to her side. Once the dog lay down, the Forest Queen turned back to Yaz with her brow furrowed. "Do I know you? I feel like we've met before."

Yaz shifted her feet, looking at the ground. "I was there when you turned into a forest..."

"Were you?"

"Yeah. There was a man who saved me, and you were there too... but then you became the forest..."

"A man who saved you..." The Forest Queen stepped closer. "What man?"

"He said his name was...Brent."

"Brent..."

Yaz continued, "He protected me from Sir Ja—I mean, Ningursu."

"Wait... Ningursu? You were the Mist Keepers?"

Yaz nodded.

"Dammit..." The Forest Queen mumbled. She dug her foot beneath a nearby root as if trying to lift it. "How did he protect you?"

"I'm not sure...but he went with them, and they vanished. And left me in the forest with you and that other woman. Lana."

The Forest Queen's gaze fell past Yaz and into the distance. "Of course he did. Dammit..."

Yaz shifted. Her throat tightened. Did the Forest Queen blame her?

"I'm sorry," Yaz whispered. "I didn't mean for him to go with them..."

The Forest Queen stared at her with tears in her eyes. "Oh, don't worry, I don't blame you. He did what I would expect him to do. If he didn't save you, I would have been worried that he had lost his way."

"Then why are you crying?"

The Forest Queen wiped her eyes and smiled. "Because I love the man who saved you... and I'm so proud of him. But it breaks my heart because I might never see him again."

"But you can save him, right?"

"I'll try."

"But you're the Forest Queen!"

"That's what people call me... but really, I'm just Bria."

"Bria..." Yaz whispered, reciting the name like a prayer. "I'm Yaz."

"Yaz. Nice to meet you."

With a slight smile, Yaz fidgeted with the flower in her hands before handing it back to Bria. "Sorry. I took this."

"Oh, you can keep it! I have plenty of flowers!" Bria ran her finger over the petal. The white flower glowed with magic and sent a warmth through Yaz, like a promise.

"Wow!" Yaz exclaimed, cradling the flower close in her hands.

"This flower is a promise to you, Yaz. Just like Brent protected you, I will protect you, too. From any monster or Mist Keeper, you are under my protection. Do you understand?"

"But we only just met..."

"That doesn't matter to me. Because you deserve to live, to have fun, and to be *you*. Got it?"

"Got it..." Yaz stared at the flower.

"As long as that flower thrives, know that I am protecting you. I promise."

Yaz closed her hand around the flower, then stared up at the Forest Queen. She said her name was only Bria, but Yaz didn't believe it. With the kindness in her eyes and the power on her skin, this woman couldn't be anything less than a queen.

"Thank you," Yaz said, her throat tightening again. But she swallowed the tears. She couldn't let the Forest Queen see her cry.

Yet, Bria certainly saw it without question.

She knelt to Yaz's level, not touching her but keeping her voice soft and kind. "Things will get better. That's something easy to forget...I forget it a lot, too. But it will get better. We'll make sure of it."

Yaz didn't respond. Instead, in one outward sob, she threw her arms around the Forest Queen and hugged her tight as if scared she might vanish into the trees.

CHAPTER NINE

S.O.S

Bria walked Yaz back to the Pit. She didn't pressure the girl to tell her anything, letting the child babble when she wanted and bask in silence if nothing came to mind. On the walk back, she learned that Yaz had been a nomad who traveled in an eclectic tower, only to be taken by Ningursu when she showed signs of mist. They turned her magic into a weapon to control "demons" and to rid the world of "evil magic." It only made sense that Brent rescued her; as much as his actions broke Bria's heart, if he hadn't, then he would not have been Brent Harley.

In all honesty, Bria would have done the same.

"I wonder if Ms. Kai and Mr. Nasr miss me…" Yaz said as they approached the tenement hall where she'd been staying.

"Ms. Kai and Mr. Nasr?"

"They ran the Curio Shoppe Tower. Gisela Kai and Yeshua Nasr were their names, but I wasn't allowed to call them by their first names at all."

"Gisela and Yeshua," Bria recited, but she didn't let Yaz see her concern. She recognized those names. Before they attacked Knoll, Gisela and Yeshua had entered the Pit and offered their services. With them, they brought Lex Dray, a woman who had only just unlocked her potential as a seer. What happened to them?

Am I really that selfish? I didn't even ask what happened to Lex.

She blinked and turned back to Yaz, forcing a smile as she said, "I'm sure they miss you."

Yaz glanced at the ground. "I don't know. They never really cared what I did."

"Well, you're with people who care about you now."

They didn't speak again until they reached the tenement hall doors. A few children peeked from the window. Were all of them orphans? Did they all have magic?

With a hug, she bid Yaz good night. Yaz swallowed once, looking as though she might cry, but after patting Nix on the head, she turned into the building and shut the door.

As the door snapped shut, Bria's mask fell. Once again, Lana didn't give her the full truth! Why didn't she mention this child? She only told Bria that Brent was gone—not where, not how, not when. Yaz was the key! Brent was with the Mist Keepers! No wonder the tunnels remained locked. They expected that the moment she woke, she would come blazing down the path to the Library.

She clenched her hands, and a gust of wind caught her hair. *Calm yourself. Focus on each element. It's in your control.* Bria exhaled, searching for the unique taste of each component of the surrounding air. Lana had given her a book called the *Rules of the Apothecary* that detailed all the elements. Perhaps on a calmer night, she would read more about each element. But for now, she could only imagine the basics of the air: oxygen and nitrogen, rising and falling against different temperatures, returning to a gentle breeze.

Bria's hands opened, and the wind stopped bellowing.

She exhaled and shifted her bag over her shoulder. *Now to find Lana.*

Despite spending plenty of time in Knoll's Pit, Bria still didn't have a clue where Lana lived. Not that it mattered; she had an idea where the woman spent her time.

With her head down, she trudged through the Pit. She smiled at a few people as they called to her but maintained her focus on the southern edge of the forest. She missed being invisible. Even back in Newbird's Arm, she kept her magic a secret. People respected her as the young gardener, never really bothering her except to gather seeds and flowers. Well, except for Christof and his obsessive advances. There, she was just a gardener.

Bria had no desire to lose her magic but for it to, perhaps, be nothing more than a secret talent. That was all—a talent.

But despite everything, Bria's magic gave people hope.

While every part of her wanted to hide, a responsibility rested on her shoulders that she could not avoid.

Outside of the main center of the Pit waited a decrepit barn. She approached it without fear and pushed open the doors.

As she expected, Lana sat on a pile of hay, staring at the wall where the so-called 'elders' met and where others performed their vices. Here, Lana sat alone. Waiting...

Watching...

"Lana," Bria stated.

"What do you want?" Lana didn't turn.

"Answers."

"Like always. Can't you ever come visit me to say hello?"

"Maybe if you told me the truth, I would come by to say hello." Everything had come back to this. Sure, Lana waited by her side in the forest. True, Bria raided Knoll to save her. Yes, they had truth between them that hung by a thin thread.

But they still refused to knock down the wall.

Lana sighed. "What did I lie to you about *now?*"

"You said you didn't know what happened to Brent."

"I don't. He vanished."

"You didn't mention Yaz!"

"Yaz?" Lana wrinkled her nose. "Oh, right, the girl…"

"That's important! She's the reason she vanished."

"You want me to imprison a child!?"

"No!"

"Then what does it matter if I told you or not?"

"Because she was able to tell me what happened, and Brent is alive. I can't get to him right now, but I know." Bria rubbed the tattoo on her good hand with her branched fingers.

"Then you have lost nothing by me not telling you."

"You're ridiculous! I deserve honesty."

"So what? You can obsess over your missing husband? There are more important things to do right now."

"Brent is important. He's part of this whole thing—"

"See? You're already fixated on him."

Bria cursed under her breath. Lana didn't get it! Of course she wouldn't! The idea of Mist Keepers, immortals, and this ongoing war went far over her head. To her, it was a battle between the Order and freedom. Nothing more.

"What about Gisela and Yeshua? Where are they?"

"Who?"

"The two curio shoppe owners! They have to do with that girl as well!"

"Oh, them? Not sure. They never returned after the battle. Didn't think that was important."

"If you spoke to the girl—"

"The girl didn't want to talk to me. We'll ship her home like the rest of them with our next working tower."

"She has no home! She told me that!"

Lana shrugged. "Then she'll be with the other orphans. We have a handful of them."

"She has magic... she's not safe here!"

"A lot of the kids have magic—"

"No, you don't understand. The people who want her are worse than the Order and—"

"What do you want us to do?"

"We need to get her out of here! I can leave with her and—"

"Bria, enough. You're being hysterical!" Lana rose from the hay pile and approached her. "You're learning a lot of information at once and struggling to process it. Now go back to your room and rest."

"No, we're not playing this! I know what's going on!"

"You don't."

"I do."

They stood there, glowering at each other. Bria sensed the walls crawling with envy. The wood wanted to bloom, and the ground yearned to shake. But she kept her focus. Lana would not win this argument.

"I'm leaving. I suggest you get rest." Lana strolled past her.

Bria sent out a root from the ground at once, ordering it to wrap around Lana's ankles. The woman froze and glowered over her shoulder at Bria. In the dim light of the barn, her eyes appeared like slits, almost as dark as the burns on the side of her temples.

"Let me go."

"You have magic. Tell the roots to leave."

"Bria—"

"Use your magic."

Lana exhaled. "What do you want?"

"What else happened during the attack?"

"That's a large question."

"Who else is dead? Micca and Timothée are fine, I've met Yaz, and I've seen Marisol. Whose lives did I cost?"

Lana stared at her root-covered feet. "Thirty-four of our people lost their lives since our last count. The numbers change every day."

"And the other side?"

"Why does that matter?"

"Because it does."

Lana groaned. "We counted twenty-three."

"So fifty-seven total?" Bria gulped. Fifty-seven lives lost because of her charge. She knew going into Knoll would result in death. But it broke her heart, nevertheless. She didn't want to spill blood...but it had to happen. She kept her voice steady when she asked, "Anyone I know?"

"Bria..."

"If you don't want to answer, use your magic to break out."

Lana huffed but gave Bria an answer: "There was a well-known sister, Sister Un Dine, found in the rubble. We found Captain Glenndal Carver's body as well."

"Captain Carver's dead?"

"Died when Ab Aeterno collapsed."

"Shit..." Bria's chest tightened. The man who had sat her down, tried to cajole a truth from her, and made her question her own identity, left her fumbling in fear. He was the man who raised the boy that taunted her for years.

And now he was gone.

Just like that.

Dead.

Rotting beneath stone.

"What about on our side?" Bria asked.

"I'm sure you'd recognize most of them...but the one you personally knew was that pale girl."

"Lex?"

"Yes, Lex."

Bria freed Lana from the clutches of the roots and returned to her room in the tenement hall without food. Her heart hung in her chest. People had died...because of her. If Brent were here, he could confirm if their souls were safe. But right now, with the Council of Mist Keepers locked away, Bria couldn't be sure if anyone had released their souls.

She sat on the edge of her bed. Nix hopped up beside her and nudged her head against Bria's leg. As she stroked back the dog's fur, Bria's mind raced. Lana might have her own plans, but Bria understood one thing: she had to get Yaz out of Knoll. If the Council knew where she was, then danger lurked around every corner. Even with Brent in their clutches, she couldn't imagine Ningursu letting Yaz slip through the cracks.

Bria reached for the bag on the floor and opened it. A bundle of wires and a radio transmitter greeted her. She had spent hours reviewing the basics of tap-code with Marisol and a reluctant Micca. Despite Micca's own distaste for the code, he provided Bria with a small radio that would allow her to transmit the code in the local area. She just had to place the radio by the window and link the wires with the tap-code transmitter.

After fumbling with the wires for a minute, so the transmitter sat on the end table, she turned on the radio. Static buzzed around the room. She winced, then reached for the small notepad at the bottom of her bag. On the first page, Micca wrote the twelve different radio stations to use. Bria scrolled through the names until she came upon frequency number 93 for Micca and Timothée.

It was weird fiddling with the dial to reach the correct number. The end of the static confirmed their connection.

She flipped to the next page in her notepad. Marisol had written down the tap-code alphabet. On the page after that, she listed out a handful of common abbreviations and codes.

Bria licked her bottom lip, placed her finger on the transmitter, and slowly tapped out:

— -.-. -.-. ..--.. / .. ... / -... -... .-.-.-

MCC? Is BB.

She waited a second to see if Micca would respond before reiterating the code.

A slow beeping followed on the radio a moment later.

-... -... .-.-.- / .. ... / — -.-. -.-. .-.-.-

BB. Is MCC.

Bria looked over the code words again before tapping again.

.... .- ...- . / -.. .-. .- --. --- -. ..-..

Have dragon?

A pause. Then followed:

-.-- .-.-.- / .-- .... -.-- ..-..

Y. Why?

Bria slowly tapped out the next code. A simple code, but the only one that would say what she needed.

... --- ...

SOS

I need your help.

CHAPTER TEN

THE SHIFTING WALLS

A h, there you are!" Brent lifted the pineapple off the ground. "Thought you gave me away there."

He blinked once. How ridiculous did that sound? A pineapple leading him to his demise?

But then again, who would leave a pineapple in the middle of a corridor but him?

After his last shift, he had dropped it as the mist took him away; now, here it lay, covered in dust, with half of it collapsing in on itself. He cradled it to himself. Perhaps this was the end of his pineapple's story. He had found a place to lay it to rest, so it may grow into another disgusting fruit one day.

I gotta get out of this corridor before someone sees me. He hurried against the wall, holding the pineapple close. Despite the past weeks of shifting in and out of the mist, it still didn't come naturally. After one shift, his body felt like a cloud, ready to fade away into nothing. The only option he had was to keep to the walls, move with them as they breathed, and listen to their stories.

Ever since Caroline visited him in the empty canvas room, his head had been a little clearer. Brent spent over three days scribbling Caroline's story across a multitude of canvases. He sank into the story, but this time it didn't overwhelm. He learned about Caroline's life, growing from a little girl who wanted to impress her mother to a woman with a vendetta and a heart hidden by a mask. In that single touch, he learned more about his old teacher than the past two years had revealed.

But with that knowledge and with more stories, he might just find a way out of the Library and a way to stop Ningursu. The answers couldn't be far; each corner of the Library told a story, and in the shadows, he saw the Mist Keepers act.

If only he could get into Ningursu's office. Then, just maybe, he might collect Ningursu's plans. The skull, as always, was elusive and cunning, never putting his plans out in the open. Did he even say them out loud? Was it all in their heads?

That was one thing Brent had escaped on his path to becoming one with the Effluvium. Ningursu never found a way into his head. Not like he saw through Caroline's eyes or whispered in the other Mist Keeper's ears.

Ningursu played the puppet master.

And a millennium of experience put Brent at odds.

But there were still visible secrets, and he would find them.

While he couldn't shift again, he did observe. He didn't notice the first time he arrived or even the second or third time, but the Library's walls moved like water. When he arrived, the Library was his paradise. His home didn't have a library. The only books he ever saw were in the Temple, in the schoolhouse, or the few he stole and hid in his mantel. But they vetted these texts; they did not have the freedom that storytelling so demanded. When he entered the Library of Mist Keeper, the freedom of words overwhelmed him.

But with the books fallen from the shelves and the mist showing the true bones of the Library, paradise had fallen. Remnants of a swamp coated the ground floor, leftover from Bria's attack over six months earlier, the Library had become more a product of nature. Hidden amongst the shelves, streams of the magical silver pool flickered without intensity. Wilted peonies lay along the artificial banks.

He took it in from the walkway above, holding his pineapple close to his chest. So many stories hid just on the bottom floor. In one blink, his own tale greeted him: he'd freed the Diabolo that restarted this endless war. Or at least brought it to the forefront of everyone's mind. Back then, he moved with uncertainty and a lack of grace. Not that he had it now, but he liked to think his confidence excelled a bit. He wasn't the same clueless storyteller anymore.

But his attention shifted to another story, following in the shadow of his past fear. In its place, a tale comprising Alojzy holding Ningursu in his hands, walking into the depths of the Library. Around him, the walls shifted.

Well, the walls of the story.

Brent moved along the veritable walls, following the tale, down the stairs and deep into the bookshelves. It took all his focus to keep the story alive. With so many years of tales pouring over him, Brent recited his mantra beneath his breath, focused only on the back of past Alojzy's balding head.

The story stopped before the intricate gate of the crypt. Brent felt before it entered his vision; that gate exuded fear. Last time he saw it, he'd encountered strange people with silver eyes and blank stares. In that abyss, the Mist Keeper named Julietta became the canvas for another Diabolo. He did everything he could then to save her, but by the time he pulled Diabolo out of her, nothing remained.

What happened to her after that? He didn't know.

But he knew that a story lay in front of him, and he refused to let it escape.

With a single gasp, he stepped forward, letting the tale wrap around him.

And for one moment, he existed only in the past.

"Everyone is in the crypt, sire," Alojzy said, holding Ningursu's head out to the gate.

"Beautiful work."

"Julietta drew the carvings. I merely commanded the mist."

Ningursu smirked. "But you had the image and heart. We are now safe."

"Thank you, sire."

"I assume you placed a protective measure?"

"Of course. Three clicks of your tongue, and the door is at your command if needed. But I doubt you'll have much reason to use it. The crypt will serve as its own protector."

"Explain."

"I designed the crypt to always be changing. They can only escape if the mist lets them."

"And that is by your decree?"

"Yes, sire."

Ningursu closed his one good eye, his smirk remaining on his face.

But the conversation didn't end, with Alojzy speaking next, "May I ask one thing, sire?"

"Of course."

"What are those monsters in the crypt? They're not the Diabolo, but they're not ghosts or demons..."

Ningursu responded without hesitation. "They are Mist Keepers."

"Then why are they like... that?"

"Because they are not what the Council needs."

"Then why not destroy them?"

"We destroy many of them," Ningursu said, "but these serve a greater purpose."

"Explain."

"Better yet, I'll show you. Let us go into the crypt."

Alojzy stepped forward, and the gate opened. With Ningursu in his hands, he stepped inside, basking in a cloak of smoke.

Brent stepped forward to follow, only to hit the gate with a thud. He pulled at it once, only to have a gasp of stories shroud him. Wisps of Alojzy building the Library flew into his nostrils while various fleeting stories of prisoners dragged down into their cells passed over him—including Bria...and the immortal, Kek.

The gates of the crypt did not budge for Brent. Whatever secrets waited for him below did not welcome him. It's locked. Three clicks of the tongue...

In a moment of hope, he clicked his tongue thrice.

Nothing happened.

Expect for the walls twisting around the entrance to the crypt. The Library shifted.

And Brent stepped back, letting the mist take him into its embrace, clutching his pineapple close.
As he traveled, he tried to direct himself, searching the Library for a place of safety and peace.

His heart landed in one place.

And once again, he found himself back in the room of countless canvases. He exhaled once, placed the pineapple on the ground, and strolled to the back of the room.

In a far corner, beneath three other canvases, he'd hidden Caroline's story.

Now, another one waited for him, pressing at the forefront of his mind. First, he had a whiff, and then it inundated him. It pulsed through his veins, it screamed in his chest, and it begged to be told.

It spoke the tale of a paranoid man who believed everyone was against him; he devoted himself to a god, and with that god as his savior, he did everything to excel. He uncovered a new potential in the mist and built a Library for the Council to hide. His story held every secret of the walls, and with these secrets, Brent might escape.

But the story also made his heart ache. This was not a tale Brent wanted to tell.

He didn't have a choice. That much he knew.

So he picked up a pen from the floor and scratched away on the canvas:

Not all stories deserve a pedestal.
Some belong in a drawer or buried in a hole.
Forgotten.

Brent glanced over his shoulder, making sure the door remained locked. If he didn't write this down now, it threatened to overwhelm him. Already, it clawed at his psyche. If he blinked the wrong way, his thoughts belonged to Alojzy.

He held to his constants.

He held to his truths.

And he wrote the next sentence:

But I'm not in the business of forgetting stories.

CHAPTER ELEVEN

THE CAPITAL

Christof had never been to the Capital. When the morning came, despite his horrid sleep in the creaking tower, he woke with anticipation, quickly dressing before Sister Jey Ma woke beside him. Her red hair fell over her face, her body rising and falling with even breaths. He brushed one strand of hair from her face. A yellow tinge surrounded her closed eyes, but he didn't mention it to her. It was part of her sacrifice.

And with that sacrifice, they would lead the Capital to victory.

His stomach churned with a mix of excitement and sadness. When he was a child, his father often left for the city, returning home with bundles of chocolate, posh clothing, and stories of order. His mother would hold

Christof on her lap while his father presented him with gifts, planting an idea of a utopia in his mind.

Christof left the room and, without a word, climbed up the stairs to the upper platform. He passed the beautiful woman with discolored eyes as he climbed. She smirked at him once, then disappeared behind the door.

He shook off her enchantment and finished his ascent to the platform. Christof's heart dropped, cradled with awe at what sprawled before him: a city guarded by a tower that scraped the sky, as tall as the late Ab Aeterno. Order reigned. Even from his spot in the tower, he could almost taste the purity. The streets, lined with a few scattered taverns, sat empty and pristine. While he was sure vagrants loitered in plain sight with tainted silver eyes or magic on their fingertips, something felt different. People respected the Order here. Even from a distance, he could see those out and about stopping to stare at the onslaught of towers arriving at the edge of the city.

And in the moment, however brief, he felt like a king.

But as Sister Jey Ma joined his side, that success vanished.

She arrived like a shadow, as silent as ever. Despite their nighttime rendezvouses, she had spoken little to him otherwise. The Effluvium followed her, maintaining her poise. Every movement turned heads, and when guards visited the Curio Tower, they watched her as if locked in a spell.

But Senator Cordova and his loyal Elder An Drew hovered over Sister Jey Ma the most. During the day, she spent most of her hours couped up in one of the small rooms on the bottom of the floor of the tower. It left Christof to mull about alone, creating scenarios in his head of what might be happening. Why did they take her away from him? Wasn't Sister Jey Ma his woman?

Some nights, with the way her gaze trailed across the horizon, he didn't know.

Besides, did his heart ever really go out to her?

He shook away the thought as Sister Jey Ma laced her arm through his arm. She stood like a statue as the tower marched to the city's edge, joining the other towers, waiting for their next order.

"Today begins everything new," Sister Jey Ma said. "There are many futures ahead of us."

"And which future do you see for us?" Christof asked.

Sister Jey Ma didn't reply.

"Are you going to answer me?"

Sister Jey Ma kept her head level, but her voice reeked of Senator Cordova as she spoke, "Trust me, Cadet. Everything will go according to plan."

"Aren't I a lieutenant now?"

"Only if you succeed."

Christof cursed under his breath.

"I told you not to use that language," Sister Jey Ma stated.

"Fine! Sorry. So what is the plan?"

"We arrive. And you prove your worth."

Christof knew better than to ask more. Sister Jey Ma's grip on his arm tightened again, though, and arm-in-arm, they left the overlook and headed back into the belly of the tower. As they walked, Christof glanced at Elder An Drew, standing by the doorway with that child from before on his hip. His beady eyes pierced Christof. They didn't seem like they belonged to a human. The little boy rubbed his eyes, then turned his gaze at the floor, like a tiny old man rather than a carefree toddler.

"Sister," Elder An Drew said, "We'll be speaking with Yeshua and Gisela later—about what they've seen."

"Regarding the erasure?" Sister Jey Ma asked.

The Elder nodded.

"Very well. Is Senator Cordova aware?"

"No."

"I'll see to it then."

Elder An Drew nodded once more in Sister Jey Ma's direction, then retired to the room behind him with the child.

"What was that about?" Christof asked.

"Do not worry. It is not for you to concern yourself with."

Christof huffed quietly at the response.

Jemma continued, "Elder An Drew has done some phenomenal work. I wasn't sure at first, but as he described his intentions, I now understand that it is the only way. I hope you come to agree with me, too." Sister Jey Ma said, poised and in control.

"What do you mean... only way to do what?"

"Protect the Effluvium." Sister Jey Ma gazed up at Christof. "What we always wanted to do."

Christof scowled, glancing back at the door where Elder An Drew had vanished with the child. Something about that situation left him queasy. Lieutenant Drayton told him to keep an eye out for strange situations. Was this what he meant? "Does it involve that kid?"

Sister Jey Ma didn't seem to notice his distaste. "The child will be fundamental in what shall occur... but in due time. We require more... understanding of the Effluvium."

"I see." Christof didn't quite understand what Sister Jey Ma meant. It sounded more like Order malarkey than an actual plan. Had Elder An Drew driven his claws too deep into her head?

He didn't want to bring up that argument again.

At the bottom of the stairs, Senator Cordova waited for them. Once again, he exchanged that sort of gaze with Sister Jey Ma that caused Christof's stomach to churn. She gave him respect and admiration. Not the dismissive glance she passed to Christof.

What happened to her honoring him? When they first laid together, it had been like a prayer.

Now she acted like the recipient of one.

But Christof was the loyal guard. The loyal servant. The loyal son.

Although he didn't understand what lay before them, he let Sister Jey Ma take his arm and guide him.

The Capital didn't glisten with the same prowess as he saw from the tower. The façade dropped the moment he entered the streets, losing the promise his father used to paint back at home. As they wandered through the streets, age and wear showed. Only did the city center shine. He had heard about the city center many times before, with its glass gallery of shops, winding roads and plazas, a marble temple, and the impenetrable capitol building. That much remained the same as he followed Sister Jey Ma through the city.

But something was missing.

The bolster of the city?

The peace and prosperity of perfection?

Yet, the silent stares, the glowers towards the towers, they all reminded him of Knoll.

Well, except for the lack of noticeable vagrancy.

The Capital served as a mere shadow of a utopia.

Not paradise.

Not lined with order.

Perhaps Sister Jey Ma would bring it. That was why he followed her, wasn't it?

She led him without flinching, undisturbed by the surroundings. The silence hung between them. Where was she taking him? She moved with such determination; it was like a plan waited in her heart.

But the silence was unbearable.

Instead, he asked, "You've been to the Capital before?"

She glanced at him with glossy eyes. "A while ago. With my parents when I was a teenager. They were trying to convince me to go to the Academy."

"Rather than be Sister Jey Ma?"

"They only saw me as a way to carry out their legacy. Run their farm. Give them grandbabies." Sister Jey Ma paused in a plaza, eyeing the different streets where guards gathered.

"That's why you agreed to be betrothed to Harley, then?" Christof asking.

"It was a compromise."

"You serve the Order and give your parents grandchildren at the same time? All while saving a vagrant?"

"It's ridiculous when you think of it that way."

"But it was what happened..." Christof squirmed, thinking back to when he would see Sister Jey Ma walk through town on Brent Harley's arm. It was a weird sight, even then; yet, at the time, it kept Bria free for Christof to pursue. But now, the thought that Harley touched Jemma caused a different thought to stir in his core. "Did Harley ever, well...you know...share a bed with you?"

"Is that all you care about?" Sister Jey Ma snapped. For a moment, yellow mist pooled from her lips. "What does it matter if we did?"

"I'm curious... damn if we're gonna be together—"

"But to ask now?" Sister Jey Ma glared.

"It was just on my mind. Think I got the right to know."

Sister Jey Ma huffed and shook her head, but before turning away, she said, "No. He had no desire for me. That was not a secret."

"I'm sorry."

"Don't be. He had only eyes for Bria. I let him go because I would not have been happy either." She turned away from Christof and stared up at the capitol building, "I do wonder if I kept a bit more of an eye on him...if all of this wouldn't be happening. If I would be home. If the

Effluvium would remain pure. If everything would be the same."

For a moment, as she finished her sentence, once again Christof heard Jemma Reds... not Sister Jey Ma. Not the young woman who had dove so deep into the Senator and the Elder's demands... but the girl who wanted to make the world better.

"Perhaps though," Christof said, "this is necessary. Maybe this path makes the Effluvium pure once more."

"I hope so." Sister Jey Ma stopped by an alleyway where a couple of guards gathered. She glanced amongst them, then up at the street sign, and nodded. "This is it."

Christof glanced around the area. Nothing here seemed special. It was merely a corner in a plaza, with a few guards waiting.

"What is it?" He asked.

"Your watch. Prove your loyalty here, Cadet Carver."

"Doing what?" He glanced around again. There was nothing special here. Just an alleyway.

"Oh, you can be a little dense sometimes, Christof. But that is part of your charm." Sister Jey Ma smiled at him. Then she said, "We received intel from the guard here in Knoll that this alley is one of the many havens where storytellers hide. Lead the charge. Deal with them."

"Why haven't they dealt with them?" Christof motioned to the other guards.

One of them spoke up, "These storytellers have a magic to 'em. They know the guard here. We can't get through their barrier."

"What do you mean?"

"It's like a shield. When we enter, no stories. But we know they're there. Same old people going in and out, no goods in hand. All the common signs." The guard eyed Christof carefully. "We got word from Senator Cordova to give you a chance. Said it might work in our benefit because the good sister here said so."

Sister Jey Ma kept her kind gaze locked on Christof. "You are the unexpected lead. Show us what you can do, Christof Carver. Be the person your father wanted you to be."

Christof turned to the alleyway. His hands sweated as he stepped forward; this was nothing more than what he used to do back home. He would find the storytellers—well, mostly Brent Harley—hiding in boxes and weaving tales. Those stories echoed, and nothing could hide them. Even the quiet gatherings could not be halted.

He held out his hand. "I need a club."

A guard handed him a club. It weighed heavily in his hands, holding his future in a single swing.

The voice that escaped his lips held a control that was foreign to him. "I'll break the barrier. Follow my lead."

Christof abandoned Sister Jey Ma's side. He never thought he would lead a charge like this again, but he strolled forward with his grip tight on the club. The alley shrank around him as he entered. The magic barrier the guards spoke of tore at his skin, but it did not stop him.

Each step moved him forward, each breath kept him going.

This was his charge.

He could not disappoint Sister Jey Ma.

And this was more than about her. It was for his father. If he succeeded, he would no longer be a mere cadet.

Right?

He could finally be more than that.

The barrier released him, like pins pricking and releasing from his body. Before him, a marketplace waited, with vendors talking in hushed tones. No one looked up as he strode forward, loitering high above a little old lady wrapped in a shawl.

Her voice belonged to demons with a story heavy on her lips.

"Once upon a time, a girl rose from a fireplace," she whispered to the vendor.

And that was all Christof needed to hear.

BUBBLING

Bria waited in the clearing where she'd woken deep in the Necrowood. It sat far enough away, basking in the green and serenity of life, that no one followed her.

Well, except for those who she asked.

She waited in silence, leaning against a tree, running her good hand over the bark. No matter how she begged for the tree to open, for the earth to welcome her, the ground remained locked. The tunnels no longer welcomed her.

Perhaps they never did.

She shook the doubt from her head and shifted her attention to the sky. A shadow fell over the clearing, wrapped in the shape of a dragon.

Despite the dragon's presence in Knoll, Bria still hesitated as it landed before her. She met the dragon back at the circus in Aeterno Village with Brent. While Brent became acquainted with the dragon, she never had the chance. Now, it landed before her in a plume of smoke, its scales moving like the clouds in the sky. Micca hopped off the dragon's back, patted her neck, then approached Bria with a wide smile.

"Glad to see you aren't dying or some shite. Saying 'S.O.S.'—c'mon, that's for important things." Micca laughed.

"This is important," Bria said.

"Damn, I was messing with you. Relax, Beebelle." Micca nudged her.

Bria grimaced, her attention shifting back to the dragon. "Zephyr, right? That's her name?"

"Yeah, Zephyr. Zephy. Zeph. Zeph-girl. Ze—"

The dragon snarled.

Micca raised his hands. "Sorry. I meant your name is Zephyr."

Bria approached the dragon slowly, holding out her hand for the beast to sniff. Zephyr nudged it once with the tip of her nose and huffed again, letting the smoke wrap around Bria's fingertips.

"She's friendly..." Bria stated.

"Yeah, considering what that prick Mr. Santiago did with her, surprised she even likes people." Micca removed a small toy from his pocket. He fidgeted with a gear on the back until the toy's feet moved.

"Does she mind having people ride her?" Bria turned to the dragon, watching as the creature closed her silver eyes.

"Nah, as long as they don't pick at her scales. Learned that the hard way."

Bria didn't turn away. "And how many people can she carry at once?"

"Uh… probably a good handful. Why?"

Bria stepped away from the dragon, glancing over her shoulder and back into the forest. No one followed her, and the trees remained silent. This was the best option.

"I need transport out of here," she said.

"What? You want to leave?" Micca asked.

"This isn't about me. There's this girl named Yaz… she needs to get out of here. Sooner rather than later."

"Doesn't Lana have a whole plan when each child is supposed to leave or something?"

"Yaz won't ever leave… she's not from Rosada." Bria inhaled once, flexing her branched fingers to release tension. "It's too dangerous for her to stay here."

"Why this kid, though? There's a bunch of kids in the Pit."

"I know, and I hate having to choose one over another, but... she's the reason Brent isn't here. He saved her, and keeping her here in Knoll any longer could be detrimental." Bria stopped Micca before he could speak. "Yes, everything has been fine right now, but that could change in an instant."

"And you wanna come too?"

"I need to protect her... to continue what Brent did."

"A'ight. I gotcha. Any others you want to include?"

Bria glanced over her shoulder again. Were there other children like Yaz out there? Did they loiter in this Pit, waiting for the Council to snatch them away? She searched her memory; were there any others that she had met?

"I can't think of any right now." Bria licked her bottom lip. "The one I need out of here is Yaz, though. I don't want to play favorites or overreact, but... knowing her history... the same people who took Brent might come back for her."

"So you're convinced Brent's alive?" Micca raised his brow.

"I know he is... thanks to Hortense's tattoo." Bria extended her good hand, showing the vibrant tattoo on her wrist.

"Ah yeah, forgot Hortense gave that to you. Have you visited the shop she opened in Knoll? Took an old empty storefront and claimed it for herself. Her sibling and some of the other performers use her basement for some fun performances and the like."

"I haven't checked it out, to be honest." Bria would have loved to visit Hortense and Ms. Honey, but so much had happened since she woke, she didn't have time to herself at all. At least, out of all the blood, some people found their passion, while others found their security.

They had taken one step in the right direction.

One step at a time—that was the mantra.

"So when do you want to leave by?" Micca asked.

"Oh, um…" Bria glanced at the sky, then back at the dragon. "End of the week? Right before the new moon?"

"Should give me enough time to convince Timothée and wrangle anything we might need."

"Thank you. I'll talk to Yaz."

"A'ight. Sounds like I'm going on a fun little adventure with Beebelle." Micca winked. "Any idea where you want to head?"

"Away from here. That's all." Bria held onto one slither of hope that maybe if they left Knoll, she might find an entrance to the Library. Then, she would rescue Brent, stop the Council, and end this war.

Well, she could dream at least.

"A'ight, sounds like fun." Micca patted Zephyr's snout. "You hear that, Zeph? We're gonna go fly away soon."

The dragon huffed, sending a puff of smoke across the clearing. Once it passed, Bria swore the dragon smiled.

Bria strolled along the silver river on the perimeter of the city. She didn't dare look inside it. Still, it haunted her like a gnawing sensation in the back of her mind; against her will, this silver substance healed her... and potentially immortalized her.

She kicked a stone into the liquid. Immortality. That was never something she wanted. If she did have it, what would that mean for her? From what she learned, the immortality created from Kek's potion acted as a temporary measure. Eventually, it would wear thin. When? How?

And was it impacting her?

Would everyone else age around her, leaving her in a permanent state of youth?

Or perhaps, if she was lucky, the silver liquid only helped her heal... and nothing more.

She shook her head as she reentered the forest, still trailing along the river. Madame Owiti had sacrificed herself for this magic. She wanted Bria to thrive.

Or she saw a future where Bria had to thrive.

But as always, Bria had no honesty or truth. Everyone kept their secrets.

And she would wander, alone.

Bria ran her fingers along the trunk of the tree as she ventured back through the forest. The silver stream widened as she continued deeper, opening into a lake. *Madame Owiti's lake.* Bria approached the edge of the water. Here, Madame Owiti took her last breath, and here they decided Bria's fate without giving her a chance to voice otherwise.

After removing her shoes, Bria took a step into the water, letting it rise around her. Each step chilled her. If only she had learned how to travel with it. This silver liquid held so many secrets. Kek created it, and since then, it had served as the lifeblood of the earth. It could cure diseases when mixed the right way, communicate when blessed with the right words, and travel when established with the right path. But Bria was no alchemist.

But in the water, she could feel every piece of the pool. If she focused hard enough, she might be able to destroy this one... like she had all the others. In its core, the liquid held the grounded hearts of peony flowers. But there were more elements bubbling within the pool. She couldn't identify them all. They mixed and churned well to transform into this masterpiece of alchemy.

But if she focused on the peonies alone, she might destroy this pool at least.

One of many obliterated, with many more standing.

Was it even worth destroying it? Would it be fruitless, at best? She and Brent spoke about destroying these pools months ago but...unless they found the source, the silver pools would remain, mocking her with their reappearance.

What would be the point?

She brushed her fingers over the surface. The pool rippled. A single breath and it would be gone. Did she have the strength? Outside of a few blossoming flowers and a couple of offshoots of roots, she hadn't touched too much of her magic. Part of her worried if she opened it up again, she might succumb to its demands.

The pool bubbled, mocking her indecision.

She clenched her fist and raised it above the water.

Only for the pool to bubble more.

And more.

Bria lost her stance and fumbled back to the shoreline.

The silver water began to rise, sculpting itself into the forms of different individuals. Bria rushed back to hide in the trees, watching in a mixture of awe and horror as, one at a time, different individuals emerged from the water.

She didn't recognize them at first. Not until the fourth person emerged.

A stout man with a thick beard and dark eyes stepped out of the water. She'd met him only twice, but it would be hard to forget him.

"Edith? Was that you?" Yusef asked aloud, stepping out of the lake and glancing around the area. "Edith, you here?"

Behind him, another familiar face emerged. With red eyes, combed-back hair, and a determined walk, Bria recognized Detective Tilda Locasta at once. She scanned the area, then locked her attention right where Bria hid.

"Edith isn't here. But someone else is…" She motioned to the trees with her.

Yusef followed Tilda's gaze. Bria shrunk deeper into the trees.

"Come on out, Bria. We know you're there." Yusef said.

Bria sighed, then stepped forward, "Hello, Yusef. Tilda."

"Thought you could hide from us? Come on now. I'm a seer." Tilda grinned at Bria as she spoke.

"I didn't know what was coming out of the pool." Bria glanced at the three others standing beside Yusef: a pale young man with fiery hair, a tanned middle-aged man with a determined poise, and a tall old woman with a hooked nose. Each one waited, watching Bria's every move.

"Edith told us to come. Said we should come through when a familiar touch lingered over the pool. We thought she meant her," Yusef said, "But I guess she meant you."

"I didn't even know I was going to be here."

"Edith probably would have come, eventually. She would have left us mulling about for a bit. That is just how she is." Tilda added.

Bria scowled. Yes, that was how Edith behaved. But it didn't make the situation any less uneasy.

"Why are you here, though?" Bria dreaded the answer. Part of her already anticipated what they would say.

"If we're going to win this war, we need to be at our strongest. We need *you* to be your strongest."

Bria shook her head.

"We're here to train you. With our help, you can become our key to success—"

Bria interjected, "Once again, you're here to turn me into a weapon?"

"No—"

"I'm not a weapon. Yes, my magic is acting up, and I'm discovering new things, but—"

Before she could finish her sentence, the red-headed man threw out his arm. A wave of flames escaped his skin, rushing towards Bria like a falling tree.

She threw her arms up in defense.

The heat hit her first.

But the pain never followed.

As she exhaled and opened her eyes, the flames fell to the side, landing on the ground and fading to a brief murmur. *What did I just do?* She stared at her hands, then back at the red-headed man.

"Tristan, that was unnecessary," Yusef said, calm as ever.

"Yes, but now she's interested." The young man, Tristan, replied.

Bria continued to stare at her hands. Her body shook, her head spun, and her heart thudded.

What's my limit? She raised her head, meeting the gaze of Yusef and his entourage. Questions continued swimming through her head. At what point would her magic stop growing? Could she ever reel it in and control it for good?

But only one question left her lips: "Why is this happening to me?"

CHAPTER THIRTEEN

UNFURLED

Bria had lost control of her life.

With the arrival of Yusef, Tilda, and the rest, she had become nothing more than a pawn.

Waiting.

That was all she ever did.

She felt it as soon as they arrived.

She sensed it as she guided them back to the Pit.

And now, as she stood outside the barn, listening to the indiscreet discussions of Edith and her entourage, everything remained in chance's court. The walls closed around her, and every time she thought she found an exit, they only collapsed further around her.

Why did she think she would ever have control over her destiny? Life had ripped it from her long ago.

Perhaps back when Lana buried her alive.

Perhaps when Brent found her tunnels.

Or perhaps when Ningursu first clawed his way into her mind.

She leaned against the wall, running her fingers through Nix's fur, listening to the soft chants of the wind. Evening had fallen with a sullen sigh, the purples drizzling over the sky like an iridescent syrup. The beauty of the earth, the silence of the forest, at least it gave her a momentary reprieve. Part of this was all because of *her*, even if she didn't intend it.

Even if it came with the blessing of death.

Lana approached with Tilda walking beside her, speaking in a low tone. For a moment, concern crossed Lana's face, then a nod, before letting Tilda disappear into the barn. She didn't notice Bria at first, attention still locked on the dirt.

After a few moments, she noticed Bria. "Oh, what're you doing mulling about here?"

"Edith's having a conference with her people. Thought that's what you were talking with Tilda about?" Bria replied without flinching.

"What do you mean by 'her people?'"

"You didn't know?"

"No. I'm not that close with Edith."

Bria glanced up at the barn behind her. "She invited some Magii here that she thinks can help train me. Tilda's one of them."

"Oh. Good."

Bria scowled. "Good!? I'd like to at least have a choice in the matter."

"A choice?"

"Yes, a choice!" Bria exclaimed. "I don't want this... training thrust upon me! It turns me into a weapon... which I'm *not*. I want a say in how I control my magic. I don't need some...strangers coming and telling me what to do."

"Then don't let them," Lana said without flinching.

"But they—"

"They won't make you do anything. You're stronger than them."

"Maybe alone, but together they surpass me."

"This is your fight. You decide how to lead it."

Bria stared at her hands. *I'm not a weapon.* Her branched hand bloomed with flowers. This was her future, negotiated behind a flimsy wooden door.

And she deserved a voice.

She turned to the barn and exhaled. Lana was right. She almost always was, despite Bria's own reservations. *This is my fight.* She stepped forward and pushed open the barn door. The wood curled around her fingers.

My destiny, I can control it.

As she opened the door, Edith turned, eyes blazing. Her lips twitched, then a smile pricked her lips.

"Glad to see our prodigy has stopped her griping outside." Edith chided. Behind her, Yusef, Tilda, and the other three arrivals sat in piles of hay, watching silently as Edith led the altercation.

"You told me to wait outside."

"Only because you ruin everyone's mood."

Bria gritted her teeth.

"Just face it. You're nothing when you don't have your reaper boy. Without him, what do you ever accomplish?"

"Plenty," Bria spoke through her teeth.

"Really? I say you need help—and that's why we're here."

"I don't need whatever help you are planning. This is my future we're talking about."

Edith chuckled, "No. This is not about *you* at all. Don't go thinking you're that important."

"I don't think I'm that important."

"Good, glad we're on the same page." Edith leaned forward on her toes. "This is about making sure we can stop the oncoming storm."

"Because I'm your weapon?"

"Because you are a necessity."

"Even if this isn't about me personally, this is about what is going to happen in *my life*, so I'd like a say in this so-called *training*." Bria kept her voice level. She channeled Lana or her grandmama as she spoke. This magic, this decision, it all came down to her choice, just as Lana said.

"You know nothing about magical training," Edith said.

"I know enough about my magic to know what sort of training I want."

"And that is?"

Bria eyed each of the Magii. Their talents differed from her own, but each had one commonality: elements. She still remembered those rules of the apothecary. Now, all she had to do was harness them in the right way.

That, of course, was another problem altogether. Each element had its own taste and sensation, but she could not for the life of her differentiate between them. A few stood out to her, and other elements breathed with such prominent life. Until Lana gave her the *Rules of the Apothecary*, she never even thought about the details of her magic. She just sensed the life of the trees and breathed with them.

But did these Magii see their magic the same way? Or did they act of their own accord?

"Give me a test," Bria whispered.

"A test?"

"You can't train me unless you see what I can do."

"She makes a fair point," Yusef spoke before Edith could interject. "I know I have nothing to teach her—we do not want to waste our time if she has a natural inclination to any other elements."

"There are always things to learn." The red-headed young man, Tristan, added. "No one is that much of a prodigy. Took me years to control my fire."

"Didn't take your sister long," Tilda joked.

"We don't talk about that," Tristan grunted.

Tilda smirked.

"Needless to say," Yusef said, "Bria is right. A test would serve as the best opportunity to see her readiness. No point wasting energy on fruitless causes."

Bria's shoulders eased. At least someone was on her side.

Edith muttered to herself, then smiled. "Very well. Let your test begin."

"Wait...what!?" Before Bria could react, Edith pulled a nail from the wall. She threw it into the air, and as it soared, it stretched, turning into a narrow knife ready for the kill. Bria shot her hand forward, bracing for the impact.

As the blade touched her finger, fear sent the knife exploding into a thousand shards. Bria questioned how to reform them. With the trees, it was like bellowing an order to the army. But even as she wished the shards transformed into a shield, they only fell to the ground at her feet with a thud.

"This isn't what I meant by test!" Bria shouted.

"War is disorganized. Life is unexpected. You cannot expect it to come to you in perfect formation." Edith paced backward, then with a single flick of her wrist, three more nails escaped the wood. They rushed forward through the air.

This time, Bria focused on their movements, and it was as if time slowed around her. Edith sent them forward with momentum, but an object only stays in motion if nothing stops it.

Bria imagined the nails were nothing more than branches unfurled from the walls.

As she reached for them, they thudded like a heartbeat. Only nature, no different from life; the elements in the nail came together to form steel. She could manipulate them like the plants.

She pictured them twisting like rope or vines. Each wire that composed the nails tied together, reshaping their identity and purpose.

The nails hit her body.

But they did not pierce.

Rather, they thudded against her skin and landed on the ground in the shape of small, round coins.

"Smart." Edith smirked. "But we're not done yet."

"Wait," Bria panted.

She should have known Edith wouldn't listen. While the nails did not fly, nor did any metal appear, a gust of wind picked up in the barn. Outside, Bria swore that Nix howled.

"Fritjof, you're up," Edith ordered.

The older gentleman with slicked-back hair stepped forward, and the wind continued to ripple. Each gasp of air tasted different, reeking of different scents. One whiff caused nausea, another caused bliss, but all made her head spin. This wasn't like the Mist Keepers; this was nature.

Her heart jumped to her throat. *Calm. Stay calm.*

The wind fought her with every breath. Serenity became its downfall, and only then did the different scents yield.

But Edith did not yield.

"Tristan! Go!"

The pyromancer unleashed his fire without hesitation. Bria expected the attack, and within an instant, she'd suffocated the fire with an inhale. Just like the previous night, she couldn't control the fire, but at least she could stop it. If she held her breath, it would flicker to embers.

"Mayim!" Edith shouted.

Bria spun. The last newcomer, a woman with long black hair, wiped her eyes. A single drop of water appeared on her finger, and with a flick, it shot out, traversing the air like a sea serpent. It slammed into Bria, sending her flying into the wall.

"Now!"

The fire returned, circling around her while the air and water twirled like a hurricane. Only Yusef and Tilda, sitting on their hay bale, did not act, watching as Bria crumbled to the floor. She stared at them, pleading for help.

But they did not come to her rescue.

Her vision grew fuzzy. Another breath of fire lassoed around her, followed by a puff of smoke. While the fire burned, the water lashed. Temperature swayed. And wind yelled. Bria fell deeper into her protective bubble, begging the elements to stop before her skin.

Then Edith emerged from the miniature storm, a sword outstretched. She placed the blade to Bria's chest.

"Do you yield?"

Bria winced.

Lana's voice cut through the air. "She yields."

Edith dropped the sword, and the storm stopped. The fire skidded to embers. The water returned to a mist. And the air gently waved to sleep. Bria collapsed, breathing heavily, as Lana joined her side.

"That was a fruitless endeavor," Lana said to Edith, placing a hand on Bria's shoulder to get her to rest. "She won't learn that way."

"War is not a classroom," Edith replied.

"But you gave her no time to prepare! She's still healing."

"Oh, boo-hoo."

"Maybe I should have kept you imprisoned..." Lana approached Edith. "You have no sense!"

"But I gave her a fantastic test... and now we know what we need." Edith glanced over at Bria. "You need to act more rather than think, girl. You have the talents, but thinking is making you delay. This is no different from your plants."

Bria looked away from Edith, glancing over at the entourage of Magii. They all watched her with curiosity, analyzing each movement and breath.

When Lana didn't respond, Edith continued, "If you don't like that, too bad. Your daughter is an adult now. It's not my fault that you missed her childhood."

Lana clenched her fists but said nothing, eyes locked on Edith. If now was ever the time to use her magic, now would be it.

But Lana still didn't unfurl her anger.

Rather, she stepped back from the scene.

"I don't let anyone harm my people. Bria is no different."

Edith kept her ridiculous smile as she turned her attention back to Bria. Her eyes flared with excitement. "Training will begin tomorrow. I look forward to our lessons."

Bria sat by the fire, peeling open an orange. Her heart rate had finally fallen, and with Nix on her heels, she watched the fire. Tristan had set it alight about an hour after the battle, not saying a word to Bria. Fritjof watched Bria with fascination. Each time he rose, Yusef forced him to sit. Only Mayim spoke to Bria, offering her a cup of water and complimenting Bria's talent. Bria responded with a slight smile, but mostly, she remained quiet, picking at food or petting Nix's head.

Edith and Lana had left with Tilda, as Bria expected. Without a doubt, they probably bickered over the training somewhere else in the Pit. Bria wanted no part of it. The test was necessary, even if it left her feeling defeated. She held her own, sure, but at what cost?

Feel the elements. Let go of your fear.

She finished removing the orange peel and took a piece. A few others had joined the fire, eating and laughing like the world no longer burned. Knoll had become a symbol of their freedom.

But Bria still felt trapped.

Would she even be allowed to leave at the new moon?

Yaz! Bria jumped to her feet. A few people glanced in her direction, but no one questioned her as she hurried from the area with Nix.

As she walked, she dropped her orange, letting a few sprouts follow her. If she remembered right, Yaz stayed in the tenement hall in the center of the Pit, where other children stayed and played. Even as she neared the building, a few children ran past her.

"Come 'ere ya vagrant!" One child barked.

Bria's stomach dropped. She remembered that game: *Guards and Vagrants.* While she never played, she would watch the children playing in the garden. They always made certain children be vagrants—like Brent.

That was before they were even friends, but she still remembered seeing him and others, the target of the game.

Things don't change.

She slowed at the building. A few more children raced out of the door, not paying much mind to her. An older woman stood guard by the entrance to the tenement hall.

"Excuse me?" Bria approached the woman.

The woman smiled, "Ah! You're Rhodana!"

"Oh, uh, yes." Bria flushed, then asked, "Do you know all the children here?"

"I'm the matron here, so yes."

"Do you know a little girl called Yaz?"

"Oh yes, she's here. Why?"

"Can I visit her?"

"You don't need to ask me, dear. Go on up. Haven't seen her leave this evening, so she must be in her room. Floor three. Room number six."

"Thank you."

"Of course, deary."

Bria entered the tenement hall with Nix behind her. Children loitered in the hallways. Some played games. Others picked on their food. The building itself wasn't quite suited for children. Similar to the shape of her own tenement hall, no central location existed for the children. In the largest room on the ground floor, a makeshift kitchen pulsed with the scent of stew. Children waited in line outside, bowls in hand, talking with excitement. This place, despite its tight quarters and broken walls, was far better than prison.

Anywhere was better than the bottom of the towers.

When Bria helped people escape Captain Palmer, she never really sought where the others stayed. It only made sense they would end up in the same buildings as her... even the lonely children.

She reached room six on the third floor. The door waited open for her, and she peeked inside the doorway.

It really wasn't a room for children. Drab, with four cots lining the wall, nothing in the room seemed remarkable. For bags, the children used old potato sacks, mostly filled with worn clothing and makeshift toys. With all the faults of Newbird's Arm, at least her home never had children living in the Pit.

Yaz sat on the cot near the far wall. Bria tapped on the door once, and the girl turned. A smile expanded over her face.

"Miss Bria! You came back!" Yaz jumped from her bed and bolted over, throwing her arms around Bria's waist.

"Of course I did." Bria brushed back Yaz's hair. She let a flower blossom from her fingertips and carefully tucked it behind the girl's ear, just like she used to do with all the children in Newbird's Arm.

"I thought you'd be busy being a forest queen and then forget about me."

"Forget about you? Never. But..." Bria paused, debating how to phrase her next sentence. "Remember how you told me about Ningursu?"

Yaz nodded.

"He's powerful, right?"

"Right."

"And I want to do everything I can to protect you from him. So...I have an opportunity for you."

"What is it?" Yaz adjusted her glasses.

"I have a friend, Micca, who can help get you out of here. Far away, to someplace Ningursu can never touch you."

"Really?"

"Yes. He has a dragon, and he can take you anywhere you want."

Yaz furrowed her brow and fidgeted. Bria could see the cogs turning in her head, imagining the adventures. It reminded Bria of when she discovered the tunnels as a child. All at once, the entire world waited for her.

"Are you coming?" Yaz asked.

Bria shook her head. "I wanted to, really, I did. But...I need to train so I can fight Ningursu for you."

"And save...Brent?"

"Yes, and save Brent."

Yaz continued to squirm, her thoughts taking her entire body by storm, like its own form of magic.

"Can I think about it?" Yaz finally asked. "I don't wanna do what I did with Sir Ja—I mean Ningursu."

"Of course. How about tomorrow afternoon, I take you to visit Micca and the dragon?"

Yaz's face lit up again. "Okay. I'd like that."

Bria couldn't help but return the girl's smile. Children like her, innocent people like her, gave her more reason to fight.

And as long as they trusted her, maybe Bria could unfurl her magic and lead the charge.

CHAPTER FOURTEEN

SOARING

Yaz squeezed Bria's hand as they walked up the path to the hill where the dragon lived. The Forest Queen gave her a sensation of peace. She walked with kindness and never held Yaz too tight. Ms. Kai never held her like that; was this what it was like having a big sister? Or a mother? She still didn't remember her mother, no matter how hard she tried. Occasionally, in her dreams, she would see a faceless figure, but nothing further than that. In those same dreams, sometimes the faceless figure became Ms. Kai.

But Ms. Kai was never her mother.

Yaz wanted nothing more than to stay by Bria's side. At first daylight, she raced out of the tenement hall, only to find a group huddled in the center square. She nearly screamed at what occurred: a man with greasy hair stood over Bria, and around him, the wind caught the trees. As he breathed, a strange scent of lavender filled the air. He held his hand out, beckoning Bria forward as if she were in a trance.

But before Yaz could react, Bria jumped back, and the air around them grew stale. The man choked, bringing his hands up to his throat.

"Yield," he gasped.

And the air returned to normal, a gentle summer breeze molding with the pine needles and the leaves.

The man bowed and stepped back into the crowd.

Another opponent stepped forward, and another battle began. For over three hours, Bria fought each of these opponents, causing them to yield one at a time. Yaz watched in awe, unsure whether she should step in and help. What if Bria hurt herself? What if the forest queen... failed?

Bria answered all of her questions as she walked up the hill. "I hated that you saw me practicing. I didn't want to do that in a public area, but Edith insisted..."

"Who's Edith?"

"She's the one who wants me to practice more with my magic. That's why I was fighting each of those people. They each have a different element that Edith believes I can use to my advantage."

"So you weren't really fighting... you were practicing?"

"Exactly."

Sort of like what Ningursu did with me. He had me practice.

"And because they want you to keep practicing, you can't come with me if I decide to leave?" Yaz asked.

"Yes."

"Oh. I understand."

And Yaz did. She didn't know how else to express it, but she did know more than anything. Bria gave her that glance all adults had, the nod that said *of course you do* but with no real sincerity. Yaz recognized the look too well. Ms. Kai and Mr. Nasr always gave her that look, and sometimes it was with the truth behind it. But after she had been through so much, shouldn't they expect her to understand?

"Yaz...what do you know about magic?" Bria asked as she helped Yaz over a fallen tree.

"What?"

"Magic. What do you know about it?"

"I know that I have Mist Keeper magic, but I don't really know how to use it. And Ningursu said lots of magic was evil." Yaz mumbled. "Ms. Kai and Mr. Nasr didn't care one way or the other... they didn't really tell me stories or anything."

"Well, I want to make sure you understand. You're a bright girl, and I don't think you deserve to be left in the dark about important things. I know what that feels like. People treat me like I don't deserve to know things."

"But you're the Forest Queen! Shouldn't your subjects tell you everything?"

Bria chuckled. "I'm not a queen with a rule or any loyalty. Just some trees." She brushed her hand along the trunk of a tree. Moss bloomed.

Yaz still marveled at it. "Wowee..."

Bria continued, "But what I want you to understand, Yaz, is that war is brewing. Ningursu said evil magic is brewing. And while there is evil magic, he is wrong. More people than you know have magic, however subtle or magnificent. Taking that away from us would not benefit the world at all. In fact, I think the world might... die without it."

"So Ningursu wants the world to die?"

"Something like that. But... whatever his plan is... I'm going to do everything in my power to stop him and protect innocent people. That is why I have to train... even if I do not want to train. I need to be ready for whatever he can do because... I've only seen some of it." Bria paused, glancing back at Yaz with a melancholy expression. "But he's not the only one. The people who control this country, Rosada, they have connections to him. I have to sever those ties and help stop their rule."

"Because they took your country from you? Are you a lost princess or something!?"

"Oh, no. I've always been a... secret queen, I guess. A legend. Rosada is not mine to rule, but I will protect it."

"Oh..." Yaz joined Bria's side and took her hand again. She asked, "And who protects you?"

"What?"

"Don't queens have guards? You're protecting so many people, but all the stories I've read say queens have guards!"

"Oh... well... I have people who help me..."

"Was Brent your guard?"

"Sometimes." Bria's gaze fell on the path, a distant expression that Yaz didn't understand on her face.

"If I ever get good at my mist magic, I can protect you too," Yaz whispered.

Bria didn't reply.

They continued in this silence for a few more minutes, hopping over roots and moving through the plants. Yaz's feet hurt from all the walking, but she didn't complain. She had to be strong. What good would whining about blistered feet do for her?

As they rounded the bend, a gentle light trickled from the trees where a clearing greeted them. At first, all seemed peaceful.

Then, Yaz saw it, basking in the sun like a rock, pulsating with wisps of smoke: a dragon.

The cocky engineer with greasy hair popped up from behind the dragon. Yaz saw him by the tower in the forest almost every day, and up close, he moved with the same clumsy swagger as always.

"Ah! You must be Yaz!" He bounded towards her and held out his hand. "I'm Micca! And this here is my dragon buddy, Zephyr!"

Yaz shook his hand as another voice piped into the conversation.

"Your dragon? She doesn't belong to anyone." Another man stood in between the trees. With a long curly mustache and slicked-back hair, he towered above Yaz like a giant. Except when he moved, it was like he danced.

But more than anything, Yaz couldn't tear her attention away from the child in the man's arms. Translucent, with a mist-like quality, the child reminded Yaz of the ghosts that haunted her dreams and loitered in the Library.

Micca stuck his tongue out at the man, then turned back to Yaz, "That's my man, Timothée. He's the real dragon master if I ever seen one."

"I'm not her master either."

"Blah blah blah, you don't like any of the words I use."

Bria interjected into the conversation, approaching the ghost-like child in Timothée's arms, "Is that Preston?"

"Yeah, this is Preston. Have you met him?" Timothée asked.

"Oh, not you going on about this invisible child too!" Micca griped. "I swear if anyone else says they see him—"

"I see him!" Yaz said.

Micca groaned and threw his hands back. "Ya'll are pulling my leg."

Timothée rolled his eyes. "Why don't you introduce Yaz to Zephyr? I want to talk to Bria."

Yaz exchanged a glance with Bria, then she nodded. With a gulp, she removed herself from Bria's side and approached Micca.

"A'ight, well, at least this isn't all too ridiculous then. Because if anything, I know this freaking dragon is real." Micca muttered.

The dragon followed Micca with her gaze as they approached, as if she heard what the man had said. Yaz stayed a few steps back, her heart growing louder in her ears with each step closer to the animal. Something about it reminded her of the demons, ghosts, and Mist Keepers pulsating with mist. This creature belonged to another realm.

Yaz stole a quick glance back at Bria, who stood at the tree line with Timothée, engaged in a conversation.

"Zephyr isn't gonna hurt you." Micca called to her, "Trust me. Unless you act like a twat, she likes people, a'ight?"

"Okay..." Yaz took another step toward the beast, throwing one more glance back at Bria. The forest queen wouldn't let her get hurt, right?

The dragon watched her with a pair of striking silver eyes, lying on the ground like a dog resting, waiting to play. Micca took Yaz's hand and held it out to the dragon.

As if the dragon understood Yaz's fear, it didn't move, letting Yaz's finger graze its warm, scaly skin.

"See?" Micca asked. "Yaz is a good dragon. She won't hurt you."

Yaz kept her fingers on top of the creature, watching as it breathed. She turned back to Micca to ask, "Where did the dragon come from?"

"Well, it was a prisoner of a circus, but Timothée over there thinks she came from a place called Spinoza. He wants to take it back there."

"If I go with you, is that where we're heading?"

"Most likely, to start at least. Unless Zephyr decides to go off track or something." Micca winked.

"So far away from here?"

"Yeah. No more Rosada for us."

"Oh..." Yaz threw another glance at Bria, but she still spoke to Timothée with focus.

"Are you scared still?" Micca kept pressing.

Yaz shrugged. "I've never flown before..." Well, that was a partial lie. She *had* flown through the eyes of the Diabolo but never on a dragon.

Never in her own body.

"You wanna try it?"

"Try what?"

"Flying! C'mon. I'll take you on a loop around Knoll!"

"Oh... really?"

"Yeah!" Micca shouted over to Bria and Timothée, "Oi! I'm gonna take the girl for a ride. We'll be back in ten minutes top, a'ight?"

Timothée waved his hand while Bria threw a quick supportive smile in Yaz's direction. That was enough to ease Yaz's nerves enough to agree to the ride.

"A'ight, c'mon on then!" Micca hopped over to the dragon. "Zephyr, wake up! Time for a joy ride!"

The dragon yawned, stretched, then stood, towering almost as high as some of the small trees. Yaz jumped in surprise but then accepted Micca's hand.

He hoisted Yaz up onto the dragon's back and secured her near the creature's neck. "Hold on to the scale right there. Atta girl."

Yaz dug her fingers into the scale, but not hard enough to bother Zephyr, while Micca reached for the rope hanging around the dragon's neck. He shook it once, and the dragon released its giant wings.

Before Yaz could second guess her decision, the dragon then pumped its wings once and lifted off the ground. Yaz yelped as the wind wrapped around her. Her knees shook as they climbed above the trees. And her heart climbed in her ears.

But once they reached high above the treeline, Zephyr's wings stopped beating.

And they soared peacefully through the summer sky. Wind caught her hair, and a few bugs hit her glasses, but otherwise, everything flew with a song of peace. Yaz loosened her grip around the dragon's scales, taking a chance to take in the sights.

From high above, she saw everything. Bria and Timothée became nothing more than specks on top of the hill, while the city below looked like a broken play set, with towers standing like a pile of broken blocks. In the distance, even the Pit where she'd been staying had a strange dead sensation to it. How many ghosts haunted it now that she had seen the one? Would they return to her? Would the Mist Keepers?

If this place was haunted, she would have to leave.

But she didn't care about that as her attention fell on the beautiful, lush forest that circled the city. It climbed over train tracks and pulsed with life like a gasp of fresh air. The forest made everything come to life around it. Even the sky appeared bluer while the water glistened with a brighter resolve.

This was indeed the legacy of the forest queen.

"What d'ya think?" Micca asked behind her.

"It's amazing!" Yaz exclaimed.

And she didn't lie about it either; it truly was spectacular. What more could she see soaring in the sky like this?

What waited for her in the world?

Yaz spent the entire trip down the mountain babbling about the dragon ride. Bria listened to each of her words, smiling every time Yaz remembered another detail. For the first time in months, Yaz felt excited. She hadn't definitely committed to leaving, but her qualms about Zephyr had vanished like the ground beneath her. The dragon would take her across the world! Not even Ningursu had a dragon!

When they returned to the tenement hall, she hugged Bria once before venturing back to her room. Bria promised to visit every day until it was time to leave. It was the first time Yaz felt a constant in her life. It might be short-lived, but she would take it with her heart.

She raced over to her bed when she got back to her room, immediately removing the white flower Bria had given her from under the pillow. *Maybe I can turn it into a necklace or a barrette or something! I don't want to lose it.* She ran her fingers over the edge of the petals, engrossed in their shape.

She didn't hear anyone else enter the room.

"Yaz!"

Yaz jumped. Chander and Anandi stood in the doorway. Anandi had her hands on her hips, while Chander looked disinterested, as always.

"Oh, hi! Sorry I couldn't play today. I was—"

"You were riding on the dragon! When did you get permission to do that!?" Anandi inquired. "We've been asking Mr. Timothée for weeks, and he always says no!"

"Oh, well... um..." Yaz fidgeted. How could she tell her friends that she might be leaving?

"She was also with the forest queen," Chander muttered.

"Yeah, I met her the other day..."

"And you didn't tell us!?" Anandi continued to rant.

"I didn't think you'd care."

"It's the forest queen! Of course we'd care!" Anandi stomped forward, continuing to glower at Yaz. "Now tell me why you were on the dragon!"

Yaz sighed, "I... might be leaving with the dragon riders in a couple days. The Forest Queen wants to protect me."

"From what!?"

"Probably Chef's disgusting gruel...again," Chander said.

Anandi glowered at her brother before turning back to Yaz. "Well!?"

Yaz fidgeted. She hadn't told her friends where she came from or what had happened. How could she?

"Well!?"

"Before I was here...I was kidnapped by bad people. And if they know I'm here, they might come back and cause worse problems." Yaz kept her voice low and her head lower. "Bria...the Forest Queen...she wants me to leave here for my own safety and go far away. I can do that with the dragon riders and Zephyr. But they wanted to make sure I was comfortable flying on the dragon and the dragon liked me. That's why I was there today."

Anandi frowned. "So you're leaving us?"

"Probably..." Yaz fidgeted with the flower in her hands.

"But you'll be alone with some people you hardly know! Isn't that scary?"

Yaz shrugged. She'd been with worse people, she supposed.

Anandi collapsed on a cot and kicked her legs out, clenching her fists to her side. "Not fair!" she bemoaned.

Yaz continued to fidget with the flower. Perhaps it wasn't the best idea to leave after all.

"Anandi, stop throwing a tantrum," Chander grunted.

"But I wanna fly on a dragon!"

"I know you do. That's why we're gonna go with Yaz."

"Wait... what?" Yaz asked.

"We're going with you. Whether they want us to or not. It's not like Anandi and I have anything here."

"But—"

"No. We're going. End of discussion. Come on, Anandi. We should probably start planning our good-byes."

As if a switch went off in Anandi's head, she bounced off the bed and raced after her brother, leaving Yaz alone and wondering what had just happened.

CHAPTER FIFTEEN

TORN FROM THE MIST

Brent rubbed the ink on his hands, staring at the last sentence of his new story. Alojzy's tale bled from the canvas, and now Brent had a glimpse of the man's true form. He always knew that Alojzy slithered with disloyalties and dishonesties, but not to the extent that he'd alienated everyone around him. Alojzy, the Architect of the Mist, took the lives of his wife, his daughters, and those he did not trust. All in the name of his god: Ningursu. People like him gave Ningursu power, and now Alojzy operated with the same intensity.

The story left Brent feeling hollow inside as he leaned against the wall. For three days, he had hardly left his hideaway amongst the canvases, engaged in the tale with such intensity that the mist failed to dissipate. But now he knew one thing: the Library, Alojzy's pride and joy, was nothing more than a product of the mist.

If he could find the right stories, then it might easily fall into his control.

But how?

When he looked at the walls, he saw a structure sprawling out before him, made of nothing more than stone. Bria deciphered its more natural elements: while the mist constructed the structure, the heart of the Library had always been the core of a tree. Alojzy had built a home that invaded the core of the world.

Now Brent had to escape it.

He glanced at his pineapple on the floor. It sat there with a lopsided smile he'd drawn on it halfway through writing Alojzy's tale. "Don't look at me like that. I know staying in here for this amount of time was... It wasn't a good idea, but I had this story and...yeah."

Brent shook his head. *This is getting out of hand.*

He glanced over the room once again. The room pulsed with Julietta's tale, but he hadn't dared venture too far into it. With painting scribbled across a multitude of canvases, her story moved about the room like a ghost... just like how she used to operate in the Library. When Brent first met Julietta, she moved with grace and elegance, but a strange mystery behind her. Even the story, sifting in a room that once belonged to her, remained an enigmatic lure.

His stomach grumbled. Brent moved his pineapple to the side and dug into the bag where he'd been keeping his dried fruits and nuts.

Only to find it empty.

Brent glowered at the pineapple. "What'd you do? You think that stealing my food will make me eat you?"

The pineapple stared.

"Yeah, no, not happening." Brent picked up the small bag and glanced around the room. If he focused, the walls shifted, blessing him with a moment of smoke. He stepped forward, letting it wrap around him.

The walls changed, and his body was transported out of his newfound hideaway. He had to focus in order to survive; one wrong move, and he'd end up in Ningursu's office.

Food. Galley. Focus. It was like a story. If he told a story of arrival, he would arrive.

That was how he saw it, at least.

And in his mind's eye, he imagined just that: arriving in the galley, hidden behind empty barrels, where no one would see him.

The mist took him there like a breath, and he exhaled as he skidded to a halt. If only the Library didn't suffocate him, if only it didn't keep the mist from carrying him outside of its walls. Then he would be free of this labyrinth.

But that was a wish he carried with every step.

He snuck along the back wall to the cellar, keeping his breaths low. His stomach growled again. More than anything, he yearned for a full meal—meat, bread, cheese, vegetables... anything. But in the cellar, he found only more dried fruits and nuts to pile into his bag.

As he filled the bag to its brim, the opening of a door outside the cellar startled him. He dropped the bag and the array of nuts scattered on the floor.

Shite. He seeped into the shelving.

No one came to the cellar door.

Well, except for their voices.

"We're preparing for the demonstration." The first voice boomed. Brent recognized it as Jiang.

"Good," the second voice said, crisp and pointed.

Jiang and Aelia... Brent gripped the wall.

"I'll be honest. This whole thing feels like a fool's run if you ask me. The reaction will not be what we want...especially in Rosada," Jiang said.

"Sometimes, to defeat the enemy, you must play their game," Aelia replied.

"And if this works... what next?"

"We'll see what Ningursu says. But I imagine we'll expand."

Jiang didn't reply, leaving a silence hanging in the air. What were they talking about, though? None of this really helped him pinpoint the topic. Clearly, the Council planned something; he knew that without thinking. But what?

"Did you brew enough of the recipe I wrote up for you?" Aelia asked Jiang.

"Working on it now. Need some more of that dried morning glory. I don't know why you don't do this yourself…"

"Pardon?"

"Nothing. Grabbing it now."

Brent shrank further back into the shelving. *I need to get out of here.*

The door to the cellar turned.

Brent focused on the mist, begging it to open its arms and let him escape.

Light trickled into the cellar like a halo around Jiang's body.

His eyes locked with Brent.

His mouth opened.

His iris turned white.

But Brent's body shifted into the mist before he could hear a word.

The smoke tightened around Brent, tugging at his limbs as he resurfaced from the mist. A new air sifted through the Library. Now that Jiang had seen him, surely the walls had sprouted eyes. Ningursu had his ways of controlling the Library, and a gasp of mist was all it took for him to take control.

"Shite," Brent cursed, glancing amongst the shelves of books. He didn't set a specific destination when controlling the mist and found himself on the ground floor of the Library, surrounded by books. His head spun, and he let the air settle, gripping a shelf for stability. Where could he run? If he avoided Ningursu long enough, he'd transform back into a phantom, haunting the walls and playing games. But Ningursu had weeks to figure out what to do if he found Brent.

And Brent did not doubt that the chase had begun.

He didn't bother waiting, weaving in and out of the shelves to hide from his invisible foe. Pressure grew in the air, like fingers weaving their way through the mist, searching for him in the shelves. The sound of books clattering to the floor gave Brent pause. In his core, he wanted to help the books find their place back on the shelves, but he didn't have the time. Instead, he kept running in his endless circle.

As he ran, the stories removed themselves from the wall, beckoning him forward with different tales. He caught whiffs of every single Mist Keeper. Of Ningursu leading his brother Nedo through the halls with Aelia wandering by his side. In another, Tomás sat cross-legged by the fire, Julietta humming to herself, and Jiang practicing sword fighting with a wall. In brief glimpses, Malaika appeared, scouring the shelves with a handwritten map. All while Alojzy ruled his structure like a king, and Caroline adjusted her lip paint in a mirror. Their stories called to him. If he stepped forward, he might learn more, but he hadn't the time.

Run. Keep running. Eventually, Ningursu will get tired, and the stalemate will return.

But the pressure did not retreat. Rather, as he tried to blend in with the mist, a new foe emerged.

It crawled from the walls, oozing like blood; tendrils of black smoke whisked through the air, growing closer to him with every movement. It reached for Brent, and despite the stories he threw in its direction, the smoke did not yield. Like ropes, it laced around Brent's wrists and ankles, bounding him in place.

He tugged against the tendrils as they pulled him to the floor. They had no story. Even as he summoned the story of a fisherman at sea, or a hunter chopping wood, the tendrils did not yield.

His face hit the ground, with his cheek pressed to the wooden floor. Before him, the mist continued its assault, tightening around him.

Darker...

Darker...

Darker...

With it, he fell deep into an abyss.

Smoke...

Air...

Nothingness...

Then cold.

The mist relinquished at once, leaving him in utter darkness. Around him, cold stones served as his fortress, with nothing more than a small grate in the wall blessing the room with the faintest gasp of light.

And that was enough for Brent. His location sank into him, resting like a lump in his throat.

The mist had pulled him into the crypts, deep in the core of the Library.

Now, he had joined the silver-eyed creature—no, people—that he had seen in the crypts.

Disjointed. Empty. Alone.

To fade into nothingness.

He gripped the walls. No stories loitered for him to ground himself. No matter where he searched, this cell had only just been born, primed for him and him alone.

His vision grew blurry. How couldn't there be any stories? Even a new book had stories laced into its spines. Someone had to build this crypt! Something had to loiter in the walls.

But here, there was nothing.

Here, nothing remained.

Here, nothing would ground him.

Would his Diabolo return? Would he find his mind slipping?

Would he even remember Bria?

No. Of course he would remember Bria. That much was a constant.

So he clung to her memory, like a precious flower, against his chest.

Even as the surrounding walls shifted and the crypt grew dark, he promised himself that the stories would return.

Because without stories, who was Brent Harley?

CHAPTER SIXTEEN

A SONG FOR THE SENATE

Christof winced as the subway rumbled beneath the plaza. Of all the things in the Capital, he could not get used to the technology that dominated the city. From wires hanging along poles, constant radio transmissions, underground railroads, and even a theater that displayed moving pictures on its wall—the city had its own manmade magic. No wonder storytellers and Magii hid in plain sight. They could use this technology to their advantage, and no one would think anything otherwise.

He glanced back at the plaza. A crystalized shopping gallery stared off with the Capital's temple, marked by the hustle and bustle of people with their heads downcast. Word had spread fast of the newest attack on storytellers. On the front of every newspaper, a photograph of the guard pulling people from the alleyway dominated the cover. Christof had avoided the shot, passing the glory onto a city native. As much as he wanted to be the one to carry the fame, to continue with pride, he had to stay in the shadows.

Otherwise, even the storytellers might know his name.

He returned his focus to the Capitol Building at the end of the road, perched above the plaza with a smirk of glory. That morning, Sister Jey Ma asked him to meet her at the Capitol when noon struck, as she had a meeting with Gisela and Yeshua from the Curio Tower.

Already a few minutes late, Christof marched to his usual beat. He had not a clue what would happen today—no one ever told him, so why bother rushing?

Sister Jey Ma waited for him on the Capitol's steps, arms crossed, eyes lost in a deep focus. She greeted him with a nod and a lack of lecturing, then laced her arm through his.

"Afternoon, Sister," Christof said.

"Hello, Cadet. You are late," she replied as she led him up the stairs.

"I apologize...but shouldn't you refer to me as 'Lieutenant' now?"

"In due time. Come."

Christof asked no more questions as they ascended the stairs. Guards lined the path; some he had met after the attack on the storytellers, and some he knew from the towers. One man caught his eye: Lieutenant Drayton. They locked eyes for a moment. *Probably should tell him about that little boy. Still don't got a clue what is going on, though.*

Senator Cordova waited for them at the entrance to the Capitol with that slimy Elder An Drew at his side. Something about the Elder still made Christof's skin crawl. He watched Sister Jey Ma with precision, and as they approached, the Elder stepped forward and handed Sister Jey Ma a small cup. She pressed it to her lips, took a gulp, then handed it back, all in one swift movement. The Elder then whispered something in Sister Jey Ma's ear before stepping back to open the door.

"Come," Senator Cordova ordered.

Christof yearned to know what Elder An Drew said to Sister Jey Ma, but he knew better than to ask as they left the Elder in the entranceway. He had to maintain his poise.

After all, he was her guard.

Her consort.

Her protector.

She was his commander.

Sister Jey Ma squeezed his arm as they followed Senator Cordova into the building. A wide marble hallway greeted them, with a pristine stairwell climbing to the next floor. They did not ascend it, though, venturing beyond the winding steps and into a small room towards the back of the entrance hall. Nothing more than a small library waited for them, but Senator Cordova acted without hesitancy.

He removed five books from the shelf, and as the last one fell, the shelves opened. On the other side, a corridor lined with stone greeted them with the glow of the candlelight.

"This way," the senator said without looking back at Sister Jey Ma or Christof.

Christof stepped into the corridor, questions lingering on his tongue. This was not his place. He had to remember that.

He was here as a guard and a guard alone.

As they strode down the dark corridor, the doorway closed behind them, leaving only a gentle candlelight as their guide.

"Was this Rose and Ada's fortress?" Sister Jey Ma asked, her curiosity reminiscent of when she had been *Jemma*. Christof knew a little about Rose and Ada, of course. They were the founders of Rosada, who fled their home after their father, a silver-eyed sorcerer, wreaked havoc. They came to this empty land with a promise that magic would not wreak havoc.

And with that promise, the Effluvium revealed its true colors.

"Yes," Senator Cordova replied, "they built their home here after their arrival. The Senate still embraces it now." The senator turned his attention to the ceiling, wringing his hands behind his back as he walked. "My father and uncle used to take me here as a boy. Quite a remarkable structure, really. Hasn't changed a bit. I can still recall all the secret tunnels and crevasses."

"I did not know your family had a history with the senate," Sister Jey Ma remarked, asking all the questions Christof wondered himself.

"Oh no, not the Senate. My father was a guard, and my uncle was an Elder," Senator Cordova replied. "I used to come here all the time until they sent my father to Newbird's Arm."

"What made him leave the Capital? Surely the best opportunities are here."

"Punishment."

The words slipped from Christof's lips. "For what?"

"Ah, nothing major. He broke a few formalities and laws when trying to stop some illegal storytelling tavern. When his superiors found out they threatened his career, so he accepted the transfer." Senator Cordova motioned them down a narrow corridor as he continued. "It may have been for the best—we would not be here today if I did not start my career in Newbird's Arm."

"I see..." Christof scowled. Storytelling taverns? The mere idea that something could operate in broad daylight seemed preposterous.

He didn't ask any more questions as they came upon a narrow door with a rusted bolt. Senator Cordova removed an equally rusted key from his pocket and lined it with the lock.

As he inserted it, he glanced at Sister Jey Ma. "Are you ready?

Sister Jey Ma nodded.

Christof interjected. "For what? No one has told me jack-shite!"

"Christof!" Sister Jey Ma tugged at his arm.

Senator Cordova waved his hand. "Sister Jey Ma trusts you to guard her as she performs."

"So that's what I am now? A watchdog?"

"Christof..." Sister Jey Ma hissed again.

"Trust me, Cadet. This is an honor few will experience. Place your trust in the Effluvium." Senator Cordova placed a hand on Sister Jey Ma's back. "Come along, Sister. Your audience awaits."

Christof trailed to the back, glowering as Senator Cordova pushed open the door. A stone balcony awaited them, staring down at the Senate Chambers with determination and resolve. Just beyond them, dim lights cast shadows onto the stone walls, extending down to the mahogany floor of the Senate, where senators gathered in discussion. Christof could not hear them, but from his perch, he recognized Senator Heartz from Newbird's Arm. With her dominating stature, frizzy hair, and boisterous laugh, it was hard to miss her.

Senator Cordova did not speak. He merely stepped forward, removed a small glimmering pistol from his pocket, and shot into the air three times.

Bang! Bang! Bang!

The senators turned.

"Good afternoon," Senator Cordova boomed.

"Donovan!" Senator Heartz rose from her spot. "What is the meaning of this ridiculous entry!? We have been waiting for you for hours!"

"Ah, Helga, you wish you could garner such attention...but you can only do that if you show up to the Chamber."

"I am here right now, am I not?"

"Only to go shopping in the Gallery later."

Christof restrained a laugh. How many times had Senator Heartz returned to Newbird's Arm with a new hat or a pristine suit? How many days had she spent hiding in her gorgeous mansion or luscious gardens?

"It is not like you have been to any recent Chamber meetings," Senator Heartz kept her defense. "You are as aloof as anyone."

"I have had a city to run."

"And destroy..." another senator grumbled.

"Do you have something to say, Franklin?"

The grumbling senator did not meet Senator Cordova's gaze as he spoke. "Everyone knows what happened in Knoll. You let some vagrants run hog-wild. We wouldn't let that happen in Hutch."

Christof recognized the senator the more he spoke; the senator of the neighboring region of Hutch, Senator Franklin Porter, kept order locked firm in the region. Other than Senator Porter and Senator Heartz, Christof could not name the other eight members standing on the Senate floor. A few he recognized from other regions, most notably the senator from Aeterno, but he could not recall their names at all. But it didn't matter, really—not now, at least.

Senator Cordova replied to Senator Porter without a hint of betrayal. "The vagrant uprising was unprecedented. We left Knoll with what we needed. At least we did not work with the vagrants like our dear Senator Heartz here."

Senator Heartz scoffed. "I would rather support my constituents than kill innocent people."

"Ah, taking after your father now?" Senator Cordova chuckled. "I have not shed blood."

"You have given the order."

"Their duty is to the Effluvium."

"Their duty is to this country!"

"Their duty is what is right. That is why we are here today, after all. To fix all the wrong with Rosada. Here, let me introduce you to Sister Jey Ma. She'll tell you what she has seen." Senator Cordova glanced back at Sister Jey Ma. She had been so still that Christof almost forgot she stood beside him.

Before any of the senators could protest, Sister Jey Ma stepped to the front of the balcony. She bowed her head, then, with a low, soft tune, she began to sing.

Here now,
Listen to me close,
It's here now,
That distant smoke,
Give it now,
A single breath stroke,
And say it now,
Pure as is remote,
It's here now,
The purity knows,
It's here now,

As she said the last word, wisps of gold exited her mouth and laced through the air. It waltzed in front of Christof before seeping to the Senate Chambers. There, it wrapped around the senators, pulling at their skin, filling their nostrils and eyes. Half of the chamber stood there, unphased and in awe, while the other half fell to their knees. One senator's head snapped backward, foam filling their mouth, convulsing in place. Another fell to the floor as if in a seizure. With each passing second, the golden smoke grew thicker, tightening around them, until the five lay on the floor, unconscious and heaving.

Christof stepped back once, unable to shake the new emptiness washing over his core. His heart stopped in place, and his head spun; what had happened?

As the golden smoke settled, the five remaining senators gawked in horror at Senator Cordova and Sister Jey Ma.

Senator Heartz and Senator Porter stood amongst them.

"Hmph," Senator Cordova shrugged, "I could have sworn you would have magic, Helga."

"What did you do!?" Senator Heartz barked back at him.

"Exposing the traitors."

"What!?"

"They have magic."

That piqued Christof's interest.

And Senator Heartz asked the question on his mind: "What are you talking about? They have never shown any magic!"

"When you get to be my age, you learn a few things… and the past few years have only exasperated these beliefs." Senator Cordova leaned against the railing, staring down at Senator Heartz. "Magic is hidden everywhere. People use it and taint the Effluvium without even knowing. We have tried to scoff it out… trap it in our Pits… and send it away. But that is not enough. It continues to reign everywhere… not just in Rosada. But every country on this planet succumbs to magic's nefarious hand. So, we must put our foot down… and end this magic… once and for all." Senator Cordova stroked his silver pistol. "Now, if you agree, you will join in this plight. If not… then you are no more a traitor than the Magii convulsing on the floor."

The remaining senators stood still, awaiting a response. Senator Porter stepped forward first, bowing to Senator Cordova. The senator from Aeterno followed suit, and then one other senator whom Christof did not recognize. But Senator Heartz and another unfamiliar face did not move, standing in place, stubborn as ever.

Senator Heartz spoke with determination, her voice unyielding. "I shall not kneel to you. I stood by my home as they fought against you. I might not be as noble as my papa, but I will continue to hold my virtues. I shall not—"

Bang!

Christof stumbled back at the noise, gripping tight to Sister Jey Ma's arm. Smoke gathered from the tip of Senator Cordova's pistol.

Then settled.

A single bullet had pierced the center of Senator Heartz's forehead.

Her eyes widened, then, with an inhumane wheeze, she collapsed on the floor.

The gunshot set everything in motion. The main doors to the Senate Chambers flew open, and in raced the guards, led by the giant Captain Rivers. One by one, they shot the traitors dead, leaving but a pile of bodies on the floor and only three senators remaining. The blood moved across the ground like a river.

For a moment there, Christof stood again in the Tower of Ab Aeterno, amongst the rubble and death. The bodies lay strewn, staring at him, watching him.

And there he saw his father's lifeless eyes, bearing into his soul.

Judging him.

Watching him.

And yelling as Christof left him to rot.

You useless kid, his father said to him often. *Just like your ma. Ain't take the lead in nothing. Always a leader, never a follower. Useless if ya ask me.*

Christof reached for his own pistol. His sweaty fingers reached for the trigger.

But he still couldn't remove the gun.

What could he do now? The blood had already planted the seeds of a new future.

This battle, this Senate, had fallen with a single song, with blood dripping like seeds on the ground. Traitors lost their lives. The first step to eliminating magic: complete.

But was it the right step? These senators might not have known they even had magic.

What if Christof had magic? Would he have succumbed to the song, too?

"Did you know this was gonna happen?" Christof asked Sister Jey Ma, voice shaking with each word.

Sister Jey Ma didn't answer.

"Jem!" he hissed.

She glanced at him. Her eyes bore a lifeless yellow.

She said only one thing, and one thing only: "It is what we must do for the Effluvium."

But was this the Effluvium that Christof vowed to protect?

That, he still didn't know.

A Drawing in the Dirt

A cloudy day marked Yaz's departure. She clutched Bria's hand tight as they ascended the hill. Since the day she met Zephyr, she hadn't seen Chander or Anandi. Were they mad at her? Or were they really sneaking onto the dragon like they said? It wasn't like she decided who would leave with them. Why were they so upset?

Even in the following days, Yaz's focus fell on her friends. She hardly paid attention as Micca gave her more lessons about the dragon or as Timothée reminded her what to pack. If Bria wasn't there to help, Yaz wasn't sure what she would do.

She squeezed Bria's hand again. Much to her disappointment, the Forest Queen would not travel with her. Yaz understood; she watched every day as Bria practiced her magic, sparring with other Magii. Each time, Yaz nearly screamed. How could the Forest Queen save herself from fire? Or rock? Or water? Sometimes, she couldn't, and she went hurdling onto the ground. But other times, she controlled the elements like the forest.

Yaz didn't understand how, but that was all a part of the magic.

As they reached the top of the hill, Bria spoke, "I wish I could come with you... away from all of this."

"I know... but you have to be a queen, right?" Yaz asked.

"I have to be something." Bria smiled down at Yaz. "You still have your flower, right?

Yaz reached into her coat pocket and removed the white flower, still as healthy as the day she received it.

"Do you remember what I said about it?"

"Yeah... if it is still alive, then everything is okay."

"And that means I will protect you."

Yaz stroked the petals. "So I'll see you again someday?"

"Without a doubt. I promise."

Yaz grinned and replaced the flower.

They resumed their trek up the hill, where Micca waited, a grin spreading ear to ear. Behind him, Zephyr loitered, huffing with smoke.

"About time you two showed your faces. Been waiting here all morning."

"It is a hike up the mountain," Bria replied.

"I could've come to get ya."

"I didn't want to draw too much attention."

Micca shrugged and glanced at Yaz. "Ya ready, girly?"

Yaz glanced up at Bria.

"You're going to be okay. We'll be together again soon," Bria said, her words gentle. "I promise."

"I know." Yaz beamed, then threw her arms around Bria's waist.

Bria hugged her back, gentle as always. "Be good."

"I will."

Yaz released Bria, smiling one last time at the Forest Queen. There was a sadness in her eyes, one that Yaz wished she could help with, but she knew that would be impossible. The Forest Queen wore the world on her shoulders.

Wasn't Yaz nothing more than a child?

"C'mon, Yaz. Let's get ya out of here, you hear?" Micca touted. "Timothée's finishing getting Zephyr ready and everything. We got a nice spot for you on Zephyr's back, a'ight?"

"Okay-doke." Yaz waved to Bria and followed Micca toward the dragon. Bria stood there, hugging herself, still watching as Yaz left.

But as Yaz joined Timothée and Micca on the other side of the dragon, Bria vanished from her sight.

Timothée loaded bags onto the back of the dragon while the strange ghost child sat on the ground drawing with his finger in the sand. He didn't look up as Yaz walked past him. For a young child, he had this lost gleam in his eye, as if he had lost something dear to him.

Well, other than his life.

"So we've made this saddle here," Micca said, pointing to a large piece of leather on the back of the dragon's back. "Timothée needs to ride in the front 'cause he can control Zephyr the best, but that saddle there will keep you secure. Don't know why he made it for multiple people, though... there's only the three of us."

"Four," Timothée called over his shoulder. "Don't forget about Preston!"

"Preston ain't real! Stop with that shite!"

"You just don't have the sight to see him—no magic and all that shite."

Yaz interjected, "Preston is right here, right? He's a ghost?"

"He's something..." Timothée eyed Yaz and Preston carefully. "So I guess you see him?"

"Yeah, he's right here!"

"A'ight, then I'll want you to keep a good eye on him, okay? He's scared and doesn't talk much, but he's a good kid. A'ight?"

Micca visibly rolled his eyes, but Yaz agreed.

"Good. We'll get going shortly. Gotta do some last-minute prep, a'ight?"

Yaz nodded again and sat down beside Preston. The little boy did not look at her, continuing to doodle on the ground. It seemed to be fruitless scribbles at first, but as Yaz watched, it took form. The boy continued to scribble, forming a circle on the ground, where two slits sat, staring like eyes. Around the slits, blobs in humanoid shapes lay scattered.

She reached out to touch the edge of the drawing. Preston stared at her.

And as their eyes locked, yellow masked Yaz's vision.

She stood in the room.

Hungry.

Starving.

Just a small taste would solve it.

And she could sleep.

Sleep. That's what she wanted.

That's what she needed.

Just a taste...

And she did scream. It exited her body in a rush. The ghost child beside her cried out.

But she only saw yellow pulsating around her, begging to be used. It was the first time since escaping Ningursu that the yellow came back to her. It pulled at her skin, begging for her attention.

She could feel people piling around her. One person reached out for her arm.

"Yaz! I need you to focus!" A boy's voice called.

"I can't!" she sobbed.

"Listen, I know it's scary...but it's not real."

"No...it's real. I feel it."

"It's not here, though."

Yaz shook her head.

"Listen!" the voice continued, "I met someone, and he said that when things are confusing, think of something important to you... something that is constantly there. It helps me with my magic, too, 'cause I think of Anandi."

"I don't have anything, though."

"You have me and Anandi. We're your friends."

Yaz blinked. *Friends?* She had friends? Since when? Sure, she had Bria protecting her, and Micca was friendly enough… but she didn't realize that Chander and Anandi thought of her as a friend!

Especially after their last interaction.

The yellow still tugged at her, but now she saw the outline of her *friend*, Chander, sitting there with his usual serious expression and thick eyebrows creased. He kept a hand on Yaz's shoulder, eyes unyielding. After Yaz blinked a few more times, Chander released her, closing his eyes once and whispering to himself.

Behind him, Anandi clutched a bag with Micca beside her while Timothée stood a few more paces back with Preston in his arms. Bria knelt on the other side of Yaz, sweat matting her brow. Everyone was there. For *her*.

They didn't cast her aside like Ningursu and the other Mist Keepers.

Instead, they stayed by her side.

My friends.

"What happened, Yaz?" Bria asked.

"I saw yellow when I looked at Preston's drawing…" She glanced at the ground. Footprints covered the markings in the dirt.

"What did he draw?"

"It was a circle and eyes and people, I think. Or that's what it looked like. It might have been scribbles…"

Bria glanced over at Timothée and Preston, mouthed something, then turned back to Yaz. "Well, you're okay now, alright?"

Yaz nodded and stared at the ground. The yellow continued with quiet wisps, but only like the hums of birds or the whisper of the wind.

"Is it really a good idea for her to fly if she's gonna be like this?" Micca asked.

"It's even more important that she leaves," Bria responded at once.

Anandi finally piped up, still clutching her bag, "And Chander and me are coming with her!"

"I told you already, no you aren't!" Micca argued back at her.

But Yaz mumbled her own response. "I want my friends with me... if Bria can't come... I need my friends."

She raised her head up to meet Bria's gaze. The Forest Queen frowned, contemplated for a moment, then turned back to Micca and Timothée. "Is there enough room for Chander and Anandi?"

"There is, but isn't this a bit rash?" Timothée asked. "They're kids—it's a last-minute decision."

"We don't have anything here or anywhere, really," Chander stated, confident despite how his eyes remained shut. "We want out."

Bria glanced in Chander's direction. Her brow furrowed. "I think it would be for the best—Yaz needs her friends."

Micca groaned but didn't argue. With that distasteful noise of approval, Anandi raced over to Yaz's side and threw her arms around her. Chander joined them, too, still keeping an arm's length from Yaz, a smirk on his face.

"Alright. Guess we've got a full group then." Timothée winked at Micca, "Guess we better get Zephyr all prepped and ready."

Yaz stared back at the ground as the adults continued talking. Her head ached, and her body quaked, the remnants of the yellow still surrounding her. But maybe, with her friends at her side, she'd be okay.

Perhaps, together, they might stop the yellow.

CHAPTER EIGHTEEN

THE ENDLESS TEST

Bria leaned against the tree, waving as Zephyr hoisted herself from the ground with Timothée, Micca, Yaz, and the other children on her back. The dragon roared once, exploding with smoke, then launched itself with steady beats into the sky. Her own heart grew heavier with each thump. That little girl, Yaz, she bore so much already on her shoulders—but at least she had the opportunity to be free. Everyone deserved that chance.

But more rode on that dragon than just Yaz. She had friends, ones that could help her stay whole; ones who knew what it meant to be taken from their home. Bria almost forgot about Chander and his sister, despite rescuing them from Captain Palmer's tower months earlier. Chander's magic was unique; any time someone touched him, or he touched someone else, their sight became his... at least until the next touch occurred. When Bria met him, he held that power with fear.

Until Brent spoke to him—and that seemed to help.

Then, of course, there was Preston—the ghost child. Bria saw the child more clearly now than she did the first time in Mert. The deceased son of Todd and Lex Dray now sat on that dragon... disconnected from his twin brother—his living brother. According to Timothée, Lex handed the ghost child to him as she said her dying words. No one had found the living brother or his father. The child, like Yaz, needed to leave here, though; if his brother had been taken by the Order, Bria could only fear what might ensue.

As Zephyr disappeared into the clouds, Bria left her post by the tree and started the descent back to the Pit. She let the trees call to her, but her focus remained on the pebbles and the air. Her training, exhausting as ever, seemed frivolous. She sensed the elements if she focused but could not manipulate them with a mere thought. They wanted her to each use the elements in a different fashion: mold them like clay, taste the air, listen to the waves, or focus on internal heat. But Bria's magic didn't work like that; everything she did, every element she wove, it had to do with *her*. Didn't they understand that her magic was not driven by some external force? All of it came down to what *she* felt.

But that wasn't the answer they searched for when "teaching" her.

As she rounded the bend, a gust of wind tossed her backward into a tree. The branches caught her, keeping her upright.

Fritjof walked around the bend, still in a pristine suit, with his hair combed. He smiled at Bria. "Ah, there you are, my lovely lady. You missed our spar this morning."

"I told you I had an errand to attend to this morning," Bria said as she removed herself from the tree.

"Edith was not fond of such choices." Fritjof beckoned her forward with his finger. As he motioned, the air thickened with an enticing scent. Like the forest, but richer, almost like she was back in the gardens back home. She couldn't control her feet as she moved forward; Fritjof's allure grew with the scent.

He took her hand as she neared and planted a wet kiss on her skin. "There you, my lovely. You cannot resist..."

No... Bria blinked. The scent kept growing stronger. For a moment, she wanted to collapse into Fritjof's arms, only so he could carry her back home.

Home...

But home is more than this.

She gasped, a wave of fear blasting through her. With the fear, a gust of wind blew, wiping away the scent and forcing Fritjof to release Bria. His smile grew wider.

"Ah, impressive. Few can avoid my allusive phero-mones."

"Repulsive..." Bria grunted.

"It is only to test your skills."

"It's manipulative."

"Those of the strongest mind can withstand it."

Bria huffed, her anger flurrying with wind as she pushed past him.

Only to feel heat rising around her.

Then, with a single flicker, fire burst to life, circling around her with fury. Her trees cried out as the flames burnt, stripped their bark, clamoring to their branches and digging into their roots. She sucked in a breath, and around her, the air pulled back from the flames. The fire cried and fizzled as Bria held her breath.

Tristan waited for her on the other side of the fire. He stood still, without a word, then snapped his fingers.

Fire engulfed his body, burning at his clothes, coating his skin.

Bria rushed forward, but he grabbed her arm, letting the flames crawl up her branched arm. If she took the oxygen, then Tristan would suffocate. If she didn't stop the fire, she might die.

Panic caught her. As the burns cut into her branched arm, tears welled in her eyes.

As did a sudden burst of rain.

The water barred down on the flames, a miniature storm picking up around her and Tristan. He released her branched arm, a few pieces of bark falling with char, and stepped back. Only fragments of his clothes remained, while his hair—still long and red—singed at the edges. He wiped the soot from his face.

As the rain continued to beat.

Harder.

Like a single monsoon rippling through the trees.

Mayim took Tristan's place, her body swaying with the rain. She mouthed the word "sorry" in Bria's direction, but then the wall of water thickened. Alone in the monsoon, the wind screamed. She couldn't panic. Not now.

This was only a trial.

A test.

And even if it wasn't, it was only a bit of rain.

Well, and embers fizzling on the ground.

Growing...

Growing...

Then, a figure jumped from the trees. Edith, unphased by the rain, wind, and fire, gripped Bria by her neck, staring hard into her face. She bore no weapon or metal. Only her fingers digging into Bria's skin.

"There's something I've always wanted to try…" Edith hissed. "Never got to try it in battle… but you might be just the perfect subject for my little test…"

"Enough of this…" Bria choked.

"No. Not yet." She pressed her fingernail into Bria's skin. Blood trickled out of the wound onto Edith's hand.

Then Edith removed the finger and smirked at the blood on her hand. "Did you know that blood has iron in it? Oxygen, iron, and more. We are all products of the same element. If you understand that, you can control anything."

From the blood, Edith focused. The blood on her finger turned gray.

Then Edith brushed the back of her hand against Bria's cheek.

A stabbing pain entered her skin. The blood transformed, with a mere smile, into a weapon. It cut into her face with force, as sharp as any common dagger.

Bria gritted her teeth in pain, holding back a cry. She wouldn't let Edith win this time. If she let Edith win, she would never finish this endless trial.

But the pain ripped through her body, causing her mind to spin. She stumbled to the ground, gripping the earth with her good hand. Her branched arm laced itself into the ground, still recovering from its own attack. *All of these elements, all of this manipulation, it's all part of the earth.*

The rain. The wind. The fire.

The blood.

And the earth is my domain.

She whimpered as the earth pulled at her.

"Do you yield once more?" Edith taunted.

"No…" Bria whispered.

"Hm? Louder, please."

"I said no!" Bria threw her good arm behind her. The earth bowed to her. In her heart, she pleaded for serenity, and the wind stopped shrieking. On her skin, she begged for sunlight, and the sun itself parted the clouds. And with her entire being, she demanded peace, and the fire diminished to embers.

Finally, in her blood, she yearned for a win, and the stones on the ground reached for her opponents' ankles, locking them in sculpted chains.

And as the commotion stopped, the burnt grass and trees flourished, returning the forest to its glory before this so-called test.

"Enough…" Bria removed her hands from the dirt. "I'm done with this training. It isn't helping me."

"What you just did says otherwise." a new voice spoke.

Bria spun. Yusef sat on a nearby rock, with Tilda a few steps behind him, rubbing her eyes.

"You stopped four of our strongest Magii after a week of training—I think that speaks volumes." Yusef continued.

"I'm not doing this anymore. This isn't helping *me*."

"Oh, it's not about you." Edith balked from behind her.

Bria ignored Edith. "I know what I'm capable of, but my magic doesn't work like theirs does. They tell me to focus on different parts of the elements, but that's never how I've conducted my magic. It's about my internal focus or something…" Bria inhaled and stared at her hands. "I need to know more about *me* to use my full potential, I think."

Yusef nodded, then glanced at Tilda. "What say you?"

Tilda crossed her arms and closed her red eyes. The forest remained silent until Tilda finally spoke. "I do not see any further need for *this* kind of training. Bria is right—she needs to pursue more about herself. Then, she might be able to stop the erasure of all we know."

"Oh, that's a load of bull!" Edith shouted.

But Yusef ignored her, "Very well, Bria. You can decide what you do next—you have passed your test."

Bria returned to her room in the tenement hall. After greeting Nix, she vanished into the lavatory for a long shower, letting the grime and soot wash from her body until the hot water died. She wandered back to her room and pulled on one of Brent's long button-down shirts, pretending he was hugging her and taking in his distant scent. In the mirror, she could almost see him, his head chin on the back of her head, arms around her shoulders. But once she focused, he vanished, leaving her standing there alone, worn from battle.

The wound on her cheek continued to pulse with drops of blood. Without saying a word, she commanded her little branch to add an extra offshoot and grow across her cheek to weave into the wound.

With every day, she was becoming more like the forest.

She collapsed back on the bed and hugged Nix. The dog nuzzled into her.

"What am I going to do, Nix?" she asked aloud.

"Don't think your dog will have the answers."

Bria glanced up from the bed. Lana stood in the doorway with her arms crossed.

"Thanks for knocking..." Bria grunted.

"The door was unlocked."

"I could have been undressed."

"I *am* your mother."

"That doesn't matter."

Lana shrugged, "Nonetheless, talking to your dog won't solve your conundrum."

"I was thinking aloud." Bria sank back into the bed. "What does it matter to you, anyway?"

"I heard about what happened in the forest. I wanted to—I needed to—" Lana sighed, "Are you okay, Bria?"

"I'm fi—"

"Don't say that fake answer."

Bria groaned, then said, "I'm happy that ridiculous test is over."

"And?"

"I'm in a bit of pain, but nothing terrible."

"Anything else?" Lana still stood in the doorway, face unflinching.

"I... am confused about what to do next. I need more answers about my magic."

Lana still didn't move; her attention had turned to the window. Her brow furrowed before she responded, "Before the ordeal with the towers and the forest... didn't you have intentions of returning to Newbird's Arm to find answers?"

Bria remembered; she had planned to leave, desperate to see her grandmama. But what could her grandmama say now that Bria didn't already know?

Lana kept speaking. "I would think, if you want answers about who you are, you would return to where it all began, right?"

"Home..." Bria whispered.

"I can arrange transport for you, if you would like—I do not think there is much more value for you here at the moment."

And with Lana's blessing, Bria made the decision.

CHAPTER NINETEEN

THE WAITING GAME

Bria pulled on Brent's tattered jacket while glancing around her empty room in the tenement hall. Everything she owned fit in her satchel except for the box of tap-code equipment. She locked the machine tight in its case and placed it on the bed. Marisol had been sending her countless tap-code messages to practice with, giving Bria a basic understanding of the code. She would bring the materials with her to Newbird's Arm; if she could master this code, then she could send messages back to Lana or the Pit.

"C'mon Nix..." Bria called for her dog as she hoisted the case from the bed. The dog crawled out from beneath the bed and joined Bria's side, tail wagging with excitement.

Before leaving, Bria slipped on a pair of gloves. Before covering her good hand, she took a quick glance at the betrothal tattoo. The flowers had gotten smaller over the last couple of days, wilting slightly. Her stomach churned. What was happening to him now? All she could do was silently pray. *Stay strong, Brent. Please.*

She covered her hand, then took her old cowl from the hook on the wall, positioning it over her face to hide the branches crawling over her cheek.

And in that moment, however briefly, she once again became Rho.

But the confidence vanished as she left the tenement hall, feet weighed down as she took each step. While excitement bubbled in her chest, there was a fear in her core. She had left Newbird's Arm in shambles with a promise to return—which she never fulfilled. What would her grandmama think? What about her father or Ric? She had left behind her family after exposing her magic to town, all to chase a boy across the world for his own protection.

But if she had stayed, she might have ended up in the Pit.

Or worse.

Just because Senator Heartz of Newbird's Arm protected storytellers and magic, it didn't mean the rest of the town might abide. They came together in a fit of fury… but for what?

What would her home be like now?

She clutched the tap-code case tighter as she headed towards the forest where Lana told her to meet. With the sun only just beginning to rise, the Pit itself remained empty. No one would be around to stop her. She did not need some dramatic, heroic sendoff by the people of Knoll.

It was best to go alone.

Bria kept her head down as she moved to the edge of the forest. Nix barked as someone emerged from the trees.

Marisol emerged, beaming wide as ever. "Bria! Heya!"

Bria stepped back, readying her lie. "What're you doing out and about?"

"Oh, relax—Lana told me to fetch you."

"She couldn't even come to say goodbye?"

"What? No—Lana's coming with you. So am I. You've got a whole crew at your leisure."

Bria shook her head. "No. I just wanted some basic transport. I don't need people coming with me."

"Well, you can't go operating a tower alone, can you?"

"I thought she was organizing a train ticket or something… Not the *tower*." It was typical of Lana to organize a ridiculous thing like this! Bria should have left on her own, trekked on foot to avoid this becoming a whole *mission.*

"I'm guessing she has her reasons. I don't know—didn't ask or anything. Though it would have made more sense to tell you straight up to meet at the tower... you know where it is." Marisol shrugged. "Lana bothered me last night about it. We've been ready to move for a while, according to Jeremy."

"Who's Jeremy?" Bria asked as she followed Marisol.

"Oh yeah, you've probably seen him. He defected from the guard two years ago. Super smart mechanic and everything—Micca hung out with him a lot. He knows all the different codes and could forge some documents and everything, so we'll be able to get into Newbird's Arm unnoticed if there are any guards. We haven't been able to pick up any news on the radio frequencies. A lot of silence from out that way..." Marisol continued to babble. "I think you'll like Jeremy. He's really sweet and has a nice smile and is good with the tower, and did I mention he's really handsome?" Marisol's cheeks turned pink as she spoke.

Bria smiled. She didn't pry but recognized that look at once. The blushing told the whole story.

It was nice having a moment of "normal" conversation. Listening to Marisol ramble about this Jeremy brought Bria back to a simpler time when she sat in the town square with some boys and girls in her class.

One memory flooded back to her. She must have been fifteen sitting around the fountain after school one day with the others. Even as a teenager, she'd been a recluse, but she'd forced herself to sit with the others, counting the moments until she could visit the tunnels and explore the world. Someone—Bria couldn't remember who—asked her if anybody had caught Bria's fancy.

Bria panicked. She *had* liked Micca until finding out his preference for men. Was there anyone else she fancied? Her attention had gone to the plaza, searching for someone, even if it was a lie.

And there stood Christof Carver. Two years older than Bria, he attracted every girl in town. It'd be an easy answer.

Until the others found out Bria hadn't even had her first kiss—so they dragged her over to Christof so he could plant one on her lips. That began the young guard's obsession with her.

All the others had been giddy with excitement, but Bria retreated to the forest, trying to wipe the kiss from her lips. No one noticed her.

Except for Brent Harley, walking home along the same path.

Kind even then, he asked if he could do anything to help her. Bria had known he was a storyteller, so in a hushed whisper, she asked one thing: "Tell me a story. Help me forget."

Bria remembered that story even as she trudged through the forest, tears dotting her eyes in recollection. It had been a simple story about a woman made of gingerbread, but it helped Bria forget the moment with Christof Carver.

When Brent was finished, he smiled with his cheeks red. That began their friendship. Soon Bria joined Brent and Micca in their usual spot in the garden, listening to their rants. Yet the ongoing anxiety remained as Christof still watched her, obsessed with brushing against her skin in the halls of school or cornering her alone.

Bria avoided gossiping after that day, but it didn't stop her from savoring Marisol's rambles. Part of it felt like she wasn't about to take on the world. Rather, she was just a young girl, listening to the chatter around the fountain, before Christof Carver stole her trust.

Marisol's babbling led Bria to the tower. Gears ground on the outer exterior, waiting to begin its roaring journey through the forest. A few engineers worked on the outside of the building. A tall man with a shaved head glanced up and removed his goggles as they approached. He smiled in Marisol's direction. Bria caught Marisol flushing again, but they exchanged no words. Without a doubt, that had to be Jeremy. Marisol was right—he was a good-looking fellow, despite the soot blending in with his skin. The way he smiled reminded Bria of Brent—kindness.

She rubbed her hands together as they entered the tower. Nix bounded ahead, sniffing every corner of the tower. Bria let the dog be, following Marisol up the stairwell. Her attention fell on the silver pool, still pulsing with her reactivated power. Whether the Order or the Council wanted to admit it, they bathed in hypocrisy. Magic fueled every part of their action; it fed the monsters the Council hid, it supplied power and fuel to the moving towers, and it became a weapon when used in the wrong hands.

They needed magic as much as Bria needed it to breathe.

Marisol opened the door to the bunk. "Here, I set up a space for you and me here. I call top bunk, though!" She beamed at Bria, eyes lit up. "This is gonna be fun-I promise! We can pretend we're roommates at the Rosadian Academy or something. I was supposed to go to the Academy, but then they took me because my magic caused some Senator to admit he was having an affair with a vagrant! Oh, jeez, that caused a whole thing, and the senator was *mad*. Didn't have a clue why he said what he said. But he said it and ran some tests on me cause it happened after I was there for the Academy acceptance letters." Marisol finally exhaled once, catching her breath. "They did a whole ceremony in Hutch for the Academy acceptances. We all got to go to the senator's house, and he shook our hands. I was the last person he met, then he got on stage and confessed his affair without realizing it. Had the local captain do a bunch of tests, and they grabbed me, and now I'm here."

A twinkle caught Marisol's eyes as her body relaxed. From what Bria could tell, Marisol had that tale bundled up inside of her for months, and with it finally released, her body relaxed.

"Sorry, I ramble a bit sometimes when I get excited." She flushed again.

"It's okay. I didn't know you were from Hutch," Bria remarked.

"Yeah, a small little town just outside of the main Hutch's Creek area. Probably why no one knew my magic."

"I spent the first few years of my life in Hutch's Creek before moving to Newbird's Arm," Bria replied. She remembered little about that time; her magic didn't truly come to life until she returned to Newbird's Arm. Her magic only had started to blossom, and those moments held some of the most crucial memories for her. If her father didn't decide to move them back, would her magic have flourished the same way? Sure, she visited Newbird's Arm often to see her grandmama and grandpapa, but those were just visits. The first time she even remembered having magic was during a visit at the age of six or seven. Her grandmama served some poppyseed chicken. Moments after Bria took her first bite, she choked. Rather than upchucking, though, a hundred poppies flew from her mouth.

That memory still made her smile.

"Ah, shame you didn't stay. We could have been friends, maybe!" Marisol interjected her thoughts.

"We're friends now, aren't we?"

"I suppose so!"

Marisol's smile was contagious. Bria couldn't help but smirk slightly, perhaps not with the same amount of glee, but with a smile.

"Right then, I have some stuff to finish here. Lana's probably waiting for you on the bridge." Marisol walked past Bria. "Remember, I get top bunk!"

With Marisol gone, the room fell silent. Bria placed her bag on the lower bunk while Nix hopped onto the mattress to take refuge in the pillows.

"Stay here. I'll be back, okay?"

Nix didn't even bother to raise her head.

Bria knew the tower well, and without hesitating, she ventured to the bridge at the top of the tower. She gripped the railing as she climbed, nerves filling her with each step. About what? Returning to Newbird's Arm? Lana's presence? Something else?

She turned her attention to the center of the tower. People hurried along the catwalks, each with a job in mind to keep the tower running.

Everyone had their own goals. Why did they choose to join this tower, to fight for this cause? What did they lose to cause a flame to ignite?

Beneath her gloved fingers, the metal railing bent.

"Shit…" she mumbled.

"Yeah, those gloves will not do much for you," Lana spoke from behind Bria.

Bria didn't flinch at the voice. "It was an attempt."

"A poor one." Lana joined Bria's side. "We will leave soon."

"This isn't quite what I thought you meant by arranging transport."

"What? You expected a nice quiet buggy ride? Newbird's Arm is a key point. You can't just go waltzing in there without backup," Lana said.

"But why do you want to come?" Bria asked. Part of her hoped Lana would admit to returning home to see the family, but she knew Lana better than that. Another plan churned in her head.

Lana responded, "The leaders here decided that Senator Heartz would be a valuable ally to the cause. They elected me to go—since I am familiar with the region. Hue and the others can handle Knoll while I am gone."

"That makes sense," Bria replied. The Heartz political dynasty had existed in Newbird's Arm for the past one-hundred years. Consistently voted in by the residents, the Heartz Dynasty won, often unchallenged, with controversial platforms: more freedom for vagrants, ending the black stamp on children, and more.

Bria continued, "Senator Heartz will help. Grand-mama is good friends with her and the family, too." Bria still recalled the day in Newbird's Arm when she broke down the Pit's wall, instigating a rebellion that would flood the country. Her grandmama joined her on that stage and convinced Senator Heartz that the fight was for the greater good.

Her grandmama would help them now too.

But Lana drew her mouth into a frown, following Bria's gaze down into the heart of the tower.

"I hope my mother will." Lana finally said.

"She will. We're her family."

"You're her family. She disowned me years ago."

"Once she hears your story, she'll understand," Bria said.

"Understanding differs from acceptance." Lana gripped the handrail.

"Yes, but you're her daughter and—"

"I'm not going as her daughter. I'm going as a negotiator. That's all. This voyage isn't about reuniting with my family."

"I don't believe that."

"Believe it. You might be returning home to reconnect with your family and find out more about yourself, but I am going as a representative for this rebellion."

"But we'll find out about you too..." Bria met Lana's eyes, "we can find out together about your magic and—"

"I don't have magic."

"Oh, don't pull that on me!"

"But I don't. At least not anymore. They took it from me."

"What are you talking about?"

"The Order. They took my magic." Lana dug her fingers deeper into the railing. "They did Level Five of the Cleanse, the Buzzing. Had that happen before, and usually, it was temporary. But then they added something new. It was like... they sent that yellow storm of nightmares after me... in a single room. And my magic was gone. So yeah, I don't have magic anymore."

Bria stared at Lana. The cleanse, a deeply religious ritual doctored by the Order of the Effluvium, had always terrified her. The three standard levels—fasting, ice baths, and humility—had been common practices. Only in the past couple of years did Bria learn of the other two: lashing and the buzzing. These two left Magii and "demons" maimed.

Now, based on Lana's story, they added another potential method of torture, a familiar one that she had seen before in her fight against the Council. Certainly, without a doubt, the nightmarish yellow storm belonged to the Diabolo.

"There has to be a way to get it back..." Bria murmured.

"I don't care if there is or isn't. It doesn't matter. My magic isn't that important to me... not like with you, at least."

"But—"

"Just drop it, Bria." Lana let go of the railing. "It's not in my cards. Now if you'll excuse me... I believe we leave soon."

Without waiting for Bria to reply, Lana marched away, her shoes thudding against the metal grate.

Bria stared after Lana. Everything kept getting worse. She hated to admit it, but with every new revelation, she sensed her own confidence falter.

Keep your head up. You can make the world pretty again. She closed her fists, feeling the burden of her magic in her fingertips.

She would make a promise to anyone who might listen: she would stop this.

Even if she hadn't a clue.

For now, she just had to fight back the constant pangs in her chest and wait.

Wait to arrive in Newbird's Arm.

Wait to confront the Order.

Wait to fight the Council.

Wait to reunite with Yaz.

Wait to find Brent.

And wait for the tower's horn to blow.

CHAPTER TWENTY

WHERE DEATH STORES HIS FAILURES

His chest hurt with each breath as his body fought the tendrils of black smoke. But despite the pain, Brent kept himself together. He sat against the wall with the black smoke laced around his arms and chest. He could only walk as far as the bucket in the corner to relieve himself, but not far enough away to avoid the constant scent. Even when the crypt seemed to shift beneath the twisting mist, repositioning his cell in a different part of the endless maze, the aroma followed.

In irregular intervals, different faceless ghosts stopped by to clean his cell and throw some old food in his direction. Bread, a clump of mashed potatoes, and worst of all...they'd somehow discovered his hatred of pineapples.

He ate with reluctance. All the while trying to keep his head in place.

When alone, his Diabolo raved in his mind. It had been getting worse, with only darkness and shadows to occupy his time. In the Library, he learned the stories of the Mist Keepers and focused on their tales. Down here, he only heard the screams of the creatures kept behind bars, the moans of those imprisoned, and the hissing of the black smoke chains keeping him captive.

So he told stories to himself instead, devising obscure tales about talking mountains, flying dogs, and king-doms of ants. By all counts, the stories were ridiculous. But at least it kept him talking to himself, no matter the language or tale.

If only he had his pineapple to tell the stories to—then at least he wouldn't feel so alone.

He slipped deeper into the mist. Languages became muddled, sights became mirages, and some days, he even forgot his name.

He couldn't be sure how many days had passed before a change came in the monotony of the cells. They'd fed him twice since his arrival and cleaned his cell once. It could have been hours, days, or even weeks. It all blended in one uneasy blur.

But it all broke with a gasp.

"Is that Brenton Harley?"

Brent neared the bars, straining against the black smoke webbing. His Diabolo cackled at him, but Brent didn't listen, squinting into the darkness.

In the cell right across from him, slumped against the wall, sat Kek—the alchemist and leader of the Palaver of Immortal Magii.

"Kek?" Brent's voice cracked. He hadn't spoken since they put him down in the crypt, except in mumbles and incomprehensible repeats.

"Thought it was you. Thought Ningursu mentioned your name... and you have a smell about you."

Brent sniffed himself and scowled, "Sorry... it's been... I mean, I've been... it's been... shite sorry." He inhaled and repeated the sentence to himself, "Sorry... I haven't been talking much and, I mean—"

"Yes, I overheard Ningursu express frustration with your...predicament," Kek said. "He is quite furious... but I find it hilarious. You have really messed with him for good."

"By surviving his... attempt to eradicate me?"

"Quite certainly. I have not heard him in such a tirade in centuries."

"Wait... how do you know about that?" Brent squinted. Wisps of stories gathered around the cells, the first he'd seen in days. His entire body yearned for the tales, begging for them to enter the bars and grant him a momentary break in the monotony.

"He's been interrogating me ever since you pulled your little magic trick," Kek said. Another wisp of their story came through the bars. Brent had already grown somewhat familiar with it; he'd seen it in the Library, in bits and pieces. After the Magii took the Library, the Mist Keepers returned in force, with monsters as their steeds. Despite the unlimited magic in the Magii's pals, the monsters won...controlled by a little girl. The same little girl Brent met and protected: Yaz. Used as a weapon against her will, she had no clue how the monsters tore through the shelves, gobbled the magic with determination, and reclaimed the Library.

The Magii fled. Ningursu only cared about one hostage: Tehuti Thema Tarek Kamilah Kafele Kek.

The story faded, leaving Ningursu's deeds after the hostilities a mystery.

So Brent could only ask, "Are... are you a'ight?"

"You know, I've had worse..." Kek audibly paused, inhaling again. "Ningursu has been running experiments, trying to increase his defenses against magic... and from rogue Mist Keepers. He had it under control until you showed up, it seems."

"What do you mean?"

Kek sighed, "You are not the first, nor shall you be the last, 'rogue' Mist Keeper, Brenton. Or perhaps the better word is a 'true' or 'pure' Mist Keeper."

"Ningursu said something about that... but what does that mean? I mean... how am I different from the others? Aren't the others pure, too?"

"No, no. The only pure Mist Keeper that currently is functioning is, well, Ningursu. And now you."

"But what does it mean?"

"It means you are completely connected to the mist. Your soul has transferred over to the mist, and you are part of that plane of existence."

"But I'm not...I'm not *dead*."

"Not in the traditional sense, I suppose. But you are more Mist Keeper than man. You can use the mist to hide or reveal yourself in full."

"Wait...so...does that mean..." Brent stared at his fingers. "Does that mean that...if I were to return home that...my ma couldn't see me? Or Bria? Am I...invisible?"

"In some places, the mist hides you...but sight has grown stronger over the last few years. Some Mist Keepers are known to also project themselves beyond the mist...and they have always had the means to interact with the physical world."

"Like with Bria..." Brent recalled back in the tunnels, back when life did not seem so heavy. Bria hadn't seen the Mist Keepers, but she had noticed their remnants. She had seen him thrown against a wall. Even the tunnels themselves were a remnant, all of which Bria accessed without sight. It wasn't until he pushed aside the mist did Bria *see* at last. He had opened the world for her.

Now, it remained vivid and clear.

"Remember, Brenton. The mist is your tool, and you can use it to your advantage. I think, in a way, it makes it so you are not just the judge and jury of the dead; you are the controller of the mist...and your powers are limitless. Think of everything Ningursu can do! You could be his equal."

Brent laughed to himself. The idea seemed preposterous to him. But he had also taken control of the mist in so many situations: telling stories with the mist, collecting tales from within it, creating physical objects, and more. While to him, they only had ever been stories, the way the mist acted reflected other Mist Keepers.

But why him?

"I can't be the only one since Ningursu... I mean... it's been such a long time." Brent said.

"You are not the only one. But... you are the only one who made it this far."

"What do you mean?"

"I only know so much, but if memory serves me right, Ningursu has kept track of everyone with mist inclinations since before I knew him. Many people have mist inclinations. Some maintain it as only magic... but some grow stronger and become Mist Keepers. They behave in contrast to most Magii, whose powers stem from the earth." Kek inhaled again before continuing. "Ningursu has always known of potential contenders with his 'all-knowing-sight,' as he calls it, who has a mist inclination. He doesn't fret over those who don't expand their magic, rather relying on groups like the Order of the Effluvium to keep them at bay. But... when their powers expand... that is when Ningursu begins to watch and wait. Only seven others have met what he deems acceptable."

"The rest of the Council, you mean?"

"Yes. And thousands of others have perished because they because their powers exceeded what Ningursu deemed acceptable. Most of them went mad... as they thought you did many moons ago. So, Ningursu eradicated them... or turned them into nothing but mist. Their souls live on as nothing more than particles in the air. Nothing else but forgotten." Kek's voice fell as if in prayer. "But there have been a handful who become pure. Ningursu maimed them all instead, turning them into half versions of themselves. They're here now... in this crypt."

Brent strained forward, glancing at the other cells where the obscure misty creatures with silver eyes lingered. He couldn't make out their forms, but he remembered them clearly from when he and Bria discovered them. They pulsed with mist and wouldn't meet his gaze. In their presence, he had seen himself in the creatures. But he never thought of it in a literal sense.

"Why am I not like them, though?" Brent asked, voice quaking.

"I believe it is a situation of circumstance above all else. Not fate. You were just in the right place at the right time... and knew the right person."

"Right person..." Brent rubbed his hands together. "You mean Bria?"

"She introduced you to magic through a different eye, protected you when you were mad, and led you to Mert. If you didn't make it to that city, I never would have met you... and thus, never would have cured you." Kek once again paused for a breath. "You have also been without Ningursu's influence for well over a year. You had the opportunity to explore the strength of your magic. These apprentices in this crypt didn't have that. Their lives were watched, regimented, and controlled the moment Ningursu discovered them. The moment their magic became too great, he ended it. That is why so many Mist Keepers fail the first time."

"Because the only ones he wants to keep are the ones that have magic he can control?" Brent asked.

"Exactly. Unless someone has inconsequential loyalty, such as with Aelia and Alojzy, Ningursu maintains control. It has always been about control. Back when he and I had a civil relationship, he expressed the desire to maintain a certain... order. I saw him eradicate countless potential Mist Keepers because he feared that lack of control."

"So there could be thousands of Mist Keepers helping to release souls? But because Ningursu is scared... he... I mean, he... he let... I mean... I..." Brent cursed and pulled on the black tendrils of fog. His heartbeat rose in his ears. A gong rang in his head, filling his ears with a loud buzzing noise.

"Scared... that is the right way to put it." Kek pondered. "I understand how that frustrates you... but perhaps you can turn that frustration into change."

Brent nodded, unable to speak. He knew Kek didn't see him, but that didn't matter.

How many Mist Keepers were out there? How many had died without knowing their potential?

Why did Ningursu not notice him all those years ago? Brent couldn't help but wonder if his magic was never supposed to grow; a victim of circumstance, an accidental meeting with a Mist Keeper, and a friendship with a powerful Forest Queen led to this moment.

And now, Ningursu left Brent to rot in jail.

How can I break the cycle? He stared again at his mist-laden hands.

You can't. Just give in to it, his Diabolo hissed, a single intrusive thought in the back of his mind.

No.

It won't be long until you lose yourself.

I know who I am.

For now.

Brent cursed under his breath and leaned against the wall. He rested his hand beside him, where a single chiseled rock remained. He laced his fingers around it and scratched Bria's name on the floor.

"Do you know what Ningursu is planning to do?" Brent finally asked.

"Hm?" Kek responded.

"To me. Do you know what he wants to do?"

"I cannot be certain what he plans to do, Brenton. I'm sorry."

"But he must have been interrogating you for something…" Brent squinted past the bars, catching a glimpse of Kek's shadow.

Kek paused, inhaling once, then said, "He was interrogating me about my knowledge of sight."

"You mean…how Magii and others can see Mist Keepers and the dead, right?"

"Mhm." Kek lowered their voice. "Ever since what I did to Merta all those years ago, I spent many years researching how sight works and how it impacts our world. For a time, Ningursu even helped me with that research."

Another pause followed. Brent waited.

And Kek continued, "The only reason why Magii, and even in some cases, non-Magii can see us is because of the power of seers. They form a…network of sorts through their magic. Unintentionally, of course. It weaves its way into the mist and allows a transaction to occur…and so Magii, Mist Keepers, and others can communicate."

Brent pondered for a moment. "So that's why people in Mert have stronger sight than, let's say, Rosada?"

"Exactly."

"But why was he interrogating you about sight? What did he want to know?"

"How it works…how to stop it…" Kek laughed. "I told him it would require powerful alchemy…and the right circumstances. The seer network is strong. To sever it would require strong magic and the right people."

"Like who?"

"I'm not sure. I never figured it out myself." Kek's voice trailed off, exhaustion seeping over them.

Brent knew better than to press, sinking back against the wall instead. Ningursu was playing a game of chess; each movement had a purpose, but Brent could not be sure which movement would put the world in check.

How could he figure out the truth?

Around him, the walls of the crypt turned again, wrapping the cells in mist and nightmares.

He closed his eyes, weaving together threads of stories in his head.

For now, he had his mind. He had his thoughts. He had his life.

And he had his constant.

But he needed *time*.

CHAPTER TWENTY-ONE

A Landing in Black and White

Flying meant freedom. At least for Yaz.

As they flew across the world, she no longer worried about the monsters. On the back of the dragon, she was free; she could dream without worry and breathe without mist. In the sky, nothing mattered.

She could be a fairy. A snowflake. A cloud.

Her dreams could be realized, even for a moment.

When she first left Knoll, the yellow nightmares haunted her. She didn't rest, clutching Zephyr's back tight, while Anandi pointed in excitement at the disappearing trees, babbling about how amazing the world looked beneath them. Chander's face paled as they reached the clouds, vomiting twice over the edge. He glowered when Anandi taunted him but said little at all.

The ghost child, Preston, showed almost no reaction to the flight, gaze locked on the horizon. Yaz joined his side, watching the sky, not speaking.

As they touched the clouds, the yellow nightmares left her.

Finally free.

Timothée and Micca heralded the dragon as easily as driving a truck or directing the tower. Beneath them, Zephyr screeched with pleasure, darting through the sky, only to be reined in when she attempted to spiral or prance. Yaz swore, if dragons smiled, Zephyr would smile indeed.

The mood changed each evening when they landed. While Chander rejoiced, and even Anandi seemed happier, the heaviness of the yellow and smoke fell back on Yaz as soon as she touched solid ground. The nightmares returned to her with a constant chant:

Yasmin...

Yasmin...

Yasmin...

She heard the voice whenever she closed her eyes. Did it belong to Ningursu? The monsters? Or something else? While Timothée and Micca always found them a place to hide, away from anyone who might try to harm them, Yaz still feared that Ningursu might find her.

Did he watch her, even from the shadows?

After the third day of flying, Zephyr landed at the edge of a forest bordering a field of black and white flowers. Yaz blinked as she hopped off, hugging herself tight as she glanced around the strange area. It almost looked as though someone planted the flowers in that specific order. But how could they? The pattern traveled beyond the horizon!

"We'll stay here for the night," Timothée said as he patted Zephyr's snout. The dragon purred in response.

"Can't believe we're actually outta that shithole Rosada," Micca replied.

"*Language.*"

"Eh, these kids have heard plenty. Ain't that right?" Micca threw a grin at Chander.

Chander shrugged without looking up from his spot.

Timothée grunted and removed the bags from Zephyr's holster. "Yeah, sure, but we aren't much better right now. I think we're on the outskirts of Kainan."

"Well, yeah, we're on the Chessboard Plains."

"Yes, but I heard from Mr. Santiago that these plains are unclaimed land. There are a lot of smaller nomadic groups here."

"So what? We're nomads too."

"Yeah, but they don't take kindly to Rosadians. And sorry, love, but you have the thickest Rosadian accent there is."

"Dunno what you're talking about." Micca grinned at Timothée.

"Just don't cause any problems. Once we get to Mert, it'll be better for everyone."

"Still don't know why we're heading there..."

"I told you, Mert is the safest place for magic. It's the best place to start."

Yaz traced her fingers through the dirt, her attention leaving the two men to stare out at the strange plains. To her left, a patch of black burnt dirt greeted her. To the right, a gaggle of blossoming tulips waved. She immediately brought her hand to her pocket where the white camellia flower sat. As Bria had promised, it hadn't wilted.

Chander sat beside her, lacing his hands together, lips pulled in his usual frown.

He spoke in a mere whisper, "I don't like it here."

"Huh?" Yaz glanced at him.

"It gives me a headache... like I'm seeing through the eyes of hundreds of people at once."

Yaz followed his gaze back towards the Chessboard Plains. At first, the plains' beauty had captured her. But the longer she stared, the more the true nature of the land came into view. She felt it now, calling to her, filled with mist.

And nightmares.

The monsters from her dreams, the yellow she had so long tried to battle, lived there. Her heart stopped, her throat tightened, and everything spun in a circle. She refused to pull her gaze away from the plains.

And in that glimpse, she was again a monster, flying above the world.

A demon hunting for magic.

A creature lurking over a city coated in smoke and fear.

She fed off the pain and suffering.

Only to let out a cry when Chander touched her shoulder.

"Yaz? You okay?"

Yaz blinked, once again sitting beside Chander at the edge of the Chessboard Plains.

She glanced at Chander. He abruptly removed his hand, only to rub it with his other one as if casting aside any semblance of touch. Concern marked his face with a frown.

"You looked a little freaked out," Chander said.

"I...I was the monster again." Yaz brought her knees to her chest. "I wanted to eat magic."

Chander raised his brow. "Just from staring at the mist?"

Yaz nodded.

"Remember what I told you, alright? Think of people who are always there for you. Like your friends. And what makes you happy." Chander reached into his pocket and removed a smoke. He quietly lit it.

Yaz pressed her head to her knees. It was hard to decide what made her happy at this point. She smiled when a dog approached her or when Zephyr snorted in her sleep. Was that enough to stop the yellow monsters?

"It probably sounds dumb, right?" Chander asked.

Yaz glanced at him, "Oh, um, I don't know..."

"It was something that this storyteller who had this mist magic—"

"You mean Brent!?" Yaz hadn't told Chander about the events in the forest. She didn't think he would believe her.

"Yeah! How do you know him?"

"He saved me... from the bad people who took me... then they took him," Yaz replied.

"What? So he's alive? Everyone said he died!"

"No... the bad people took him." Yaz fidgeted.

Chander furrowed his brow. "I was wondering what happened to him. He said he would help me with my magic 'cause it seemed like his."

"What do you mean?"

"When he met me, I was...I was having problems with my magic. Y'know how I see what people see? It was constant, and there was a strange mist and everything. So Brent told me to think of the most important thing in my life when the magic got bad. So I thought of Anandi... and it wasn't so bad anymore." Chander shifted slightly. "He said he'd help me figure out my magic more, but then he never came back."

Yaz's mind raced. If the storyteller, Brent, had an interest in Chander... did that mean Ningursu would too? Did that mean that Chander had magic similar to hers?

"Does that mean you're a Mist Keeper?" Yaz asked him.

"A what?" Chander cocked his head to the side, his smoke nearly falling from his mouth.

"A Mist Keeper. They...use the magical mist to do things like control monsters, tell stories, and release the dead. Brent was one of the good ones...but the bad ones captured me." Yaz stared at her hands. "I still don't get everything that it means. I just did what they said."

"Oh, that's cool—but I don't know if I'm one or not."

"Oh."

"But maybe...Brent might? And if we ever see him again, we can find out for sure."

Yaz agreed. She didn't know how they would find Brent. But the mist worked in strange ways. Perhaps Brent would seek them out and help them train.

After all, the Council had those magical tunnels that traversed the Earth. Perhaps she could use those to find Brent one day.

"Mist Keeper." Chander recited. "I like the sound of that."

Yaz swore she saw him smile. It was the first time she'd ever seen a smile cross his lips. It made him look kinder.

They didn't speak again, joining Micca, Timothée, Anandi, and Preston by the fire. The ghost child sat in the dirt, drawing with his fingers. Yaz sat beside him and watched his nonsensical drawings take form. Zephyr slept behind them, and Yaz used the dragon's body as a backrest, waiting as Timothée cooked what looked like a dead squirrel over the flame. Anandi complained about the meal, saying that the squirrel didn't deserve such an untimely death.

But ultimately, when the food was served, she ate it in full... with a few mild complaints thrown in the mix.

After they ate, Micca removed a wind-up toy from his pocket and let it loose around the fire. That caught Preston's attention, and he watched in awe for a time.

They really had all come together to form an interesting little family. It was more of a family than Yaz ever had with Ms. Kai and Mr. Nasr. Even if laughter remained a limited commodity.

But cries existed in surplus.

Preston broke the serenity. He raised his eyes from the wind-up toy and pointed his small hand to the sky. An indecipherable cry escaped his lips, followed by an echo of mist.

Everyone, except for Micca and Anandi, looked into the sky.

Yaz's stomach dropped at the sight.

"What is it?" Anandi pulled on her brother's arm. "I can't see the magic stuff!"

"It's a monster…" Chander gripped his sister's hand.

Yaz stared as one of the yellow demons, the Diabolo, as Ningursu had called it, lurked on the horizon. With each passing second, it grew closer, plumes of smokelike tufts of hair sprouting on its head. It moved like a spider, crawling along on all fours. One mere glance and it sent Yaz's head spiraling into nightmares.

And again, she saw through its eyes. It moved across the Chessboard Plains like a pawn or a queen, searching for its next piece to claim. Upon spotting the group in the distance, with a mist-laden dragon, it roared.

She listened to its call from where she stood, but her own mouth opened in unison.

She was the monster.

She was coming for herself.

She couldn't stop it.

Think of something important to you.

She couldn't see her hand, but she guided it into her pocket, where the Forest Queen's forest remained. The petals reminded her of a warm embrace. That embrace held every bit of love, every bit of care she'd ever experienced.

If only she could hand it off to the monster on the horizon.

"Go away... go away..." Yaz mumbled.

She closed her eyes tight, once again only seeing from the monster's eyes. Thrice more, she reiterated the command.

"Go away. Go away. Go away!"

Through the monster's eyes, she felt the beast stop. It continued staring at its victims on the other end of the plains.

"Go... away." Yaz reiterated one last time.

The monster grunted, as did Yaz, then turned to sulk back whence it came.

And Yaz opened her eyes. She stood still amongst her friends, sweat matting her brow, her body trembling.

They all stared at her, except for Preston, who hugged Timothée around the neck while snuggling into his chest.

She shrunk back. Did they fear her now? Would they want to leave her behind in the field?

But of all people, Chander broke the silence. "That was amazing, Yaz! If the Mist Keepers taught you how to do that... I can't wait to find out what they'll teach me! We gotta find Brent!"

"Mist Keepers?" Timothée cocked his head.

"And what about Brent?" Micca added.

Yaz stammered, "Oh, um—"

"Yaz told me some about it!" Chander kept talking, fast now, jumping between his feet. "C'mon Yaz! Tell us more!"

Yaz glanced at her feet. "I don't know if I'm allowed—"

"Aw, come on!"

"Chander, don't force her." Timothée scolded.

"But—"

"Let her tell it in due time."

"But—"

"Leave it. You too, Micca." Timothée glanced at the other man in the group. "The girl has been through enough."

Chander and Micca huffed in unison, then they both wandered off in separate directions. Yaz watched Chander leave. In due time, she might tell him what happened.

But she still didn't quite understand everything that had occurred.

But without a doubt, she managed to control the monster.

All without Ningursu's help.

A Family Reunion

Bria leaned against the railing of the tower's overlook, watching as the mountains marched past the tower. These mountains that she had called home for so many years almost seemed unfamiliar. No longer bursting with the green that she'd grown accustomed to, they hung in drab gray. A thick mist traveled down the edge of the mountains, the arms of the Effluvium itself overtaking the landscape. Its decree ruled.

While the green faded.

Even without the flourishing evergreens of the mountains, she recognized each one without flinching. They arrived at the foot of the first mountain one day after leaving Knoll. She had grown up beneath that mountain in Hutch's Creek, and as they passed it, she and Marisol exchanged a moment of understanding of silence.

But that mountain bore more demons than just the Order: there, she had seen Brent go head-to-head with a Diabolo. He almost died.

And upon searching for help from the Council, she became forever embedded in their game of puppet mastery.

The other mountains did not carry the same. She had ventured on all of them at some point or another. Back when she and Brent first tried dating, before his betrothal to Jemma Reds, they had explored the one bordering Newbird's Arm. They found small hideaways to kiss and innocently touch. That was before Brent knew of her magic.

Although one mountain bore a memory of watching Newbird's Arm from afar, soon after Brent met her magical alter-ego, Rho. They sat there for the whole night.

There, Bria had maintained her lie.

At least it was all in the past now.

Her stomach churned as they passed around the final mountain. The tower navigated around each of them with ease, flooding the riverbanks with each step. Once they passed this mountain, Newbird's Arm would make its presence known.

Home.

The word sounded foreign. Was Newbird's Arm her home anymore? Was anywhere?

"We'll be arriving in Newbird's Arm shortly." Lana's voice didn't shock Bria, coming up from behind her.

Bria didn't respond.

"I recommend getting one of your disguises together. We must act fast." Lana said.

Bria still didn't move, and Lana took her leave. Her stomach performed somersaults. *Home.*

She stayed at the lookout for a few more long minutes, then headed back inside to her room. Upon opening the door to the bunks, she sank onto her bed. To her relief, Marisol wasn't in the room, giving Bria a chance to breathe while changing into her disguise.

She and Lana had already reviewed the plans. Once the tower arrived, a few of the other members of their brigade would meet with the local captain, hiding any true intentions. All the while, Bria and Lana would venture to see Madame Gonzo to, as Lana put it, arrange an appointment with the senator. Once those wheels started turning, everything would follow.

Or so Lana claimed.

Bria sighed and removed a yellow fedora from her bag. It was one Brent bought on a silly whim over two years ago, and it would do well enough to hide her hair. She then pulled on her long overcoat and a pair of glasses that Marisol had found for her. The ridiculous disguise would be enough to get her to Madame Gonzo's house undetected.

At least she hoped it would.

Lana knocked on her door a few minutes later. Dressed in a hooded shawl, she covered the black stamp on her cheek with cosmetics. She didn't have to hide her face with the same tenacity as Bria did, but it was a good enough disguise.

"Are you ready?" Lana asked.

Bria glanced at Nix, sleeping on the bottom bunk, then nodded. She'd be back for the dog later.

In stride, she and Lana walked from the room to the entrance of the tower. The engineers worked on securing the gears. One bellowed orders, while another pulled on a guard jacket, boring the most convenient disguise of them yet.

"Have you met Jeremy? I'm trusting him to deal with the Guard. He'll keep them distracted with formalities," Lana said.

Bria said nothing, choking down the fear building in her throat. Part of her worried that the Guard would already circle them, that the moment she stepped foot in Newbird's Arm that her life might end.

She inhaled as she stepped through the front of the tower.

On the other side, the familiar Newbird Forest greeted her. Its tall oaks and stringy pines seemed to sigh at her presence. She had to resist their call and the way they begged for her magic to bless them. If she brought back the life of the forest now, everyone would realize she'd returned.

And everyone would once again chant her name.

Rhodana...

Bria cast her gaze to the ground, strolling alongside Lana in pace. Lana seemed to recall the forest like an old friend, moving through it without a moment of thought. Much to Bria's surprise, she showed no semblance of emotion, staring on as if walking through the Pit.

The forest opened on the other side of the train tracks, just where the tracks crossed over the winding river. Beyond it, the town center of Newbird's Arm waited, situated beneath the watchful eye of the year glass. The temple always stared over the town, perfectly situated to capture the Effluvium in its ruby-jeweled stare. Beneath it, the town square slept. A few merchants prepared their stalls for the day, but otherwise, the early morning kept its grip on the town.

When Bria had last been here, she'd left a path of destruction in her wake. Shops had fallen, a wall had lain in shambles, and rubble turned over in its spot. The remnants of that battle remained, but as the town had rebuilt. Newly erected buildings gazed throughout the town, and as Bria crossed the train tracks into town, she counted each of the new bricks lain with the old ones. Newbird's Arm, despite everything, had rebuilt.

But it didn't thrive.

Bria felt it in the dying forest, she sensed it in the empty marketplace, and she tasted it in the air. Hope no longer ran through the rivers. Instead, towers stood along the riverbanks, casting a shadow from the marketplace to the farmlands.

And with the towers, the Pit's wall once again stood above the rest, repaired after her destruction.

Her rebellion had ended.

For now.

Lana strode forward, keeping her pace fast and disinterested. Bria tried to keep up, but her attention kept falling on different discoveries: the dark house on the corner that used to bustle with light, the old man selling broken toys in his shanty stall, and the garden in the distance hanging with weeds.

Bria froze, staring over the bridge at the garden where she spent her childhood. The Senator's Garden had long been a pinnacle of Newbird's Arm. Her grandpapa kept it alive. After he passed, her father's partner, Ricard West, did his due diligence... but Bria kept the garden thriving.

Without her, the garden turned to weeds, glowing with yellow and brown.

Except, of course, for the camellia bushes, still bolstering in white.

Her camellias.

"C'mon," Lana tugged on Bria's arm.

Bria stumbled along after Lana. She swallowed the heartbreak and the tears. *It couldn't be helped. I did what I had to do.* But the weight of responsibility still hounded her. What could she have done differently?

Her grandmama's cottage sat at the edge of the market square. As the matron of the market, she had eyes over the entire town. People respected her; people loved her.

At least they *did*.

What did they think now? Did they harbor anger towards Madame Gonzo for hiding the supposedly dead *Rhodana?* Did they blame her for the destruction?

Would her own grandmother turn her away?

No. She won't. Of course she won't.

Bria froze a few paces from the door, gulping back her fear. Lana joined her side.

"Go on," Lana said.

"Aren't you coming?" Bria asked.

"I'm here on business, and business only. You go share your tears first. Then I'll discuss business with her."

"But she's your mother."

"Doesn't matter."

It was pointless to argue with Lana. Rather than pushing the question, she stepped towards the door. She removed her yellow fedora, then, with a trembling hand, knocked.

A light flickered on in the cottage window. Bria pictured her grandmother grumbling as she climbed out of bed, pulled on her robe, then bumbled to the front door.

The locks clicked.

The door creaked open.

"By golly, it is the crack of dawn. Can you not wait an hour—Briannabella?"

Madame Beatriz Gonzo, Bria's grandmama, stood in the doorway, draped in a long robe with a head wrap around her hair. Her dark eyes softened.

"Hi, Grandmama," Bria squeaked. Tears already betrayed her.

"Oh, look at you..." Her grandmama placed both hands on her cheeks. "It really is you."

Bria nodded, unable to speak.

Madame Gonzo pulled Bria into a hug, holding her tight in her arms. Bria melted like a child in her grandmother's arms. She missed the way her grandmama used to hold her like this. She missed the scent of lemon tea and freshly baked bread that followed her, and she missed the lulling of her voice. She never wanted to let go again.

But her grandmama did.

She kept her hands on Bria's arms, but her gaze passed her. The next words came like the wind.

"Angelana?"

"Hi, Mama," Lana spoke from behind Bria. "I've come home."

Madame Gonzo placed a tray of tea and lemon cakes on the table. Bria found her favorite spot on the sofa, curled up in a ball, knees against her chest. Her body had given out, ready for another long slumber, but her mind remained attentive. She monitored Lana as the woman paced the room, bringing her hand to the curtains or running a finger along the table. The tension in the air could sharpen a knife. Madame Gonzo watched as Lana paced, the two women holding the same wordless conversation.

And Bria participated as well.

Where to begin? How? Could she tell her grandmama everything that had happened that led her to Lana?

What would her grandmama think?

Lana broke the silence, "So... you kept my daughter from me."

Bria gawked at Lana. *That* was how Lana would reunite with Madame Gonzo?

Madame Gonzo shared the same sentiments, "We haven't seen each other in twenty-one years, and *that* is what you want to bring up first?"

"You didn't come searching for me. You didn't even write. You threw me to the dogs. The least you could have done was tell me that my daughter lived."

"It was for her safety." Madame Gonzo sat down beside Bria and stroked a hand through her hair. "Though it did little good, did it?"

"It kept me safe until I was an adult... but..." Bria glanced at Lana and back at Madame Gonzo, taking her grandmama's hands in her hands, "a lot has happened."

"I can see that. How did you two even meet?" Madame Gonzo whispered. "Lana... she lost her mind—"

"Oh, there you go, talking like I'm not here." Lana snapped.

"Are you here, though? Last time I saw you, you were mad!"

"They tortured me!"

"For what?"

"Because I had magic!"

"No, you did not."

"Yes! I did! Perhaps not like Bria, but I had magic. *Papa* helped me with it. You know Papa had magic, right?" Lana shook. It was like looking in a mirror. Suddenly, Bria saw herself standing in the forest, facing Lana.

The anger. The uncertainty. The confusion.

It all ran in her blood.

"Of course I knew Tulio had magic!" Madame Gonzo replied. "But he didn't want to use it. There were risks! I never knew it passed on to you."

"Because I didn't tell you! You would have made me hide it."

She made me hide it. Bria stared at her gloved hands. She removed the one covering her branched hand and flexed the twig fingers.

"What, do you think Bria has spent her life flaunting her magic publicly? Of course not! The only way to keep her safe was to hide it! So, of course, we would have done the same with you!" Beatriz argued. "Tulio kept his hidden. It is part of being a Magii."

"Oh, what do you know? You don't have that burden!"

"Angelana—"

Bria interjected the conversation, redirecting the conversation. "Why didn't you tell me that Grandpapa had magic?"

Madame Gonzo glanced at Bria again, tearful. "*He* didn't want to tell you. He thought if you didn't know, your magic might go away."

"Pah." Lana laughed, "Fat load of shit that did."

"We were wrong. That much is obvious now. For better or worse, we were wrong."

"Even after you saw my magic continue to grow, you didn't tell me," Bria whispered. "There's so much I've wanted to learn about my magic since I was a little girl... but you used to say it was a miracle. I had to end up in the Pit and meet my... my..." Bria couldn't bring herself to say that Lana was her mother, so she settled on a different statement. "I had to meet Lana to learn the truth."

"Briannabella..."

"I've been through so much now, Grandmama. I just want to learn the truth. If I had known... maybe some of this could have been avoided."

"Your grandfather and I made some mistakes. But I hope you'll forgive us...because I am just... so happy you're here." She took Bria's hand, unaware of the roots hidden within the glove. Then, she glanced at Lana. "Both of you."

Lana crossed her arms and huffed.

"Please... please eat." Madame Gonzo motioned to the lemon cakes. "We can't just sit here in silence. Please."

Bria sensed her grandmama's heart breaking. She didn't need Brent's empathetic ability to see stories to understand everything that ran through Madame Gonzo's head. Regret, pain, loneliness; it all hovered in her eyes and in the excessive lines on her face. She saw how her grandmama had aged over the last two years. Her hair had grown thinner, while she'd lost weight in her face from worry. As much as Bria wanted to be angry with her grandmama, she couldn't. Not after she spent months yearning for their reunion.

"Will you talk to us?" Bria pleaded. "Will you tell us the truth?"

"I don't know much." Madame Gonzo stared at the ground.

"Please, Grandmama."

Madame Gonzo once again brushed back Bria's hair. "I can tell you that your grandpapa had immigrated from Perennes many years ago with a bit of magic in his palms to avoid being drafted into the war between Perennes and Proveniro. He found work here as a gardener... and a few years later, he met me in Grover's Marsh. We fell in love, and I moved here. But he kept his magic hidden from me for some time, fearful of my reaction. During those years, the Guard had been cracking down more on storytellers and magic. Despite the late Senator Calvin Heartz's protection, Tulio worried he would be found out and sent to the Pit." She blinked the tears away from her eyes. "I promise. That is all I really know."

Lana huffed again from beside the wall.

"Oh, don't give me that, Angelana."

"Did you ever bother asking him? Did you even care?" Lana kept glowering. "Probably not. You were too busy running your stupid market!"

"You know very well what that market meant to me."

"Maybe if you hadn't been so busy with it, you would've noticed *me*."

"I loved you!"

"If you did, you would have *seen* my magic. But no. You didn't. So you thought I ran away to rebel against you, never knowing that the Order spent *months* torturing me. Did you even look?"

"I searched everywhere for you! The Newbird Guard declared you a missing person. Some people thought you were *dead*. Then you came knocking on my door years later, pregnant. I was overjoyed! At least until you tried to *kill* your daughter!"

"I did it to save her!"

The bickering continued. Bria's head spun. She understood both Lana's frustration and her grandmama's reservations. This was fruitless, wasn't it? They wouldn't be able to mend their wounds with a mere conversation.

Bria rose from the sofa and, without looking either woman in the eyes, mumbled, "I'm going to bed."

"Briannabella..." Madame Gonzo reached for her hand.

"I'm okay. Just... need to think and rest. You two have more to discuss, I think." She pulled away from her grandmama and wandered into the backroom, where she would often sleep without looking back at either woman.

The small backroom welcomed her. With an old quilt sprawled across the rickety bed, it was like she had never left.

Bria collapsed on the bed and shut her eyes tight. Everything had changed... but really, nothing did at all.

WHISPERS

Christof took his position outside the Capitol building, still as a statue, watching as civilians passed, unsuspecting. No one knew but a select few of what had occurred in the Capitol building. As far as they were concerned, the Senate ran as always, with every Senator alive, well, and pure.

But despite keeping his stature, nerves raced through Christof's body. Every time he saw Sister Jey Ma, part of him wanted to flee. She held secrets to her chest, ones that Christof could not find. No matter the questions he asked, no matter how much he pressured, Sister Jey Ma provided one answer: "It is for the greater good."

So Christof kept his post, wearing the burden close to his chest as he watched the crowds. Since he led the at- tack on the storytellers in the alley, people walked with their heads down, murmuring their prayers beneath the watchful eye of the Year Glass. He had checked a few other alleyways, but mostly, they remained vacant. One raid was all it took: one example. Just like they had done in Newbird's Arm.

"Afternoon, Cadet."

Christof turned. Lieutenant Drayton approached, stiff as a board, lips curved in a permanent frown.

"Lieutenant." Christof let the word sit in his mouth. Would he soon be more than a cadet? Would he wear that same rank?

"You are dismissed for the day. I believe Sister Jey Ma wishes to see you."

"Thank you, Lieutenant," Christof said. As he walked away, he paused, recalling the events of the past weeks. "Lieutenant, may I speak freely?"

"Do as you wish."

"You asked me to report anything odd."

The lieutenant perked up ever so slightly and asked, "And have you discovered anything... odd?"

Christof paused. Should he tell the lieutenant everything? Part of him yearned to tell Lieutenant Drayton about everything that had happened: the Senate had fallen. Magic had taken its roots. But then he would be betraying Sister Jey Ma—and then what? What would Lieutenant Drayton do?

After all, they had all seen the magic on the outskirts of the Capitol. This was none the different.

"There is one thing I found strange…" Christof recited slowly. "In that tower, they've been keeping a child…a little boy."

"A little boy…" the lieutenant whispered.

"I didn't get a good look at him or anything, but it was definitely some kid. Don't know why they would have a kid like that either. Elder An Drew and Senator Cordova never let him out of their sights. I just thought it was kind of weird."

Lieutenant Drayton didn't speak. Eyes cast ahead, brow furrowed.

"I'm sorry. That is all I know," Christof finished.

The lieutenant did not lift his head, speaking in a dull, vacant tone. "Thank you, Cadet. Please, if you learn anything about that little boy, let me know."

"Of course, sir." Christof saluted, then left with a dismissal wave of the lieutenant's hand.

Christof jammed his hands in his pockets and, taking two steps at a time, hurried up the stairs of the Capitol. The building itself glowered at him as if judging by the comments he made to Lieutenant Drayton. What did it matter? He kept everything else quiet. The state of the Senate remained locked behind closed doors. Sister Jey

Ma had decided to include him in this outcome, and he would not betray that trust.

Even if it made his skin crawl.

What would become of Rosada now? With Senator Cordova at the helm, surely the Effluvium would remain pure and undeterred.

Surely order would reign.

A guard opened the door of the Capitol as he approached, letting him step inside without questioning. He had complete freedom within the Capitol building. No one stopped him as he ventured along the corridors, checking inside the different empty offices. The building, once a bustling hub, lacked life. Instead, only Senator Cordova's loyalists and guards occupied the paths.

If an outsider entered, surely something would seem amiss.

But no one did; Captain Rivers made sure of that.

Ever since Sister Jey Ma performed her song in the Senate, Captain Rivers became a constant presence in the Capitol as well. His hulking body and long black hair demanded attention. He moved with a scowl, and everyone stepped to the side as he marched down the hallways.

So as Christof ascended the stairwell to the second floor, it was almost impossible to miss Captain Rivers as he stood with Elder An Drew in a heated discussion. Christof slowed his pace, watching the two men talk.

Elder An Drew controlled the conversation, his harrowing gaze like daggers at Captain Rivers.

They didn't notice Christof approach at first.

"I need you to use it. We cannot let people suspect what happened until it is time," Elder An Drew said.

"You should know that I will not. I made my vows."

"Even if he commands it?"

"He'll have to force me."

Elder An Drew relaxed his shoulders and glanced down the stairwell at Christof. He spoke without looking at Captain Rivers, "We shall discuss this more later. Forget your personal reservations for the good of the Effluvium."

Christof shrank as Elder An Drew's eyes bore into him. Was Elder An Drew talking to Captain Rivers or to him? It could have applied to either.

But as Elder An Drew inferred, the answers would come later. The Elder swiftly left his place on the staircase and ventured down the hall. Captain Rivers clenched his own fists, glowered at Christof, then disappeared down a corridor.

Once again, Christof stood alone, with secrets haunting his every step. Everyone spoke in whispers; no one preached any grand plan to him. Everyone expected Christof to act, to behave, and to worship their words.

His mother always told him to listen to his superiors but not to be afraid and ask questions. She told him: *Christof, people will always whisper behind your back, but if you are loud and commanding, then they will tell you the truth in full.* He clung to those words but failed to act upon them. In contrast, his father had insisted that Christof behave loyally; the Guard worked as it did because no one asked questions. A constant tug-of-war between asking and listening pressed against Christof's stomach. He wanted answers, but he had learned not to ask.

Only in Newbird's Arm did he feel powerful. There, he was the leader of a brigade of cadets. Vagrants cowered at his very movements. Storytellers begged for his forgiveness. And even there, he could woo whichever woman he so desired.

At least, he *thought* he could.

Bria Smidt became the object of his fixation for years. After kissing her once, at the request of a few girls in town, she never left his mind. Her beautiful complexion, her thoughtful eyes, and her sweet smile haunted his dreams. Two weeks after that kiss, he courted her for marriage.

His pursuit started with walks in the garden over the next few months. As he grew more comfortable in his command, he coerced her into gentle caresses and touches. Then he found his lips against her thrice more, desperate for her to return his desire.

On the last kiss, right before he was due to leave basic training, Christof pulled her close and told her of his plans to marry her when he returned.

Bria had responded in silence and rejected any further advances.

Christof took that hesitancy as nerves and left for a year to begin his training. Only when he returned did he find Bria Smidt in the forest, kissing that ridiculous Brent Harley.

He had hoped after Brent's betrothal to Sister Jey Ma that Bria might come back to him, but she grew even more recluse. All the control, all the command that Christof held, vanished, and he spent years trying to reclaim it.

Only to remain a cadet.

Only to lose his home.

Only to lose half his face.

And only to lose his remaining family.

He had Sister Jey Ma now, but she had a command over him that left him powerless. Plans happened around him; he had no say in his destiny. Did he ever?

"Fucking shite…" He cursed to himself as he walked. Why did he keep thinking about Bria? Why did he keep thinking about the past? Now, he was Sister Jey Ma's loyal guard, soon to get a promotion, and a confidante for

Senator Cordova. Surely, this was worth everything he had experienced over the years.

For the Effluvium.

For Order.

He had to keep going.

Sister Jey Ma sat in the suite they shared on the third floor of the Capitol. She didn't turn from her vanity as Christof entered.

"You summoned me?" Christof remarked.

"Yes, thank you for joining me." She ran her hairbrush through her red locks, focus still on the mirror.

"How can I be of service?" Christof stepped behind her and placed his hands on her chair.

She brought one of his hands to her lips and kissed it. "I just need you here for comfort."

"Oh." Christof stiffened. So was that all he was then? Her consort? Her pet?

But this time, Sister Jey Ma continued, "I am fearful, Christof. Something quite tremendous is about to happen... but it fills me with a great amount of fear."

"And that is?"

"Our next hymn, of course." She faced him. "I am to recite the hymn in the next couple days for the entire country. If it goes as we intend... every Magii from Newbird's Arm to Ab Aeterno, to the border of Volfium and the border of Kainan, will succumb to its rhythm."

"And then what?" Christof asked, hanging on her every word.

"We work to restore the Effluvium." Her eyes lit up, a hint of yellow around her irises. Despite the yellow, Sister Jey Ma spoke more like Jemma Reds than a puppet of Senator Cordova and Elder An Drew. "We help the Effluvium breathe again at last. That is why we are doing this. For the Effluvium."

"And how do we help the Effluvium?"

"Elder An Drew says he'll tell us in due time. But first, the hymn must be successful. Otherwise, the Effluvium will remain tainted."

"I'd be lying if I told you I understood." Christof stroked back a strand of Sister Jey Ma's hair. Her beauty still drew him in, like a beam of sunlight cutting through the clouds. When she spoke of the Effluvium, life filled her body. But it vacated quickly, leaving her a corpse with hints of smoke about her mouth, nose, and ears.

"I do not expect you to understand entirely. Let us handle the magic, Christof Caver. Your job is merely to listen."

"For storytellers?"

"For everything. That is your job as a guard, is it not?"

Christof agreed without speaking, twirling Sister Jey Ma's hair around his finger.

Yes, his job was to listen. To wait. To learn.

But with everyone whispering, it made focusing difficult. Each word might have belonged to the wind.

"Where shall I listen first, then?" Christof asked Sister
Jey Ma.

She smirked at him and squeezed his hands tight before saying, "To me, of course. Come. It has been a long
day."

BROKEN GLASS

Bria folded the quilt and placed it on the bed, listening to the bustle outside her window. The midday market woke her with its usual bustling. For a second, she wondered if the past two years had all been a dream, and she had woken up in her grandmama's house after a night in her tunnels.

But she could not ignore how the earth called to her or the obvious missing hand replaced by a bundle of weeds.

She ran a hand through her hair, untangling a few strands, before weaving her hair in a clumsy braid. For a few moments, she fidgeted with the loose strands, but unable to get her branched hand to behave, she gave up and pushed them behind her ear. Her hair still lacked the vibrance and health from before she became the forest, but at least the matting had disappeared.

After putting on her gloves, Bria peeked out of the room. The scent of lemon cakes and tea whistled into the room and pulled her toward the kitchen. Her grandmama sat at the kitchen table, staring out the half-shuttered window.

"Hi, Grandmama," Bria said as she took a seat at the table.

Her grandmama took her hand, and they sat there in silence for a moment. Bria swallowed, squeezing her grandmama's hand, relishing that moment of silence.

"Eat. Please." Her grandmama pushed a plate of lemon cakes toward her.

Bria obliged, picking at one as she asked, "Did you and Lana reach any sort of resolution?"

"We talked. That is all I can say about it. It is all hard for me to piece together..." Madame Gonzo shook her head. "How did you two even meet? It seems highly unlikely... unless you were in Knoll?"

"It's a long tale..." Bria whispered.

"Tell me."

Bria squeezed a few crumbs between her fingers. With her voice low, she told her grandmama what had happened since the Storm of Nightmares in Newbird's Arm—well, within reason. She skipped the parts about the Mist Keepers, the Palaver of Immortals, and the silver pools, focusing instead on the role of the Order. Her grandmama knew about the tunnels, at least, but she didn't need her grandmama fretting about evil death gods.

So spoke about her time in Mert, about being captured by the Guard, about her marriage to Brent, and about taking down Knoll. With her voice cracking, she explained Brent had sacrificed himself and was now a prisoner with some 'Order loyalists.' Everything came together like a puzzle, the right pieces falling and allowing her to meet Lana and grow her magic.

Madame Gonzo nodded, listening to each word.

"So now we're here. Lana came to meet with Senator Heartz… but I just want to understand my magic more." Bria finished.

"Oh, my dear Briannabella…" Madame Gonzo squeezed her hands, her eyes staring off into the distance. "This is not what I ever wanted for you."

"You did everything that you could."

She still didn't shift her gaze. "In some ways, I am happy you… have found peace with your mother. I doubt she and I will ever reconcile. Though, it was good to see her again…" Madame Gonzo smiled slightly. "She is still herself, frankly."

"Just as determined as her mother?"

"Oh, yes." Madame Gonzo rose from the table. "That much was obvious. She took no time at all, once she finished ranting, to demand that I take her to see Senator Heartz. Shame for her because the Senator hasn't been home in the last month."

"Of course, the Senator isn't home," Bria remarked.

"Is she ever?"

"Point."

"I gave her the information to contact Helga's assistant, though—perhaps the dear senator will grace us with her presence soon."

Bria nodded and brought a piece of lemon cake to her mouth. The mere delicacy made her body swoon. Oh, how she missed her grandmama's cakes. For some time, she enjoyed the cakes in silence, pretending for a little while that everything was okay and that she could stay in her grandmama's kitchen forever.

A knock pulled her from that reality.

"Oh, who is it now?" Madame Gonzo grunted as she climbed to her feet. "Stay back here. It probably isn't best that anyone sees you."

Bria stayed in her seat, watching as her grandmama shuffled through the kitchen and into the front room. Once the door to the kitchen shuttered closed, she pressed herself against the doorway, listening as her grandmama welcomed the visitor.

"Oh... Janette!" Madame Gonzo said.

Bria's heart stopped. *Brent's mother...*

"Afternoon, Beatriz. I've come to drop off your laundry," Janette said, her voice low and monotone.

"Thank you. Here, let me get your payment." Madame Gonzo shuffled around the room. "Here we go! This should cover it."

"Ma! Ask her if she wants one!" Another voice piped. It belonged to Alexandria Harley, still speaking the same excitement that Bria remembered.

"Oh, right..." Janette sighed, "Alexandria here discovered my mother's old cookbook. She has taught herself how to make rugelach if you want one."

"Oh, rugelach! I haven't had that in years!" Madame Gonzo exclaimed.

"I filled them with chocolate because we don't have apricots. Ma said they were too expensive. I want to make a babka next!"

"Well, you're going to have a little baker on your hands soon enough, Janette. This is delicious, Alexandria!"

"Thank you," Alexandria spoke with confidence. "I like to think that the cookbook tells a story—"

Janette interrupted, "Don't you *dare* start that again. You're already being watched enough as it is!"

"We can trust Madame Gonzo, though! She always listened to Brent's stories."

"We are not talking about your brother. We're talking about you."

"Why not?! He would love that food tells stories!"

"Enough. Your brother is dead, and I won't let you be taken by the same demons as him!"

"Now, Janette, let the girl have her fun. She's a child," Madame Gonzo said.

"Fun? Where did fun get Brenton? He's dead now because he couldn't stop telling those ridiculous stories!"

Bria didn't know that she had reached for the doorknob, nor did she plan to open it. But with her heart pounding, the door swung open to the living room, where Janette Harley stood, towering above Madame Gonzo. The woman's hair had gone gray, her eyes marred by dark circles, and her skin as white as paper. Alexandria stood against the wall, hugging a box in her arms. Upon seeing Bria, her eyes lit up behind her round glasses, but she did not speak a word.

Bria's voice shook as she spoke. "Those ridiculous stories have saved Brent's life. He's not dead... I promise."

"You..." Janette's face darkened, "What're you doing here?"

"Mrs. Harley... I—"

"You have quite the nerve coming back here after what you did!"

"Janette!" Madame Gonzo interjected.

"No! She killed my son!"

"Mrs. Harley, I promise you, Brent isn't dead." Bria stepped toward the woman. "I promise. The stories are keeping him alive."

"Then where, pray tell, is he?"

How could she answer that? She couldn't tell Janette Harley that *death gods* took her son. She exhaled, then said, "They captured him for his stories and magic. But he's alive. I promise, he's alive. I've... received information that he is alive." She rubbed her hands together.

"Why would they tell *you*?"

"Because I'm his wife!"

"Wife?"

Bria gulped and fidgeted with her gloves. "We married a few months ago... before he was captured..."

"Liar..." Janette gripped the entry table. Beside her, for just a moment, Alexandria's face lit with happiness.

"Why would I lie?" Bria asked.

"He was going to marry Miss Jemma Reds!"

"Ms. Harley, he was betrothed to Jemma, but he called it off... he never loved her." Bria gulped, her words shaking. "He and I had been in love since we were sixteen."

"Then why didn't he tell me?" Janette's eyes narrowed.

"Because he wanted you to be happy."

"Are you implying that I didn't care about my son's happiness?"

"What? No. I just—"

Ms. Harley wrapped her hand around a vase on the table, shaking. "I know my son. He would never fall in love with Magii Scum like you." Tears stained Ms. Harley's face. This woman, who Bria always knew as kind but stern, no longer bore any such kindness in her eyes. A system designed to destroy her had beaten and broken her. So here she stood, clinging to what gave her hope: a perfect image of her son, no matter how false.

"Ms. Harley, please—"

"I should turn you into the Guard right now. The new captain would be very pleased to have you here."

"Janette..." Madame Gonzo approached her. "Let us talk about this for a moment. Bria isn't lying. We all saw them together in the market—"

"Enough!" Janette yanked the vase from the table and threw it against the wall, just missing Madame Gonzo and Bria. The glass shattered on the floor.

They stared at it for a moment.

Then Janette Harley brushed her skirt and grabbed her daughter's hand. Without speaking, she marched out the door, leaving the glass shattered behind her.

Bria rushed to her grandmama's side, helping the old woman sit down in the chair. She held back her own tears, shaking as she sat on the couch with her grandmama. In the early days of her relationship with Brent, she'd only met Ms. Harley a couple of times. She never had a chance to really speak with the woman, but from what Brent told her, his mother only saw Bria as a friend. She didn't notice the way they used to hold hands or the way Brent would spend hours in the Senator's Gardens. To Ms. Harley, it was a friendship.

Perhaps she didn't want to admit her son had grown older.

After all, Ms. Harley only ever wanted her children to have success. She saw Jemma Reds as that option for Brent: a pious religious woman to balance Brent's so-called demon eyes and storytelling tendencies.

But one thing was certain: nothing could take stories from Brent Harley. Even after all the times the Guard beat him, or the times they threatened him with cleansing or the Pit, he remained a storyteller.

Bria finally asked, "Do you think she'll tell the guard?"

"Doubtful. They already targeted Alexandria with that black stamp on her own wrist. Janette doesn't want to remind them." Madame Gonzo pressed her head against the back of the couch. "I'm not upset with her. She has always wanted the best for her children, and in her mind, she truly believed that Brent marrying Miss Reds was the best option."

"Surely Jemma could clear the air."

"She tried to before she disappeared."

"Wait... Jemma's missing?" Bria had heard nothing about Jemma Reds. Very little news of home had reached her at all.

"She joined the Order as Brother Roy Al's subordinate. Soon after Brother Roy Al left and Elder Lau Rel took charge, she left. Some blamed a vagrant; others say her heart was broken; no one can really verify what happened." Madame Gonzo frowned, "Her parents are a mess. She left a note, but they believe it was forged. But I don't think so. I think she left on her own accord."

"I didn't know..." Bria mumbled.

"How would you?" Madame Gonzo wiped a tear from Bria's face. "Do not take what Janette said to you personally. She was wrong, of course, but she had been like an animal in flight for years. Between her husband in the Pit, everything that happened with Brent, and now Alexandria's black stamp... I think she is at her breaking point."

"It just...hurts. Because I know Brent would love for his mother and me to get along."

"And you will. If I know anything about you, Briannabella, it is that you will not let Brent die. You're stubborn like that."

Bria almost smiled.

"Now, let's go finish those lemon cakes."

Los Gardeniros n'e Diversito

Once the sun set, Bria left her grandmama's home and headed back toward the tower. She wanted to visit her father, but they agreed to wait a day or so; the last thing she needed was to be spotted by more people. Her heart still hung heavy against her chest, the altercation with Brent's mother fresh in her mind. But her grandmama had been right, as usual; Bria would not let Brent die. He wasn't *allowed* to die. That was her promise, and she would keep it close to her chest.

But if the forest told her anything, no promise could be kept in certainty. Once full of green and beauty, the forest now stood with the same skeletal stance as the Necrowood. A little over a year without me here, and you've already withered. I didn't know I kept so much alive... she slowed as she trampled over a few fallen trees.

Trees that she had caused to fall.

For a moment, once again, she was running through the woods, trying to escape the Guard. The large, hulking Cadet Chet Lawry's voice boomed as he followed her. In her own panic and confusion, she sent the trees flying.

Only to kill the cadet.

Bria blinked, pulling herself from the memory. She knelt beside the fallen tree, her hands shaking. Who was to say she didn't do the same to Brent? Who was to say she hadn't killed more innocent people?

She buried her head into her knees, trying her best to choke back the sobs. But it didn't matter; nothing mattered anymore. She could say she would save Brent, but the tunnels no longer called to her. She could claim to fight for the greater good, but blood was on her hands.

No matter what she believed, the Order would hold her up as a destructive force. What happened to the days of just being a gardener? What happened to those days of weaving baskets with her father, baking lemon cakes with her grandmama, or planting seeds with her grandpapa?

What happened to the days of kissing Brent in the hedge maze?

What happened to her quiet dreams?

She sniffled, hugging herself. "Why did it ever have to be me?"

"Well, because you're special," a voice answered.

Bria jumped, reaching for the nearest branch. A light mist had gathered at her feet, and a shadow stood within it. An obvious smile parted its murky face.

She squinted. It couldn't be...but who else would stand there, smiling at her like that? It was a smile she never thought she'd see again. "Grandpapa?"

"Hello, Briannabella." Her grandpapa stood before her, wrapped in a haze of mist. His ghostly figure looked exactly as he had a few weeks before his death: healthy, with wide shoulders and slicked-back silver hair. He held out his worn hand out to her, then said, "You have grown into a fine young lady, haven't you?"

Bria continued to stare at her grandfather. She wasn't shocked to see a ghost—all that time with the Mist Keepers had made her sight ever so stronger—but she hadn't expected to see *him*. She had expected him to pass on, become one with the earth, and never return. But here her grandpapa stood, as clear as a reflection in the water, offering her a hand.

"Now there, you look like you've seen a ghost." Her grandpapa guffawed at the statement, "Haven't you seen a ghost before?"

"Yes, but... I didn't expect you to still be here." Bria replied.

"You mean you expected me to return to the Earth?"

"Yes."

"Well, I suppose I had unfinished business." He winked at her. "Had a granddaughter, you see, who needed my help. I just didn't know how to reach out to you. Well, at least I didn't, until that odd-ball storm that happened right here all those months ago, and you became some legend."

"The Storm of Nightmares?"

"Yes, that. If you had stayed around after all that, I might have had the time to speak with you. But then you vanished."

"I had to..."

"I know, I know, Briannabella." Her grandpapa sat beside her, still grinning as he spoke. "If you had stayed, I would have wondered where your mind had gone. You were always a bright one."

Bria fidgeted with her gloves, unsure what to say. It was weird, sitting here with her grandpapa after all those years. It was like she had seen him years ago, still smiling and welcoming. But his eyes shimmered with understanding. "You have been through so much now, haven't you?"

Bria nodded. Once again, the tears started to catch her throat. She had to stop crying; if she let herself sob, the storm clouds might rain. And if the storm clouds rained, then she'd be discovered within minutes.

Especially since the sky gazed at her with clear stars.

"You're a legend even amongst the dead, you know. Word has traveled through the mist about *Rhodana the Forest Queen*. I always knew you had strong magic…" Her grandpapa took Bria's hand. "I never thought it would be like this."

"Why didn't you tell me about your magic, though?" Bria asked. "Grandmama never told me either."

"My magic was more of a parlor trick. I had a green thumb, easy to hide. Could hardly be considered magic, really."

"But you still had it and knew it ran in our family." Bria removed her glove, revealing her branched hand. She flexed her twig-like fingers. "I always thought I was an abom—"

"A miracle," her grandpapa corrected her.

Bria shook her head.

Her grandpapa squeezed her branched hand tight to his chest. "I had every intention of telling you when you got older…if you continued to flourish. But part of me hoped that as you got older, you would abandon the magic, that it would be a subtle part of you."

"Like with Lana?"

"Lana?"

Bria huffed. "My mother."

"Oh. Yes. Angelana..." Her grandpapa frowned. "So you met her?"

"She's in town right now."

"And she's... okay?"

"She explained everything to me. It's why I returned home. She told me you had magic. I came back here to get answers from Grandmama."

"Beatriz didn't really know much about the magic. I preferred to keep that part of my life a mystery to her... to protect her. She knew I had magic, and she knew I came from a long line of those with magic... but that was it," her grandpapa said, "It was best she didn't know much... for her safety."

"And for mine?"

"And for you."

"But it could have helped with all of... this."

"What could I have said? You were a child."

"I was ten when you died."

"But hardly mature enough to carry the weight of this knowledge on your shoulders."

Bria stared at the ground. Back then, it had been so easy; magic was beautiful, and the trees sang her name. She never thought it might be like this.

"You wouldn't have understood as a child. But now, you are more than ready. Twenty-one... a young woman... carrying the weight of the world on your shoulders. Yes, you are quite ready."

"Then tell me. Please." Bria would have gotten on her knees and begged if her grandpapa had insisted. She'd been searching for answers, deconstructing riddles, and asking "why" for over a decade. Why could she access the tunnels? Why did magic course so loudly through her veins? Why did her magic continue to shine, even at the darkest hour?

Why her?

Her grandpapa stood and paced between the trees, weaving his hands behind his back. Bria watched him, a lump forming in her throat. She never thought she'd speak with her grandpapa again. Even after Brent helped her see past the mist and her sight solidified more, she never considered it a possibility.

But here he stood, like any other day, a ghost... but himself.

Would he give her the answers she wanted? Would he let her thrive?

Finally, he spoke, "You know I wasn't born in Rosada, yes?"

"You told me you came from far away when I was a little girl."

"Yes. Perennes. You know where Perennes is, yes?"

"It's on the southern continent, isn't it?"

"Yes, correct." Her grandpapa recalled. "You see, back when I was a boy, I moved here from Perennes. There was a large migration from the southern continent during those years. Famine had struck, and there had been some... constant burdens between Perennes and its neighbor, Proveniro, for over three centuries. Constant war. Constant uncertainty. It wasn't a good place to live. People with magic had grown sick and weak; we were commissioned to the army if we had enough strength, but for the most part, what once flourished in our souls left us debilitated." Her grandpapa stared at his hands. "When I was about sixteen, just when I started displaying mild signs of magic, my parents had my sister and me join a caravan north, hoping we'd be able to make it to Heims or Mert. Unfortunately, most caravans never made it past Rosada."

Her grandpapa stopped for a moment to pluck a leaf from a twig. He then frowned. "My caravan stopped between Grover's Marsh and Newbird's Arm. My sister and I weren't all that young at the time, so we made an agreement: one of us would go to the town of Grover's Marsh while the other would continue towards Newbird's Arm. As you know, I am sure, I came to Newbird's Arm and took up a job as the gardener's apprentice. My sister fell in love with another in Grover's Marsh... and it was when I went attend her wedding that I met your grandmama."

"I've heard the story." Bria smiled. Her grandmama had recanted it to her many times: how she saw a man with slick hair climb off the train, how he offered her a pack of seeds from his pockets and told her it would grow like his love, how her inability to garden to kill the seeds, but nevertheless the man returned to save them. It was the first story of love she ever knew.

It used to be the love story she wanted.

"I do miss Beatriz quite frequently..." Her grandpapa sighed. "But she has done well. It must run in the family." He smiled at Bria.

"Like magic?"

"Yes...magic..." Her grandpapa ran his hand over the tree leaves. "Magic is all I had left of my home after leaving. I never returned, never saw my parents again. They stayed behind in what we called la Propriedad."

"La Propriedad?"

"Yes, la Propriedad...or the Property. Specifically, la Propriedad d'los Gardeniros n'e Diversito. It was once a grand garden, much like the one beneath the Senator's home but far greater. It sat just inland from the coastal town of São Caméliosa..." Her grandfather licked his bottom lip. "The story goes that a couple centuries ago, someone burned la Propriedad to the ground, but people stayed to hold on to the legend."

"Legend?"

"The legend of *Los Gardeniros n'e Diversito*."

"Los Gardeniros n'e Diversito," Bria recited. "I never heard of it."

"Most people wouldn't know it. After all, it is a *story* and one not as commonly distributed in the shadows as *Rhodana the Forest Queen*." He winked at her before continuing. "The legend tells that millennia ago, the Gardeniros served as the guardians of the Earth, Life, and everything. They kept the world flourishing. While their story died and their magic faltered, a lineage remained, though their names ultimately changed. Gardensito... Gareno... Gonso..."

"Gonzo," Bria whispered.

"Exactly."

"So in this legend... these Gardeners protected the earth with their magic. They had plant magic, like me...like us?"

"Life magic. Not just plants."

Bria stared at her hands. Her fingers trembled while her branched hand sprouted a couple leaves. *Life...*

"Plants have always been the easiest, but there is so much more. The world is linked through so many different elements, and our ancestors controlled it all. In my death, I have met others as well with similar magical inclinations, all tied together by *life*."

Bria stared at her hands, unable to speak.

Her grandpapa reached forward to take both of her hands. "I've seen your magic grow. If anyone has the Gardeniros inside of them, it's Rhodana the Forest Queen."

"I'm not Rhodana," she objected.

"She was in our legends too. A child born of life, earth, water, and air; she can control the forests, knock down walls, and grant life to the dying."

"It's a coincidence."

"You've done all of that, haven't you?"

"I haven't given life to the dying." Bria almost laughed. The idea was preposterous.

"What was it that you said to me when I fell ill? That I wasn't allowed to die?"

"I was a child; I didn't want my grandpapa to die."

"But after that, did I not keep breathing for over two more weeks despite what the doctors said?"

"It was luck!"

"I only stayed alive until the day I asked you to let go. Remember?"

Bria stared at her grandpapa. She tried not to remember, but of course, she couldn't forget. A flood of memories came back to her. After her grandpapa fell ill, she almost never left his side, bringing flowers from the garden each morning. She would then tell him he wasn't allowed to die and hold his hand until her father or grandmama led her back to bed.

After a fortnight of staying by her grandpapa's side, he whispered to her that it was time to let go. She refused at first, but after many tears, she let go.

She let *him* go.

"I wasn't ready to say goodbye," she whispered.

"So I stayed. And I am convinced it was because of you." He wiped one of the tears from her eyes. "You carry the legend in your genes."

"But why me? Why not Lana? Or you?" Bria couldn't stop trembling. All of this raised more questions than answers; sure, she knew it ran in her family, but why did it all congregate in her heart?

Her grandpapa said, "The world needed you."

"That doesn't answer the question! Even if it's because I practiced more, it doesn't explain why I can control even *more* elements other than plants. This is more than life... It's nature, it's stone, it's...*everything.*"

"It's all part of the earth. It's all needed for life." He glanced around the forest. "You were planted at birth. That might have begun your transformation. But beyond that, the circumstances of your childhood and everything you have gone through have given you the chance to flourish. And who knows what magic is hidden deeper in your lineage? Your father after all, has his own family."

"Daddy never had any inclinations to magic."

"Yes, it seems so. But you never know what lies in your blood. Remember, we are but the accumulation of stories passed down through generations."

Bria didn't have a response. Every word her grandpapa said hung heavy in the air like rain.

"I know, I know, you don't like the attention. You don't like feeling special. You didn't even as a child. But everything that you have done has made you special. Because no matter the legend you believe in, if any at all, there is one thing that remains the same: Rhodana or whoever you choose to sing about is always self-made. She takes the tools handed to her and grows. And you have grown so much, Briannabella. And I am proud of you."

Bria shook her head. Tears finally started to fall, and the air around her grew thick. "I don't want this..."

"Oh, my sweet Briannabella. I know it is a lot. But remember, it is okay to cry and to step back from the world. Sometimes you need to prune the hedges so they can grow stronger."

"Grandpapa, this... It's too much for me."

"It's a heavy burden, I know. But you are so strong. Stronger than I could ever be."

Bria buried her head in her hands and heaved. She used all her energy to restrain the storm clouds from growing overhead.

Not now.

They retreated slightly. Bria dug her heels into the ground, focusing on the roots and the weeds. The forest moaned for her, begged for her to give life. She could only spare a handful, enough to pull the energy away from the clouds.

And enough to cause the nearby trees to sprout with green.

Her grandpapa laughed. "Amazing. Like a dream."

Bria shook her head.

"Oh, Briannabella." Her grandpapa wrapped her in a hug. She leaned against his ghostly chest, almost firm enough to be alive. He brushed back her hair. "Do not fret. Just take it one step at a time... and in that, you will thrive."

Bria couldn't speak, another lump forming in her throat. She wanted nothing more than to lean against her grandpapa's chest and fall asleep, only to wake up safe in her bedroom.

For now, she could only feel the temporary embrace of safety as her magic continued to take root and fill the Newbird Forest.

CHAPTER TWENTY-SIX

DRAGGED DOWN

Every day that passed, Brent felt more like he'd been skinned alive. On the floor of his cell, covered in black chains, every breath labored. All the while, the stories came few and far between. Some days, Kek sat within speaking distance, while others, he heard only the screams of the silver-eyed creatures—no, apprentices—locked away in the crypts. He tried to speak to them, only to receive shrieks and moans as replies.

The black smoke continued to form, webbing across his body, locking him tighter to the wall and floors. With each passing day, it dug deeper into his skin. At times, screams escaped his lips, only for the other apprentices to join in a chorus of cries.

Then the mist shifted around him, and for a moment, the pain stopped, only for it to begin all over again with a fresh round of screaming. He tried to ignore the pain. He tried to tell himself stories and remember Bria's face.

But even his constant couldn't keep his head sane.

His Diabolo came back in force, cackling with each of his cries.

Please make this stop. He begged silently, but he never spoke, fearful of what Ningursu might tout in front of him to end it all.

Then the prison shifted again, and the tendrils of torturous smoke retracted.

They didn't return, and Brent slipped into sleep.

He dreamt of his wedding day. Blindfolded, smiling, his stomach flipped in anticipation.

Then his soon-to-be wife spoke, and the voice belonged not to Bria but Jemma.

He ripped off his blindfold at once, face-to-face with Jemma Reds draped in wedding blues. His stomach dropped, and he turned to the pews. Bria sat there with Christof, his hand squeezing her leg, while her head hung bowed in shame.

This isn't right.

People called his name for defiling the ceremony. His mother watched in horror from the front row.

This isn't right.

Captain Carver rose from his spot by the wall, glowering.

This isn't right.

"This isn't right!" he shouted, bolting upright from his sleep. A bright white light blinded him, and unable to lift his head or body, he sank back onto the...bed?

He blinked a few times. No longer in the crypts, Brent lay on a bed in the Library's infirmary. The black smoke weighed on him as if a thousand pounds of brick sat on his chest.

Despite how he knew stories loitered in this room, he could not see them. Even the mist seemed distant, separate, and foreign.

And all remained calm and untouched until a shadow fell over him.

He squinted at the familiar figure. "Caroline?"

But as Caroline leaned over him, her face shifted.

Ningursu bore down on him, in control of Caroline's body, gaze fixated.

"At last, we see each other, eye-to-eye," Ningursu said.

"Gave you a run for a bit, didn't I?" Brent chuckled.

"Now is not the time for games, Mr. Harley." Ningursu's voice, usually booming and confident, had fallen into a hoarse rhythm. While Ningursu had always been nothing more than a skull, his face had changed even more. Skin peeled from the side of the head. "We do not have time."

"As far as I'm concerned, we have all the time in the world," Brent said.

"It's time to give into your fate."

"What fate? Dying? We already tried that."

"You're right. So we must rewrite your destiny—you are like me, after all. Pure and true. *A god.*"

Brent scoffed.

"You just need to embrace it. And I can show you how."

"Sorry, not interested." Brent yanked against the black smoke again.

"You don't have a choice. We have worked on this for months after you escaped. This is not just your destiny—it is the Council's destiny." Ningursu directed Caroline's body to step out of eyesight, and once again, Brent only saw the white walls and pristine floors. The skull's voice hung over him like a nightmare, pounding in his ears.

My name is Brent Harley.

And I don't want to be a god.

Brent strained against the black chains, trying to get a glimpse of the room. He couldn't make out Caroline or Ningursu anymore, but an unfamiliar figure stood by the far end of the room. Moving with the dexterity of a spider, the figure lifted a syringe and flicked it once before strolling to Brent's side. The figure placed a hand on Brent's forehead, forcing him to lie back on the bed.

Aelia stood over him, holding a goblet. Carefully, she lowered it to his lips. A foul-tasting liquid entered his mouth.

Brent choked.

Aelia said nothing, proceeding to remove a syringe and a vial from her apron. Her fingers moved like a nimble dancer as she tore open the buttons on his shirt. She did not speak, nor did she flinch; every action fell with precision.

Brent tried to find her story, but the black smoke tugged back his magic. Only a single moment flashed before him—a woman sitting in a throne room, calculating and wise. Was it Aelia? A relative? Or someone else entirely?

The story vanished before Brent found his answers.

"It will all be over soon," Aelia said. She lined the syringe between his third and fourth right ribs.

Then jammed it into his skin.

Brent gasped. An odd tingling sensation worked its way over his body, fluttering through his veins and leaving behind a trail of cold.

Did he have arms and legs anymore? What about eyes? Were those his breaths growing heavy?

What was happening to his heartbeat?

I'm not allowed to die. Hadn't he made a promise?

But even Ningursu said this wasn't death. This was something else.

Something worse.

"This will make the process easier for everyone." Aelia sounded as if she were underwater.

Brent couldn't open his mouth. Everything grew hazy and distant.

I'm not allowed to die.

I'm not allowed to fail.

My name is Brent Harley.

And I am the story collector.

A black cloak approached him again. Caroline strode forward, Ningursu's skull replacing her face. Mist protruded from his orifices, reaching for Brent's skin and wrapping around his mouth, nose, and ears.

It is time to face your destiny. You will be mine. The mist called.

No...

His vision faded.

As did this name.

But this time, he didn't see yellow.

Instead, every potential future bowed to him, different tales with different endings.

First, he stood upon a tower, hands laced with another. He turned to see a woman with red hair smiling back at him. As around him, guards shouted for victory.

Then it changed. This time he stood in a forest, walking through the swamp and touching each leaf of the trees. They turned gray.

Everything died.

The stories kept changing. In some, he lay defeated, breathing his last breaths. In others, he led an army. And in some, he even became king.

Then he stood amid the white and black tulips of the Chessboard Plains. A body lay at his feet, mouth ajar, blood pooling. It painted the tulips red, and he fed on life as it finally ceased.

At last, a victor.

At last...

At last...

"Enough!"

The voice sliced through the air and pulled Brent out of the dreams. Caroline's body had stepped back, gripping its head with force as if trying to yank Ningursu's skull from its neck. It stumbled backward, crashing into Aelia and against the table on the far side of the room. The jars and vials clattered to the floor, followed by an object resembling a skull.

As the objects fell, Caroline's body straightened. In place of Ningursu's skull, Caroline's face returned. She rushed to Brent's side.

"I can't move," Brent mumbled.

Caroline said nothing, hoisting Brent's body off the bed. The black tendrils of smoke snapped, and without speaking, she carried him into the plumes of smoke.

All the while, Brent's vision blurred again.

When the smoke finally parted and Brent could see, he found himself once again in the room of canvases. His pineapple lay on the floor, rotting away. He tried to reach for it, but he still could not move his arms. Only his sight had returned, and to his relief, Caroline was by the wall with a blindfold across her face.

"Caroline?" he choked out.

"Good. You have awoken. Can you move?"

"Not yet. I can't feel anything."

"I am sure you will soon..." Caroline sighed. "I am sorry I could not assist you sooner, Brent. Ningursu's grasp is hard to fight."

"I understand." Brent licked his bottom lip.

"I would give you water, but I do not want to risk him seeing you. For now, I created a distraction by putting my face in every mirror...but I do not know how well that will work."

"That's new for you."

"Something I have been practicing with for a few months." Caroline smiled slightly.

Brent returned the smile, only for a wave of pain to wash over him. He cursed under his breath.

"Oh, the paralysis must be wearing off," Caroline remarked.

"Probably." Brent closed his eyes. "What was Ningursu doing to me? That was…I…it was…it was almost like when I became the Diabolo."

Caroline hesitated.

"Please, Caroline. Tell me."

She huffed, then said, "He wants your body."

"I…I'm sorry? What?"

"I do not quite understand exactly, but from what I gathered, his physical skull is getting weaker. You are powerful, and he sees your magic as a benefit. So he wants your body. He decided that after he failed to eradicate you. That is why he has let you be free in the Library…so he could prepare for his possession."

Brent grew dizzy. It was like the Diabolo all over again; Ningursu saw him as only a vessel. He had almost succumbed to that fate, and he would have if it hadn't been for Caroline.

"You saved me," Brent whispered.

"You are my apprentice. It is my job to protect you." She raised her head as if peering around the room. "But I do not know if this will work again. We need to get you out of here."

"How?"

"I do not know. But now is the time. Both Alojzy and Jiang are not here—only Ningursu, Aelia, and whatever ghost lackeys and Diabolo they have mulling about the Library."

Brent peered around the room, layered with canvases. On the far wall, his scribbling of Alojzy's story gawked at him.

"How long until my paralysis wears off, do you think?" he asked.

"I cannot be sure. Not too much longer, I would imagine. Ningursu will want to use your body quickly."

Brent shivered at the thought but pushed it into the back of his mind. He would fret over that later. For now, he had an idea.

"Well, I don't have to move yet," Brent noted, still eyeing the wall.

"What are you thinking?"

"Simple. I'm going to tell you a story."

CHAPTER TWENTY-SEVEN

THE SONG OF THE EFFLUVIUM

Elder An Drew stood beside Sister Jey Ma.

And Christof loathed it.

The way the man fawned over the girl made Christof's skin crawl. He would place a hand on her arm, on her back, or brush a hand through her hair.

Christof hadn't noticed it until she asked him to join breakfast one morning. He sat beside Senator Cordova and Captain Rivers. Across from him, Sister Jey Ma smiled, only to direct her attention to the Elder as he kissed the back of her head. Christof sat still, gripping the edge of the table.

No one spoke as they ate. All the while, a flurry of questions riddled Christof's mind. He knew better than to speak, but he couldn't help but wonder why they had summoned him today. When they first called him, he left his room in a hurry, expecting a promotion when he entered. But after Senator Cordova sat him down at the table and Elder An Drew's fawning over Sister Jey Ma, Christof knew something far heavier weighed in the air.

"Are you ready for today's hymn, Sister Jey Ma?" Senator Cordova asked from across the table.

Sister Jey Ma did not touch her food, staring at the far wall. "As I must be. Elder An Drew has helped me prepare over the last few days."

"It will be far more trying than the events in the Senate Chambers, but the good Sister has done her training well. We have spent countless hours preparing," Elder An Drew remarked.

"And how will we negate any protests? Has that been resolved?" Senator Cordova asked.

"Indeed. Captain Rivers has made sure of it."

"Good." Senator Cordova turned to Christof. "And you, Cadet... Are you still devoted to Sister Jey Ma?"

Christof straightened his back. "Yes, sir."

"Then you will keep her from harm?"

"With my life," Christof said, trained to speak and never to think. But was it true? Would he save Sister Jey Ma again? He did it once, stopping his beating of Bria Smidt to keep Sister Jey Ma from falling to the pistol barrel of some vagrant woman. But would Christof take the bullet for Sister Jey Ma instead?

Christof inhaled, then asked a follow-up question: "If I may…why must I protect her today?"

Elder An Drew scowled, but Senator Cordova answered without criticism, "Today is the day we take back the Effluvium."

No other explanations followed. Christof knew better than to push the question further and instead returned to his meal. Like Sister Jey Ma sitting across from him, he hadn't any appetite. With every breath, smoke rose from her lips and nostrils. If Sister Jey Ma had prepared a hymn, as Senator Cordova said, then it must be the same as what occurred in the Senate a week prior. With a prayer, magic would arrive.

If all went well, then the Magii would bow before the Order and accept Death as their only friend.

But who was a Magii? That was the question, wasn't it? Christof didn't expect over half the Senate to fall to the first Song of the Effluvium. What would become of the Guard? What would become of the city?

He had to have faith in Sister Jey Ma. She would not let the Effluvium fall.

She would let Order reign.

Christof just had to have faith.

Like any loyal guard, Christof walked behind Sister Jey Ma, posture straight and eyes pointed. He did not wear the fear growing in his chest, following in step as they headed to the front of the Capitol Building. Elder An Drew trailed beside Sister Jey Ma, speaking without inflection, voice too low for Christof to hear. Captain Rivers and Senator Cordova had already gone ahead, leaving Christof alone as the sole guard.

His hand fell to his pistol. Part of him wanted to shoot Elder An Drew dead—something about the man just felt *wrong*. The way he touched Sister Jey Ma, the way he moved about like he owned the Capitol, made Christof's skin crawl. Something was amiss, but Christof had no evidence. Only a gut feeling.

And that would not be enough to protect him.

Elder An Drew opened the doorway to the front of the Capitol Building. As the doors creaked open, sunlight trickled in, washing over Sister Jey Ma in a ray of yellow. She stepped forward, her stride determined, her focus unyielding.

As Christof stepped outside behind her, he froze. Sitting in the ten chairs behind Senator Cordova waited, none other than the other senators, including the ones he had seen fall dead. Senator Heartz rested in the chair farthest to the right, staring, hands crossed in her lap.

Upon further investigation, the senators held a clear lack of life. Their eyes did not blink, and their bodies did not breathe. Color had vanished from their skin, leaving behind a dull tone resembling paper.

But they weren't corpses, either. Every few seconds, they moved, however slightly. From wiggling their fingers to opening their mouths like wooden puppets controlled by a master puppeteer.

Christof turned away, meeting the gaze of Captain Rivers for a moment. The giant captain wrung his hands together as he stood behind the senators, his head bowed as if in prayer.

Senator Cordova welcomed Sister Jey Ma to the top of the stairs, helping her stand upon the podium. In the square, no one waited. The Guard stood in their usual formation, and while a few people stopped to watch the scene, many kept their heads down, going about their business. To the commoner, this was nothing more than a Senate performance, with a blessing from the Order. If Christof did not have a position, if he did not protect Sister Jey Ma, he might have walked past as well. Who needed the popery of the Senate? There was a job to be done.

Senator Cordova exchanged a glance with Sister Jey Ma. Silence beat.

The wind hissed.

Then, Sister Jey Ma opened her mouth and recited her song:

So it goes.
So it goes.
All the world will bask in gold.
As the Effluvium, it cries.
Tears must fly.
So it goes.
So it goes.
The sky will be painted gold.
And in it, our souls must fold.
Pure, they go.
So it goes.
So it goes.

This one differed from before, but the effect remained the same. Golden smoke poured from Sister Jey Ma's mouth like a river. It rushed through the air, then expanded across the plaza, encapsulating everything in its sight.

Like a storm, it rallied. Christof did not move as the curtain of yellow ate away at the Capital. This was more than a gentle mist, but a monsoon pouring from Sister Jey Ma with no signs of stopping. As it traveled, Christof swooned, nightmares following each bout of smoke.

With a blink of an eye, he was a child again, sitting in the foyer as he learned of his mother's death.

In another blink, jealousy ensconced him as he watched Bria Smidt kiss Brent Harley in the hedge maze.

A third blink, and he stood over his father's dead body.

And then came the scream.

The blood-curdling scream.

He pulled himself from his nightmares and squinted into the plaza. A guard lay on the ground, blood bubbling from his mouth.

Then another fell.

And a third.

Soon, fell a fourth.

These guards he recognized; he might not have been their friends, but they were loyal guards, never displaying a hint of magic. Why did they fall now? Did they really have magic in their blood?

What if I had magic? Would they let me fall too?

Sister Jey Ma showed no sign of stopping her song. It echoed around the Capitol and down into the plaza. Constant, persistent, with a promise.

So it goes.
So it goes.

Christof's head spun. He was supposed to stand here and protect Sister Jey Ma... but for what? What could he do in this situation? She held power far greater than he ever imagined. How could he protect her?

Was he just an object for her to tout?

Would he ever get his promotion? Or would he once again be a useless guard, as his father always said?

He had done everything they asked; he stood in his place; he obeyed their orders.

Now he trembled in fear.

This is magic. Whether or not she says it... it is magic.

Magic that destroys magic.

How would this protect the Effluvium? With walls of yellow, with gasps of nightmares, he saw no purity or prosperity.

He only heard screams.

He only tasted fear.

And he only dreamt of nightmares.

"I can't do this," he said aloud.

No one responded. Sister Jey Ma's song only continued to roar, beckoning the yellow through the city and beyond the walls.

"I...I can't..." He stepped back from Sister Jey Ma. She did not flinch, and he did not call her name.

With no one watching, with no one caring, he darted off the platform. He had no clue where to go or what to do, but as he ventured into the wails of bleeding Magii, Christof Caver knew one thing.

This was not the Effluvium he had vowed to protect.

CHAPTER TWENTY-EIGHT

EGGS OVER HISTORY

Bria stayed in the tower until the early morning, unable to sleep, her mind still locked around her grandpapa's tale. *I am but the product of my family's story...* she pondered, running her fingers through Nix's fur. As far as everything was concerned, no one suspected the tower to be anything more than a typical guard tower. Whatever Jeremy had done, it worked. Marisol babbled in excitement about it the previous night while messing with her tap-code machine, but Bria had paid little attention to it. Her mind would not relax.

She considered mentioning it all to Lana, but the woman hadn't shown her face. *If only Brent were here. He'd figure out this story.* Bria shut her eyes again. Of course, as her grandpapa had mentioned, secrets may hide on her father's side of the family as well. While her father showed no signs of magic, it didn't mean it didn't hide in his past, like the rings of a tree.

Did she want to know everything about her family? Would it really make much of a difference?

Either way, her heart yearned to see her father. So as dawn painted the sky purple, she and Nix sneaked out of her bunk and from the tower, once again wearing the yellow hat as a disguise.

The forest greeted her with a gentle gasp of green. With her grandpapa by her side, she gave just enough life back to the trees, far enough away from town so no one would see. The Newbird Forest swooned with the brief touch of life, but as much as Bria wanted to expand upon it, she held back her magic.

The earth yearned for her touch, but it had to wait.

It always had to wait.

She stayed close to the trees as she returned to town, avoiding the shadows of the towers bordering the town. Hadn't she promised to protect Newbird's Arm? Now, its freedom had fallen to the wayside.

Her promise was broken.

How could she bring peace to her town again?

How could she bring back the green?

With her heart weighing, she entered the path leading towards the Senator's Gardens. She kept her gloved hands close, exchanging a brief glance with her dog, before walking into the gardens. Every part of her wanted to bring back the greenery. But she couldn't.

Only her camellias continued to bloom.

She smiled at the white flowers and brought one to her fingers. It crooned at her touch.

"I'll be back someday soon... I hope."

She let the flower fall from her fingers and continued down the path.

The small gardener's house sat on the edge of the hedge maze. Well, it was once a hedge maze. Now, it sat as only a skeletal pathway, with a few leaves hanging by thin stems. She ran her fingers along a branch, and with a gasp, a few green leaves sprouted from the buds.

Even the grass beneath her feet blossomed, tugging at every bit of life trailing from her skin.

She pulled back on the magic. *Careful,* she kept reminding herself as she approached the gardener's home. It was so easy to bring back her magic. Even as she knocked against the wooden door, she could feel the long-lost whisper of life from trees. As she watched the doorknob turn, the brass metals sang to her.

Everything sang.

The door opened. Mr. Ricard West stood in the doorway, his few strands of hair combed over his balding head, a strap to his overalls hanging off his shoulder. He glanced down at Bria, then covered his mouth as he audibly whispered, "Bria. Is that you?"

"Hi, Ric…" Bria smiled.

He threw his arms open, allowing Bria to embrace him in a thick hug. Ric had always been there for her. As the Senator's head gardener after her grandpapa died, he'd acted as her mentor. And as her father's partner, he acted as a guardian…and a friend.

"You look so tired," Ric said as he stepped back, looking her over once more. "Are you okay?"

"I've been better."

"Of course you have, of course. Come, I'll make lemon tea and wake Noah." Ric motioned Bria inside the house.

Almost nothing had changed in the small gardener's home since she left. A few half-finished baskets lay on the floor while family portraits and old paintings intermingled with the cobwebs on the wall.

"Your father has been struggling with some of his crafts as of late…" Ric said as he removed a half-finished basket from the table.

A twang of guilt seeped into Bria's heart. She used to sit with her father every day, weaving baskets, and helping him in the market square. His tremors always made it hard to focus, and each day, Bria would guide his hand, helping him correct his errors. That had always been his magic, though; even during his worst days, he always came up with new elaborate designs.

Like a sculptor of stone and clay.

Or a painter gazing out to sea.

Ric smiled half-heartedly at Bria, then disappeared down the narrow hallway. She took her seat at the table, the same place where she always sat for dinner, and eyed the room. What stories did these walls hold? She remembered spitting poppies out on this table back when her grandmama and grandpapa lived in this very house. There was the day she learned how to summon the tree branches and broke the back window. Her father had chalked it up to the wind, and no one asked any more questions. Then, of course, there were the times when she would sneak up the ladder to her attic bedroom with Brent. Everything had always been innocent then, but they would laugh and kiss until falling asleep in each other's arms.

Her gaze fell to the portraits on the wall. She never gave half a mind to them. Growing up, Bria never met her Nanni Safiyyah or Pappy Gilbert. They'd passed away before she was born while her father fought in the Smoke Riots. She never thought that they might hold the key to her past. Not until her grandpapa said otherwise.

Footsteps trudged down the hall. At once, Bria rose to her feet, feeling her stomach twist in knots as her father's shadow entered her purview.

"Beebelle?" Her father stepped into the room with his dog, Gato, on his heels. He had lost weight, his face gaunt and oak-colored eyes heavy. His tanned skin had paled, while his usually short hair hung to his ears.

"Daddy?" She approached him. It hurt more than when she reunited with her grandmama.

At least he had.

"Beebelle..." He took another step toward her. His eyes didn't blink. Tears gathered in his eyes.

Bria hadn't realized how much she missed her father. She ran over to him, throwing herself into his arms and letting untethered tears fall down her chin.

"Daddy..." she sobbed.

He rocked her close, brushing back her bangs so he could see into her face. "It's really you. You left..."

"I had to. I'm sorry."

"You've been in the paper... is it true? Are you... hurting people?"

"Of course not, Daddy, of course not. I would never..." Bria gulped back another dash of tears. "Please believe me."

"I do, I do. I… just never thought… my Beebelle… wanted by the Order. You were always a good girl. A perfect girl. A sweet girl."

"Sometimes you have to find other ways to make the world pretty."

"Yes, right, of course. Make it pretty…" Her father released her and sat in the chair.

"Bria, sit." Ric entered from the hallway. "I'll prep some food for us, and we can talk."

Bria obeyed, sitting next to her father with a weak smile. He took her hand and squeezed it.

Where would she even begin?

Bria devised a story over the next couple hours, like the one she'd told her grandmama while eating a breakfast of eggs and toast. Nix and Gato played with a dirty sock on the floor, undisturbed by the conversation. In her narrative, she tried her best to avoid scaring her father, but sometimes his eyes flickered with worry. She did not tell him the details of how she lost her arm nor about her near-death experience in Knoll. As far as her father was concerned, she had led a rebellion. Some injuries occurred, some lives were lost, but all fought for survival.

With hesitation, Bria told her father that she had reunited with Lana. Her father stiffened at the news, but as Bria elaborated on the tale, his posture once again loosened. She didn't expect her father to forgive Lana or to fully comprehend what happened, but at least there was an understanding.

"I... remember when I met your mother," her father whispered as she finished the tale. "She was... lost. I had come from Hutch's Creek as reinforcements for Knoll... but upon seeing her broken and branded... I couldn't stand with them." He blinked a few times. "I wanted to help her. I think... after that... we grew attached and... and..."

"I understand, Daddy. Really." Bria took his hands.

Ric placed a hand on her father's shoulder and squeezed it.

"I thought I loved her. I *did* love her... but after we escaped... she grew distant and fearful. Paranoid. Or something..." He wiped his eyes and glanced at the window. "I was too. While I tried to stay by her side, I was lost and afraid... and then she fled. I found out she was pregnant with you when Beatriz sent a letter. I wasn't even there for your birth 'cause I was mourning the loss of my mamma..."

"Daddy, I don't blame you." Bria kept his hands close. "I'm here now."

"Yeah... Beebelle is... my Beebelle is..." his gaze fell away from her.

She took this as her moment to ask the questions hanging on her mind since talking with her grandpapa. "You never told me too much about Nanni Safiyyah and Pappy Gilbert."

"My parents?"

"Yes. I never knew them... not like Grandmama Beatriz and Grandpapa Tulio."

"Yes, that's right... Mamma died right before you were born... and Pa was many years earlier." Her father's eyes glazed over as if lost in a story from long ago. "They would have loved you."

Bria half smiled. "What were they like?"

"Hard workers, but kindhearted. Mamma was a miner... and Pa was a blacksmith. Always working. Put me to work at a young age too, except my hands always got these tremors... so they didn't want me touching anything dangerous." Her father flexed his trembling fingers.

"Were they good at their jobs?"

"Amazing at them. Mamma... she had this way of... finding ores exactly as Pa needed. She said her family back home always had a knack for it as well."

Bria gulped. *Nanni was an amazing miner... no, it has to be a coincidence.*

Bria kept the conversation focused, though. "Where was Nanni from?"

"She never talked about it… didn't want to, really. I just know she immigrated to Rosada for work… met my father. Pa was from a long line of blacksmiths. I ended that lineage… but Mamma encouraged me to find a new craft." Her father reached for a basket. The tremors quivered along his fingers, and he pulled back. "Oh, without you here, Beebelle… it has been so hard. I try to do other things… but I can't and… and… and…" He lowered his head and shivered.

Bria took his hands again and squeezed them. For a moment, she swore she felt a spark beneath his fingers, like disconnected magic trying to break to the surface. But unlike the spark she felt in Lana, this was missing something. It was like the wax of a candle without a wick—the potential was there, but not the spark.

She tried to keep her father talking. "Did you ever meet anyone from Nanni's side of the family?"

"Yes."

"Once… when I was a little boy…" he recalled. "An aunt, uncle, and cousin were traveling through to Volfium but stopped to visit. I can't help but remember a funny conversation while there… they said to her, 'Safiyyah… have you built a house of diamonds yet?' Mamma just said, 'That's a silly thing to wish for when everything looks like mud.' Don't know what it meant or anything, but I called our home our 'mud house' forever, much to my mamma's dismay." Her father chuckled. "Hutch's Creek is made of mud."

Bria smiled. She didn't find it all too humorous, but it made her father happy, and that's all she could ask for, really. What piqued her interest was the story; did her distant aunts and uncles really believe that her nanni could build a house of diamonds? Was there really magic?

Was that why it all sat in her soul?

She couldn't even be sure about her pappy's side, either. He was a blacksmith from a long line—could he have magic to manipulate ore? Or perhaps to control fire?

Or maybe none of it. He might have been a normal man from Hutch's Creek, and Nanni might have been an immigrant who enjoyed mining.

She doubted her father had any more answers.

"I would have loved to meet them." Bria finally said.

"I'm sure they would've loved you."

"I'm glad."

"I wonder if my cousin, Avan, is still alive. He came for Mamma's funeral, but I haven't seen him since..." Her father scratched his fingernail into the table. "He was a nice man. A kind man. A nice one. I wish I knew him better. Could have been like a brother. A nice man. A kind man... a nice man..." her father continued to recite the phrase to himself, digging his finger deeper into the table. His eyes widened with each word.

"Noah," Ric gripped his shoulder, "I need you to breathe. You're in our house, not at your mother's funeral."

"I'm sorry, Daddy." Bria continued, gripping her father's hand. She'd seen her father get like this before. With a bit of grounding, he would return to them, but they had to wait.

She whistled for her father's dog, Gato, to abandon the sock. The dog bounded over at once, and Bria guided her father's hand to Gato's fur.

On the floor, Nix stole the sock Gato had been guarding.

"I'm alright. I'm here..." Noah whispered.

"Are you going to be okay, Daddy? I'll have to leave again soon. I can't stay here..." Bria swallowed.

"Yes... but I worry you are not happy or safe." Her father looked at her. "Are you happy and safe?"

Bria chose her next statement carefully. "I have security. I have friends. And I have love. I'll be okay."

"Love?"

Bria flushed and rubbed her hands together. "I... didn't mention. He's not here right now... he's taking care of some things... but... Brent Harley and I got married."

Ric nearly jumped out of his spot, while even her father broke into a smile.

"Always knew about you two!" Ric exclaimed. "Never said anything, of course, but I always saw you two necking—"

"Ric!" Bria felt her face turn red.

"What? He was a good kid! Always liked him."

"Yeah. Good kid. Very good kid." Her father murmured. He was back to his distant self, lost in stories and tales from long ago. It was fortunate that her father had Ric for support. There were so many other men and women who couldn't thrive. Brent's father had been one of them; despite his mother's support, he couldn't stay out of the Pit. With two children and a full-time job, Janette Harley had to decide where to put her resources.

"Daddy," she whispered, "I promise... I'm safe, okay? I'll be okay, and I will return to you. Just like I have now."

"Okay." Her father whispered, and she knew that would end the conversation. He had returned to whatever world drew him in, and she knew it would take a while to pull him out.

She kissed his forehead and rose from the table, taking a few of the empty plates of breakfast to the kitchen. As she began washing each one, she glanced out the window.

In another life, she'd still be washing plates here on a regular basis.

In another life, she might have even had her own little home.

But in that life, she might have had a different husband.

A husband who forced his way to her with threats and demands.

Bria shuddered at the thought. She still recalled the day in the garden when Christof tried to force himself on her. She avoided him, then tearfully ran to the edge of the field where Brent usually sat, smoking and naming the cows.

Brent... I miss you so much... She placed the plate on the rack and eyed the hedge maze. There had been countless times when she and Brent got lost in there. He would tell stories while she wove flower crowns together to stack on his unkempt curls.

It was so simple then.

She jumped at the sound of a knock on the front door. It reminded her of all those times Brent would come to her home, asking to go for a walk or to sit by the fire. But as she entered the foyer, her momentary excitement waned.

Lana stood there, arms crossed, eyeing Ric.

"What're you doing here?" Ric asked, his voice dripping with distaste.

"Bria, we need to get out of here," Lana spoke without acknowledging Ric.

"How did you know I was here?"

"It was obvious. C'mon. We don't have time."

"You're not in charge of me."

"Not here," Lana hissed.

"No, just tell me what's going on!" Bria approached the door. Behind Lana, the sky bled with a distant pulse of yellow. Her anger fell, her stomach dropping. *Not again...*

"We intercepted a tap-code message. Something is coming, and we have to leave... now!" Lana continued.

"I can fight it—"

"No, not this one!"

"Lana, I've done it before. I can fight—" The yellow continued to thicken behind Lana, marching forward like an army. It rushed towards Bria, whipping around her.

It was like someone was choking her. She couldn't breathe or move.

And as she withered to the floor, a single scream escaped her lips.

All went black.

CHAPTER TWENTY-NINE

MONSTERS IN THE CITY

Yaz squinted through the fog. From aboard Zephyr, she could make out the shadow of a city. They had voyaged across the black-and-white checkered plains over the last few days, with Yaz riding the momentary breath of confusion and serenity. Sometimes, when she closed her eyes, she saw yellow. But Chander helped her come back, focusing on the present.

Some nights, the monsters still came. In her nightmares, at times, Yaz ran with them as they tore through the world. Other times, she stood beside them as they towered over their next victim. She would whisper pleas for them to stop. If she shouted loud enough, sometimes they listened.

But while Anandi didn't understand, and Micca and Timothée shared their quiet concerns, Chander stayed by Yaz's side.

Since she told Chander about her experience with the Mist Keepers, the boy had been a bit more interested in life. He pestered Yaz to tell him more, and rather than scowl at every remark, he would spend time staring across the plains. Yaz didn't pretend to understand his magic. But Chander wanted to belong.

Just like she did.

"I'm gonna have Zephyr land outside the city," Timothée said over his shoulder. "Don't know the state of Mert or anything. Rather not risk her."

"I'm just happy to be getting a clean bed!" Micca shouted over the wind.

"Remember, we're here for the kids. Not you."

"Oh, come on! I deserve a clean bed!"

Yaz squinted again at the approaching city, ignoring the two men bickering. It didn't have the towers she'd grown accustomed to seeing in Rosada. Rather, buildings joined together like friends holding hands, with winding roads and broken columns. It almost seemed familiar. But where would she have seen it? When she traveled with Ms. Kai and Mr. Nasr, they stayed on the Rosadian continent. She'd never been this far east.

Or, well, not that she knew of, at least. The Council had brought her many places, but she didn't learn their names.

As Zephyr turned her body down towards the earth, preparing her wings for a landing, Yaz continued to wrack her brain. The movement through the air felt like that of a diabolo.

Had she seen the monster in this city?

She gripped onto Zephyr's saddle as the dragon came to a halt on the ground. Timothée and Micca helped the children off the dragon before exchanging a glance.

"Right-o then." Timothée picked Preston up in his arms and glanced at the rest. "Everyone, stay close. No wandering. Understood?"

Preston squirmed in Timothée's arms and blinked twice. Tears welled in his eyes. For a moment, Yaz thought they might have been blood. But ghosts didn't bleed...so it couldn't be blood, right?

Before she could point it out to Timothée, Preston wiped his eyes with his hands, and the tears vanished.

"Are we really going to Mert?" Chander asked, pulling Yaz's attention away from Preston.

"Ay."

"But Mert is... My grandfather used to tell us about Mert!" Chander marveled. "He said it was a place where we could be safe. We were planning to go there when the Guard captured us!"

"Well, guess you've made it, huh?" Timothée motioned the children along. "C'mon now, let's find a place to stay... then we can figure out what to do with you lot."

"You mean you don't have a plan?" Micca asked.

"I told you I didn't. You don't listen."

"But then, what're we gonna do here?"

"We'll figure it out. Maybe we start living here. Mert's supposed to be safe." Timothée started forward along the path, "What'd you expect our life to be? All hunky-dory?"

Once they gathered their bags, Zephyr took into the sky, beating her wings once before disappearing into the clouds. Yaz still marveled at the way the dragon moved. It understood everything they said. And that in itself was amazing.

Yaz took the rear with Micca while Timothée strolled forward towards the city. Chander and Anandi walked hand in hand beside her. As far as Yaz could tell, they'd been getting along. While Chander still snuck off at night after stealing Micca's smokes, the siblings weren't fighting.

They continued on in silence. Anandi pointed out different landmarks, like a gravesite on the edge of town and a rickety bridge, but otherwise, no one bothered to speak. As they passed the tombstones, a headache prodded at Yaz's head, but she ignored it. It was as if the voices called to her, yearned for her.

Mist Keepers save the dead. That's what Sir Jama—Ningursu said. But I don't know how to save the dead. They never taught me. She stared at her hands as they approached a bridge crossing the canal. She only learned how to control monsters. How would that save the world?

Upon crossing the canal, the serenity of the Chessboard Plains broke. The fog opened, and before them, a city in shambles greeted them.

Chander froze. Timothée stepped back from the scene, holding the ghost child tighter.

"Way to go, Tim," Micca grumbled. "This ain't the haven you told us about."

"I also told you there were rumors of war but didn't want to scare the children!" Timothée barked. "Don't you read the paper at all?"

"Yeah, but for the jokes."

"Pah."

"What happened to Mert?" Anandi asked. "Grandpa always said it was safe here."

"Nothing is safe..." Chander mumbled.

Yaz nodded in agreement. Nothing was ever safe. If Mert was indeed a haven for magic, as she had heard, then monsters like the Diabolo surely hunted it.

"Micca, why don't you take the kids back to camp? I'll find out if we can get a room or—"

"Oh no, I ain't gonna be on babysitting duty again."

"Yeah, but you don't know how to deal with all of this!" Timothée motioned to the destroyed town square. What must have been the city hall stood as a skeleton, its roof concave in on itself. Above, a few airships gathered while guards and police lined the street. Yaz felt their eyes.

Watching.

Waiting.

"You don't trust me to do nothing." Micca snapped. "You're just as bad as Jem. You think of me as worthless. I got my talents, y'know!"

"We don't have time to do this now," Timothée grumbled.

"Now's the best time! Because right now I could leave! I can take Zephyr and go back home while you futz around with magic here or whatever shite you want."

"Micca, we're all tired. Let's talk about this later."

Whaamp.

A siren drowned out the argument. Yaz threw her hands over her ears and closed her eyes.

For a moment, the siren sent her back into the Diabolo's embrace. She soared through the sky, hunger seeping through her veins. With each second, her mouth grew wider.

334

And she shrieked with the siren.

Only for her cries to break with gunshots ripping through the air.

"Yaz! Get down!" Chander grabbed her arm and pulled her behind a bench.

She blinked, staring at him and Anandi. Commotion had already begun to tear open the plaza. With the sirens, police and guards marched into the streets. The guards bore the insignia of the Order, while the police bore a symbol she'd never seen. They each took a stance, waiting... watching...

Yaz gripped Chander's hand. He didn't budge, his gaze fixated on the guards.

"Something is coming..." he whispered.

Yaz waited, holding her breath.

And then, in a fit of smoke and gunshots, an army of individuals in pinstriped suits, dark hats, and billowing coats entered the plaza. They loaded pistols and open fired.

"We gotta get out of here!" Chander shouted as the pinstripes and guards battled. Yaz covered her ears. Each gunshot reminded her of the monsters pounding in her head; each fallen body, a meal of the Diabolo to feast.

She could feast upon it.

She wanted to feast upon it.

"Yaz! C'mon!"

She blinked once, then nodded.

"But Chander! What about Micca and Timothée?" Anandi asked.

"I dunno where they went! It got all chaotic. But we gotta get away from this mess, or we're going to be killed!" Chander tugged on both Yaz and Anandi's arms. "Come on!"

Yaz followed Chander, letting the eldest of them take the lead. In the commotion, the plaza transformed into a battlefield. Yaz couldn't tell what direction they'd come from or how to escape the madness.

"We came from the north…" Chander mumbled to himself.

"Which way is north?" Yaz asked. She'd never been one to study maps.

"If I could see the sun, I could tell you. But the blasted fog is too thick…" Chander cursed as another round of gunshots exploded. A few pedestrians fled past them.

Where did Micca and Timothée go?

"Come on, let's get out of this mess. Here, down here!" Chander guided Yaz and Anandi down the alleyway. A white stone building towered over them. From the other side of the walkway, Yaz watched as a group of medics unloaded a stretcher from a vehicle and took it inside the building.

"North... we gotta head north..." Chander kept mumbling to himself. "If only I'd touched Timothée or something before we got separated. Then I'd see where they are..." he blinked a few times. "I just see triple right now."

Yaz didn't quite understand what he said but ignored it, keeping pace with her friends.

"Chander... wouldn't it be better to sit here and wait?" Anandi finally asked. "Grandpa always said if we got lost not to go running about—"

"Well, Grandpa is dead!" Chander snapped. "If we didn't stay put, the Guard wouldn't have found us, and Grandpa would be alive."

"But—"

"We keep moving!"

Anandi pouted, but she didn't fight as Chander continued to lead them through the alleys, departing from the commotion in the main square.

They turned down another path, and before them, a bridge crossing the canal greeted them. Chander laughed, "See! Told you!"

He sped up their pace. Yaz held her breath. A thick fog crossed over the bridge, and as they neared it, she could make out the shadow of a figure.

Mist Keepers? Are they coming for us?

But as they neared and Chander's own pace slowed, she breathed a sigh of relief.

A Mist Keeper did not wait for them. Rather, a blonde woman in a pinstripe suit stood on the bridge. Despite the pistol in her arms, her hazel eyes bore a layer of kindness that Yaz found herself trusting—for better or worse.

"Lookie! Who goes there?" the woman asked.

Chander gulped and squeezed Yaz's hand before speaking, "Excuse me, ma'am—"

"Ma'am? Do I look old to you?" The woman took a step closer. "I'm only twenty-three! Do you think that is old, young man?"

"Oh, sorry, but you're older than me," Chander said.

The woman's eyes narrowed. "What are a bunch of kiddos doing out and about? You should know by now that noontime brings the slaughter!"

"We're not from around here."

"Yeah! We got separated from our friends!" Anandi added. "We came to visit Mert, and then the shooting started."

The woman raised her brow. "Now, how'd you get on here from Mert? All the transport has died. You didn't walk all the way, did you? No one survives that trip unless they're well prepared."

"We came on a dra—"

Chander interrupted his sister. "We had our way of getting here. Please ma—miss. Our camp is a bit out of the city... can we pass through?"

"Ain't gonna let that happen. Sorry kiddos." The woman repositioned her pistol.

"But—"

"Nu-uh. No one is allowed in or out during noontime. Really, no one is allowed in or much at all. But..." she frowned, "it ain't much like me to let kiddos be without safety. Why don't'cha come with me to the safe house? We'll give you a warm meal and help you find your friends once this is all said and done... deal?"

"I don't know—"

Yaz decided to interject Chander. "Deal!"

Chander glared at her.

"We can't stay out here while they're fighting. We don't even know why they're fighting! Timothée and Micca would want us safe, wouldn't they?"

Chander continued to scowl but didn't argue.

While Yaz knew it wasn't the wisest to trust this stranger, they couldn't stay in the streets. Each gunshot sent her head ringing. If it went on for too long, she might just explode.

And who knew what she might become if that happened?

"Right-o then! C'mon, kiddos, let's get you safe." The woman motioned them away from the bridge. Yaz swore Chander would make a run for it, but he stayed by their side, his lips pursed in a frown. The woman kept talking, "What can I call you three, if I may ask?"

Anandi spoke at once, "I'm Anandi! And this is my brother Chander and our friend Yaz!"

"Nice to meet you. You can call me Mitzi, second in command to the Pinstripe Gang. Glad to welcome you to the family."

CHAPTER THIRTY

FAREWELL TO PARADISE

Brent approached the door, gripping tight to Caroline's arm. The pain continued to roar through his body, but he wouldn't let that stop him. Caroline stayed faithful at his side, blindfolded, but with a determination in her walk he had never seen. Both of them agreed: they had to get out of this Library. Brent would not become Ningursu's... vessel, for lack of a better word.

Frankly, he tried that out with his Diabolo Frankie... and he did not like it one bit.

He took a couple of hours to let the stories wrap around him. Now, despite his trembling knees, he was ready.

As he stepped across the threshold and exhaled, the mist washed over him. *Stories.* He chuckled silently. They filled the room with pride, riding on the edges of the words he'd inscribed on the canvases and in the history locked within the Library's walls.

"Keep me steady, please. I have the story." Brent muttered.

Caroline obliged without asking questions. They had a mutual understanding; if she learned too much, then Ningursu would know his plan. Well, if Brent could call it a plan.

It was only an aggregation of ideas.

And using Caroline as his support, he let the ideas and story carry him forward into the mist of the Library.

With each step, he inhaled, balancing the stories between his mantras.

My name is Brent Harley.

I'm gonna get out of this shite hole.

To his surprise, his Diabolo didn't reply.

He let the smoke wrap around him, focusing on one destination where the stories did not linger. The mist pulled him forward, over the debris of dried-out swamp, past the murky pool and withered peonies, and past the dismantled bookshelves. One place; he had one place in mind. There wasn't time to ponder the destruction of the Library.

No. He had to go where stories ended.

And the mist brought him there, not to the exit or to a hideaway, but to the iron doors of the crypt.

He released Caroline's arm and brought his fingers to the gate. Upon touching it, he fell back into Alojzy's story: a tale of a man determined to leave his mark. He took all his anger and transformed it into a maze. There, the maze served as the ultimate prison, a location that felt endless but never moved.

A place where confusion replaced stories.

And a place where people became monsters.

But Brent stood outside it. All he had to do was take the story, pocket it, and end the charade. Then everyone would be free.

He traced the gate again. *Need a story to break this thing open. Come on... think.*

A reply still never came from his Diabolo.

Brent stole a glance over his shoulder. Black smoke gathered around the bookshelves. Dread tugged at Brent's stomach, but he didn't dare fall into it. Ningursu could not sense his fear.

He turned back to the crypt. *C'mon. Focus. This is nothing more than a story... now you just have to tear it down... like a woodsman or... a miner...* The story came to him in a rush. No longer was he Brent Harley. No, he was a strong man from Hutch's Creek, working day and night in the mine,

lifting a pickaxe and grinding it through the stone. For
his daughter, for his son, for his wife, he would break
open each wall.

"I'mma do this for ya, my love," the story spoke
through Brent. He bit his tongue on the last word. *Focus.*

He wore the story close, and as the tale around him
took form, so did that of a pickaxe in his hands. Brent
lifted it, swearing he could feel its weight, then slammed
it into the crypt's door.

Once.

Twice.

And again.

The sound rang across the Library, echoing with a
high-pitched scream. If Ningursu didn't know where he
went, he surely did now.

But Brent didn't dare stop.

He slammed the pickaxe into the door again.

And again.

One more time.

He refused to let this jail stand. Criminals did not live
deep in its walls.

His future lay there.

And his past.

Everything that he could be and once was.

He would not let it happen again.

A voice spoke to him through the mist, "Brenton!"

He didn't look back, his focus locked on the crypt. It didn't matter who called his name. Nor did it matter that the black smoke pummeled around him. Or that the pain rippled through his body.

It didn't matter.

Only the stories mattered.

"Brenton Harley, do not ignore me!"

But Brent did just that.

"NOW!" Black smoke raced around Brent and turned him around, pulling the story away forward. Brent toppled forward and glared at Ningursu as he sat in Aelia's hands. Behind them, Caroline lay on the ground, blindfold still laced over her face.

With Ningursu in front of him, Brent could take a better look at the skull. With skin peeling from the skull's cheek, teeth rotting, and a vacant stare, without a doubt, Ningursu had weakened. Was it because of Brent? The child apprentice, Yaz? The onslaught of Diabolo and magic? Even the stories didn't know.

Brent snarled, "Are we going to constantly do this? The back and forth?"

"You're growing weaker. I can see it in your eyes, boy." Ningursu pressed. "You cannot keep this up forever."

"Neither can you…"

"I've gone on much longer. What is one more battle?"

Brent gritted his teeth. He kept his head high but knew in the depth of his heart that Ningursu was right. Every passing day wore on him. He survived on fear alone.

But yearned more than anything to sleep.

It would be so easy to give himself over to Ningursu and forget this life.

But he refused.

"You've become a pure Mist Keeper now, boy," Ningursu continued. "You have entered a new realm of existence. You won't age, not like normal, at least; how will you live a life with your Briannabella if she grows old? How will you live as you outpace your mother and sister? You are trapped in this state for good. Stop trying to return to a world where you don't belong."

Brent shook his head. He hadn't thought of that, but it didn't matter. It was an issue for another day. Ningursu was trying to cajole him; it would not work.

"I don't belong in... in your world, either," Brent replied as he backed into the crypt gate. He searched along it with his fingers for the cracks made by the mining story.

"Then you'll live a lonely, pitiful existence."

"Sounds like you already live that life."

Ningursu responded by opening his mouth again and sending tendrils of black smoke toward Brent. The smoke laced around his ankles and pulled.

But Brent resisted the tugging, digging his fingers deeper into the story of the gate. Instead of a miner, he imagined himself a giant, pulling apart the stones and letting the door collapse.

And it did just that.

The crypt door fell to the ground. Out of it, pure mist escaped. It suffocated the black wisps and then dissipated, leaving the air untarnished and clear. Brent snapped free of Ningursu's grasp and took a step backward.

But the God of Death did not relinquish. With a singular nod, he directed Aelia forward. Another tendril, another twirl; Brent took each arm of mist and sent it in another direction. Every attack tugged deeper at his soul. He wanted nothing more than to stop, to give in, and to forget.

It had been easier, in some ways, when he had become the Diabolo. At least then, it was like a deep sleep.

Nothing more.

You're not allowed to die. Bria's voice rang again in his ears.

So he wouldn't die.

He refused.

He would do more than that.

Brent threw his arms back, feeling the story of the prison wrap around him. These cells didn't exist. They were no more than a story composed by Alojzy himself.

But Alojzy wasn't here to continue the tale.

If the man had been here, Brent might not have had the energy to fight it. But now, the stories shifted easily beneath Brent's fingertips.

"You know..." Brent glowered at Ningursu. "Everything can be destroyed. A hurricane can destroy a fortress."

"You don't have the strength." Ningursu hissed.

"Not for a hurricane... but perhaps... a tornado..." Brent inhaled. He caught a story of a man chasing a tornado on his lips. The man prayed to the storm gods of his region as the tornado ravaged his village. He watched, he begged, as the tornado ripped open the jail.

And with a gasp, the same tornado spiraled from Brent's fingertips and raced into the crypt behind him.

A beat passed.

Another.

Then a bang.

A new swarm of mist embraced Brent, and in that moment, the stories of all the prisoners flooded over him. Free at last, they were coming.

Fast.

But Brent couldn't keep them together. He stumbled forward, gasping as each tale wrapped around his head. He couldn't decipher them anymore. One belonged to Kek, another belonged to a woman who claimed the wall as her friend, and another to an individual who was more mist than a man. Each story dragged him down as their owners moved closer.

He took a knee and exhaled hard. His head spun. Where was he? Who was he?

Brent. Your name is Brent.

"Enough," Ningursu boomed.

The stories continued their assault.

Even through them, Brent could feel the hand of Ningursu's mist wrap around him. It worked its way from his throat to his mouth, up into his nostrils. Brent froze, choking as if his own life were being torn from him.

Perhaps this was all he could do. His last hurrah.

Sleep sounded all the better.

"Brent! Watch out!"

He raised his drooping eyelids. Caroline had hoisted herself from the ground, blindfold removed, eyes flaring. The mist barreled behind her. Brent had never seen her act with such determination, but without hesitation, she yanked Ningursu from Aelia's arms and threw him into the mist.

In a blink of an eye, he vanished.

Aelia shrieked, "Sir!"

Caroline shoved Aelia back into the mist, too, then raced over to Brent. He gawked at her, one eyelid drooping, his mouth half ajar.

Around them, the Library continued to shift, its image faltering beneath the weight of smoke and stories. All the while, Brent's head continued to droop, his head growing heavy and tired.

Sleep.

Whose voice was that?

"You are okay." Caroline reiterated. "You survived. You will continue to survive."

"I'm tired..." Brent mumbled.

"I know, I know," Caroline wrapped her arm around Brent's waist and hoisted him from the ground. "But we need to get you out of here."

"But everyone else..." Brent glanced back towards the crypt.

"They are coming. They will follow. But we need to get out!"

"I..." Brent glanced towards the glass ceilings above him. Cracks formed along them. With his prayer of a story, everything had begun its collapse.

He turned back to the crypt. Figures moved down the hall, led by none other than Kek. They nodded in Brent's direction.

"Brent... please! We need to get out of here before Ningursu returns." Caroline tugged on his arm.

"A'ight... yeah... a'ight." Brent turned to her. "Where're we going?"

"Someplace safe. Come along. Before the exit collapses."

"A'ight..." Brent took a wobbly step forward, only for his body to collapse just like the Library.

CHAPTER THIRTY-ONE

HUNGRY FOR PRETZELS

Yaz kicked her heels together as she sat on the bar stool, watching as the woman in the pinstriped suit—Mitzi—raced around the bar. She had led them to a speakeasy beneath a group of dilapidated shops. Anandi kept her grip on Chander's hand the entire way, her eyes wide in awe as they continued along the path. Yaz mimicked Anandi's own fascination; Mitzi bore a presence around the bar, bellowing orders to different individuals while keeping a pistol close. When two other individuals in pinstriped uniforms entered the room and asked her what had happened, she merely dismissed them.

Mitzi fed them a basket of salted dough she called a pretzel, a delicacy that caused Yaz to giggle, and each a glass of cranberry juice. Yaz and Anandi ate with excitement, but Chander didn't dare touch the food.

In fact, he didn't say a word until Mitzi left to shout at someone in the kitchen,

"I don't trust her. We gotta get out of here." Chander said.

"And go where? We dunno what happened to Timothée and Micca!"

"Then we find Zephyr and wait. I was listening to those two over there... Freddie and Billie are their names. This a gang. They're not good people."

"Yeah, but they didn't hurt us."

"But they might later!"

"I don't wanna leave! I like Miss Mitzi! She made us food!"

"Who's saying I'm a miss?" Mitzi returned from the kitchen.

"Sorry...ma'am?" Anandi flushed.

"All good, love, all good." Mitzi sighed. "I had a lover once. He done up and kicked the bucket, but then he came back...then disappeared again. Went through all that just so he didn't have to marry me. Guess that's how it goes..." She shook back her long blonde hair. "Very well. If you want to go, you can go. You're not a prisoner. We just don't want to see children in the streets when we go to war with the Order."

"The Order isn't in Mert!" Chander crossed his arms. "I've read the history."

"Oh, but this is new. A few months ago, the Order arrived, and bang! All Hell broke loose. We here in our pinstripes have been trying to subdue the chaos... but you won't hear that from those pesky newsies, y'hear." Mitzi took a glass and filled it with an amber drink. "Just trying to claim back what's ours. We're the natives of Mert, not some damn Rosadians elitists."

"See Chander! We can't go out there! We'll get hurt!" Anandi remarked.

"Well, we can't stay here either!" Chander hopped off the stool and approached the windows. A few of the pinstripe gang glowered as he pushed past them, but he didn't react, keeping his hands laced in his pockets. Yaz watched him. Was he going to leave them behind, just like everyone else? Chander said he was her friend.

But as he peaked through the curtains, his body froze. Rigid like a statue, he did not move.

"Well, are you leaving or not, Chander?" Anandi shouted.

Yaz jumped off her stool and walked towards Chander. She kept her head down, not daring to look at the different pinstripes in the eyes. One with a scar on his face eyed her while drinking a glass of wine. The two, who Chander called Freddie and Billie, shouted something at Mitzi.

But Yaz focused on Chander.

"What is it?" She asked.

Chander didn't move.

"Chander?"

Yaz peered through the window. Wisps of gold floated in the air and wove through the streets. The few people in the street wobbled, their faces growing pale with each floating wave of yellow.

"What's with all the gold?!" Anandi asked beside Yaz.

The gold continued to pulse, growing stronger and breathing something Yaz knew all too well.

"It's like a Diabolo," Yaz mumbled.

"What?"

"A monster."

"But it doesn't look like a monster! It looks like golden rivers!"

"But it is..." Yaz pressed her hand to the glass. She already felt the monster tugging at her soul. She couldn't see the beast yet, but it was there.

"What're you doing?" Chander whispered to her.

"I dunno, but I feel it coming, and I want to stop it, but I don't know how."

"You can't destroy this!"

"Mist Keepers can though..." Yaz's fingers trembled. With a single exhale, mist bubbled from her lips, with hints of gold lacing its way into the air.

Just like the gold in the streets.

I'm not a monster. I can do this... She tried to inhale again, but more mist gathered at her fingertips.

Chander placed a hand over her shoulder. "Remember what I told you, Yaz? Find something that is constantly there to fight for—like your friends."

"A constant." Yaz recited the word once again. *Constant.* The word warmed her heart. It settled in her mind like a lulling dream. And as she breathed, as she focused, the yellow around her faded.

But then she closed her eyes.

The nightmares didn't come.

But she was the monster approaching the city from the north.

She stood upon the Chessboard Plains, claws extended, mouth curled with vengeance. The city on the horizon smelled of honeycomb and desire, with streaks of gold flitting through the air. Her stomach growled.

Food waited.

So she walked.

Then ran.

And flew.

As she touched the clouds, she inhaled the city's scent.

But this time, rather than desire, it reeked of rot and flesh.

Enough to pull her back and remember her name.

Yaz.

She froze in place, reciting the name. She was not the monster in the sky.

Freeze, *she ordered.*

The monster obeyed.

What to do next? She had to change the direction of the storm.

Turn.

The Diabolo turned its back on the city.

Move.

It flew a few paces away.

But it fought her at every move, roaring and crying, tugging at her thoughts.

Family, *she recalled.*

And she could breathe peacefully once more.

But the monster didn't want to leave. It obeyed her command but fought at every crack. If she let it go, it would only return.

So she marched it away, as far as she could, flying...

Flying...

Flying through the clouds.

Only to freeze upon a shadow of another beast rising from the mist. Its wings extended, its mouth unhinged, the dragon soared towards the Diabolo with determination.

And struck.

"Zephyr!" Yaz cried out as she toppled to the floor. Mist poured from her body, but it harbored no yellow. Chander raced to her side.

"What about Zephyr?" he asked.

"She's gonna take care of the monster." Yaz giggled to herself slightly. "I lured it away from the city. I was the monster, but I stopped it!"

Chander glanced out the window again, "The yellow is retreating too..."

"Aw! It was so pretty!" Anandi complained.

Yaz removed her glasses and wiped the sweat from her brow. Slowly, she moved back towards tables and chairs. Every step made her head pound.

Louder.

Louder...

She couldn't hear Anandi and Chander's continued bickering over the noise. People watched her. That much was obvious. She could feel their eyes on her. No one approached her. Did she scare them? Or had they only seen three kids playing a ridiculous game?

But it wasn't a game.

Didn't they understand it wasn't a game?

"That was quite impressive."

Yaz nearly jumped. The man with a scar on his face that she had seen earlier took a seat at her table.

"Huh?"

"Your magic there—it was impressive."

"You...you saw?"

"Ah, yes, I did." He smiled. Despite the scar on his face, he had a kind smile, and his eyes glimmered.

"What did you see?" Wasn't everything in her head?

"Quite a bit," the man said. "You protected us, didn't you?"

"How did you—"

"I know things, Yaz." The man tapped his forehead.

"Like my name?"

"Like your name."

"And what's your name?" Yaz inquired.

"You can call me Tommy," the man said.

"Tommy..."

The man continued to smile as he spoke, "I wonder... with what you did... could help me with something?"

Yaz gulped. The last time she *helped* someone with something, she ended up with the weapon of a talking skull.

"Do not worry, you do not have to if you do not want to... but it would mean a lot to me," Tommy said.

"What do you want me to do?"

"My boss is quite unwell. I think you may be able to help her."

"But... I see monsters. How can I help her?"

"I think you'll understand when you meet her."

Yaz glanced around the room. "But who is she? Is it Mitzi? She seems okay."

"No, no, Mitzi isn't my boss. My boss is sleeping right now."

"Oh..."

Tommy rose from the table. "If you would like to meet her, she'll be awake later tonight. Again, it is only an ask—your decision matters."

The man left, sending one last smile in Yaz's direction, before disappearing down the corridor. As he vanished, the tavern went back to normal. People continued their gambling and drinking while laughing and bickering. No one paid any mind to her.

Yaz had to admit, though, Tommy piqued her interest. What did he want with her strange magic? What did that have to do with anything?

"Yaz, wanna another pretzel?" Anandi called to her from across the room.

Her friend held up another one of those salty dough pastries.

Yaz *was* hungry.

But this time, not for magic.

CHAPTER THIRTY-TWO

GAS MASK

It was like being strangled.

She couldn't breathe. She couldn't see.

And then came the gasp.

Bria shot up at once, her vision blurred. Something clung to her face, covering her mouth and nose while distorting her eyesight. She reached for it and yanked.

"Bria! Keep the mask on, okay? You need to keep it on!" Lana shouted.

Bria clawed at the strange contraption on her face. A nozzle covered her nose and mouth; goggles masked her sight. She could hardly see Lana through the lenses.

"What is this? What's on my face?" she cried.

"It's a gas mask. Relax. Just breathe normally."

"Why am I—"

"There was an attack with yellow smoke. Just breathe. You're okay. Just breathe."

"Attack? What attack? What're you talking about?"

"I'll explain. Just breathe. Relax. Please."

Bria inhaled again, her head spinning as she slowly glanced around the room. She lay in her father's home on the sofa, with Nix and Gato resting on the floor beside her. Lana sat on the arm of the sofa, holding a bloody rag to her nose, face pale and eyes bloodshot.

Lana continued, gazing past Bria towards the window. "We received a tap-code message from one of our insiders in the Capital. Senator Cordova called a meeting on the steps of the Capital. He had some sister of the Order join him, and she sang a hymn. Yellow smoke poured from her mouth, and people started collapsing throughout the city. It seemed to do with magic or something, and it was spreading out across Rosada." Lana removed the bloodied handkerchief from her nose, still not looking away from the window. "I grabbed a gas mask as soon as I heard and went searching for you. If it reached here, I thought, it would harm you the most. So I thought, if it was mist or smoke... then it would impact you through your lungs and... so a gas mask might protect you."

Bria raised her fingers to the gas mask again. This time, she didn't remove it but let it sit beneath her fingers. *Lana wanted to protect me.*

"It hit you pretty badly," Lana mumbled. "As soon as the yellow smoke entered the gardens, you started choking. I wasn't sure if you were going to survive..."

"My magic is ingrained in me. It only makes sense..." Bria hoisted herself up slightly, glancing at her branched arm. It lay at her side, unwoven, more like a tree than an appendage. With a single breath, she willed it back into place. At least, despite everything, her magic remained.

And with each breath, she knew it waited beneath her fingertips, ready to ignite.

"It still looks quite yellow out there, so I would keep that on if I were you," Lana said.

"What about you? Are you okay?"

"It didn't hit me too badly since the Order took my magic away." Lana wiped her nose again.

"And what about Daddy? Where's he?" Bria squinted through the mask at the living room. Ric and her father did not reside in the room.

"Ric took him into the backroom to rest. He started panicking as soon as you collapsed." Lana furrowed her brow and placed the bloody rag on her lap. "Oddly enough, his nose started to bleed, too."

Bria's stomach twisted. Then...did that mean her father had magic somewhere in his blood? Was her hunch about her paternal grandparents correct?

Carefully, Bria lifted herself from the couch, taking each step one at a time across the room. The two dogs watched her, heads tilted.

"What are you doing?" Lana asked.

"Checking on my father. Don't worry... I'm not going anywhere."

Lana relaxed and crossed her arms. "I am not worrying."

Bria smiled beneath her gas mask. The cracks in Lana's demeanor glowed like the sun through the clouds. Some days, the clouds hid light, but today, it shined through to the world.

"I promise I'll be just down the hall."

Bria continued her slow walk. Gato and Nix joined her, one on each side of her body. They kept her secure and balanced as she approached her father's bedroom. The walk itself felt long, and by the time she reached the door, her lungs ached. Even with the gas mask, the effects of the strange yellow flickering in the windows remained.

She knocked on the door. "Daddy?"

"Come in," Ric's voice answered.

Bria poked her head into the room. Her father lay in bed with Ric sitting next to him. As Lana said, blood trickled from her father's nose.

He raised his head as Bria entered. "What are you? Are you here to take me—no, I won't go back! Don't take me back!"

"Daddy! It's me!" Bria took a deep breath and, for one brief second, lifted her mask. At once, her head spun.

Once the fear in her father's eyes subsided, she let the mask fall back over her face.

"See, Noah?" Ric said to her father, "Beebelle is all good. She just needed some protection."

Her father nodded, his eyes glossing over as he stared past Bria.

"Gato, to his side, now," Bria said to her father's dog. The dog obeyed, leaping onto the bed and nuzzling between the covers. Meanwhile, Bria kept to the wall, staring at her father with a sunken heart. All this time, he held a secret. He never knew it, and she doubted he ever would, but it provided a small piece of the puzzle.

However small.

However insignificant.

Her father spoke, still without looking at her, "Are you a'ight, Beebelle? You fell. Did you hit your head?"

"I'm okay, Daddy. Really. Just rest, okay?"

"My poor Beebelle, falling on the floor. I hope she's okay... She better be okay..."

"I am, Daddy. I promise." Bria wanted to approach her father's side, but with the gas mask, she worried she might send him spiraling once again.

"My Beebelle is okay... She's okay... My Beebelle..."

He continued to trail off, his eyelids drooping further with each breath. The last thing Bria ever wanted was for her father to see her weak; she needed to be strong for him. She had to remain strong. It wasn't a choice. It was an obvious fact. Succumbing to pain would only destroy her father. He'd done everything to care for her, but on his own, it hadn't been enough.

Bria was his rock. She knew that more than anything.

And she left.

And she would leave again.

"He's asleep finally..." Ric murmured. "He's gotten worse since you left... and I think seeing you collapse was... a lot."

"I'm sorry. I... I never wanted him to see me like that," Bria whispered.

"I know," Ric approached Bria and placed a hand on each of her shoulders. "You've been so strong for him. Always so strong. Noah is lucky to have a daughter like you."

Bria sucked in her lips, happy that the mask hid her tears.

"Go with Lana... probably not the best idea to hide around here while whatever... magic thing is happening."

"Are you sure?" Bria asked.

"Positive. I've taken care of Noah plenty. This is no different."

Bria hugged Ric. Unlike her father, Ric's hug exuded warmth and confidence. He tended to her father like he did the dying gardens; no matter how many weeds stood in his way, he would always mend the dirt and help the flowers grow.

After releasing Ric, Bria called for Nix to follow, then returned to Lana in the front room. The woman waited by the window, fixated on the deep yellow haze washing over the town. She didn't flinch as Bria joined her side.

"Guards..." Lana muttered.

Bria followed her gaze out the window. In the distance, out past the dying hedge mazes, guards marched along the paths, shouting orders and bellowing commands. Bria couldn't hear what they said, but her stomach churned. If this strange yellow smoke impacted her, Lana, and her father... then surely others felt it, too. How many people in Newbird's Arm unknowingly had magic? How many had collapsed like she did?

"I was going to say we should leave... but I guess it's not a good idea..." Bria said.

"But how long until they come knocking is the real question? I am sure they're going to check every household."

"And do what?"

"I imagine they're going to take anyone impacted to some secure location. A new Pit... worse than Knoll..."

Bria clenched her fists. Her nose itched beneath the gas mask, but she did not remove it. "We can't let them..."

"Oh, don't start with your heroics again."

"But it's true! That's what all this is for, isn't it?"

Lana didn't respond.

"They don't know that I'm here. I have the advantage." Bria placed a hand on the doorknob. "After all, this is my home. I made a promise to protect it."

"We need to plan. Any movement must be done with cause."

"This is my home. I vowed to protect it, and I failed. This time I won't let them fall again."

"Bria—"

"Please, Lana. Trust me on this."

"But you can't stay here forever. What will you do if you defeat these guards? Leave Newbird's Arm to its devices again, alone?"

Bria gritted her teeth. *No, not again.*

"I won't leave until things are secured this time." Bria rubbed her hand. *Brent isn't here this time to distract me.*

"This is ridiculous."

"It's what I need to do. I'm sorry, Lana." She cracked open the door and called over her shoulder. "Stay here, Nix!"

Before Lana protested again and before her dog could bolt, Bria slipped out into the elements. The yellow smoke bombarded her, slapping against the gas mask. But Bria still breathed. She still felt.

And her magic still danced.

Alone against the strange mist, Bria did one thing she hadn't done in weeks.

She took to the trees.

CHAPTER THIRTY-THREE

THE QUEEN'S WALL

The trees welcomed Bria with excitement. They wrapped their branches around her, creating an armor of bark across her skin and covering her gas mask. She felt like a monster, born of the trees, the power given all to her little branch. This time, rather than her giving life to the trees, they gave it back to her.

It was their way of saying, *Welcome back.*

She didn't look back at her childhood home as she let the canopy act as her guide. With each passing second into the trees, she took a moment to familiarize herself with their stories. She knew these trees; she knew their histories; these were the trees that taught her about magic, about life.

These were the trees she would use to protect her home.

Guards dominated the market square, set up on each corner and bellowing orders. The makeshift tower yard in the fields glowered in the distance, moving closer to the heart of town. When she visited her grandmama, everything sat with silence, a sort of serenity that almost made the town seem normal. Now it reminded Bria of the certain truth: this was Rosada.

And in Rosada, the Order ruled.

Bria squinted from the trees, watching as guards dragged different people away from their homes. She'd known these people; none of them had ever showed magic, but now blood dripped from their noses and mouths, followed by cries and pleas. They didn't know they had magic! Why should they be taken away?

Well, why should anyone?

Amongst the commotion stood a familiar face. With her gaunt face and straight posture, the notorious Captain Palmer stood amongst the lieutenants and cadets, bellowing orders in her baritone voice. Bria couldn't hear what she said, but her mere presence sent nerves through her body. Captain Palmer captured Bria back in Aeterno Village. She brought Bria to Knoll; she caused Bria to lose her arm, and she set off the chain of events that led Bria back to Newbird's Arm.

Bria could have sworn the captain was dead. But then again, during that time, Bria had been unconscious, her arm septic, and her body weak.

"What is she doing here?" Bria wondered aloud.

Captain Palmer hoisted an old man from the ground. Already, blood dripped from his nose, and he swayed to the side. But the captain did not hold back, jamming an elbow into his ribs and tossing him to one of the other guards. The scene was a common one. These guards would never make the world pretty.

They're going to tear apart the town.

Bria's mind raced. What if she surrendered? That wouldn't be enough to stop them. Captain Palmer didn't even *know* she was here. And even if she turned herself in, she'd be imprisoned, and the circle of pain would continue.

If she fought them here, her home would be destroyed.

If she killed them, she would be no better.

Then it all came together. If she took away their power, like they tried to do to the Magii, wouldn't that be enough? But how?

I can't tell a story like Brent... but I can make the world pretty. She placed a hand on the tree and listened to the earth. With a prayer of success on her lips, she imagined the flowers sleeping in the garden around the fountain.

Their seeds remained, pulsing and breathing, just waiting...

Waiting...

And with a burst, they came to life.

Then another.

More and more sprouted in the crevasses of the bricks.

Until finally, a lieutenant shouted, "Captain! Look!"

Captain Palmer's nose wrinkled, and he mouthed clearly, "It's her..."

Perfect.

Bria hopped into the next tree, and with each movement, she commanded more flowers to grow. Each bundle of flowers bounced in different directions, some heading toward the Gardens, some toward the Pit, and others toward the Temple. The guards quickly dispersed in different directions.

Make it unorganized. The more, the better.

Every few trees, she sent flowers in different directions. Flora soon covered the market, and as Bria continued to circle, more ascended across the town. They crawled up the walls of the

Temple, reignited the brown of the Pit, and crawled into the Senator's garden. The roads flourished with grass.

Everything lived.

Newbird's Arm would be a gem once again.

But Bria had one destination in mind.

As the Guard continued to follow her foliage, Bria directed each of the clusters to lead to one place. Groups of guards traveled from the market, from the Pit, and from the Senator's gardens; they ran with anger, with Captain Palmer's order as their guide.

"Get her. Trap her. Do whatever it takes. She can't kill us all!"

A few guards tried shooting into the trees, but her trees acted as a shield. For a shining moment, Bria felt invincible.

She reached the last tree before the farmlands, where the towers waited like a constant wall. Their gears groaned and their bodies rocked while the yellow smoke continued its angry reign. This would be her final resting ground.

Here, she only commanded the camellia bushes to blossom solely for the purpose of protecting her, then she disappeared behind the stones of the tower. *No one will die today.* She promised herself. *Not even the Guard.*

Guards swarmed the tower yard where Bria waited.

Be nothing more than the wind.

Captain Palmer stepped forward, shouting, "Get out here! Don't think that your little flower game will scare me!"

Bria didn't move. *Please let this work.*

She turned her focus away from the trees, recalling to herself what the *Rules of the Apothecary* said. It said that every element interacted, every element helped create the earth. Clay composed the bricks, and in clay came the nutrients that fueled the trees. She just had to listen.

She thought of the way each nutrient worked in the trees, giving them the resilience to survive. Despite the way magic suffocated and how the land turned brown, the trees remained. Determined. Strong.

And the same nutrients screamed within the towers. Fueled by anger.

By determination.

By life.

Move with that anger. Move with that power. Bria dug her hand into the stones. She pictured the towers shifting, moving one brick at a time, like giants wandering along the landscape. One step at a time.

Just one step...

One shift.

One gear.

"Captain!" someone cried, "The towers are moving!"

"What!?!"

As Bria had hoped, the towers did indeed move, crawling across the earth, merging in closer together like one structure.

Side-by-side, the towers circled the group of guards. She commanded the doors and windows to cave inward, leaving behind just a plain stone wall. With nowhere to escape, nowhere to slip through, the guards stood trapped in their new prison.

It wouldn't be a permanent solution, but at least it would give the people of Newbird's Arm time to protect themselves.

And a chance for Bria to establish her protections.

As Bria released her hand from the nearby tower, she exited her own shadow and turned to face Captain Palmer.

"You might wear a mask, but I know it is you," Captain Palmer said.

Bria did not reply.

"Very well." Captain Palmer removed a pistol. She rubbed the barrel and cocked it back with a click.

Then…

Bang.

Bria reacted at once. With a single stomp of her foot, she formed a sinkhole around her. She inhaled once, letting the dirt pull her down into the earth.

The roots acted as her transport. In the past, they would carry her down to the tunnels, but this time, they passed her within the earth, away from the towers, and far from the Guard. In their embrace, exhaustion seeped through Bria's body. Her mind burned, her head ached, and her stomach twisted.

The earth spit her out in the heart of the Senator's Garden. She collapsed on the ground, exhaling sharply.

With a gasp, she pressed her head against the ground.

Her magic drifted from her fingertips.

And in that moment, Life returned to Newbird's Arm with a bow of green.

CHAPTER THIRTY-FOUR

JEWEL

Mitzi gave the children a room to sleep in for the night on the second floor. With bejeweled sheets and piles of pillows, the beds welcomed the children with open arms. While Chander and Anandi immediately fell asleep, Yaz tossed and turned. Her mind ran; Tommy's request haunted her. What did he want? Could she trust him?

Coupled with her shouts, outside gunshots ripped through the night. Followed by screams.

And sobs.

She peered out the window from her bed. It was more than just weaponry. With the strange strips of gold gone in the depths of the night, magic reigned. Most common seemed to be variations of fire, glowing. But also came siren songs, nimble acrobats, and mist.

So much mist.

Maybe the Mist Keepers are near here.

She squinted at the sky, hoping to see Zephyr come to her rescue. Only an airship floated above, surrounded by fog.

She glanced back at Chander and Anandi. The two slept soundly, despite the noise. Not wanting to disturb them, she slipped through the door and headed downstairs to the bar. She at least had to hear what this Tommy person had to say.

She moved like a shadow amongst the droves of pinstripes. They drank, smoked, and passed drugs, laughing as if celebrating a victory. Yaz stole a bowl of pretzels from the counter and, meeting no one in the eye, hurried to the table in the back of the room to wait for Tommy.

No one paid any mind to her. Perhaps that was the benefit of being a Mist Keeper; people overlooked her like she was nothing more than a ghost.

It allowed her to observe the tavern. People spat curses, waved magic, and held drinks. Unlike the poised behavior Ms. Kai taught her or the proper language exhibited by the Council of Mist Keepers, people here spoke without filters and ate with improper manners. *Freedom.* Was that what it was? People could live without worry, tell stories, practice magic. Whether it was just this tavern or the city beyond it, people here *lived.*

As if someone had turned off a light, the commotion in the tavern stopped. Everyone turned, attention directed towards the stairwell.

And upon seeing who stood in the stairwell, Yaz understood their awe.

A woman, draped in a golden suit, with eyes as haunting and hair as pristine, walked down the stairs as if floating. Her smile glimmered, a twinkle in her eyes. Tommy followed two steps behind her.

"What is the meaning of this commotion? The tavern is a mess." The woman remarked as she stepped into the room.

"What's it to ya?" One pinstripe asked. "We've been here longer than you."

"But I'm the boss, am I not?"

"Only 'cause you killed our old boss."

"Your old boss was, frankly, an asshat. He deserved what he got." The woman strolled through the room. No one dared to go near her. Despite their language, the respect wove deep into their core.

Yaz didn't dare move, her eyes locked on the woman. She danced between the tables, checking each person while stealing sips of their drinks. The jewels on her fingers glistened, and her long necklaces clacked against her chest.

Tommy caught a glimpse of Yaz at the table and sent a smile her way. He touched the woman's shoulder without fear and led her toward where Yaz waited.

"I am glad you came down here, Yaz." Tommy pulled back a seat for the woman. She took a seat without even acknowledging Yaz.

"I was...curious," Yaz mumbled.

"As many are."

Yaz glanced again at the woman, but still, she did not say a word.

"I'd like you to meet the boss of the Pinstripe Gang, Jewel." Tommy stepped back from the boss, his smile still a permanent fixture on his face.

"Nice to meet you." Yaz held out her hand.

Jewel did not take it, gazing straight at Yaz. There was something about her—Yaz could not look away from her. She was alluring, yes, but something more. It drew Yaz forward, like a song playing deep in the shadows.

Or like a monster calling her name.

Jewel narrowed her eyes at Yaz. "Why is a child in my tavern?"

Tommy straightened at once. "I believe Mitzi invited them to stay. She found them in the street during noon-time."

"And she did not report this to me?"

"She did not want to wake you."

"Unacceptable. Send her to my lounge at once," Jewel rose from the seat. One of her rings fell from her finger, clanging against the tabletop and rolling onto the floor. She watched it fall. Once it finished spinning, Tommy picked it up and placed it back on Jewel's finger. She wrung her hands together and nodded to Tommy. "I'll be waiting for her."

With another gasp of gold, Jewel waltzed from the table and back up the stairs. Her long golden coat bellowed behind her.

As did a brief touch of yellow smoke.

"What did you notice about her?" Tommy asked Yaz.

"What?" Yaz glanced back at Tommy, breaking the spell cast by Jewel.

"About Jewel? What did you notice?"

Yaz licked her lip, unsure what to say. She recognized her beauty and riches. But she also saw the smoke.

Just like the smoke that had been outside earlier that day.

"She was gold."

"Yes, she wore gold."

"But it was everywhere. She glowed with gold." Yaz gulped. The gold was everywhere, just like the yellow monster.

But Jewel wasn't a Diabolo. How could she be glowing like one?

Tommy closed his eyes. "Yes. Very good."

Yaz fidgeted with her sleeve, unsure if she should say any more.

But Tommy continued, "I was wondering if you would notice."

"Why?"

"Because Jewel has not been herself for a long time."

"What do you mean?"

"Jewel encountered a monster a few months ago. This monster...well, it has taken a place in her heart. After I saw your magic, I couldn't help but wonder if you may be able to help her banish the monster in her heart."

"I... I don't know. I'm... confused what you want." Yaz inched away from Tommy. What did he mean by that? Did he know about the Diabolo?

Tommy furrowed his brow, but he did not approach her, merely wringing his hands behind his back while taking a step away from her. "We will discuss more later, Yaz. I must go—if I do not do what Jewel wants, then she may punish me punctually."

"Oh. Okay."

"We'll talk more later. Just... ponder your magic, and consider this: how do you banish a monster?"

Yaz didn't say a word as Tommy strolled back through the crowd. No one really acknowledged him, nor did he acknowledge him. *How do you banish a monster?* The question echoed in her head. What did that mean? What did it matter?

Did it have to do with the Diabolo? Or the Mist Keepers?

Yaz popped a pretzel into her mouth. She didn't feel like going back upstairs to Chander and Anandi. If they heard her return, they'd ask questions. Right now, she didn't even have the answers.

She could speculate all she wanted, but what good would that do?

Why is everyone always so secretive? Yaz picked at the salt on the pretzel. If adults just told her what they wanted and didn't lie to her, then perhaps she wouldn't be in this mess.

At least she had Chander and Anandi.

And Bria.

They were honest with her, at least.

"TOMÁS!" someone screamed.

Yaz perked up, dropping the pretzel on the table. She caught a glimpse of Tommy, standing in the stairwell, shock on his face as he stared towards the entrance. Yaz followed his gaze.

She yelped.

In the doorway stood none other than Caroline, the woman who helped teach her under Ningursu's guise.

But also the same woman who helped her escape.

That wasn't all, though. Hoisted up by Caroline's arm, teetering to one side, stood none other than the man who helped her escape from Ningursu.

"Brent!" Yaz bounded from her seat, racing to the front of the room. Caroline looked exactly as Yaz remembered her; her skin melted from her face in black and blue blotches while her blue eyes shone brightly. Her black cloak resembled the night.

But beside her, Yaz almost didn't recognize Brent. His curls fell over his face, eyes bloodshot and skin pale. Part of him looked more like a skeleton than a human. Each movement caused the tendons beneath his skin to stretch, and each step threatened to knock him over like a tree in a storm.

Despite that, Yaz couldn't help smiling as she joined Caroline and Brent by the entrance.

"It's you!" Yaz piped.

Brent lifted his eyes. With shadows hanging over him, he looked like a skeleton.

But then he smiled, and light returned to his face.

"You... You're okay," he whispered.

Yaz nodded.

"What're you doing here, Yaz?" Caroline asked.

"Miss Bria sent me to Mert to protect me. Chander and Anandi came too!"

"Bria..." Brent breathed, glancing over the room. "Is she here?"

Yaz shook her head. "No... she had to stay behind in Knoll to learn more about her magic."

Brent's head fell again.

Yaz rushed to reclaim his smile. She reached into her pocket, finding the white flower that Bria gave her, and held it out to Brent. "She gave me this... but I think she might want you to have it."

He stared at it. A single tear fell from his eyes. "Her camellia..."

Yaz placed it in his hand. He ran his trembling fingers over the petals.

His smile returned, then he said, "You keep it. She wants you to have it."

"Are you sure?"

"Yeah... just take good care of it... a'ight?" He handed it back to her.

Yaz beamed, closing her fingers around it. "A'ight."

Brent's smile remained, but as he stepped forward, his eyes rolled back into his head, and he collapsed. Caroline caught him by the arm. Another person walked past Yaz, catching Brent's other arm to keep him upright.

"How'd you know we were here, Caroline?" Tommy asked as he positioned Brent's arm over his shoulder.

"Malaika told me where you were hiding a few months ago. I ran into her in Spinoza when Ningursu was preoccupied with Yaz here. Kek and I agreed this would be best."

"Understood. Let us get Brenton to bed then—I imagine Kek will send some medication over presently?"

"I would assume so," Caroline said, walking in step with Tommy as they carried Brent out of the tavern.

Yaz stood there as they left. She continued to grip the flower tight, her heart racing, unable to keep her eyes off Tommy.

The realization hit her with a wave of panic.

"You're a Mist Keeper!" she shouted after him.

If Tommy heard her, he didn't respond, disappearing down the hall with Caroline and Brent, wrapped in a plume of smoke.

TAPPING IN THE TAVERN

Christof woke to his head pounding. What happened? The night was a blur.

It was only when he rolled over did he discover the two vagrant women lying naked next to him. He blinked before sitting up in shock.

The night raced back to him at once: he left Sister Jey Ma at the Capitol, confusion and rage coursing through his body. He walked for hours from the Capitol, down a path where taverns and farmlands waited. Upon finding a strangely empty tavern, except for an elderly woman sitting in a rocking chair, collecting coins on her lap.

She gave him a room for the night for only a few coins, but he instead headed straight to the tavern. After a few drinks and a whirlwind, rambling story—well, he hoped they weren't stories but truths—the barkeep led him to a bustling speakeasy in the basement. The noise had been so great, he couldn't be sure what was happening. And after a few more drinks, a lot of rants about magic—which people laughed off in disbelief—he found his way into the arms of two women dressed in red.

And those same women lay in his bed now.

"Fuck!" He shoved them from the bed. "Get outta here! I don't want nothing to do with you fucking harlots."

"Oi! You wanted everything to do with us last night!" One girl remarked.

"Yeah, you ain't allowed to treat us like shite." The other added.

"I'm a guard, and you're fucking vagrants. Get back to the damn Pit where you belong."

The first girl grabbed her dress and glared at him. "You know, we got plenty of dirt on you. So you better behave yourself."

"You got nothing."

"Yes, we do… Mr. Storyteller," the second taunted.

"I don't tell stories. Only truths."

"Yeah…because there's definitely a forest queen and a demon lady. Pfft. Watch out, or we're gonna report ya."

"There is!" Christof objected.

The two women smirked at each other, then shared a mutual laugh. Christof quickly glanced over their bodies once, licked his lips, then looked away. *At least they're attractive. Glad I didn't go fucking some old broad.*

"You've already paid, so we'll see ourselves out." The first woman said as they finished dressing. Before Christof considered inviting them back to bed, they vanished through the doorway.

He cursed under his breath. What would Sister Jey Ma do if she found out?

Did he care?

It wasn't like he planned to tell her.

Granted, he wasn't even sure if he would go back.

Christof slowly climbed out of bed and headed into the lavatory. He let the steam from the shower embrace him. It did little to get rid of his headache, and by the time he stepped out, all he wanted to do was lie in bed.

Instead, he pulled on his undershirt and uniform pants, then headed down the stairs. The scent of bacon and eggs drew him into the kitchen, where the barkeep from the night before cooked. A newspaper sat on the table.

"Can I look at this?" Christof asked.

"Yeah, go ahead, kid." The barkeep didn't look away from the food.

He stole the newspaper. As expected, not a single statement of the night before crossed the page.

They wanted it silent. For everyone, it would only be a dream.

"They're scared..." Christof mumbled.

"Hm?" The barkeep turned.

"Nothing." Christof retorted.

The barkeep shrugged and returned to his eggs.

Christof read through the article one last time, glancing over at the image of Senator Cordova at the Senator Prime's pedestal, a determined gaze on his face. Elder An Drew stood on one side, and Jemma on the other. Christof tried his best to discern Jemma's expression; was she hurt? Pained? Did she feel anything at all?

Christof didn't turn when the barkeep placed a plate of eggs on the table. Despite his earlier hunger, all he could do was pick at the food. Every time he closed his eyes, he saw blood. Not that he was a stranger to blood, but so many people had fallen.

And how many didn't even know they had magic? How many had turned away from it and prayed to the Effluvium?

How many people were *good*?

Sister Jey Ma's emotionless determination would forever break his heart.

In all honesty, it brought him back to when he saw Bria use magic for the first time. She became a demon then… but now, Sister Jey Ma may have been the same.

Everything brought him back to think of *that* girl. Why? He hated her! She killed his father.

And she broke his heart.

He'd been obsessed with her since he was sixteen. It had happened outside the schoolhouse. She was sitting with a few girls, and they'd all been talking about their crushes. So many of them fancied him, and he loved hearing their ogling phrases.

When the girls asked Bria, she merely shrugged. Christof hadn't paid attention to her before, but over the last year, she had blossomed. In that springtime light, her dark skin radiated, and her eyes glazed like the bark of oak trees. He couldn't take his eyes off her.

The girls continued to pressure her. They asked her if she had ever kissed a boy, and when she said no, they kept asking who she liked.

They brought up Christof's name to her, and she once again shrugged and mumbled something. To Christof, it sounded from the distance like, "I guess I like him."

So he took his chance.

He swaggered over to Bria, smiling at her. The other girls all giggled as he asked if she wanted to be kissed.

Bria agreed. It was a soft one, but she agreed.

So he kissed her.

And he dreamt of kissing her again ever since that day.

But then she'd avoided him. All the while, he didn't stop his pursuit. Always, he thought, she was playing hard to get.

About a year after that kiss, he convinced her to eat dinner with him despite constant attempts to court her. It was a perfect day, Christof thought. He courted her like a gentleman, wearing his finest clothes.

Over dinner, she sat quietly, proper and behaved. She would've been the perfect wife.

After that first date, he pecked her gently on the lips.

Over the next year, he took her out three more times, trying his best to woo her with his strength and prowess. He got closer to her, and on the last date, he told her point blank, as he pinned her against a tree in the garden, that he would marry her when he returned from his two years of cadet training.

She merely stared in shock, but she didn't say no.

So he kissed her hard, grabbed her tight.

But she stopped him from reaching beneath her clothes.

He respected that boundary, expecting her to be his when he returned.

But when he came back after his first year of training and found her in the gardens, in the spot beneath the camellias, she was kissing none other than that vagrant Brent Harley.

He'd nearly bashed Brent's head in that day, but the altercation was enough for his father to cut his cadet training short and force him to stay home. His father said he didn't belong in Knoll if he couldn't control his emotions.

Until then, he would be a permanent cadet.

And that still hadn't changed.

Bria still avoided him. She still didn't stop seeing that damn Brent Harley, either. Even after Brent became betrothed to Sister Jey Ma, he caught them together.

She'd only agreed to marry him because he nearly killed Brent in the forest that one day.

And despite everything she had done, despite her magic, and despite her evident hatred of him...he still couldn't shake those years of obsession.

Nor could he get rid of the years of longing aching through his body.

His body throbbed now as he stared at his now cold plate of eggs. *Dammit. Where's that damn barkeep? I need to get outta here.* He took one bite of the eggs and scowled. *I'll go find him.*

Christof pulled himself from the chair and glanced into the main dining room.

He immediately pulled himself back into the kitchen.

In the other room, the two strange individuals from the Curio Shoppe Tower, Gisela and Yeshua, sat with the old lady who ran the tavern. The barkeep stood behind the old lady with his arms crossed.

Christof pressed his ear against the wall, trying his best to hear the conversation.

The first thing he heard was a rhythmic tapping on the table. It reminded him of the tap-code a few of the guards used. He never bothered to learn it or the telegraph system beyond how to read the tap-code alphabet. Truth be told, he didn't get the point when people could simply use the radio.

After the tapping stopped, the barkeep said, "My auntie asks why she should help you after you, pardon my language, fucked her over all those years ago?"

"Oh, Nan, are you still upset after that whole incident with what's-his-name? Yeshua, do you remember?"

"Ralph..." Yeshua muttered.

More tapping followed.

The barkeep translated, "That so-called incident took her tongue."

Gisela replied, "Oh, you can still talk, dear. You're being stubborn. Come now—"

The tapping stopped her.

The barkeep recited, "You were not part of her life. You just left when things got bad. Never even told her your motive. She owes you nothing. Did I get all that ,Auntie?"

The old lady must have nodded.

"Nanette, please," Yeshua spoke. "It's a child. A little boy. If they get their way, then all progress will be *erased*. Everything will fall. We need to get that child out out of their clutches."

Are they talking about the little boy that Elder An Drew keeps carrying around? Christof pressed his ear against the wall. He still couldn't help but feel torn about this situation; if he rescued the child, it meant treason.

If he didn't, then it meant losing all order.

He had always believed in rehabilitation for children. Not all of them ended up like Brent Harley. Some of them thrived.

If they tortured the child, he would never find the Effluvium.

The old lady didn't respond to Gisela and Yeshua at first. Then she tapped.

Her barkeep responded, "She says of course she'll help a child…but she has no reason to believe *you*. Auntie does not want to see either of you in her tavern again. Find someone else to help."

"There is no one else. If we do not act soon, then they'll erase—"

"I said leave."

The barkeep and the old lady rose. Christof ducked into the kitchen, pretending to be preoccupied with a painting on the wall.

Footsteps retreated down the hall.

"At this rate, it is inevitable—the first phase has occurred already," Yeshua said. "Sight is at risk. You know how the prophecy goes."

"We could find the child, love."

"No. We cannot. They'll recognize us. It is too late."

"It cannot be."

"It is. You know the prophecy."

"Yeshua..."

"When the brothers no longer touch, and the books have met their match, she will rise as a queen, and the sky will become vermillion."

"We cannot be sure what that means."

"It means my days are numbered. They're going to take everything that I am." The man choked out, "I'll lose everything."

"No. You will not. We will save the boy."

"We can't. You know that, Gisela."

Christof's heart lurched. He didn't understand what the two talked about, and he couldn't be sure what compelled him out of the kitchen and into the dining hall, but he stepped into the room, voice raspy as he spoke. "I can help."

CHAPTER THIRTY-SIX

THE QUEEN'S KINGDOM

Bria nursed her lemon tea, slipping it through the bottom of her gas mask before securing it on her face. The yellow smoke outside had dissipated, but she still felt it tugging at her magic. *Better safe than sorry,* Lana had said after finding Bria in the gardens.

After Bria completed her tower sculpture, the roots brought her back to the garden, where she lay there enamored by the foliage. Her heart pounded in her ears for what felt like hours until Lana found her and hoisted her off the ground. With each step out of the garden, bark fell from her skin, and by the time she reached her grandmama's house, she stood as nothing more than herself.

Her grandmama fawned over her arrival, forcing Bria to take a seat on the couch while Lana disappeared into town. There Bria stayed throughout the night, huddled beneath the blanket, while the gas mask dug into her face, leaving her skin yearning for a scratch. Her grandmama never left her side, brushing the leaves from her hair, all while mumbling about the ridiculousness of the Order, of the Government, and of Bria's action.

Bria let her ramble well into the morning, tuning out most of her complaints. Really, she wanted Lana to return with answers. Did the Guard remain trapped behind their towers? What was going to happen in Newbird's Arm now?

People had seen her. Without a doubt, word would spread fast: the Forest Queen had returned to her Kingdom.

Madame Gonzo peeked out the window as Bria finished her tea. She said nothing, closing the curtains again before teetering across the room.

"What's going on?" Bria asked.

Madame Gonzo waved her hand, "Nothing. Just people being... people."

Bria picked herself off the sofa and approached the window. Her grandmama grabbed her arm.

"Don't fret over it."

"I'll fret more if I can't see."

Madame Gonzo dropped Bria's hand.

Bria took that as permission to part the curtain a crack.

Her stomach twisted.

Nearly half the town waited in the marketplace. She didn't have to hear their chants; she knew they sang the song that haunted each movement.

Rhodana,
The forest queen,
She loves to laugh,
She hates to scream,
She promised the world a reverie,
Rhodana.

Bria stepped back, letting the curtain fall.

"They know you were the one who stopped the Guard," Madame Gonzo said.

Bria gulped. Every action she took only reaffirmed the song. She didn't believe in prophecies, but how could she ignore it? The story always changed.

And it was the one story not even the Order could stop.

"What am I supposed to do now?" Bria whispered.

"Hm?"

"I can save the day all I want, be some sort of hero. But... someone has to pick up the ashes and rebuild." Bria stared down at her hands. "I... jump in and destroy. I'm not a leader. I'm not like you or Lana…"

Madame Gonzo took Bria's hands. "Sometimes, we need people who will act. People like Angelana and I will sit and plan for months. But nothing will ever get done. When people like you act, change becomes imperative. You are young, Briannabella, so very young." Madame Gonzo placed a hand on Bria's cheek. "You will learn to lead. Until then, be the hero… and keep those of us with the knack for planning closer."

Bria pulled away from her grandmama and looked back toward the window. "Then what should I do?"

"Well, Angelana went out to assess damages and connect with Lieutenant Randall. Do you remember him? He's one of the few guards that Senator Heartz trusts. I think she is going to see if he can keep the town under control until the Senator returns."

"When is she returning?"

Madame Gonzo shrugged. "I don't have a clue. She's been gone about two months now…which is a normal time frame. So hopefully soon. I've sent some messages but haven't received a reply."

That wasn't unusual either.

Madame Gonzo continued, "After the last time, after you left… a few of the prominent leaders and I created a small council."

Bria winced at the word. *Council.*

If Madame Gonzo noticed, she said nothing. "Ric is involved, as well as Old Dr. Ortega, Lieutenant Randall... and a few others. We all hold the same beliefs; we just want our town to thrive. Unfortunately, as we were putting together our proposition, Elder Lau Rel arrived, and she recruited Captain Palmer a couple of months later. But all this is just me rambling."

Bria didn't reply.

"What I am saying, Briannabella, is that we can take care of this town as long as you come back as you promised every now and again."

"Okay..." Bria whispered. In the silence of the house, she did not hear the forest beckon her. But the song of the Forest Queen continued to ring.

Bria turned to the door, her hands growing sweaty. Did they want to see her? What would she say?

This is my kingdom. And it needs a queen. She placed her hand on the doorknob. *Show them you won't run. Let them trust you. If Newbird's Arm is on your side... you won't ever be alone.*

Bria adjusted her gas mask and opened the door to her grandmama's house. Outside, the sunlight trickled into her gas mask with a yellow glow and with each step onto the porch. The entire town waited in the market square outside the house, vagrants and civilians alike, all watching. Some held handkerchiefs beneath their noses, while others appeared pale and weak. The number of people gathered dulled the presence of the Temple's Year Glass on the other side of the square. These people came for her and to stand with what she believed.

She scanned the audience. So many faces she had seen while growing up: from vendors to farmers, to miners, to vagrants, and more.

In the back, she caught a glimpse of Janette Harley holding onto Alexandria's hand. She stared at Bria, but not with any vengeance. A seeming appearance of melancholy acceptance marred her eyes. Beside her, Alexandria beamed.

Of course, her husband, Robert Harley, was nowhere to be seen.

What do I do now? Bria scanned the audience. Trembling, she removed a glove from her branched hand, then raised her palm in the air. Out of it bloomed a single white camellia flower.

As it bloomed, the crowd jeered.

Bria didn't stay long. After the cheers subsided, she slipped into the trees, letting flowers dance in a flurry behind her. With the trees as her guards, she returned to the forest, holding her grandmama's words close. *Just come back every now and again; show them you are still protecting this town.* Her grandmama was right, of course; there were people with far more experience to lead a charge. Without them, where would she be?

Bria let the trees part as she approached the tower. Alone in the forest, the greenery followed, tracking like footsteps on the ground.

It even climbed up the steps to the tower, only halting when Bria waved her hand. Her body ached as she entered the tower, and even as Nix bounded towards her, all she wanted was to climb into her bunk and sleep.

But despite her body's pleas, she walked past her room and towards the bridge.

As she expected, Lana waited by the tap-code machine, writing notes on the pad. Her eyebrows remained furrowed, and she didn't even raise her head as Bria entered the room.

"Wish you didn't act like some hero," Lana muttered as Bria entered.

"They were going to take people. I couldn't let that happen."

"All of Rosada has felt the effects. What good does saving one town do?"

"The same good as us reclaiming Knoll."

"And that was just as irresponsible."

Bria clenched her fists. "I feel like I never do anything right! I saved countless people from a life in the Pit, and you say it is pointless! What would you have me do? Sit around and look pretty?"

"I would have you think before you act."

"I do."

"Oh? Then what is the plan with that *wonderful* tower sculpture you erected in the fields? That won't be so easy to move. Lieutenant Randall has found some explosives. With luck, he'll be able to get those guards out alive for interrogation."

"But now those towers will be useless. Captain Palmer's crew cannot contact their superiors." Bria adjusted her gas mask. While Lana seemed unphased now, she worried one breath of the tainted air might take away her own magic again. "I know it leaves behind a path of destruction... but... it was all I could think of doing without spilling blood or harming most of the town. Newbird's Arm will not fall to whatever is happening. That is a promise I made."

Bria couldn't be sure what was happening. Senator Cordova was planning something; Lana reported that this yellow smoke started in the Capital. But this was even greater than Senator Cordova. This was the Council of Mist Keepers. And more importantly, this was Ningursu's domain.

"Well, luckily, Lieutenant Randall expressed excitement in blowing up those towers." Lana grunted as another tap-code message came through the machine.

Bria listened to the beeping and clicking. While still not fluent, she could pick up a few words in the code: *Capital, Knoll,* and *yellow.*

Lana scribbled it down on her paper. "As I said, that yellow smoke attacked the entire country. There are reports it spread as far as Mert... but that's where it seemed to stop. It is retreating slightly, but I would keep that mask on for the time being. There are reports of people passing out... or worse." She glanced over at Bria. "Did you hear that Elder Lau Rel here in Newbird's Arm had a reaction?"

"Really?" Bria never imagined an Elder having any magic. Didn't the Order vet their leaders?

"Seems it. Lieutenant Randall found her dead."

"Dead?"

"Yes. Blood was coming from her nose and mouth like all of us damn Magii. But from what Lieutenant Randall told me... it looked like she killed herself. Found her hanging in the Temple. Guess she couldn't handle the truth."

Bria sucked in her lips. *If she didn't know about her magic... how many people don't know about theirs? How many people are in danger now?*

Lana rose, holding her notebook close. "Hue sent a message. One of our contacts in the Capital is hiding a good hundred or so Magii. They need transport and medical care."

"I'm guessing she wants us to go there?"

"She wants the tower to transport them someplace safe."

Bria stepped towards the bridge's window, staring out at the green forest. She had gotten her answers from Newbird's Arm. Now she had to use it.

As her grandmama said, change only occurred because of action.

"When do we leave?" Bria asked.

"Hm?"

"When do we head to the Capital?"

Lana furrowed her brow. "I thought you would want to stay here."

"Of course I *want* to stay, but I can't. Not when people need our help."

Bria expected Lana to protest. Yet, to her surprise, Lana merely nodded as she said, "We'll leave early tomorrow morning. Need to tell everyone else and take care of a few affairs. I suggest you do the same."

With that, Lana left the room, notebook in hand.

Bria glanced at Nix, lying by her feet, then back at the forest. Through the trees, she could make out the distant outline of the Temple. This time, it didn't glower at her; rather, it stood there, faded like the mist.

Yellow tainted its purity.

No one, not even the purest Elders, was safe from the truth haunting Rosada: magic never vanished.

And it never would.

A Sober Awakening

Brent woke feeling like a pit of molten lava. His entire body ached, his head seared, and sweat covered his body. His vision blurred as he blinked, skipping between reds, yellows, and blacks. *I belong in a volcano.* He blinked a few more times. Despite the blurred room, his thoughts remained more lucid than they had in months. Stories didn't mar his every movement, and it didn't feel like he was bouncing from one state of existence to the next.

He shifted his arm. Intravenous lines wove their way into his arm, pumping him with his silver medication. Brent sat up, groaning as he flexed his shoulders. The events rushed back to him. Caroline had punted Ningursu across the room, and when he vanished, the Library followed. Floors cracked, walls fell, and shelving fell. With the collapse of the walls, freedom welcomed Brent. With Caroline leading the way, they limped into the tunnels, only to emerge in Mert, where Caroline brought him to a tavern. Tomás greeted them... as did that little girl, Yaz. After that, everything became jumbled and dark.

His stomach grumbled, and with one aching leg at a time, Brent swung himself off the bed.

As he took his first step, he fell to the floor.

"Dammit," he cursed and tried to return to his feet. But his legs remained too weak, and he lay there, pressing his face into the tile.

He didn't know how much time had passed, slipping in and out of consciousness, before the door finally opened.

"The floor cannot be that comfortable, can it?"

Brent raised his head as Caroline entered the room. Behind her, Tomás strode in on the arm of the giant and seer, Varden. With his deep red eyes, Varden eyed Brent carefully, then hoisted him back onto the bed.

"It wasn't where I wanted to be..." Brent mumbled. "I was hungry."

"Tom, can you get him food?" Varden asked as he fixed the intravenous line on Brent's arm.

Tomás obliged with a bow of his head, disappearing back through the entrance.

"According to Kek, it will probably be a good few weeks before your energy returns. If you weren't a Mist Keeper, the long-term effects of stress and this attack on your body would have killed you. But luckily you're more mist than man at this point." Varden finished adjusting the line, then stepped back from Brent. "So rest."

"I—"

"Brent, do not argue." Caroline crossed her arms. To Brent's surprise, she did not wear a blindfold.

"You can look at me now?" Brent asked.

"I think I have severed the connection for Ningursu… at least for now."

"And lucky for you, Ningursu still did not create one with you," Varden said as he stepped back from the bed. "That much Kek determined so far."

"Kek escaped too, then?" Brent asked.

"Yes, they escaped with all the others," Caroline replied.

Varden added, "The spirits, as Kek is calling them. They are all at the Sanatorium right now so they can heal."

"The Sanitorium? That would… they shouldn't be there." Brent recalled the time he spent in the Sanitorium. In its own way, it was like a prison. Not intentionally, but extreme cases of magic lived there, with people struggling against their own psyche. "They need... someplace they can thrive."

"Yes, but first, they need to heal. Like you. We need to figure out what Ningursu did to you."

"He attacked me... but I'm... I'm me. I don't... I'm me."

"Yes, but not in any way we had seen before. According to Kek, that black smoke is new. We have yellow smoke attacking Magii, and we've seen Phantom Rot in the blood... but not like this. Here, let me show you." Varden took the edge of Brent's undershirt and lifted it. Beneath it, a black smudge spread out across his abdomen. It almost looked like veins, but it moved with each breath, a permanent fixture of smoke.

Brent touched it and let out a gasp. Pain tore at his side like lightning. Bile rose in his throat, but he choked it down.

Varden stepped back and wrung his hands together. "It reminds me of Phantom Rot, but it's not. Phantom Rot is an allergic reaction to magic, often due to the suppression of one's own magic. It's like a clog, leaving the body to react poorly to all magic. If the individual's magic does return, it often is fatal."

"But I'm not a Magii... my magic isn't suppressed."

"But you have a suppressed Diabolo." This time, Tomás spoke, standing in the doorway with a tray of snacks.

Tomás strode in, his good eye solemn and lips curved in a frown. He approached Brent, placed the snack track on his lap, then sat at the edge of the bed. Tomás's talent lived in mind reading and control, something that always struck Brent with uneasy fear. But he had learned to trust Tomás through Nedo's story after learning it almost a year early.

He still felt uneasy in his presence.

"What do you know, Tom?" Varden asked.

"I've been working on piecing it all together, but I think I have an idea." Tomás crossed his legs. "You may remember some of this, Vardy. If you recall, after the One War, the Council and the Palaver of Immortals made a treaty. There were multiple concessions on both sides: limitations on immortal Magii for Kek, discontinuing of the Pools, and of course, the destruction of the Diabolo."

"Sounds like both sides failed to keep up with their side of the bargain," Caroline grunted.

"Kek did not create any new immortals. Merely, people found their way to immortality. And as far as the Pools are concerned, it's hard to destroy something ingrained in the world," Varden argued.

Brent could not doubt that. He and Bria set out on a quest to destroy the Pools before realizing how deep they ran through the earth.

"You still *used* the Pools!" Caroline replied.

Tomás raised his hand to stop the argument. "There were difficulties in adhering to the treaty on both sides. That much we realize in hindsight. As is clear with the Diabolo as well. Ningursu honestly tried to destroy them. He and Aelia worked relentlessly for hundreds of years, but only for each concoction to aggravate magic. It created issues such as Phantom Rot and other magical ailments." Tomás glanced at Varden before turning back to Brent. "Of course, Ningursu would not try curing Phantom Rot. In fact, I would say it did exactly what he wanted by limiting magic. After multiple failed attempts, he abandoned his quest to destroy them and merely jarred them, where they remained for centuries. Well, at least that is... until you entered the equation, Brent."

"As I said, it was an accident," Brent said.

"An accident that led to quite an ordeal," Caroline chimed in, smirking.

Tomás waved off the statement as he continued. "The rest is just conjecture, but I imagine as his distaste for you grew, Ningursu whipped out his old projects to defeat the Diabolo. I remember seeing a black smoke like this a few centuries back when he was working on destroying them. What I'm guessing, and I could be wrong, but after Ningursu failed to destroy you in his usual methods, he targeted the piece of Diabolo inside of you."

Brent placed a hand on his wound. "So he wants to rot me from the inside out?"

"All conjecture, but yes."

"Can I do anything to stop it?"

"I couldn't tell you." Tomás sighed. "I wish I could, but I can't. That will be up to Kek to figure out, I'm sure."

Varden nodded in agreement.

"How long do you think I have, though? Will I ever be cured?" Brent continued to press.

"I couldn't tell you. Not until I have done more research."

"Great..." Brent groaned.

Always told you I'd be the death of you, his Diabolo whispered. It was feint now, like a disorderly song.

"I imagine we will not stop until we figure this out, correct?" Caroline asked.

"Yes, of course. Do not fret, Brent. We are working on it." Tomás replied.

"I'm not worrying. This shite happens to me daily. It's just a question of what will kill me first." Brent half-laughed, wincing at the slight pain in his side. Yet, despite the pain, the laugh was... satisfactory. It meant, if anything, he was alive.

For now.

"Well, don't go starving to death. Eat." Tomás tapped the tray as he rose from his seat. "Now."

Brent glanced at the tray of food. He sifted through some of the notes before resting on a twisted hard bread covered in salt. It tasted like heaven on his lips. Perhaps not as good as a lemon, a chocolate sundae, or pizza... but good enough.

Tomás and Varden took their leave, but Caroline remained. She paced the room before taking a seat and twiddling her thumbs.

Brent tried to make conversation. "You knew Tomás was here?"

"Malaika told me a couple of months ago. I would not be surprised if she made an appearance soon. She told me she has been spending a lot of time on the Chessboard Plains and everything with an old friend."

"What about her airship?"

"Well, apparently, one of her crewmates on that airship went and stole it. That is the problem when you get mixed up with pirates." Caroline smiled, a twinkle in her eye.

Brent placed another piece of the salty dough in his mouth. A brief story crossed over his head, and he learned the word for the snack: pretzel. Eager to get out of the room, he imagined the stories in the tavern below him.

What could he learn?

What other secrets would unravel now that he had escaped the Library? Stories waited for him about each Mist Keeper. What spawned Malaika's rebellious attitude? Why did Jiang hold such distaste for magic? Why did Tomás yearn to keep the peace? And the others remained too. What secrets did they hold in their pasts? How could they help Brent shape the future of the Mist Keepers?

A knock on the door served as one answer.

Caroline rose. Slowly, she approached the door.

A beat passed as she opened it.

"Is Tommy in here?" a woman asked.

Caroline stood there, not moving.

"Well?"

Finally, Caroline responded, her voice like the wind: "Julietta?"

Brent sat up, catching a glimpse of the woman in the doorway. With pleated blonde hair, wide green eyes, and paper-like skin, he knew Julietta at one glance. He had spent countless hours on her canvases.

And he remembered, most of all, the way her eyes blanked when he removed the Diabolo from her body months earlier.

Julietta narrowed her eyes at Caroline. "I do not know a Julietta."

"Do you not remember? It is me... Caroline." She took one of Julietta's hands. "Please, remember."

Julietta smacked Caroline's hand away. "Do not touch me!"

"But—"

"Ah! Jewel! There you are!" Tomás raced to Julietta's side.

"Tomás! What is—"

Julietta interjected, "Tommy! I want you to escort this woman out of my tavern. She is acting like a fool."

"What did she do, boss?"

"She touched me!" Julietta raised her hands. Jewels covered her fingers, and from Brent's spot, a shimmer of gold glistened.

"Julietta!" Caroline objected.

"I told you I am not *Julietta*."

"I am so sorry," Tomás spoke, an obedient servant as he turned to Caroline. "You must be confused. This is Jewel, not Julietta. I assume you have confused her with someone else."

"Which is ridiculous. There is no one like me, Tommy."

"Of course, Jewel."

"No... no... Julietta..." Caroline bemoaned, "please... remember me. Please."

"Tomás! Get her out of here!"

"Of course. Come along," Tomás beckoned.

Brent still didn't speak, watching from his bed as Julietta stood there in her golden aura. Muddied stories sifted around her. Despite her newfound role, there remained a vacancy in her tale, almost as if another story had taken residency.

Or a Diabolo.

"No! Julietta! Please!" Caroline sobbed.

"Caroline! Come!" Tomás grabbed her arm.

Caroline swung her arm back, throwing Tomás into the nearby wall with a plume of mist. In a fit of desperation, she snatched Julietta's hands, her entire body shaking.

Brent could only imagine what went through her head; once again, if his recollection of the story was accurate, Caroline was losing her dearest friend.

"Please! Recognize me! See me! Please... I can't lose you again!" Caroline begged.

Julietta stared.

Then...

Bang!

A gunshot pierced the air. Brent nearly fell out of the bed, causing his tray of snacks to fall to the floor. His ears rang as he clutched the bed, squinting as the smoke parted in the room.

Caroline stood there, paler than usual, her hand on her stomach. She turned to face Brent and Tomás.

Blood pooled from her abdomen.

"Leave," Julietta hissed, clutching a small golden gun in her hand.

"Caroline!" Brent shouted. As he climbed from the bed, his legs gave out.

"You stay there! Or I'll shoot you too!"

Tomás stepped in front of Brent, "Stay there, Brent. I'll take care of it."

"But she's bleeding!"

Caroline had found her way to the wall and slowly sank to her knees.

"She's already dead!" Tomás rushed to Caroline's side. "Jewel, I'll get rid of her. Is that understood?"

Julietta placed the gun back in her coat. Without another word, she turned, leaving Tomás to hoist Caroline off the ground and leaving Brent with a trail of incomprehensible tales.

CHAPTER THIRTY-EIGHT

REMOLDED

Brent waited for Tomás to return, unable to take his eyes away from the bloodstained on the wall. He played the story on repeat, trying to understand what had happened.

But no answers came.

Whether it was his own injuries or the jumbled nature of the story, it left Brent with a constant headache.

Much to Brent's relief, Tomás did not wait long to return. He entered the room without knocking, rubbing the scarred side of his face as he took a seat in the chair next to the bed. He didn't say anything at first, crossing his legs in front of him before letting out a deep sigh.

"What the hell is going on?" Brent finally asked.

"Caroline's fine. Don't worry. As I mentioned, she's already dead. Mended her wound, and she's sleeping. If

Ningursu can survive his head being chopped off, she can survive a gunshot wound." Tomás still didn't look up from his spot.

"Good…" Brent gripped the blanket on his legs. "But what is going on with Julietta?"

"Trust me, it is for the best."

"Tell me." Brent felt the tales of anger coursing through his body. He wouldn't act on them.

Not yet.

"It is not important—"

"Enough. I have the right to know. The last time I saw her was in the crypt. You said she was… *gone*." Brent scowled at the word. "Lack of information… that only makes things worse."

"It has nothing to do with what is going on."

"Every one of the Mist Keepers' stories has to do with what is going on. I've been… I mean… down in the Library… I collected stories. I'm still figuring them all out, but… I've learned that you're not as powerful as the stars. You're humans making human mistakes, and you gotta… you gotta start acting like it." Brent held Tomás's gaze for a moment. "Tell me the truth."

Tomás scowled, letting a beat pass, before responding, "I remolded her mind."

"Wha—what?"

"Julietta was a blank slate after the incident with the Diabolo in the crypts. I restructured her mind so she could be more than an empty shell."

"So you reformed her into what?"

"Into Jewel, a wannabe mob boss." Tomás adjusted his pinstriped suit. "Of course, she still has elements of Julietta; she loves to paint and adores a good romance novel, and some days I'll find her meandering in a haze. But at least now she's not an empty shell... she is *somebody*."

"You remolded her... like clay..." Brent stared at Tomás, "You turned her into a Diabolo..."

"She's not a Diabolo."

"I had my mind taken from me for months!" Brent didn't mean to shout, but already his voice bounced around the room in utter dismay. "I was nothing while the Diabolo ruled my body... did things outside my control! You... you've created a new person inside Julietta's body! She won't be able to return!"

"I took facets of her and made her something new. It is possible she can remember someday... although—"

"Bullshite!"

"It's not the first time I've done it."

"What?"

"Her name was never Julietta," Tomás said.

Brent shook his head, trying to catch a whiff of Tomás's story, but his head spun with each new revelation.

Tomás continued, "When I first met her, and she became my apprentice, her name was Julyana, the crowned princess of Spinoza. Have you studied any Spinozan history?"

"I didn't learn much outside of Rosada in school." Brent spat. He struggled to quell his emotions. Fear battled with anger, sadness battled with hate; he breathed in once to level his head, but the pangs didn't disappear.

"Well, never mind that," Tomás said. "She was the heir to a powerful kingdom. A smart girl. Loved to read and adored painting. But she always wanted more... so when I took her under my wing, she went with me eagerly.

"But she was too eager, and upon learning that she had to die to join the Council—"

"Another load of bullshite," Brent remarked.

"That's another discussion."

"I'm proof you don't have to die."

"You are dead, though."

"I'm a true Mist Keeper. It's not quite what all of you had to go through."

"Hm." Tomás scowled but didn't argue any further. "Can I continue?"

"Yes. Go ahead."

"As I was saying, upon learning she had to die... she stabbed herself in the heart." Tomás blinked a few times.

"She killed herself to join?"

"That, at least, is what I observed. It happened soon after she learned about her fate. But I may never know the true story."

Add it to my list. Brent eyed Tomás but said nothing.

Tomás continued, "However she died... well... she wasn't ready. So she wandered in her personal Hell, and I moved on because I thought she was gone. So I resumed training three more apprentices. All of them ultimately failed. One of them, Elmer, you met in the crypts. He lost control, and Ningursu imprisoned them. The others, well, they died... and I had to release them traditionally. They could not escape."

Brent had plenty of questions about Elmer, but he waited. For now, he focused on Julietta. "Why didn't you release Julietta that way?"

"I could not find Julyana's soul whenever I looked. She wandered out on her own about ten years later..." Tomás inhaled and wiped his eyes. "She was confused. Lost. Disoriented. At once, Ningursu locked her away, where she painted endlessly. Her magic solidified but made no sense; she painted moving portraits, but most were meaningless.

"Ningursu saw her as a perfect test subject. He was still livid after Kek beheaded him, so while he was trying to eliminate the Diabolo... he also reshaped them for a future war. Julyana served as a perfect vessel."

"Why didn't you stop him? Aren't you the peace-keeper?" Brent spat.

"Because I didn't know." Tomás snapped back. "This was long before we had the Library, long before we had a home. The Mist Keepers were nomads. I did not discover it until I wandered into her prison one day, years after Julyana returned, to find her screaming on the floor. She was an empty shell, and the only way to beat out the Diabolo was to put a new soul in its place.

"So I remolded her mind based on an author and painter she admired: Julietta du Ville Ciel. With Julyana's determined and kind personality mixed with Julietta's stories and words, she became a new person. And the Diabolo returned to where Ningursu had kept it. From then on out, she was Julietta: an obedient, kind, and perfect Mist Keeper. She was everything that the Council needed.

"And she no longer was tortured by the Diabolo. That was the most important thing to me."

"And that's what you did by creating Jewel?" Brent asked.

"Exactly."

"But…" Brent licked his lips and glanced at the smoky sky, "I removed the Diabolo from her! She could have been herself again—"

"You removed more than the Diabolo. You removed *Julietta*. She returned to that same shell she was before I intervened."

"Or maybe that was her chance to rediscover everything about herself! Maybe she could have been brought *back*."

"There was nothing there, Brent."

"How do you know?"

"Because I looked into her mind! All I saw was a white void! So, to protect her, I gave her a new identity. How hard is this for you to comprehend?"

"So she's just an empty vessel for you to manipulate?" Brent's body shook as the words left his mouth.

"No… not like that."

"Then what is she?"

"She's Julyana, she's Julietta, and she's Jewel. She's all three women… but different parts of her personality have shown through to help her survive."

Brent leaned his head against the pillow. His eyes twitched with frustration as he lay there, bottom lip quivering. *They're all part of the same story. You just have to weave the tale together.*

"You owe her the chance to find herself..." Brent finally spoke, "without interference."

"She's a child. I can't let her be free."

"She's over a thousand years old!"

"But she's a newborn now."

"No... this is the problem with all of you! You think you know shite, but you don't! She deserves the chance to write her own story... not be manipulated by... by someone like you!"

"She wrote her own story for almost a thousand years. In the end, it still faded."

"No. You erased it." Brent tried to ignore the gong playing in his head. It vibrated back and forth, sending shivers through his spine. He kept his final statement level. "Everyone deserves to remember their story."

"It isn't that simple, Brent."

"Everyone deserves their story," Brent repeated. He flexed his fingers, watching the mist weave its way between them.

"I understand why you are upset, Brent, but it is not that easy." Tomás rose to his feet and turned toward the door. "I'll leave you now. Rest. I understand if this tale was too much for you... but I hope you understand it is for the best."

Brent didn't reply, continuing to glower toward the window on the far wall. Through the smoke and distant lights, he vaguely made out the white bricks of the Sanitorium. Julietta was like the spirits loitering in that building now. He could try to be objective. That was the job of the Mist Keepers, after all.

But the Council had lost its objectivity the moment they decided to become gods.

No one had the right to sit on a pedestal.

If I'm to be a true Mist Keeper, I have to stand for something else. I can't allow this manipulation between the spirits... Julietta... Caroline... me. I have to stop this. He closed his eyes. *If only I knew how.*

CHAPTER THIRTY-NINE

SPEAKEASY

Bria braided her hair, watching from her window as the landscape marched past the tower. She had said goodbye to her father, Ric, and her grandmama the previous day, and now the tower rumbled along the country. Inside, now that they had filtered the air, she could remove her gas mask. But even with the protective walls of the tower, she could feel the yellow begging for her. Magic did not bend the same way, more like a distant breath than a dream. So as the tower rumbled, she spent her time in her bunk, brushing her hair and studying the tap-code notes that Marisol left behind.

At night, Marisol helped her study the tap-code. As long as she had her notes, Bria managed to decipher tap-code when recited slowly and multiple times. It wasn't realistic for future use, but it would take time.

It'd be useful to be a Mist Keeper right now. They just... know languages. She brushed the edge of her hair. Outside, a deep yellow haze followed them as they left the Newbird Region and headed west to the Capital. Mostly, everyone kept to their tasks in the towers. She saw Lana sparingly, often sitting in the cockpit, listening to telegraphs and reviewing maps of the city. The plan now was simple: meet with Hue's contact and get the hidden Magii to safety.

It sounded simple, at least... but Bria had her doubts.

She rose from the bed as the tower slowed to a halt. Peering out the window, she saw nothing more than empty plains. *Why'd we stop?* Bria scratched behind Nix's ears, then headed out of the room and towards the control room. Surely Lana would know.

As Bria expected, Lana waited in the control room with Marisol and the engineer, Jeremy. The radar blinked loudly on the control panel.

Beep.

Beep.

Beep.

"What's going on?" Bria asked.

"Towers have shifted," the engineer said. "They're blocking our path."

"Can we go off the rails?"

"It'll delay us a day or so. We can't waste time. The longer we wait, the more likely we won't be able to find them."

Bria eyed the radar again, then turned to the window. The Capital wasn't far now. Perhaps an hour of walking.

"We can send a scout," Bria stated.

"Too risky," Lana muttered.

"*I can go.*"

"No."

"I've explored the Capital since I was a child. I know the alleys and the networks that can help us." Bria argued. Every time she visited the Capital, she made a point of hiding in the shadows. But she had learned how storytellers hid, how magic thrived, and how vagrants survived.

She'd seen it all while she navigated the tunnels and traversed the city.

"It's not safe," Lana stated.

"Nothing is."

Lana exchanged a glance with Jeremy and Marisol. She scowled to herself, then nodded. "Fine. But I want someone to go with you."

Bria glanced at Marisol. "Do you want to come? You're better at tap-code than me."

Marisol bounded to Bria's side, "That sounds like a swell time!"

Lana grunted, "Fine. Stay together. Both of you."

"Thank you," Bria replied.

"Jeremy, chart a course to the cliffside. I'll send a message to Hue to meet us there." Lana glanced at Bria. "Be ready to leave on the hour. I'll provide you with the address. And please... be safe."

"I will."

"When you get there, send us a telegraph, please. The code is CAM-RO-7."

The moment the tower dropped off the rails, Bria and Marisol took their leave from the tower, leaving Nix behind for her own safety. She balanced herself on the platform, and while the tower roared with each step, she summoned a branch to pull her and her friend into its embrace. Lana watched from a window, and once Bria had made it safely to the trees, she vanished without so much as a wave.

Not that Bria expected one.

After Marisol calmed from the excitement, they followed the dead tree line toward the city. Marisol bumbled on about Bria's magic and how impressive it was overall. Bria smiled but said little, focusing instead on the forest. The branches bowed and snapped beneath her feet while the trunks begged for her to give just a taste of life.

Not now. I can't right now.

The trees continued to demand her help. She would if she could, but she needed her strength. What if she arrived in the Capital, face-to-face with guards?

If magic thrived without fear, and she could be whoever she wanted, perhaps her job would be to bring life to the forest. To protect life, just like her ancestors.

But right now... she couldn't.

The forest thinned out along the fields. Bria knew this spot well. Just past the fields, on the edge of the road, stood a tavern that she held close to her heart.

She had brought Brent there and watched as his magic took root. It was a haven for him, a hidden realm of stories and magic. And there, they finally opened to each other and embraced their vulnerabilities.

She checked the address again. *It's here.*

Bria snuck along the field, adjusting the gas mask on her face and hiding between the brush with Marisol. As usual, the tavern sat in silence, completely untouched by the Guard. The times the Guard came, the old tavern owner, Ms. Doris, would deter them without flinching, composing a natural lie she had practiced for almost sixty years.

The front step creaked as she climbed onto the porch. When she opened the door, it screeched even louder.

Old Ms. Doris sat in her rocking chair, a pile of coins on her lap. When the door opened, she woke with a start.

"Who goes there?"

Bria lifted the mask from her face. To her relief, only a few gasps of the strange yellow smoke wiggled through the tavern.

A smile crossed the old lady's mouth. Her speech came out garbled as she tapped her fingers on the arm of the chair.

"That's tap-code..." Marisol whispered.

Before Bria could respond, the old lady spoke.

"Ah. I know you."

"Hi. Yeah. It's been a bit." Bria glanced around the room. "Is everything okay here?"

"We survive." The old woman struggled with each hard consonant but still kept confident with every word. "Do you need a room for tonight?"

"Hue sent us." Bria glanced around once before lowering her voice. "She said you had information about some Magii."

Old Ms. Doris climbed from her rickety chair and motioned Bria and Marisol to follow her down the hall and into the kitchen, where her barkeep cooked at the stove. She closed both doors, then turned to the graying barkeep. Then, she tapped her fingers on the counter.

"She's asking him to talk for her," Marisol whispered to Bria.

"Of course, Auntie." The barkeep confirmed, then turned to Bria and Marisol. "I'm Lester. Auntie doesn't speak well, so I can answer your questions."

"Oh, okay." Bria glanced between the two, then launched into what Lana told her about Hue's discovery. Marisol added a few pieces to the tale but ultimately let Bria take the lead. Lester and his aunt listened intently, exchanging a few understanding glances.

Once Bria finished, Lester spoke. "Hue gave you the right information. We've been in touch with Knoll since we heard it fell, and our network sent a message out there after the Yellow Smoke attacked. Hundreds of people collapsed. We got them to safety via the Witch Tunnels, but it's a temporary solution."

"The Witch Tunnels?" Bria asked.

"We try not to use them much after the subway system was installed. Guard discovered a whole network of them. But there's still a few lingering beneath the city. They were built after the Order started its assault on magic, according to what my late mother said." Lester motioned Bria to the cellar door. "Here. I'll show you."

Bria followed Lester and Doris down the stairs, with Marisol close behind her. It was odd entering the little speakeasy while it was empty. Everything sat covered in blankets, as if abandoned from years past, except for the bar glistening with an array of liquor bottles on the far wall. Bria still remembered when she sat at the table in the corner of the room, listening to Brent's stories. She remembered how she approached him, placed a flower crown on his head, and they shared a kiss.

Back then, she still had hope for a future.

Doris tapped her fingers along a couple of bottles on the wall in rhythm. As if controlled by magic, at the final touch, the bottles turned, and a door swung open, leading deep into a tunnel.

If Bria didn't know any better, she would have thought they were *her* tunnels. But these didn't reek of the mist. Made by hand, carved by Magii or miners or something else.

"Wow!" Marisol exclaimed.

"Uncle Ryon and Aunt Doris dug these out over the years. We've hidden Magii all throughout the network in different speakeasies." Lester said, placing a hand on his aunt's arm. "People have been using witch tunnels since magic was outlawed. A lot has been destroyed... but these still stand. The Guard could never figure them out. Once the rest of your people are here, we'll send a message to the others and get them here."

Bria peered into the dark tunnel. The lack of mist and extent of magic called to her. She turned back to Lester and Doris. "This is wonderful. Thank you for doing this."

"It is what we have been doing for years," Doris spoke, each word careful and precise.

"It's amazing!" Marisol exclaimed.

"Yes, thank you." Bria smiled, then asked, "Do you have a telegraph machine? We'd like to send a message to the others as soon as possible."

Lester responded, "Of course, come with me."

"Thank—"

The creaking door stopped her.

"Nan, are you down here?" Someone called.

Bria clenched her branched hand.

Footsteps sounded down the stairs.

Doris spoke as she approached the stairwell, "I thought I told you..."

Bria ducked behind the bar, pulling Marisol beside her. Two figures appeared in the stairwell.

Her stomach fell.

Gisela and Yeshua. She held her breath as the two appeared in the stairwell. *What are they doing here?* It had been a while since she gave the two a single thought. They abandoned Knoll after the attack. To go where? Bria could only guess. But not only that, she had learned of Yaz's tale. The girl spoke of the two with admiration, but they never searched for her.

They'd abandoned a child. Whether they knew it was to a death god or not, it didn't matter. Everything they did should have been for Yaz.

"I thought we said you are not welcome here," Lester interjected.

"We came to say goodbye—" Gisela stopped mid-sentence and sniffed the air. "Someone else is here."

"We run a tavern. Of course, someone else is here."

"But they're hiding right behind the bar."

Sweat gathered on Bria's brow. The air around her warmed as if someone had pushed her into a sauna. She crawled along the floor, trying to ignore the wave of heat prodding her with a migraine. It came so suddenly, as if tossed directly at her by someone.

"It doesn't matter," Lester said. "Leave."

"They might be here to hurt you, Nan. Have you ever thought of that?"

"Why would they hurt us?"

"Because your auntie is a traitor," Gisela stated.

"No more than you."

Bria crawled around the edge of the bar. She eyed Gisela and Yeshua from her spot.

Then, as another wave of heat pushed her down, she sent her little branch flying straight toward the couple and into the wall.

TRAITORS IN THE WALLS

Gisela and Yeshua toppled into the wall. Bria scrambled to her feet, stepping in front of Doris and Lester before glaring at the two Magii.

"What are you doing here?" she demanded.

Gisela raised her head. Her dual-colored eyes brightened. Around Bria, the air chilled. Her little branch retreated as if in winter.

Gisela rose and helped Yeshua to his feet. She stepped forward as Bria crumpled against the frigid temperatures. Marisol grabbed her arm, keeping her steady.

"You...abandoned...us." Bria shivered.

"You won the battle. What does it matter?" Gisela's fingers flicked through the air.

Focus on the air. Focus on the elements. Come on... She rubbed her shoulders and glowered at Gisela. "I'm sure you left with reason."

Yeshua spoke, "We only acted in the best interest of the future."

"And what is that?" Bria winced as the air chewed at her skin. *Elements... What impacts temperature? Think.*

"It doesn't matter anymore."

"Money," Doris mumbled.

"You don't know that," Gisela spat.

"My mother was enough of a fashion enthusiast for me to see those are new clothes," Lester interjected. "I'm sure you're being paid a nice little penny from the Order again, hm?"

Gisela's eyes narrowed. She flicked her fingers again, and the room grew frigid. Doris and Lester both withered slightly against the change in temperature.

"You wouldn't be attacking if you didn't do something wrong," Bria replied.

"You attacked us first."

Bria couldn't argue with that. But these two people had left Knoll. For what? For fortune? For fame?

I need to get them talking...but it's too cold for my plants. She licked her lip. *Oxygen...hydrogen... Focus on the air. The elements are there. Just listen.* Oxygen sang a song of life.

Hydrogen ticked like a clock; if she focused, the two sang together, like the gentle thudding of the waves in the sea.

Focus. She shifted her hand forward, playing the song of the air. With enough pressure, enough focus, water droplets formed a low cloud in the air.

With the chilled air, the water froze.

Bria didn't hesitate. She threw her arms forward, and a snowstorm slammed into Gisela and Yeshua. It threw her backward, almost toppling over Doris. Her head spun from the mere action, but she couldn't stop there.

With Gisela and Yeshua thrown to the ground, Bria sent her little branch flying into the stone wall of the basement. She ordered the branch to lace through the wall and pull it apart.

It took all her focus to make sure the stones fell in an orderly fashion. The last thing she needed was more death and pain because of her own mistakes.

Instead, the stones fell around Gisela and Yeshua, forming a prison with no light.

Bria gasped and stumbled back. Lester caught her arm.

"Sorry...I'll fix this later," Bria mumbled. *Too much in one go after what I did in Newbird's Arm. It's still not instinctual yet, like my plant magic.*

"I've had worse happen." Doris took Bria's other arm and helped her to the table.

"That was some impressive magic."

"Yeah, that's what people say." Bria lay her head against the table.

"Rest."

"But—"

"Bria, rest. I'll send a telegraph to Lana," Marisol said.

"And we'll bring you some food. Sound good?" Lester added.

Bria nodded. She didn't have the energy to speak or move.

Even Gisela's and Yeshua's muffled cries did little to stop her exhaustion.

All she could do was count her breaths…and wait.

Bria stayed in the basement. She teetered in and out of consciousness, waking when Doris brought her a bowl of rice and some flatbread. The food went down without taste, and she gorged herself on water.

Despite the calls from the Witch Tunnels, Bria waited until she received a telegraph message back from Lana to explore them. For now, with the empty speakeasy, everything was safe. Her prisoners could not escape. And for now, her magic thrived.

Marisol returned a couple of hours later.

"Heard from Lana. They'll be here in a day's time." Marisol said as she sat beside Bria.

"Thanks."

"What're we going to do about those two?" Marisol glanced at the wall.

Bria scowled at the prison. She had thought little of Gisela and Yeshua. But certainly, they had answers.

"They can tell us things. Do you think you can help?"

Marisol smirked and flexed her hands. "Ask them anything you want. I'm here to cajole the truth from them."

Bria thanked Marisol and approached the stone prison. She rarely asked Marisol to use her magic; how Marisol could pull truth out of someone just by looking at them terrified Bria in some ways. But this time, it was necessary.

Bria placed her hand against the stone prison. Her voice shook as she said, "Are you ready to talk?"

"You aren't a very good captor. There's fear in your voice." Gisela hissed. "And I can sense you're sweating."

Bria wiped the back of her forehead and straightened her back. "You're right... but I still trapped you. So I think you can answer my questions."

"And if I don't?"

Bria paused. Would she leave them in there? She never considered keeping prisoners... but what ultimatum could she give?

"You don't have it in you to hold us hostage. Your body heat deceives you." Gisela kept her voice level. "You're small and scared. Confidence burns at a different temperature."

"Oh, just answer her!" Marisol shouted.

Gisela chuckled.

Bria closed her eyes, considering her options. What would scare two Magii... potentially *immortal* Magii... but another immortal Magii?

She took her chance. "I know Edith. I'm sure she'd be happy to deal with you." Bria said. The last thing she ever expected was for Edith to be on her side, but she proved to be a useful alley. Bria didn't agree with Edith's ways, but she struck fear through others with a mere glare.

She filled Bria with fear as well.

"Ooh, good one!" Marisol giggled quietly.

Gisela's prying stopped. She said something in an unrecognizable tongue before saying, "Very well. Ask your questions. But could you be kind enough to give us some light?"

"As long as you promise to behave." Bria approached the concrete.

"There is no benefit to me attacking you."

Bria knew it was the truth. With a tap of her fingers, three stones disintegrated, giving enough space for Gisela to peer through at her with one eye.

Bria stepped back and watched Gisela for a moment. The woman hardly blinked, her dual-colored eyes glaring at her.

Finally, Bria asked, "Why did you betray us?"

"Betrayal implies that we damaged your plans. You escaped the Order, and Knoll fell," Gisela replied, voice level.

"You were supposed to help get people out of the towers. Instead, you left, and by the sound of what Lester said, you helped the Order. Just tell me… Why? Why join a group that hates magic when you have it yourself?"

"If you've been around as long as we have, you'd know one fact: the Order only hates magic that it cannot control. When it serves a purpose, they take it and pocket it." Gisela paused. "It is why they have formed an advantageous relationship with the Council. We *betrayed* you to stop that relationship."

"How? It doesn't seem like it has worked."

Gisela glanced back into her cell. "Yeshua has seen the details…"

"Then tell us." Bria glanced back at Marisol, confirming she still sat there. It was strange watching her magic work. There was no physical effect but a clear determination and focus in her eyes. She knew Marisol didn't understand everything about the Council or Order. If she asked later, Bria would explain. But for now, she just needed to collect the answers.

Bria turned back to the prison. The couple shifted, and Yeshua appeared in the slot. He licked his lips before saying, "It goes back a long while. About nine years ago, I had a vision about a child and how she would be the tipping point for a war. I couldn't see much of it, but we decided we had to do our part to protect her. We adopted her as our ward... and for eight years, we kept her safe. That is... until she disappeared..." Yeshua's face fell. "We searched for her, which is what initially brought us to Knoll... thinking the Guard took her. But in Knoll, my vision shifted. It had a few outcomes: in one, she remained missing, and her disappearance would ultimately lead to the Council and Order separating."

"How?" Bria kept pressuring.

"I don't know. I only saw glimpses. It isn't a science..." Yeshua said. His red eyes continued darting around the room. "That would be a favorable outcome... but at the same time... we hated the idea that something bad happened to her."

"Then what were the other visions?" Bria asked. They had to be talking about Yaz. But she didn't want to give away anything until they finished.

Yeshua didn't notice her hesitancy. "In the second vision, she returned to Gisela and me. If that happened, the

Order and Council would remain separate but equal. Communicating but not entwined. So we had to prepare ourselves to find her…" He licked his lip, "That is one reason we did what we did… to make sure we were within reach. The vision showed us many potential reunions—in the Necrowood, in the Opal Desert, and even here in the Capital. The best way to move to those locations was with the Order… especially if they were connected to her."

"And the other reasons were monetary based, weren't they?" Bria inquired. It was rare for her to be on the side of the interrogator. She still had flashbacks to the holding cells in Newbird's Arm, where Captain Carver questioned her for hours.

She would never be like that.

She could never be like that.

Yeshua glanced back at Gisela, then said carefully, "When we arrived in Knoll, Captain Carver reprimanded us for an unlicensed tower. It was either jail or acting as an escape if things went south for the Senator. We chose the latter, with the condition that we receive payment for fuel, food, and other wear and tear. Gisela negotiated it all… and we may have asked for more than we needed."

Because, as Lester said… you only ever cared about riches. Bria didn't vocalize her opinions, instead giving a half nod. "I see."

"We must find a way to survive." Gisela said from behind Yeshua.

"Even at the cost of others?"

"Unfortunately," Yeshusa said.

Every person for themselves, I suppose. But then again, hadn't she been selfish as well? How much had she sacrificed for her own survival? What about Brent? Who had she hurt in the process?

She could name them.

She still dreamt of them.

"What about the last vision?" Bria asked.

Yeshua's face darkened. "This one was always murkier. Our ward... in the vision at least... she escaped the Council in a shroud of mist. With her disappearance, the Council of Mist Keepers grew in power... and a cloud of Death and blood fell across the world. Even the way it looks is like a blinding darkness. And with the way things have gone recently... we fear the worst. We highly doubt that she is still the Council's prisoner."

Bria's chest tightened. "And you aren't able to see if light prevails in the end?"

"No. It's like... I lose all sight beyond the darkness." Yeshua stroked one of the stones. "We played our cards and tried to deter them...but as things have played out, we fear we made the wrong decisions. We fear that other prophecies will unravel now as well."

"Like what!?"

"There's one that says the Council will erase all we know and see."

"What do you mean? Stop speaking in riddles!"

Gisela pushed next to Yeshua, "It means you won't be seeing anyone any time soon."

"What?"

"We'll all be blind soon."

"Stop!" Bria's fingers twitched. "Give me a straight answer!"

"We've given you what you deserve to know. You've imprisoned us, and we have a right to refuse interrogation."

"Only because you attacked me!"

Gisela smirked. "Girl you have a hefty price on your head, and we want out of here before things get too dark. Any rational person would attack."

"So it's always about *you* in the end."

"It's about survival."

Survival. There was that word again. People were just trying to survive. But at what cost?

"Well, I can't help you if you don't give me straight answers. Because those prophecies are happening," Bria finally said as she turned away to rejoin Marisol. She only paused to add, "Yaz escaped. She's safe. No thanks to you."

CHAPTER FORTY-ONE

STALE BREAD

Christof kept to his room in the tavern. Other than venturing downstairs for food and drink, he wanted nothing to do with the storytelling tavern beneath him. But even more, he had no desire to return to his meaningless position beside Sister Jey Ma. While he sent her a message containing a half-baked lie, saying he uncovered a group of secret storytellers threatening to undermine her power, with it, he sent none of his heart.

Instead, he waited. After hearing the two nomads, Gisela and Yeshua, talk about the child held hostage by Elder An Drew, he agreed to be their eyes and ears. While he would have left at once, the two strange individuals told him to wait. "A bargaining chip will come soon. Be patient. If you act in haste, then the child's life will be at risk," Gisela had said to him.

So Christof didn't rush out the door, nor did he tell Sister Jey Ma where he waited. While he didn't really trust these nomadic Magii, it at least gave him an excuse to do, well, nothing.

At least for now.

His hunger spurred him from bed. The insulation in the tavern made it so no sound escaped beyond the walls. Other than the shadows of footsteps beneath his doors, he might have been in this strange tavern alone.

Probably did this to hide the storytellers. Christof grunted as he left the room, taking a quick peek down the hallway that no one loitered. The idea of talking to anyone made his skin crawl. These people were nothing more than traitors.

But was he any better? Hadn't he abandoned his post?

No. This is different. He marched down the stairs and into the kitchen. The barkeep did not loiter as he usually did, leaving Christof to mull through the icebox and cabinets until finding a loaf of bread and some butter. He served himself half the loaf, then threw the plate onto the dining room table and kicked back a chair.

As he stared at the bread, he fell back in time, sitting with his mother at the table as she hummed a hymn. She would delicately butter each slice, remove the crust, then lay them out evenly on a plate for Christof. It was a simple meal, and Christof didn't appreciate the simplicity of it.

He picked at the bread, removing the crust to just pick at the white innards. Then he brought it to his mouth.

And scowled.

It's stale.

He took another bite. Where was that damn barkeep? Surely there was some good food around here somewhere.

Christof kicked his feet up on the table and crossed his arms. *I can wait until he gets back.*

Waiting; that was something he had learned in the Guard. He had waited plenty. Whenever that barkeep returned, he would give a piece of his mind. How dare he leave without providing his guests with food?

Behind him, in the kitchen, the cellar door creaked open. Christof turned at the sound.

A lovely young woman with tanned skin and wavy brown hair exited the cellar. She glanced behind her, not taking any notice of Christof.

He immediately looked away, staring back at his piece of bread. *Probably another guest. Wonder if she'll be around tonight.*

Just as he went to take another gander, the woman spoke.

"You owe me a whole explanation, you know."

What?

Another woman replied from within the stairwell. "I will. It's...complicated."

Christof sank deeper into his chair. *It can't be...*

The first woman said, "Like, what were they talking about? Prophecies? Councils? I have heard none of that!"

"You wouldn't believe me if I told you..."

The two women grew fainter as they left the kitchen. Once Christof was sure they had left, he shot up from his spot and snuck behind them. With each step, he paused, ensuring the old rickety floorboards didn't creak beneath his weight. He snuck around each corner, following the women's shadows as they climbed upstairs to the bedrooms.

Their voices echoed in and out of the hallway. He didn't care what they spoke about, his focus on one thing: *her*. It had to be *her*. That voice was too familiar. He still dreamt about it some nights. Now, he could finally avenge his father.

He kept against the wall in the stairwell, taking a quick second to peer into the hallway. The first woman he saw before stood, arms crossed, in front of one of the bathroom doors. Beside her stood a shorter, dark-toned woman with a heavy coat over her body.

Bria Smidt.

Christof knew *her* without seeing her face. He'd memorized her body from afar. And he knew her now.

It took all his restraint not to kill *her*.

The appearance of the barkeep from one of the rooms gave Christof the restraint. Rather than jumping out and grabbing the girls, the old man's authority over the tavern told Christof to stay.

It wasn't worth it.

Christof could make out what the barkeep said. "So I guess we'll leave those traitors down there, huh? Aunt Doris seems fine with that until reinforcements come."

"The stones are secure," *she* spoke. Her voice held so few emotions, stolen from her by this magic in her soul. Part of Christof wanted to scream; couldn't she see what the magic was doing to her?

She used to be so happy. Her smiles were golden. Christof used to search out her smile in the market. Her eyes would twinkle, and she would laugh.

Even if it wasn't for him.

No. She smiled at me. I remember her smiling at me.

The other girl piped up, "Lana and her crew will be here in the morning. The tower has a secure prison. I'm guessing we'll be able to get some more information out of them."

Bria nodded. "I think they know even more information that can help us."

"You don't need to tell me." The barkeep raised his hands. "I'll tell you, though, that Aunt Doris has known Gisela and Yeshua since she moved here. They still look the same, but we don't care. We see enough magic here to shrug it off. Though I don't forgive them for what they did to Aunt Doris back then."

"What'd they do?" the first girl asked.

"They're why she's missing part of her tongue."

"And that's why she uses tap-code?"

"Mhm. It's quite the story, let me say."

Christof stepped away from the group, sneaking back downstairs towards the kitchen. *So those two nomads are locked downstairs? What is that damn Magii up to now?*

He stopped before the cellar door, hands sweating. Why didn't he attack Bria then and there? Why was he scared of a little girl who could control plants? It'd be so easy to wrap his hands around her neck and squeeze.

But the mere idea caused his fingers to twitch.

Focus, Christof. He reached for the doorknob.

The door didn't budge.

Behind the door itself, a bell chimed. Muffled by the stone, Christof could hardly hear it. *Designed to be an alarm system...* He flared his nostrils. Why did it feel like everything in the tavern aimed to fend off the Guard? Didn't the old tavern owner understand that the Guard existed to protect her? Why did all these people rely on

Magii? Or listen to storytellers? If they behaved, then things wouldn't be so... *disorderly*.

Why didn't they get it?

His father always taught him that order came from authority. But when he closed his eyes, he envisioned authority without Order. This authority used magic. Would it turn to stories next? Would it unravel the Order granted by the Effluvium?

He cursed, then slammed his hand into the door. Pain shot through his knuckles with the splintering wood.

Christof cursed again.

His own profanities masked the footsteps coming down the stairs. The barkeep peaked his head around the corner.

"Ah, it's just you! Sorry, the speakeasy's closed tonight. We'll be open tomorrow, most likely. Can I get you anything in the meantime?" the barkeep asked.

Christof huffed and glowered back to the dining room where his stale bread sat, half-eaten.

"Yeah. A warm meal would be great."

CHAPTER FORTY-TWO

SPIRITS

Brent snuck out of his room before sunrise. With a makeshift cane, he limped down the stairwell, catching whiffs of the stories as he walked. Exhaustion seeped through his body, but he ignored it. After Tomás told him Julietta's tale, Brent spent hours scribbling it on a few pieces of parchment and pocketing them in his coat. He would need to collect more details, but her tale served as much of a purpose as Caroline and Alojzy's tale.

With her story in his pocket, Brent carried a heavier burden. In the Sanitorium outside his window, more lost souls waited. Elmer, as Tomás mentioned, was one of them. Who else? How many Mist Keepers existed before Ningursu rid them of their talents?

He kept his head down as he entered the empty bar. With the new medication, the stories did not assault him. He could feel them reaching for him; there was a familiar air about them as if he had spent time in this tavern, dressed in a pinstripe suit, laughing.

Laughing...

He stared around the empty tables. *I stayed here when I was the Diabolo...when I was temporarily Reggie or something like that. Wasn't there the other pinstripes? Freddie, Billie, and Mitzi?*

Brent shook his head, pushing the story back from his mind, and stumbled out of the tavern.

The autumn air greeted him with a quiet gasp. It was strange, being in Mert again. He knew these streets, but there was something different about them. Less magical? Less peaceful? He couldn't quite pinpoint it.

Brent didn't spend long pondering it. Using the mist as his cloak, he strolled towards the Sanitorium. His skin pricked as the mist washed over him. Despite everything Ningursu had done, he was still a Mist Keeper. His knees quaked, and his heart thudded with discontent, but he could still harness the mist.

The Sanitorium waited only a few blocks from the tavern. As he approached, he let the mist take a different form around him. He told a story of a doctor walking to work. The mist surrounded him, and if anyone noticed him, they held no suspicion.

And with no one stopping him, Brent walked straight through the lobby of the Sanitorium and into the ward.

It took all his focus not to fall into the onslaught of stories. The ward greeted him like a scream. Stories of people injured and dying loitered in the halls.

But even more, so did their souls. The true job of a Mist Keeper called to him; he was supposed to be their judge and guide. Had anyone completed the task since they imprisoned him in the Library? Wasn't that the whole reason they protected the mist?

I can't do it right now... I'm sorry. He stared at his fingers. Pale and dry, the mist pulsed from his nails. The mere presence of the crying souls pulled him in two directions. Once he healed, he would come back. It was a promise he kept close to his heart. No one deserved their death without judgment; no good person deserved an eternity without peace.

Brent avoided the stories as he stumbled along the corridor towards the stairwell. He kept the doctor's story close, and the few times he passed others, he adopted the doctor's wide smile and jolly greeting.

"G'morn, dear! Hope you're well." The words felt weird on his lips, but he maintained the act until reaching the stairwell up to the magical ward: Ward Nine.

He held tight to the handrail as he ascended the stairwell. His knees trembled with each step. Brent had considered waiting for Tomás or Varden to take him, but they would have made him wait. They would have claimed he was too weak. But he owed it to these Mist Keepers, these spirits, as they called them, to help.

How? He didn't have a clue.

His fingers trembled at the locked door for Ward Nine. The story of the doctor abandoned him, and this time he put on Varden's tale. In the story, the giant removed a ring of keys and inserted them into the lock. Brent forced the mist to create the same item, following Varden's pattern, to unlock the door.

The story slipped away as he stepped into the ward. Sweat trickled down his face, and after the constant tales, exhaustion became his new fixation. He shuddered as he walked past the rows of doors and windows. Here, Kek had tended to him back when his Diabolo became a constant companion. In one of these rooms, Edith had dug the word "reaper" into his skin.

He eyed his right arm. It really had become quite the collection: with his old black stamp, his null betrothal mark, the reaper scar, the sun-shaped contractual brand from the circus, and his magical betrothal tattoo. He could be a museum.

Brent refocused on the ward. Filled with magical patients without cures, their stories hit him like a wall upon entry. He winced, biting on his lip and repeating his mantra as he stepped through the corridor. History from the past hundred years flourished before him, filled with blurred tales of Kek, Varden, Edith, and more managing the wards. Were they actually here?

With a blink, they vanished.

And Brent continued.

In a haze, he followed the stories down the hall, passing the rooms where a woman's nails never stopped growing and where a woman who could communicate only with music resided. If he dared stop too long to look, their stories reeled him in, but instead, he kept walking, pushing forward the doors to a separate edge of the ward.

Mist fell from the open doorway. It gathered around his feet as he entered, tugging him forward by an invisible string.

His heart sank at the sight. Lines of windowed rooms greeted him. Smoke battered the walls.

And inside, the withering Mist Keepers from the crypts waited.

Quintessentially, they were human. Almost every one of them stared forward, eyes glassy, a layer of film covering their irises. Mist plumed from their skin. Yet, they still bore some semblance of humanity. A woman with frail hands popped her lips in and out. A man whose once dark skin had paled from lack of light paced and mumbled. Another individual played with their stringy red hair. Their individualistic mannerisms remained hidden behind layers of torture and dragging tales.

Brent enthralled himself with each of these so-called failed apprentices. He counted thirty-seven of them total, each with varying degrees of ailments. Some seemed more aware as Brent stared through the glass. A woman who created orbs of mist around her even seemed to stare back at him. In each of their hollow, silver gazes, he saw himself. This was the future he had brushed fingertips with, and somehow, despite everything, he escaped it.

"I have to do something," Brent said to himself. What was the difference between these Mist Keepers and Yaz, Julietta, and himself?

"That's why they are here."

Brent turned. Kek stood there, arms crossed. Now that Brent could see them, he noted how horrid they looked. Without the sun, locked away in a crypt filled with mist, they had lost some of their youth. In some ways, with the bright light, they looked more like ghosts wandering for thousands of years.

Brent tore his gaze away and back to the spirits. "Why are they in cells?"

"They're in hospital rooms, not cells. That is all we can do until I can give them full examinations. They are wary, as I'm sure you can imagine. But... I think they will be safest here." Kek joined Brent's side, peering into the windowed room. "You, on the other hand, should go back to the tavern. I don't know what you're doing up and about."

Brent clenched his cane. "I had to see them..."

"You do not owe them anything."

"I owe them everything." Brent's confidence surprised him. But he kept his voice level. "I owe them answers because *I* survived what they didn't. I'm still here. I'm free... but they got locked away, tortured by Ningursu... and all the other Council members did *nothing*."

"But it is not your responsibility to fix their mistakes."

"If it's not my responsibility, then who? There are children who are Mist Keepers... people who are suffering... and... and I'm the one who is collecting the history to all this... this... bullshite. Knowing the past gives me the tools to create a future." The next idea came from his mouth before he registered the thought. "I mean... maybe... if there's *more* of in the world... there needs to be a school or an academy or something. You know, a place where others with an inclination to the mist could learn. That way... their future is not only a choice but a success."

Kek scoffed, "Do you honestly think the rest of the Council would allow that?"

A voice piped up from behind them. "I would be all down for it, but I don't think my opinion matters much."

Brent spun. Malaika stood in the doorway, a wide smile on her face.

CHAPTER FORTY-THREE

THE GHOSTS IN THE WINDOW

Yaz watched out the window at the early morning mist pacing in front of the tavern. Ever since Brent had arrived in the tavern, her stomach had done somersaults. Now that she'd found him, surely Ningursu wouldn't hurt her anymore!

So when she saw Brent leaving the tavern that early morning, she nearly jumped out of bed. She removed her glasses once, cleaned them, then pressed her face to the window. What was Brent doing? Was he abandoning her?

"Yaz, what'cha doing? It's early..." Anandi yawned from her bed.

"Brent's leaving..." Yaz mumbled.

"Who?"

Chander stirred in his bed, and in his half-sleep state, he mumbled, "The guy Yaz was telling us about."

"Oh. I wasn't listening."

Chander groaned and sat up in bed. "You sure it's him?"

Yaz nodded.

"A'ight, then let's go after him."

"What?"

"People are just gonna keep leaving you if you don't stop 'em. C'mon." Chander pulled his shoes on and headed to the door.

"Chander! Where're you going!?" Anandi protested.

"To help Yaz!"

"We're not supposed to leave—"

"Well, I don't give a damn. I wanna talk to this guy, too."

"But Mitzi said—"

"I don't care." Chander opened the door. "Yaz? You coming or not?

Yaz glanced at Anandi, pouting in her corner, then back at Chander. She wouldn't let Brent leave her, not again! So with an apologetic glance at Anandi, she followed Chander out of the room.

Once away from the door, Chander let out an exasperated sigh. "I love my sister... but she's so damn annoying."

Yaz giggled.

"Like… she doesn't get it or nothing. I dunno. Maybe it's 'cause she doesn't have magic." Chander shrugged. "Whatever. C'mon. Let's go stop that guy from leaving us."

Yaz followed Chander as they snuck down the stairs and into the empty tavern. The early morning still held the tavern hostage, with no one gathered around the tables. Even the streets outside appeared vacant, except for a newspaper delivery boy and a few people heading to work.

Awe struck her as she gazed amongst the buildings. Curiosity had a habit of getting her into trouble, but she always loved adventuring. Back in the Curio Tower, she used to wander off all the time. She had forgotten the thrill it used to give her.

Ningursu had taken that away from her.

Part of her still itched for the excitement. And with Chander by her side, she knew she would at least be… mostly safe.

At least she wouldn't be alone.

"Right, we better hurry if we wanna keep up with him." Chander motioned Yaz to follow.

If anyone saw them leave the building, no one stopped them. They blended in seamlessly with the few people walking around the street. Perhaps it was the mist that protected them, loitering behind Brent and joining both Yaz and Chander like a loyal companion.

Or perhaps people minded their own business in Mert, unlike in all those other countries where Yaz traveled.

In Yaz's home country of Jrin Ayl, from what Ms. Kai said, everyone always walked with purpose, moving from one place to another without much talk.

In Volfium, the swamp-riddled nation south of Rosada, people told stories and laughed.

And in Rosada, everyone walked with their heads down, speaking only in facts and never of fiction.

But in every place, outsiders garnered attention.

Not in Mert, though.

In Mert, everyone belonged. That much seemed obvious to her.

"Yaz! Stop dilly-dallying! C'mon!" Chander tugged on her sleeve, careful not to graze her skin.

Yaz hurried along beside her friend as they left the market square, turning down an alley of white stones. Windows gazed from above while a set of double doors swung closed.

Chander peaked through the window. "Dammit."

"What is it?"

"There's a stupid receptionist at the front desk. She won't let us in."

"Stupid's not a nice word," Yaz mumbled.

"You're fine with me cursing, but stupid is where you draw the line?"

Yaz shrugged. "I don't like words like that."

Chander sighed. "Fine. It wouldn't be in their best interest to leave it open, I think."

"That's better." Yaz smiled at Chander and joined him by the window.

As Chander said, a receptionist sat at the desk.

She scowled.

"Told you!" Chander hissed.

"Then what're we gonna do? Brent went in there."

"He might return. You said he didn't look good when we saw him? This looks like a hospital, so he might be getting a checkup."

"I don't know. What if it's something important, though? Like what if it's someone bad that wants to hurt him or... or..."

"Yaz, he's an adult. I'm sure he can take care of himself."

"But you were the one who said we should follow him!"

"Yeah, 'cause I thought he'd take us someplace cool. Not to the... *hospital.*"

"I don't want to lose him again 'cause he can help..." Yaz reached into her pocket, feeling for her camellia flower. Why did everyone she trusted leave?

Chander frowned and shoved his hands into his pockets, eyeing the building. Yaz sat on the ground. If she waited just a little, he might exit the building.

But when would that be? Would she have to sit there for hours for him to appear?

Chander leaned against the wall next to Yaz before glancing down the alley, where a short woman with curly hair approached the building. He perked up as she approached.

"I got an idea."

"Huh?"

Chander approached the woman as she neared the doors. "Excuse me!"

The woman turned, "Oh, hullo!"

"Yeah, my... uh... sister and I have a question." He glanced at Yaz briefly, then turned back to the woman. "Our older brother is in the hospital, but we're not allowed to see him without an adult present. But he *is* our adult. So you can imagine our problem. We want to make sure he's okay... you know?"

The woman smirked before saying, "And you want me to be your 'adult,' hm?"

Chander nodded his head.

"Alright, I can do that. C'mon. Just be on your best behavior, okay?"

"Thank you!" Chander motioned Yaz to his side.

Excitement filled Yaz's core. She couldn't believe it; they were going inside the hospital!

The next step would be finding Brent.

Yaz stayed close to the woman as she bantered with the receptionist, while Chander stayed a few steps away from her. Once she'd worked her magic and they entered the infirmary doors, the woman waved both Chander and Yaz goodbye to disappear down a narrow corridor. Part of Yaz wanted to follow her, but she knew that right now, she had to find Brent.

But how?

Chander vocalized her uncertainty. "So... how are we gonna find him? Didn't think this place was so big."

"Uh..." Yaz glanced around the hall. "We search for mist, I guess."

"Mist?"

"Yeah. Just... um... follow the mist? He's a Mist Keeper... so why not?"

Chander squinted around the hallway. "There's a weird mist over there."

He motioned down the path where the woman who helped them went. Yaz peered down at it. Chander was right—a fog loitered in the hall, like a ghost beckoning them. It did not haunt her like the Diabolo but welcomed her.

It was like the Library of the Council or the tunnels where they loitered. What if she followed it and she ended up back in Ningursu's clutches?

No. No. Ningursu couldn't touch her anymore.

"Okay. Let's check it out," Yaz stepped towards the mist.

Chander kept close to her, their footsteps echoing along the corridor. A few patients lay in the rooms along the path, but none of them held a familiar face. Yaz held her breath. What if they ran into Micca or Timothée here? They hadn't gone looking for the two men. What if they were here in the hospital now? Did the fact she never thought to check make her a bad person?

She stayed silent as she climbed the stairwell where the mist loitered. As they climbed each step, she held her breath. What if they got in trouble? What would they say?

At the top of the stairs, an open door and a bright white light greeted her. She squinted past it, and as they entered the threshold, a white corridor waited. Windows lined the path.

"What is this place?" Chander whispered to her.

"I dunno..." Yaz reached for Chander's hand. Much to her surprise, he didn't shy away, squeezing her hand in return. Together, they walked through the hall, focused solely on the mist. She didn't peer into the windows. Something told her monsters lay within those walls. She felt them crying for her. Not like the Diabolo, but still filled with pain.

The mist gathered at another set of doors towards the far end of the corridor. There, leaning against the door frame, stood the woman who they met in the alleyway.

"...don't think my opinion matters much," the woman said.

"Malaika!?" someone beyond the door exclaimed.

Yaz almost bolted towards the door, but Chander held her back. Brent was there! They had found him!

But who was Malaika?

"You don't think I wasn't watching you, hm? As soon as I saw you here, I made my way over," the woman said.

"Yeah, but Caroline said that your airship was stolen—"

"I got my ways."

Is she a Mist Keeper?

Yaz took another step towards the doorway. As she stepped behind the woman, mist washed over her.

She blinked it away as she peered around the woman.

A scream exited her lips.

Through a glass window, just behind Brent, stood a Diabolo. It stared at her with lopsided eyes and a distorted smile. The gaze locked onto her, and she couldn't stop screaming. Why was it here? What was Brent doing with it?

"Go away... go away..." She fell to her knees and pressed her hands to her head. There was no buzzing, no yellow, but this had to be a Diabolo. Why else would it look like that?

"Yaz!" Chander's voice cut through her fear.

"No...no! They're coming..." She hugged herself.

"Yaz..." This time, the voice belonged to Brent.

She glanced up at him. He still had those kind eyes.

"It's a'ight. They're just a person."

"But they look like the Diabolo."

"They're not. They're someone who suffered... that Ningursu used."

Yaz stared at the monster—no, *person*—again. Looking at them now as they watched her, she still couldn't shake the image of the Diabolo. But they weren't pulsing with yellow smoke, nor did they cackle with anger and ignite fear. Rather, they were like the milder version of the Diabolo, not yet transformed into their monstrous state.

"Did Ningursu use them to make the Diabolo?" she asked Brent.

His face fell, brow furrowed. He glanced back once at the misty person. "Even if he did... it doesn't mean they're bad. We're gonna help them, like I'm gonna help you, too."

"Are they Mist Keepers?" Chander asked from Yaz's side.

Yaz glanced at her friend. He kept his hand on her shoulder.

"How do you know about Mist Keepers?" Another person, dressed in a long white robe, asked from beside Brent. There was something familiar about this person, but Yaz could not figure out what.

"I told him... because I think he has mist magic too..." Yaz mumbled.

She expected Brent or Malaika or this other person to lecture her. But Brent merely smiled.

"Thank you, Yaz," he said, then glanced at Chander. "It's good to see you again."

Chander shrugged.

Brent continued, "To answer your question, yes... they were Mist Keepers. But Ningursu, the Head Mist Keeper, didn't want them anymore. So he locked them away. I came by to visit them because... I want to help them."

Chander said nothing, his attention returning to the window where the strange Mist Keeper lingered.

Would I have ended up like them? Yaz wondered. Was Ningursu trying to turn her into a Diabolo, just like them?

"Are you okay now, Yaz?" Brent asked.

"Yeah... I'm a'ight. They just surprised me. I'm sorry that I screamed."

"It's a'ight. Don't worry." Brent rose to his feet. His knees trembled as he leaned on his cane, glancing between Malaika and the other person in the doctor's coat. "Why are you here, Yaz?"

Yaz fidgeted and shuffled her feet. "I thought you were leaving me..."

"What? No. I had an errand to run."

"An errand that could destroy your health..." muttered the doctor.

"He looks fine, sheesh!" Malaika interjected.

Brent ignored both of them, continuing to speak only to Yaz. "If I plan to leave permanently, I promise that I'll tell you. I would hate for you to think I abandoned you, a'ight?"

"A'ight..." Yaz mumbled.

Brent smiled at her, still with that same kindness. How could he be a Mist Keeper like Ningursu? He was so nice to her.

"Now c'mon. Let's get back to the tavern." Brent held out his hand to Yaz. Chander joined their side, hands deep in his pocket.

"Can we get pretzels?" Yaz asked as she took Brent's hand.

"Anything you want."

"What about chocolate cake?"

"Now, don't get carried away." But despite his response, Brent kept smiling.

"Chocolate cake for breakfast it is!"

CHAPTER FORTY-FOUR

FOREST AND WEEDS

Bria paced the foyer. The night had been quiet. She spent time with Marisol, listening to the girl talk about her new romance with Jeremy, the engineer. Bria couldn't help but share in her friend's excitement. After talking for couple hours, they studied tap-code before falling asleep in their respective beds.

Once Marisol got her coffee, Bria and she moved Yeshua and Gisela to their room early that morning, all the while waiting for Lana and the tower to arrive. After securing the prisoner, they returned to the speakeasy to prepare for the hidden Magii. Lester reported he had contacted the others in his network, and once Lana arrived, they would be ready for transfer.

Once they prepared the speakeasy, with tables pushed against the wall and the Witch Tunnels ready for their guests, Marisol retired to her room to send a tap-code message to Jeremy.

Bria gave her the privacy, instead occupying her rushing thoughts by looking over the paintings on the foyer wall. One showed two women with a gaggle of children, and the other a beautiful young lady with long dark hair perched next to a red-headed man with a scraggly beard.

Doris joined Bria's side. She spoke slowly so each word did not trip over her tongue. "That there is my sister Elodie and her wife, Marietta." She pointed to the two women standing in the group of children. "Lester is right there on the left, and the others are his siblings. Only Lester stayed here, though."

"Sounds like it was a full house," Bria replied.

"Oh, it was. But I loved it." Doris placed her hand on the other portrait. "This is my husband Ryon and me, soon after we got married."

"You two look happy."

"We were. He helped me form this tavern here. Couldn't have done it without him, really." She smiled to herself. "I miss him very much."

"I'm sorry for your loss."

"Don't apologize for something that isn't your fault."

Bria bowed her head, running her branched finger over her betrothal brand. *Once this is all done, I'll find you, Brent. I'll scour the earth until we're back together. I promise.*

Doris left Bria alone to pace. Every passing second granted with another wave of anxiety. Why wasn't Lana here yet? What if the Magii never arrived?

What if this was all a trap?

As Bria paced, she caught a glimpse of a tower as it moved across the cow pastures. Its presence was daunting, but she recognized its march and its colors. Vines drooped along its edges, and even it marched with a less menacing waltz. It moved with a call for protection rather than death and destruction.

After pulling on her gas mask, Bria stepped out of the tavern to greet it with the same determined stride.

Even if inside her core, she felt like she might break.

The tower stopped and lowered to the ground. Bria held her breath as the door opened, readying her focus around the nearby trees as a precautionary measure.

She recognized Lana at once as she stepped from the tower. Clad in a dark jumpsuit, she strode towards Bria with an air of calm and determination. On her hip, she wore a pistol.

Lana unhooked the pistol and held it out to Bria as she approached. "Take the gun."

"What?" Bria stared.

"In case you use too much magic. Take the gun."

"What? This is how you greet me? With a gun?" Bria continued, staring at the pistol. "I don't need one!"

"Please!" Lana's voice quivered. "I was thinking... and this... we don't know what will happen."

"We're just transporting people, aren't we?"

"We were until I received another message..." Lana gulped.

"What're you talking about?"

"Last night, I got a message from Hue. She received a note from someone in the Capital. Three-fourths of the Senate is dead."

Bria froze, still eyeing the gun.

"Senator Heartz was one of them."

Bria still couldn't wrap her head around it. "How has this not been in the newspaper? This is... if the people of Newbird's Arm knew, they would be up in arms!"

"They've been keeping it quiet. Hue's contact is a defector or something and has witnessed it occur." Lana licked her lip. "Hue is sending reinforcements. We may have to act soon... once we get civilians out of here. If we don't, ... the Order wins. So what I'm saying is... take the gun. We don't know what we're going to encounter over the next few days."

"I can fight without it."

"But what if you lose your gas mask? What if you overexert yourself like last time?"

"But—"

"Briannabella! Please! Don't be ridiculous!" Lana's eyes flared with tears. "You might have magic, but they have guns. They have so many weapons. Please... just take it so I don't lose you again!"

Bria slowly wrapped her fingers around the pistol, holding eye contact with Lana. The woman's eyes filled with tears, her bottom lip quivering. It was almost as if the new revelation had broken Lana. Not losing her magic; not the attack on the town; not even reuniting with Madame Gonzo. No—something else had shaken her. Was it the fact that the Order could win? Or something else? What made her shift?

Lana's voice continued to shake. "I've already lost you once. I already came to terms with that loss. Then I found you almost dead again. Don't make me do it again."

"I won't." Bria attached the pistol to her belt. "I promise."

Lana shut her eyes tight.

"What happened, Lana? You seem like something is bothering you."

"Nothing happened. I ... I want you safe. That is all."

"Lana... what is it?" Bria whispered.

"Nothing. It's nothing."

"Mom! Tell me!"

Bria paused. She hadn't realized what she had said until it exited her mouth. *Mom.* The word tasted foreign on her lips. But she said it, owned it, and now it was out in the open.

Lana stared at her. The silence weighed heavily in the air.

Then she whispered, "I do not know how much time we have left as mother and daughter. Every day, I worry that the Order might finally win. I think... I ... I want you safe. You have a life to live."

"And you have one too."

"Not like you."

Bria shook her head, "Lana... Mom... what... I..."

Before she could finish her sentence, Lana pulled Bria into a hug.

About fifty people filled the speakeasy bar beneath the tavern. Once Lana arrived, Marisol sent a tap-code message to Hue, and their contacts sent the hidden Magii to the speakeasy. Bria sat on the countertop with Lana, counting all the people as they arrived through the Witch Tunnels. All of them spoke in hushed tones. They held their bodies with pain and uncertainty, worn away by the yellow smoke.

Bria stared down at the Witch Tunnels as the last people exited. While they weren't her tunnels, they had the same sort of magic to them. Could they be her secret weapon?

"Alright then," Lana said as she counted the Magii. "We're gonna get you all out of here. We got a tower that should fit most of you. I promise you're going to be safe. Alright?"

Murmurs filled the tavern.

Bria continued to gaze over the Magii. She reached for the gun on her hip, watching them. While she and Lana hadn't spoken since their hug, there remained that fear in the air. There was no plan to attack but a constant worry that something might happen soon. If the Senate had fallen, who was to stop the Order from implementing their agenda?

How long would it be until every child with silver eyes, an inclination for stories, or with a hint of magic received a black stamp on their wrist?

How long would it be until their deaths stacked up in the Pit?

"Can I say something?" Bria asked Lana.

Lana nodded.

Speak from your heart. Bria licked her lips, then said, "I wish I could say something here... something motivating. But I'm terrified... and I'm sure you are all scared, too. And... that's okay. We're all trying to live here and learn about ourselves, but this Order has decided that we are not worth anything. Whether it is because they fear us or something else entirely, they have decided that we do not belong in Rosada." Bria wrung her hands together before continuing. "All I ever wanted was to understand *why*. Sometimes though, learning the why makes you notice all the injustices in the world. The Order... they are the least orderly group I've ever known. They're riddled by fallacies and hatred... all of which is fueling their desire to police who *exist* in their world. And I can't stand for that. I hope you can't either. So, I guess what I'm saying is..." Bria glanced at Lana, then back at the crowd. "If you want to join in this fight, and I'm not saying you should, but if you truly *want* to fight... we will happily accept it. I just... wanted to say that."

Lana placed a hand on Bria's shoulder. "What Bria is saying is that we need help. But we will never force you to help us."

"And why should we join you?" Someone called from the group. "How can we know whether to *trust* you?"

Bria and Lana exchanged a glance.

Then Bria spoke carefully, her stomach dropping further with each word, "Because... I'm Rhodana the Forest Queen, the so-called *terrorist* from Newbird's Arm, and the one who liberated Knoll."

Hushed whispers filled the crowd. For the first time, the words hung as she accepted her fate. She never wanted. She never desired the attention.

But with freshly planted seeds of vermillion, she could no longer watch the injustice. This had to end.

She glanced at Lana... her mother.

At least she didn't have to operate alone.

And together, they would fight.

Daughter and Mother.

Queens of Forests and Weeds.

CHAPTER FORTY-FIVE

NEORAMA

After returning Yaz and Chander to the tavern and sharing an odd breakfast of pretzels and chocolate cake, Brent joined Malaika for a walk through the city. Tomás protested, begging Brent to return to bed, but the last thing Brent wanted to do was sit around and do, well, nothing. His mind kept racing with potential options for the spirits in the hospital, as well as for Yaz and Chander. The mere idea of a school for the Mist Keepers danced in his mind. But where? And how? Before he did anything, he would need help from Tomás and Caroline. But would they even agree?

Malaika invaded his thoughts with her boisterous exclamation. "Well, Brenty-Boy... glad to see you didn't completely lose your mind again! Would hate to chase you around the world!"

Brent smiled slightly.

"Listen, I was waiting for you to escape the Library. Knew you would. That place has its holes in it. Al always thought he was some great architect, but it's all an illusion, lost in his pursuit for grandeur." Malaika chuckled to herself before continuing, "And I know Caroline brought you here because she heard Tom was here, but listen... I've got a safer place for you in mind."

"I'm listening."

"Got a place on the outskirts of the city. Trust me, you're gonna love it. I can hail a buggy here and everything if you're interested."

"And Ningursu can't find it?"

"He hasn't in over six-hundred years. Trust me. I'll call us a buggy. It's a bit of a hike, and you don't look good at all. Don't need you passing out on me. You're a head taller than me."

"Oh, um, a'ight."

"Let me see where a nearby one is..." Malaika waved her hand through the mist, and a map appeared before her. Brent always marveled at the way she composed her maps, and with her magic forming, he caught her story in the air. It filled him with a momentary gasp of happiness.

Not every story has a dark beginning. Brent made a mental note to recall the story later in his room. It'd be another tale for his almanac.

He turned back to her, staring at the map. His free hand traveled to the tattoo on his wrist. "Um, could you look up where—"

Malaika guffawed. "You wanna know where Bria is, don'tcha?"

"Am I that obvious?"

"Oh yes. I still remember the first time we met. Ahem," Malaika cleared her throat, "Briiiii-aaaah. Briii—"

Brent's face warmed.

"Let's look here…" Malaika rewove the map. She furrowed her brow. "Okay… she's definitely in Rosada. Yes, that's right… let's see… it's toward center… in a tavern…"

"Is she in the Capital?

"Come see for yourself."

Brent joined Malaika by the map. He hadn't looked at her maps in too much depth. Typically, they resembled any sort of navigator's aid. But this time, she had enhanced the location, where Brent saw straight into a familiar tavern.

It was there he told stories.

And there, he and Bria tore down their final walls.

In the heart of the scene, Bria stood with Lana before a handful of people. He couldn't hear them, but Bria was right there! She looked exhausted, more like a part of the forest than the last time he saw her. But she was there. Alive. Standing.

With Lana right beside her.

Tears gathered in Brent's eyes. He wanted more than anything to be there with her.

"If we go to the tunnels now…we could get to her," he mumbled.

But Malaika deterred that thought. "I already checked the tunnels. They're a complete wreck. Al wasn't going to let those stand."

Brent's shoulders fell.

"Don't worry—we'll get you back to her soon. C'mon. A buggy's just past the city hall. We'll want to get out of town before High Noon strikes, anyway."

After acquiring a buggy, Malaika paid the fare so the driver could take them to the outskirts of Mert. The whole way there, Brent didn't speak. He picked at his hand, tracing along the betrothal stamp. What was Bria up to right now? What was happening in Rosada? He tried to keep himself preoccupied, but he kept returning to Bria. He missed her smile, the way her slight overbite caused her grin to extend from cheek-to-cheek, and the way it lit up her eyes. In recent times, the smile had been less vibrant.

He would give anything to see her smile like that again.

His heart twisted, and he glanced at Malaika. Her story waved through the air just like her enthusiasm. The pieces came in choppy excitement, and he pocketed each part in the back of his mind. Later it would come together, just as Caroline's story had.

The buggy pulled to a halt where the roadway ended. Brent fumbled out of the car while Malaika tipped the driver a hefty sum. As he drove off, Malaika placed her hands in her pockets and exclaimed. "I gotta get myself one of those."

"You don't want another airship?"

"The Cheer gave me a good ride, but it isn't very discrete. A buggy would let me get to Mert and the likes without a problem..." Malaika stomped a few paces ahead. "Plus, we wouldn't have to worry about this last bit of the walk."

"How far is this place?"

"Uh..." Malaika spun her hand through the air. A map appeared of mist. She traced her fingers along what Brent could tell was supposed to be the Chessboard Plains. For a moment, the shadow of a dragon appeared on the map, then vanished. "Not far. You can handle a ten-minute walk, right?"

"Yeah, I'll be a'ight."

"Right, then c'mon then. We'll want to catch Szyman before he goes off wandering or something."

"Szyman?" As he said the name, it was like he'd spoken it before; but he had no recollection of ever meeting someone named Szyman.

"You'll meet him. Don't worry about it."

Brent followed behind Malaika as she led him across the Chessboard Plains and into a thick miasma unraveling over the black and white tulips. His head spun as each step took him further from Mert. Any other day, this would have been an easy trek—but by the time he reached the top of the hill, he had to catch his breath.

"We're almost there, c'mon. See." Malaika pointed just beneath the hill.

There, the mist broke. Like a story, in its place, a town rose from the fog. With a single road and old wooden structures, it extended out across the plains. If Brent didn't know better, he would have believed the town had always been there. But the way it pulsed with mist reminded him of the Library.

But different.

Unlike the Library, ghosts bustled in the single street, going between the buildings. People smiled, and as they conducted their business, it was as if they were still alive.

"Welcome to Neorama!" Malaika exclaimed.

"Neorama..." Brent recited to himself.

"Yeah, that's what Szyman calls it. His pride and joy and the likes, y'know." Malaika motioned him down the hill. "C'mon. He'll be waiting for us."

Brent grunted to himself as he followed Malaika down the hill. It hurt more walking down than uphill, but he kept his complaints to himself. Tomás or Varden might lecture him later about overusing his body. But for now, he would keep his head up, walking with a curiosity through the mist and towards the eerie ghost town waiting for them beneath the hill.

The town glimmered with the true beauty of the mist. Often hidden away by the smoke and yellow, Brent had forgotten the way it struck him when he first ventured with Caroline to release souls. It felt like a lifetime since he ventured to Yilk with Caroline, staring at half-giants and admiring the fire-filled glow of their funeral pyres.

It felt like an eternity since he pocketed the story of the woman who hated cats and unlocked an understanding of the world.

But Neorama brought that all back. Cohorts of ghosts occupied the single street, watching as Malaika led them towards what looked like a stone box sitting in the center of town. Yet, as they neared, Brent noticed the misty glow around its exterior.

"Ah! Malaika! There you are!" a ghost called from the side of the box.

Brent instantly recognized Dobroslawa, Malaika's first in command, from his time on her airship. She nodded in Brent's direction, her eyes like stone and scarred lips in a pout. There was something familiar about her, though, even beyond the airship.

But he couldn't pinpoint the story.

"Any news on June?" Malaika asked Dobroslawa.

"Nah. She's gone and taken that damn ship like nobody's business. There's a dragon flying around here that we might convince to go after it. Don't know where she went off to, though—"

"No big deal. It is fine. I can track June on my accord." Malaika tapped the misty air with the tips of her fingers. "Is Szyman around?"

"Yeah, he's mulling about inside."

"Thank you. We'll talk later."

Malaika motioned Brent to follow her closer to the stone box. She removed a single stone brick from the wall, and the remaining stones fell away, revealing an entrance into the cube. Brent used the wall for support as he entered a room pulsing with smoke.

He fumbled forward, squinting while reaching for something to grab hold of in the smoke.

"Ey! No touching!" a voice called.

With the voice, the smoke cleared. Brent raised his hand up from whatever he had grabbed, holding it above his head.

The smoke cleared, and they stood in a room basking in mist. Levers, gears, and cranks laced through the smoke. In the center of them all, sitting in a chair overlooking maps, sat a bearded man at least half a head taller than Brent. His black hair hung in disorderly strands down his face while a pipe sat precariously in his mouth.

He blew out a puff of smoke. "If you had pulled on that lever there, you would have sent us all the way to Kainan. I don't want to deal with that place again."

"Oh... um..." Brent furrowed his brow. The story in the room carried hundreds of years on its back. It was hard to pinpoint the true 'Szyman' amid it all.

"Szyman! Glad you didn't move the town without consulting me first," Malaika said, arms crossed as she paced the room.

"Yeah, well, I'd hate to upset you." Szyman winked at Malaika. "Besides, it only has enough energy to go back to Kainan. As I said, I don't want to go back there."

"Well, good, 'cause I'd like to introduce you here to Brent Harley."

"Ah, he's the rogue one you mentioned, isn't he?"

"That's right. Pain in Ningursu's side, really."

"Glad I'm not the only rogue player here now."

"What... what do you mean?" Brent still struggled to put the different stories together as they assaulted him from each angle.

"You could say I've been a pain in Ningursu's side for quite some time now." Szyman took a whiff of his pipe. "About six-hundred years now, I'd say, if my math is correct. I'm sure it still bothers good ol' Alojzy to this day."

"Alojzy..." Brent blinked. Parts of the man's tale whistled by him.

"Szyman here was my apprentice before Alojzy. We'll... not that I trained Al that much," Malaika said. "He decided not to pursue releasing souls or anything... but he still got that mist talent."

"Then Al killed me when he thought I was sleeping with his wife," Szyman chuckled.

"Too bad he didn't know it solidified your mist."

Szyman shrugged. There was a banter between the two that reminded Brent of his relationship with Caroline. What if more Mist Keepers were friendly rather than just colleagues? Would the dynamic be different?

"Well, listen, you two should chat. I got some things to do. I'll come back to retrieve Brenty-boy here in a bit," Malaika patted Brent's back. Her story flittered over him, bubbling with the same excitement that she carried.

"Oh, um, a'ight," Brent said.

"Behave. Both of you." Malaika left the room without looking back.

Once the door slammed shut, Szyman leaned back in his chair. "I swear, she's been here a month and think she runs this show."

Brent shuffled between each of his feet.

"I love her. She's great, but damn, she can drive me mad. Thinks 'cause she was my teacher, she knows everything." Szyman shook his head and placed his pipe down on the table. "Granted, I didn't picture you much like this at all. Malaika made it out like you were some crazed kid."

"I mean... I've had my moments."

"We all do. Isn't that part of being a Mist Keeper?"

"Well... yeah. Guess so."

Szyman smirked, then adjusted the lever. "I know I had my moments. It's why I made this town... to escape irrationality. It's hard, y'know, not belonging. But I realized... I could be an annoyance for the Council and their irrational ways. Do my part to protect people. No reason for the afterlife to be ruled by chaotic death gods."

"That's one way to describe them."

"Am I wrong?"

"Not at all." Brent glanced around the console room. "So you built the ghost town outside... so people can hide?

"Yeo. For ghosts, for others like you and me, and anyone who needs it. Not for the benefit of the Council."

"But... you said you've managed to hide from the Council?"

"Ningursu might control the mist, but it's also the greatest defense against him. He can't see something hiding in plain sight." Szyman rose from his spot and turned open the blinds on the single window in the strange room. The dusty one-road town greeted them with a kiss of mist. "Ningursu and I never met, but Malaika told me enough about him where I knew I wanted nothing to do with him... nor for him to know I existed. So I built this town from the mist and used it as my defense. With new technology over the past couple of centuries, I refined it. I used to make it disappear and reappear as a temporary home... but now it can travel with everyone else. That's what all this can do, y'see?" He tapped a lever.

"The town can... move?" Brent asked.

"Mhm. Just like a Mist Keeper can travel through the mist. This town does the same and brings everyone inside with it."

Brent scanned the room. He could see Szyman constructing this little box and testing each lever and how it controlled the mist. Different stories of different countries and scenes flew by the window. The man did not lie. The stories promised a future. *A town that can be moved... hidden from Ningursu...*

"This is amazing," Brent remarked.

"It's something. Takes a lot of energy to move. Can't go very far. Basically, from this location, I can go to Kainan or Evylain with its energy expense." Szyman tapped the gauge above the levers. "Powered by the mist, but still can only take so much."

"Have you traveled the entire world with it?"

"Honestly, I try to avoid countries with prejudice against magic. Not worth my time."

"So no Rosada?"

"Not yet."

Someday, soon maybe... The idea that he may transport to Bria soon crossed his mind. But clearly, they didn't have the power to get there.

Nor would he have the support yet.

But he still couldn't deny the safety of the town. Malaika had wanted him to visit Neorama, and it had been with reason.

It was perfect, really, for what he wanted to do. Finally, he had found fortune in the mist.

He turned back to Szyman and asked, "Do you have room for others?"

"Hm?"

"I... um... it's an idea. Really, it's just an idea... but I think it'd be a good one. I know Malaika likes it." Brent paused, trying to find the right way to describe it. "I mean, there are so many people that don't understand their magic because it is based in the mist. As well as Mist Keepers that don't have a clue of the truth because Ningursu played God. So I thought, I mean, that... I could create a school. And Neorama might be an ideal location... once I figure it out, I mean.."

Szyman raised his eyebrows. "Now that's something I find a little interesting."

The tension in Brent shoulder's fell.

Szyman continued, "Yeah, I think I got some room in an old inn down the road. Let me ask around, kay? I'll stand by anyone who wants to take down Ningursu.

CHAPTER FORTY-SIX

SANDWICHES ON THE FLOOR

The tavern was boring. Yaz didn't say it aloud, but it was boring. After seeing all the different people and exploring each unlocked room, she sat at the table, waiting for Brent to return. Anandi occupied herself with helping Mitzi, spending time in the kitchen learning how to bake. She spent more and more time with the woman, less with Yaz and Chander. Was she angry at them? She had said nothing.

When Yaz asked Chander, he merely shrugged, returning to the word puzzle in his newspaper. Yaz didn't badger him further, pressing her face to the window to watch the people of Mert race past the tavern to avoid the chaos of high noon.

Any other day, the commotion might have interested her, but her lack of sleep caught up with her. Every few minutes, she drifted into a dream, then snapped back with a sudden gasp. No, she couldn't fall asleep! She might miss something important and—

The door to the tavern opened.

And a familiar voice spoke.

"Yeah, well, this is ridiculous. If you didn't go running off after an invisible child, we would have found them and gotten out of this shite hole! Fuck this. I'm getting a drink."

Micca stormed into the tavern with Timothée close behind him. In his arms, he held Preston. The little boy stared around frantically, eyes wide and bloodshot.

Yaz almost jumped up to greet them, but Chander held her back and placed a finger to his lips. She wanted to ask why, but the two men continued their bickering, overriding her thoughts.

"Why won't you listen to my idea? We can take Zephyr flying. The kids will run after her!"

"She's enjoying the Chessboard Plains. I'm not going to force her into flight."

"Bull."

"You didn't like my ideas. We could have split up, but you clung to me like a lost puppy," Timothée argued as he followed Micca to the bar.

"I wasn't going off on my own in some creepy magical city that has a scheduled battle every freaking day. I'd be fucked in a second."

"Language," Timothée grumbled.

"You sound like Jem! *Language, language,* blah, blah, blah! Are you gonna try converting me and run off when I say no?"

"You're exaggerating again."

"Am I? Ever since Knoll fell, you've been acting weird. Why do you care about a fucking invisible child when there are real people right here? You're losing it, Tim!"

"You don't understand."

"I never do, apparently!"

Yaz glanced at Chander as the two adults continued to argue. She gripped the edge of the tablecloth. If they turned around, they would see her. Then they could stop arguing, right?

But they were too busy bickering. They didn't even notice as the door to the kitchen swung open, and Mitzi came out carrying a tray of food.

"I'm so fucking sick of this bullshite! We lost the kids. We fucked up, and they might be dead!" Micca threw his arm back. It hit straight into Mitzi's side.

She dropped the tray.

And the plates clattered to the floor.

The tavern fell silent as she glowered at Micca.

"Oh, sorry." Micca held his hands over his head. "My bad."

"That was Jewel's meal," Mitzi snarled.

"Who?"

"Jewel. My boss. She'll wring your neck."

"What!?"

"We apologize. It was a mistake," Timothée interjected. "How much is it? We'll pay."

"Paying won't make her food reappear. Her lunchtime is here right now." Mitzi's eyes flared.

The altercation froze Yaz in place. Why did Chander stop her from greeting them? That would have stopped this whole ordeal.

"What is your boss, a child?" Micca asked.

"What?"

"She can wait five minutes for a..." He picked a piece of bread off the floor. "A sandwich."

"That was a special sandwich that took time to prepare. And now it is wasted."

"Oh, c'mon. This is ridiculous."

The door behind Mitzi opened again. Anandi peaked her head out.

She cried out, "My sandwich! I worked so hard on that!"

Micca and Timothée both turned.

Chander let out a sigh. "That's why Mitzi was upset..."

"Because Anandi made it?" Yaz asked.

"Yeah…"

Tears filled Anandi's eyes. Micca and Timothée glanced around the room, pausing as they spotted both Yaz and Chander before turning back to Anandi.

Mitzi had joined the girl's side and pulled her into a comforting hug.

"Anandi! I am so sorry!" Micca exclaimed.

"Did you ruin my sandwich?" Anandi sobbed.

"Well, I—"

"Yes, he did." Mitzi stepped in front of Anandi, glaring at Micca. "And he will help you make a new one. Or I will take care of him myself."

The rest of the day involved making sandwiches. Chander and Yaz helped in the kitchen while Micca assisted Anandi in perfecting a new sandwich. All the while, Timothée disappeared into one of the rooms upstairs with Preston. Part of Yaz wanted to grumble about the chores, but each time she opened her mouth, Chander threw a glare in her direction.

No one really spoke.

There was no grand reunion.

Yaz still wondered when Brent might return. At least he would tell her the truth.

Mitzi continued moving in and out of the kitchen, racing to tend to patrons. It reminded Yaz of being in the Curio Tower. Always working. No play.

Anandi thrived with the tasks, but Yaz grew impatient. While she was bored in the tavern, sitting around doing nothing, she also hated this minuscule task of preparing tomatoes.

Mitzi peaked her head into the kitchen, "Micca! Can I get a black coffee? Make it stat. My old squeeze is here, and he wants one. Bring it out to table four once you're done."

"I thought I was only helping with a sandwich?" Micca huffed as he removed a mug from the cabinet.

"You're doing a great job here, though. Might have a job for you in the future if you keep up with it."

"I don't want to work in some gangster tavern."

"Eh, well, there's always a pinstripe suit for those who want it. Just get that coffee. Don't want him getting impatient." Mitzi slammed the door to the kitchen.

Micca cursed under his breath, then brewed the coffee. Outside the kitchen, Mitzi giggled loudly, talking with her old lover as if she had never lost him. Yaz tried to listen, but the door provided too much of a barrier.

"Yaz, focus…" Chander hissed beside her.

"Why do I have to do this?" Yaz asked him. "I didn't drop the sandwich."

"Because we're helping Anandi."

Yaz huffed.

As she continued organizing the produce, Micca sulked out of the kitchen with the cup of coffee.

As soon as the door closed, Micca exclaimed outside, "Well, well, well... Look who came crawling back to little ole me!"

"Micca!" a familiar voice replied.

Brent! Yaz dropped her knife and ran over to the door. She peaked her head out, catching a glimpse of Brent sitting at the bar.

Micca climbed onto the neighboring stool and smacked a hand on Brent's back. "Why do I keep running into you in unlikely places, hm?"

Brent winced as Micca's hand fell on his back.

"Sorry," Micca scooted back, "shouldn't have done that. You like shite."

"Sorry. You look like shite, though." Micca said.

"Yeah, I always look like shite."

"Nah, but even worse. You need to shave. You can't grow a beard... it looks like brown patches of grass."

"I mean, you're not much better."

"At least I'm attractive." Micca laughed. "Does that coffee got liquor in it? I need a drink."

"Mine doesn't..." Brent glanced at the cup again.

"No drinking! You need to get back to work!" Mitzi called from across the room. Yaz temporarily shut the door, only to peer out again a few moments later.

"Dammit..." Micca glowered in Mitzi's direction, then turned back to Brent. "Need a drink. Today's been a rough one."

"Cause you're working?" Brent asked.

"Nah, 'cause I got in trouble. Tim's not happy with me. Granted, he's never happy with me lately. We haven't been solid since that ghost child got involved—"

"Ghost child?"

"Yeah. Tim calls him Preston. I can't see him, so Timothée is always stressed about it, and frankly, I don't get it. Then we gotta take care of Yaz, Chander, and Anandi, and I don't know shite about kids. We keep fighting and everything."

Brent raised his head, glancing around the bar. He locked eyes with Yaz for a moment, gave a half smile, then turned back to his friend. "Wait... if you're watching Preston... what happened to Lex?"

Micca's eyes fell. "She didn't make it. Her magic was too much for her frail body and... yeah."

Brent's shoulders visibly fell.

Micca continued, "Beebelle is okay, though, despite how she turned into a forest and everything."

"I knew she was okay... but I didn't know about her being a forest."

"Yeah, yeah, that was something special. I gotta tell you—"

Yaz watched as Mitzi approached Micca. She took a clump of his hair and yanked him off the stool. "Back to work!"

"Dammit, woman!"

"Now!"

Yaz used Mitzi's lecture over Micca to sneak from the kitchen and behind the bar. As the two venture back, she peaked around at Brent.

He smiled.

"Hi..." she whispered.

"You like sneaking around, don't you?" he asked.

"Yeah."

"Eh, I do too." Brent leaned back in his seat.

"I like to know things."

"Did you ever go to school? To learn things?"

Yaz shook her head. "Ms. Kai and Mr. Nasr always taught me."

"So you never learned different stories, huh?

"No."

Brent lowered his voice. "Then you're missing out. Stories are my favorite."

"Because you're a storyteller, right?"

"Exactly."

Yaz leaned forward, keeping her own voice low. She never asked Ms. Kai or Mr. Nasr this question; Brent, on the other hand, she could: "Can you tell me a story?"

The smile on Brent's face reminded her of a little kid. He opened his palm, and on his fingertips, images that looked like fairies appeared, flittering in the air.

"Of course I can tell you a story. But bear with me... it's been a little while since I told one."

A SILLY LITTLE IDEA

Brent told stories late into the night. It felt liberating. For the first time in months, he could be himself. He had to admit that he was a little out of practice. The stories rambled a bit more, and some came to an awkward conclusion. But he told stories, and around him, everyone in the tavern gathered. Yaz listened with intent, and as he told each tale, with the mist conjuring around him, more and more people joined. Soon, Chander and his sister came out from the kitchen. Micca joined a few minutes later. Even the different members of the pinstripe gang listened in awe.

About an hour into his storytelling, Timothée ventured into the tavern with the ghost child on his hip and took a seat. The child perked up at the story, but he remained distant. His heart still weighed heavily for Lex.

She hadn't crossed his mind much, but hearing of her death left a vacancy in his chest. When he last saw her, she was racing from the tower with Preston on her hip. He had followed after her until getting derailed by the Council.

Now, he could only assume she had never found her other son, Garrett.

It surprised him even more when Caroline walked down the stairs with Tomás and Varden. They took seats in the back, watching Brent with interest. Exhaustion marked Caroline's face, but she had recovered from her ordeal with Julietta at least.

Brent continued his tales before settling into a booth to chat with Micca after saying goodnight to the children as they went upstairs with Timothée. His side hurt as he settled into the seat, but he ignored it, focusing only on Micca's rambling.

With the floor his to rule, Micca launched into a tale, covering everything that had happened since Brent left. It'd be easy enough to look at the story, but Micca was a storyteller in his own right. He detailed Bria's time as a forest, turning the bonelike Necrowood into a flourishing haven. How Bria returned in full force, ready to tackle everything, made Brent's heart flutter. He knew, without a doubt, she thrived. Whatever she was up to in the Capital, he had no doubt she would succeed.

From there, Micca detailed the trip over to Mert from Rosada with the children on the back of Zephyr. The dragon now loitered outside the city, waiting for the next adventure.

"But I don't know what's happening with Tim and me. Won't stop arguing. The kids stress him out. Like yeah, I was all down for this too... but I miss what we used to have."

"Guess things change?"

"Guess so..." Micca leaned back in his seat.

"Well," Brent continued, "Now that I'm here, I can watch the kids. I think I'll be able to help them."

"You got enough on your hands, mate. I ain't gonna make you a babysitter."

"No, it's a'ight. Really..." Brent held back on telling Micca about his school. It was just a silly little idea. He still needed to talk with the others about it.

And he needed time.

So much time.

"A'ight, man. Well, I'm gonna go get a nice tall glass of something strong before heading to bed. You want anything?" Micca asked as he climbed to his feet.

"Nah, I'm good. Go enjoy. I gotta take care of something."

"A'ight, man. Your loss."

Brent waved as Micca turned towards the bar. A drink would be great right now, but he decided against it. What would alcohol do for him now? He had only just gotten his head back on his shoulders. The last thing he needed was a reason for the Diabolo to strike.

Wincing, he climbed to his feet and limped towards the back of the room where Caroline sat with Tomás and Varden. While the two men talked in a hushed tone, Caroline dug her fingernail into the table with a downcast gaze.

"You doing a'ight?" Brent asked her.

She didn't look up from her spot.

Brent took a seat next to her. They sat without speaking, taking in the somber reality. Through Caroline's story and his own experience, he'd seen her closeness with Julietta. How would he respond if Bria had forgotten him?

"Tomás spoke with me," Caroline whispered.

"Are you okay?"

"My stomach hurts, and my heart is broken, but I am standing as I must." Caroline's bottom lip quivered.

"If you ever, um, wanna talk, we can talk. I mean... I've seen... she meant a lot to you... and learning what Tomás has done is... hard." Brent clutched his cane. "It's okay to be sad and scared and... yeah. It's okay."

"I just... wonder who she was before all of this... and if she would have still loved me."

"She loved you as Julietta. And Julietta is still part of her identity... now and forever. That's all that matters."

Caroline said nothing, her attention drifting to the window. Tears stung the corner of her eyes, but Brent didn't pressure her to talk further. *Julietta... or Julyana... or whatever her name is... was a victim of Ningursu's ploy. Just like all of those from the crypt. Just like Yaz. Just like me. That's why this is so important now.*

"What if we stopped this from happening again?" Brent asked.

Caroline raised her eyebrows. Out of the corner of his eyes, Brent also saw Tomás perked up in his seat. He hadn't spoken to the man since he found out about Julietta. While he had expected Tomás or Varden to corner him upon arriving back at the tavern, when Mitzi saw him enter, it gave him a reprieve. The woman fawned over him upon arrival, clinging to the idea of her late Reggie. Brent had few recollections of his time with the Pinstripe Gang. He had become friends with two members, Freddie and Billie. They gave him his dog, Nix. But other than that, except for the whiffs in the tavern, he didn't remember a thing.

Brent returned to his idea. "What if we reform the Council in a new image? One that focuses on supporting all Mist Keepers." Brent licked his lip, "Chander and Yaz are proof that more than one apprentice exists at a time. There are probably hundreds of Mist Keepers around the world. Imagine... if we could protect these people and educate them."

"You want to change everything Ningursu built?"

"What he built was wrong."

Caroline shook her head. "Consarn it, Brent. That is crazy. We cannot reform what has existed for thousands of years."

"I have to agree with Caroline. Ningursu created this structure thousands of years ago... it would be a foolish errand to deconstruct it," Tomás added.

"The Council has already fallen. If we defeat Ningursu—"

"That is ridiculous," Caroline interrupted.

Brent ignored her. "If we defeat Ningursu, the Council no longer exists. We have a chance to make a better future. Not just for us, but for the entire world."

"Brent, you are speaking with too much optimism. You have only been a part of this for a couple of years."

Varden spoke, "Let him finish. Sometimes you Mist Keepers get stuck in your ways. That's the problem with being dead... you don't grow. But he's new blood. He might be right."

Caroline huffed.

Brent glanced between Caroline, Tomás, and Varden. He chose his next words with care. "This morning, when I was visiting Kek and the spirits, I came up with an idea. Malaika heard the idea as well, and she loves it. What if... what we... I mean... these people with an inclination to the mist, like Yaz, Chander, and the spirits, don't have any guidance. There are clearly tons of people in the world with this type of magic. So why not use it to make everything better? I mean—we would be able to release more souls and help maintain peace. Isn't that what a Mist Keeper is?" He licked his lip, waiting for a response.

No one said a word.

"Shite. I might not be making sense. What I'm saying is... if there are more people with the potential of becoming Mist Keepers, why not create a way where people who have this inclination can search for answers? And if they choose to help the Mist Keepers, to release souls, and to enter the mist... it is their *choice*? We could create a school, or an academy, or something where people could learn. There's no reason to hide when magic prevails. We're part of this world... and... I mean... yeah, I want to create a school of mist. It's a silly idea... and I might be overzealous. But yeah. A school. That's what I want to do."

Still, no one responded. Was the idea ridiculous? Kek seemed to think so.

Brent followed up, "Malaika showed me the ghost town she's spending time in... and they have an empty old house that we can use. Ningursu can't track it. All the spirits, the kids... they'd be safe. We can just try with who we have first because... I mean... I'm still learning, too."

Still no response. Blood rushed to his face. Perhaps it was just him being overzealous. He only just came up with the idea.

But if he knew anything about storytelling, sometimes the best ideas arrived like a comet. First, a twinkle, followed by a momentary explosion of light.

"I think it is worth investigating further," Tomás said at last. "We need to reform... and we cannot deny the spirits their chance to recover."

Varden added, "I can talk to Kek about the state of the spirits. We'll have to prepare their care... especially if we plan to go to Neorama with them."

"Neorama?" Caroline asked.

"We'll tell you more later."

Caroline flared her nostrils. "I do not know if I like this. We cannot change everything in a day!"

"And we won't. It'll take time," Tomás said. "It will take time... but, as Brent mentioned, we already have children with mist inclination. They deserve answers like any others."

Caroline fidgeted. Brent saw her hesitancy. She always tried to follow Ningursu's rules. Stepping out of that rationale to help Brent escape had been one of her biggest acts of rebellion. Now Brent wanted to change everything to which she had grown accustomed. It was hard to change the habits of a three-hundred-year-old woman.

Brent turned to her and said, "We may even help Julietta if we get this school up and running. I don't know how, but... I think it'll benefit more than just the kids, you know?"

Caroline nodded, her attention falling back on the table. "I suppose we'll see."

And the conversation ended. Brent felt the pressure of the idea leave his body. Caroline might have been reluctant, but she accepted the idea: they would build a school. If it came together, as Brent hoped, it would be a place for the story of the Council to live, to stop history from repeating itself.

That was his job as a storyteller.

He collected the stories even now in the tavern of Tomás and Varden, as well as additional pieces to Caroline's tale. They filled him like breaths of air, and he stored them like a journal in his mind.

As the story collector, he would teach these stories.

The Order might have wanted stories to remain hidden, so they controlled the agenda. Ningursu may have wanted to dictate the story of the mist and lie about its past.

But humanity always told stories. The tales lived everywhere: in the buildings, in pathways, in nature, and in the way people walked.

Stories inhabited every person's soul.

And those stories would change the world.

CHAPTER FORTY-EIGHT

FIGHT, CONTROL, ORDER

Christof stayed in the shadows, watching as Magii filled the tavern. He could tell they were Magii by the way they carried themselves, even though they didn't announce themselves. They constantly looked over their shoulders, hid their wrists, and kept their eyes downcast. Demons rode on their back, and the Magii knew it too. They could not escape their reality.

He had tried to talk to Gisela and Yeshua earlier that day, but whenever he went to their room or the basement, Lester or Doris cornered him. While he easily surpassed them in strength, the last thing he wanted was for Bria to suspect him.

Wait. No one expects a thing. Just wait.

As far as he was concerned, the tavern owners thought he was a defector of the guard. Perhaps he was—but he still held some sort of loyalty. Sure, he planned to help the child. But that was it; he still stood for the Effluvium.

No one expected a thing.

Although he really had no clue what occurred in the tavern. His imagination circled with ideas: were they planning an ambush on the Capital? Would it be a repeat of Knoll? What would happen to Sister Jey Ma? Or Senator Cordova?

Or that boy who Elder An Drew held hostage?

He camped in the second-floor lavatory, one of the few rooms without sound insulation. From there, he heard everything: people climbing up the stairs, the barkeep humming a tune in the kitchen below, and the conversations in the hallway.

Bria couldn't hide from him forever.

Now that she was here, his path to helping that child in the Capital was obvious. She held more value than anyone; if Christof gave her to the Order, then why wouldn't they let some poor child go?

Someone knocked on the bathroom door.

"Oi! Taken!" he called.

"Haven't you been in there for an hour?" someone said from the other side.

"There's two bathrooms on this floor!"

The person huffed and left Christof alone.

It'd been longer than an hour, to be honest. Already, the sun had set, dusk whistling across the farmland. In the distance, a single tower marched.

I should leave. Forget all of this. The idea struck him a few times. It was a thought he had as a child after his mother died. Why stay when no one cared? He had even told Sister Jey Ma where he was—and she didn't even come running towards him.

He remembered wanting to disappear when he saw Brent and Bria together for the first time. She had never touched his arm or smiled at him like the way she did with Brent Harley. His late friend Chet Lawry had laughed when Christof told him. *You can't even compete with a fucking vag!* Despite his embarrassment, he stayed in Newbird's Arm.

And he stayed here now.

Loyal. Obedient.

Always in Order.

He pressed his head against the far wall and huffed once. Where was she? Had she left? Did he miss his chance?

"Go rest. Now," a voice called from up the stairwell. It was clearly a mother commanding her child.

"I am. Don't worry."

Christof rose.

Finally.

He approached the door.

A knock sounded against it.

Perfect.

"Anyone in there?" *she* asked.

He opened the door.

Her eyes widened.

Before she screamed or acted, he grabbed her by the collar of her shirt and slammed her face first against the porcelain rim of the toilet.

It took one hit, and she collapsed. Blood oozed from the wound.

And her body crumpled at his feet.

"Not so strong now, huh?" He knelt beside her and stroked a strand of hair behind her ear. Despite everything, why was she still so pretty? Why did he still want to drag her into his bedroom and show her the true prowess of man? He ran his hand down the side of her unconscious body. It would be so easy.

Then he stopped. On her belt rested a small pistol. He removed it and placed it on his own belt.

He brought his hand back to her cheek, then ran his finger over her lips.

She was still a Magii. Still a terrorist. Still a symbol for everything he hated.

He couldn't.

He wouldn't.

Not now.

He lifted her body over his shoulder, then approached the window over the bathtub. The drop from the second story was short. First, he dropped Bria's body into the bush beneath the tavern. Then, without looking back, he jumped down behind her and into the night.

Christof snuck back into the city, taking to the side roads and using the buildings as his hiding spots. The yellow smoke continued to sift through the air. It wasn't as strong as it had been after Sister Jey Ma's song, but it still lingered. All Magii who had fallen to it no longer lay in the streets. A peace had fallen over the city.

Yet Christof's anxiety remained heightened as he ducked behind another building. Every now and again, he turned around, swearing someone had followed him. Only the empty road greeted him. All while guards patrolled the roads. Sure, he could approach them, ask for their help, and get transport... but why? This was his victory dance. Even the most honorable man would take a chance when heroism was on the line.

Bria stirred over his shoulder and coughed.

"Don't you dare say a word or I'll snap your neck," he hissed.

She squirmed once, then fell limp.

"So much for the ever-so-powerful Forest Queen, huh?"

She still didn't respond.

Christof chuckled and hurried along the path. Night had fallen with a vengeance, with only the glow of the gas lamps providing light.

The main plaza approached from the west, with the glistening gallery and prestigious temple acting as a beacon. He was so close now. After all this, they celebrate him in the plaza? Would women gather around while he conducted his victory lap?

Him. Christof Carver—the one who stopped the Forest Queen.

Surely they would promote him now! Maybe even make him a captain!

He snuck out of the alleyway and along the capitol building. Guards stood watch at the stairwell.

Swallowing his own pride, he stepped towards the guards. There was something strange about them. With gas masks covering their faces, he didn't recognize them.

They raised their pistols.

"Oi! I'm one of you! Got something for the Senator!" he called.

"Oh, we know," another guard stepped out of the shadows behind him. Short, with a low, feminine voice, there was something familiar about this guard. Had he served with them in the towers? Or somewhere else?

"Great, then let me go—"

"I don't think so." The guard stepped forward. As she moved closer, grass sprouted from the ground and reached for his feet.

He glanced back at Bria on his shoulder. She didn't move.

The grass continued to grow.

"What—"

The stones beneath his feet crumbled.

His body lurched.

Before Christof knew what had happened, he hit the ground.

And Bria toppled a few paces from him.

Around her, the grass continued to flourish. How was her magic working? The yellow smoke should have stopped it here, right?

Then she raised her head.

Just like the others surrounding them, she wore a gas mask.

"You're rather thick, aren't you?" the supposed guard said behind him.

Christof dug his fingers into the ground. Around him, more grass, vines, and roots gathered.

"I followed you the whole way here. Even handed Bria a mask. So much for your little crusade, huh?"

It reminded him of his father taunting him. *What type of useless guard are you? Can't even save the day. Pathetic...*

Pathetic...

Pathetic.

How many times had his father said those words to him?

Now, a nameless guard spoke to him. She wasn't even brave enough to show her face.

But she spoke with a twinge of mockery, belittling him, calling him thick.

With each word, the magic around him continued to flourish. The roots, stones, and grasses climbed up his body, tying him to the ground.

Bria would not win this battle.

Why don't you fight? His father said to him once as a child. The older kids had picked on him, calling him a "mama's boy" after he greeted his mother with a hug in the market square. When he told his father, a laugh responded.

Fight, you damn pathetic boy. You won't ever get anyone to fight your battles.

Act.

Fight.

Control.

Order.

Christof slowly climbed to his feet, fighting the rushing vines and roots. It felt as if time had frozen.

He never really fought, did he? When his father kept him as a cadet, why didn't he fight? He gave in, like every time.

Sure, he fought Brent when he discovered the vagrant kissing Bria, but there was no control over the situation.

He did not maintain order.

Did the Effluvium judge him for it? Did it waver because of his indifference?

He could have kept everything in control. He could have killed Bria in the bathroom hours earlier. Why didn't he? Why did he need to bring her to this plaza alive?

He wouldn't make that mistake again.

No thinking. Just act.

With a single movement, he leapt from his spot and reached for the gun in his holster.

His finger found the trigger.

His eyes found the target.

Bang.

Bang.

Two shots. Nothing more, nothing less.

Bria screamed.

A body fell.

Christof dropped the gun, fleeing the scene before anyone could stop him.

CHAPTER FORTY-NINE

THE TAINTED SOUL

The gunshot filled the silence of the plaza.

It echoed.

Roared.

And everything froze.

Bria stared through her gas mask at Christof. He held a silver pistol in his hands. Smoke bubbled from its barrel.

As soon as the smoke cleared, he darted towards the Capitol.

Bria glanced behind her, following the trail of smoke.

Then screamed.

"Lana!"

Her mother rocked in place, still wearing her gas mask, with blood gushing from her chest. She stumbled, rocking to the side.

Then hit the ground with a thud.

"Lana! No! Lana!" She raced to her mother's side, not bothering to monitor Christof.

She didn't recall how she ended up being lugged across the city by Christof. One minute, she was knocking on the bathroom door. The next, she woke with an excruciating headache, only to see Lana sneaking a few paces behind Christof. Her magic dwindled as the yellow smoke battered her body.

But Lana had acted with speed. She raced behind Christof and, with the dexterity of a mouse, handed Bria the gas mask.

She vanished again, only to reemerge as they entered the plaza where a few Magii they recruited had neutralized guards. There, they waited with the same gas masks and faux guard uniforms.

Now, Lana lay on the ground, blood pooling from a wound in her chest.

"No... Lana... come on. Please. It's... it's just a wound. Please... please wake up..." she reached for Lana's gas mask and yanked it off her face.

The woman's eyes did not blink. No breath exited her lips.

And beneath Bria's fingertips, the last few moments of pulse flittered to a halt.

"No... no... Lana? Please... Lana... you have to... Lana!" She tried to find any piece of life. A heartbeat, a breath, anything she might heal. "You're not allowed to... you're... Lana?" Her fingers trembled as she touched the woman's face. "Mom? Please... Mom?"

She pressed her forehead against her mother's head. Bria didn't try stopping the tears, letting them flow down her cheeks. Around her, the clouds thickened with her tears.

"You can't do this to me... you can't..." She had finally come to terms with parts of her family history. Why did the world decide it would take it from her now? This wasn't right. It wasn't fair.

"Please..." she whispered one last time. "Mom. Please."

And then came the silence of Death.

It hung in the air with the storm clouds. Death had its way of playing a tune. But now, Bria didn't even have the solace that the Mist Keepers would come to save her mother from Hell. For all she knew, Brent remained imprisoned in the Library.

The tunnels remained locked.

Everything she knew, every constant in her life, no longer remained.

"Bria..." Marisol joined her side. "We should go."

"No..." Bria shook her head.

"We should go back... no reason to garner any more attention."

"No!" Bria climbed to her feet, tears still falling down her cheeks as she stared out across the plaza. *No.* She wouldn't leave now; she had gone to save Lana once. This time, she would avenge her death.

And not just Lana, but the life lost years earlier. If the Order hadn't scared Lana, Bria might have had a childhood with her mother by her side. She might never have to deal with any of this—she may have just existed.

But now, it was obvious: she was Rhodana the Forest Queen.

The queen of the forest who lived in every prophecy.

The one who loved to laugh and hated to scream.

Who promised a reverie.

Only to be placed on a pedestal, only to wither in pain.

And alone, fighting for the world she believed in.

That Rhodana.

She snatched the silver pistol from the ground.

"Bria!" Marisol cried out.

"Don't follow me! Get everyone out of here!" Bria shouted at her.

"You need to get out of here too!"

Bria eyed the Capitol. "No. I don't."

"Then let me come with you!"

"Marisol, I have to do this on my own."

"I won't let you."

"You don't have a choice."

Bria raised her hand. Around her, the plaza beat; not just with the distant hum of trees, or the chaotic whir of the wind, but with the soft begging of stone. Between her and Marisol, the ground split, a physical crack forming between her and her friend.

"Bria!" Marisol shouted again.

"I'm sorry. Please…get everyone out of here. I'll see you soon." Bria took another step away. From the crack, she summoned rows of hibernating trees from the dirt, their seeds brought to life by her single breath of will. Across the plaza, they formed a wall, twisting and turning, thickening with every step.

If Marisol called out to her again, she didn't hear.

Bria darted through the plaza, calling forth more of her defenses. With every step, more stones overturned, and the storm continued to bellow. The trees became her protectors. She was their queen, and they were her loyal guards. Without her talents, it would take anyone time to slip through the cracks. *Let the Order know I'm here. I'm done hiding in these shadows.*

With a forest lacing through the plaza behind her like a maze, Bria raced up the stairs to the entrance of the Capitol. She didn't even bother pausing at the doors.

With a single wave of her hand, the wooden doors splintered.

Use your magic with your emotions. Let it run wild.

This is what you do.

All the elements can interact.

The empty entrance hall to the Capitol greeted her. No guards waited for her. Just like when she used to rule the tunnels, she called forth the vines and trees, using them as her protectors as she crept into the shadows and moved along the walls. They would be her guide and tell her if Christof, or anyone for that matter, loitered.

If they attacked, she could destroy this building with a wave of her fingers.

But if they had any civilians, any prisoners, the last thing she wanted to do was cause undue harm.

She hurried along the corridor. Christof had to return to the Capitol! Where else would he go? Throughout her life, he had tormented her, stalked her, assaulted her, forced her into a betrothal, and now... he killed her mother.

It was too much. It had to end.

She started up the stairwell to the next level of the building. As she reached the top of the stairs, she pressed her body against the wall.

A shadow flickered at the far end of the hallway.

Bria snuck along the hall. Each step moved slowly, light like a feather as she walked. Her heartbeat thudded. It threatened her with every movement.

And with each step, doubt crept into her thoughts. Was this worth it?

Lana is dead. She would have done the same.

So she took another step. Another breath.

And rounded a corner, readying her magic.

Only to pause.

Around the corner, in a long blue robe, her red hair woven in a complex bun, stood Jemma Reds.

"Who's there?" she exclaimed in a whisper.

Bria lifted her gas mask as she stepped towards her. "Jemma?"

"Bria!?"

"Yeah... it's good to see you, Jemma."

"That's Sister Jey Ma now. But yes, I am so happy to see you." Jemma glanced around nervously. "Are you here to take down the Order?"

"What? I—"

"I'm trying to escape. They've been holding me hostage here. Can you help me?"

"I... um..." Bria hadn't seen Jemma since she helped Brent escape in Newbird's Arm. She was on their side. Things had changed. Could she trust Jemma now? Micca had told her of his voyage across Rosada with Jemma.

Part of that story made Bria believe Jemma, but on the other hand... didn't she vanish in Aeterno? Didn't she abandon Micca?

"I joined their ranks a while ago, but since then have discovered terrible things about how they torture people and use magic and... oh, I hate it! I've been trying to stop them... but they caught wind. They haven't let me leave the Capitol building since we arrived! Please, I wouldn't lie to you." She held out her hand. "Come on, I've found a secret exit!"

"Jemma, wait!" Bria exclaimed, "Please. I... I have to get things done here first. I'm trying to... I—" What was she trying to do? She ran in here, blinded by rage over Christof. But now what? Did she really have the heart to kill Christof? Or Senator Cordova? Or the rest of the Order?

That was not in her blood.

Was this all a mistake? She let her emotions take hold, and now she stood here, questioning her own decisions. *What am I thinking?*

Bria gulped. "I'll stand guard while you lead the way. I don't want anyone hurt."

"Thank you so much! It has been quite a predicament, and... thank you, Bria! I've been following the reports on you, and I just *knew* you'd come to rescue me. There was no way you would let the Order get away with what they are doing."

Bria kept a few paces behind Jemma as she led the way. Something still didn't feel right; could she trust Jemma? She didn't want to leave Jemma a prisoner, of course, but what if it was all a ruse? The suspicion was like a distant hum tugged at her, warning her of impending doom.

All while pulling at the cords of her magic.

If Brent was here, he would know.

Jemma opened the door to a dusty office. Bria continued a few steps behind, checking the walls and shelves while holding her gas mask close to her chest. The yellow smoke did not loiter in the building, and her magic continued to pulse.

"Just right here..." Jemma removed a book from the shelf. The shelving swung open, revealing a stone stairwell diving deep into a dimly lit corridor.

Without elaborating, Jemma led Bria down the stairwell and into the dark, musty hallway. Everything remained quiet.

But no one waited.

No one looked.

And Jemma walked with pride in her step.

Jemma stopped halfway down the hallway and placed a hand on Bria's shoulder.

"It's good to see you again, Bria. You've made quite the name for yourself." Jemma said as they walked. "Your name is always in the papers. Between Newbird's Arm, Knoll... and everything."

"Do you believe it?" Bria asked.

"I was there."

"You were there? You mean in Newbird's Arm."

"In Knoll."

"You were in... Knoll..." Bria stopped, pulling back from Jemma, eyes wide. "What were you—"

"I told you... I was trying to get into their ranks—"

"You're lying." Bria took another step back. There was a strange glimmer in Jemma's eyes. She didn't trust it; it reminded her of Ningursu.

"I do not deceive. That goes against the Effluvium."

"No... you are... I... I need to—"

Before Bria moved, Jemma exhaled, and a stream of yellow smoke emerged from her mouth.

Bria froze. For a moment, her world tightened with the yellow smoke, her lifeforce placed in a chokehold. She struggled to access her magic and choked on her breath. Vines wrapped around her heart, and if she didn't fight against it, she worried she might collapse.

"I do not deceive," Jemma recited as she knelt beside Bria. But it wasn't the Jemma that Bria had known in

Newbird's Arm; she spoke with determination, ambition, and guile, not benevolence, introspection, and hesitancy.

"Jemma... please..." Bria gasped.

"Then come with me. I only want what's best for you."

Bria nodded, and the vines around her heart loosened. A few twigs fell from her branched hand as she rose, like a single breath that escaped. But there remained a cage around her magic, and every second Bria tried to fight it, spots filled her vision and threatened her consciousness.

Jemma climbed to her feet as well, adjusting her robe as she rose. Then, she continued down the hallway, her shoulders back and marching with poise. Bria's mind raced; what was happening? Was this actually Jemma?

What was she going to do?

What could she do?

She thought of running, but the strange magic kept her in place. Immediately, she went for the gun she had latched onto her belt. For once, she was glad that Lana had given it to her.

As much as the item made her stomach churn.

But upon placing her hand on her belt, she found the holster empty.

Her fingers twitched, and sweat trickled over her brow. What now? Where was Jemma leading her?

Nausea wrapped around her as Jemma knocked on a door at the end of the hallway. There was nothing remarkable about it, much to Bria's surprise, just a simple wooden door. No mist; no engravings. Just wood. Yet Bria yearned that her magic no longer ached. Anything to escape...

As the door opened, another wave of mist washed over her. When it finally parted, no more than a gasp of vapor, Bria stood on a platform overlooking the Senate Chambers.

There, sitting in their chairs around a long table, sat all eleven senators. At the head, Senator Cordova looked over his subordinates.

But, as Bria stayed a few paces behind Jemma, she realized something was not right. Her eyes landed on Senator Heartz.

Well, the corpse of Senator Heartz.

She did not breathe with life, nor did she even react to any movements. Her eyes stared forward, lifeless.

Only a couple Senators breathed, engaged in conversation around a pile of documents. If Bria hadn't known of Senator Heartz's death, she might have thought that it was a normal Senate meeting.

But death reigned.

Its silence deafening.

"Ah, Sister Jey Ma!" Senator Cordova rose from the table. "What brings you to me at this hour?"

Bria squirmed against the magic wrapping around her again.

"I have something for you, Senator."

Before Senator Cordova said another word, Jemma removed a pistol from her robe. It happened in a blink. One moment, all was quiet. The next came the gunshot.

And after that, Senator Cordova's body fell to the floor, bleeding out from the center of his forehead.

She shot a few more times, hitting the other senators and sending them into pools of deep red blood.

Bria reached for her own gun, only to find it missing from her holster. *Shit.*

The yellow smoke still prevented her magic from sparking, despite the obvious truth: Jemma had killed the Senators, all the Senators, in cold blood. She hadn't even flinched. And now, standing before their bleeding bodies, covered in droplets of vermillion, she did not flinch. Darkness rested in her eyes, deep-rooted with the acceptance of her judgment.

As she turned to face Bria, any semblance of the girl Bria knew growing up vanished.

"Now they will no longer serve as an obstacle for the Effluvium." Jemma put the gun back in her robe and turned to Bria. "But now... what about you, Briannabella?"

"What about me?" Bria's fingers flinched again.

"You were here at the time of the Senator's death. Who would believe that I, an innocent Sister, killed him? Surely, they would see you as the killer..." Jemma approached her, cocking her head to the side. "You... the terrorist of Newbird's Arm... wanted across Rosada..."

Bria stepped back, trying to find any drop of magic in the air. The yellow smoke did not disappear. Any more, and she worried her entire body might collapse.

"So you have a choice. Join me. Be my partner in this. Your magic will help the Effluvium thrive again."

"I don't trust you."

"Think about it, Bria!" Jemma spoke now, her tone once again sounding more familiar. "I have the ear of the Order, and you have magic that might bring life to the world again! Side-by-side, we'd be like... two queens. Just like the Sisters Rose and Ada who founded this nation. We'd banish all darker forms of magic, bring back life... and let the Effluvium thrive."

"The Order has destroyed my life!" Bria shouted.

"Oh, don't be ridiculous, Briannabella." This time, Jemma's voice boomed as if someone else used her as a mouthpiece.

Bria stared. "Why do you keep calling me Briannabella?"

"I am part of the Effluvium's Soul now. It speaks through me—"

"The Effluvium's Soul... Ningursu!" Bria stumbled back and instantly tried to sprint away from Jemma. It had to be him. But... since when did Ningursu control nonmagical humans?

Or was it the same as how he had tried to control her?

Before Bria managed to escape, the yellow smoke returned, knocking her off her feet with a single gust. Jemma approached her with the smoke dripping from her mouth, eyes dark, gaze determined. Spots filled Bria's vision. The smoke didn't only sever her magic but her life. Why wouldn't they just kill her? Why couldn't they let her sleep?

It might be better that way.

"Bria, please, if you cooperate... you will not be harmed." Jemma pleaded with her.

"No..." Bria hissed. She watched the lights flicker behind Jemma. She counted them to herself. There were only three. Even if her vision blurred, she had to remember there were only three lights.

"Think about everything that we could do—all this violence would end!"

All the violence would end... Bria gulped. It was tempting. But what would that look like? She couldn't see the future. She couldn't even imagine one. Would the violence end without Magii? Would the violence end because her magic fell to the Order? Or to Ningursu?

Was there even a line between the two anymore?

Gisela and Yeshua had mentioned an unclear prophecy; if Yaz didn't return to them, then the line between the Order and Council would fade.

That world was not one of peace.

It might not have been violent, but it wasn't peace.

Rather... it would be Hell. Ordered, linear, and controlled.

But Hell, nonetheless.

She tried to focus on the yellow smoke. What elements did it hold?

As she scoured the area, she found nothing. There was no hydrogen or oxygen to detect; it was something else, something far more sinister and outside of her realm.

It was a product of death.

She couldn't fight it.

But she refused to give in to the lights.

"Jemma... please... I thought we were on the same side... in Newbird..."

"Things change, Bria." Jemma approached her, "I've changed."

"But can't you see this is all wrong?"

"Can't you see that what you are is wrong? I was there in Knoll and watched as the towers fell. I saw the men who died. *I* could have died." She circled Bria as more smoke poured from her lips. "You didn't even think about all the innocent Brothers and Sisters who fell because of your own negligence."

"You don't think I recall that every day? I hate myself for every single person I've killed. By accident. Always by accident. My magic is a curse and a blessing... but I will not be giving it to you!" Bria held the confidence in her voice close. She wouldn't let Jemma, or Ningursu, or whoever she was speaking to now win.

Her magic was her own.

Her magic was her family's blessing.

And she would not falter.

Jemma stepped back. "Very well. I see how it is."

She exhaled. The yellow smoke thickened.

Bria held her breath. Where could she go? Her magic failed to come to her. She had nothing and no one.

She moved along the side of the balcony overlooking the Senate, still refusing to take a breath. With every passing moment, the smoke continued to thicken.

With nowhere to turn, she leapt from the top of the balcony and onto the Senate floor. The smoke raced after her. Bria couldn't hide from it. She just had to get out, find a gas mask, then she'd be free.

She would not let what happened in the Senate Chambers die.

Gasping for air, she searched her blurred vision. Where was the door? The walls blurred. They had to be somewhere... anywhere!

She placed her hand against the wall and began feeling along it, unable to see. Her vision spotted, and her head pounded louder. *Give me a minute. Please... I have to get out... I have to—*

Her branched hand found what felt like a doorknob. Without investigating, she turned it and tumbled forward into the entryway.

No door closed behind her.

But the yellow smoke ceased.

Heaving, she raised her head.

Her tunnels welcomed her with a breath of fresh air.

CHAPTER FIFTY

VERMILLION

Christof found an entrance to a sewage tunnel on the far side of the plaza. He didn't stop to consider where it might lead, hopping into it before anyone could stop him and sliding the door shut behind him. He fell to the damp ground. A single-lit gas lamp lit the path.

As well as the unconscious bodies of a dozen guards on the ground.

Christof checked their pulses. *Good. They're alive.* He recognized a few of them, including Lieutenant Drayton, the man searching for so-called "anomalies" in the Order.

Or, in this case, for a little boy.

"Sorry. I tried to get him back, Lieutenant. I failed," Christof said.

He did not wake.

Christof didn't stay long, following the tunnel away from the scene. While he thought it was a sewage tunnel, the path remained clear. He relished the lack of human waste, picking up his pace, one step at a time. Where would these tunnels take him? What if they took him right into the arms of the Magii, ready for slaughter?

He moved along it, slow and careful. One step, two—and then another. In the tunnels, time didn't exist. With one turn, then the next, it wove like a maze. If there was an exit, would he even be able to find it?

Did he already pass that rock? Or see that gas lamp? It blended together, all the same...

All the same...

Until a shriek.

Christof burst into a run, following the shriek down the path,

Closer and closer...

Until he reached a door.

He tugged at the knob. It did not budge.

"Shite!" He glowered at the door. Etchings covered its wooden exterior in the shape of dashes and dots.

-.-. — -... .-.

Christof eyed it. *That looks familiar. Like... tap-code.*

He couldn't translate tap-code for the life of him, but he knew the sounds. Did he have to say them? Or tap them against the wood?

Or both?

He gave it a shot, repeating brief taps for the dots and long taps for the dashes. While he said them aloud, he tapped it on the surface of the door.

With the last dot, the door opened.

Christof found himself standing in the Senate Chambers. At the meeting table, the Senators sat, limp and lifeless. Christof approached them.

Bile rose in his throat.

The bodies of the already deceased senators rotted in their seats. Beside them, the few remaining senators had collapsed face-first in their documents. Blood pooled across the table. While at the head of the table, Senator Cordova sat in the chair, eyes open, a gunshot wound between his eyes.

Christof stepped away from the scene.

Another scream ricocheted about the room.

Christof turned towards it. It came from the balcony, but he could not see its culprit.

He raced up the stairwell and to the balcony, where he found Sister Jey Ma knelt on the ground, coughing up that strange yellow smoke. Tears marred her face while another scream threatened to escape her lips. A silver pistol lay on the ground beside her.

"Sister!" He joined her side. "Sister Jey Ma... are you okay?"

Sister Jey Ma raised her head, smoke pouring from her lips as she spoke. "I tried to stop her. She was too powerful."

"What? Who?"

"Bria!"

"What? She got in here?

"Yes! Didn't you see!?" Sister Jey Ma pointed into the Senate Chamber.

Christof peered over the edge at the bodies of the senators.

"She killed all of them, Christof," Sister Jey Ma hissed.

"Killed…" Christof stared at the carnage, "But… doesn't she got magic? Why would she use a gun to kill them?"

"I don't know, but I saw her! Are you saying I'm lying, Christof? I thought *you* would believe me!"

"I do… it just seems odd."

"That is not of importance right now." Sister Jey Ma hoisted herself from the ground. Christof joined her side, offering his arm for support. He kept glancing over his shoulder, searching for Bria. Where could she have gone? What happened? How did she escape?

Was she more powerful than Christof ever believed?

"Weren't there other guards in here?" Christof asked her. Surely, the Senate wouldn't have operated alone.

"There were a few outside, but Captain Rivers wanted to conduct a training exercise, which you would have known if you had been here!" Sister Jey Ma snapped.

"But leaving the Senate completely defenseless?"

"I do not know, Christof! But we cannot keep arguing. We must tell Elder An Drew at once." Sister Jey Ma climbed to her feet and brushed the dust off her dress.

"Are you sure? Don't you want to rest?"

"No... we don't have time."

"For what?"

"If we don't act now... I'm afraid that the demons win."

"Sister!" Christof cursed. "You need to tell me what the hell is going on! You were attacked!"

Sister Jey Ma's eyes darkened. She bit her bottom lip, then hissed, "How I feel does not matter. This must end." She turned and left the chambers. As she walked, that yellow smoke followed. It still made Christof uneasy; why did she have such magic wasting away at her fingertips?

But he didn't question it, rushing to keep pace with Sister Jey Ma. Despite her ordeal, she walked as if she had only just left her bedroom or finished a daily sermon. Yet, the smoke that followed her acted as a cloak, and no matter where she went, it followed.

She rushed up the stairwell and back into the small library, not saying a word. She seemed to know exactly where Elder An Drew waited.

Every puzzle piece fell into place.

All in order.

Sister Jey Ma led Christof to a long, abandoned hallway he didn't even know existed. Offices and empty rooms lay scattered, with papers and old telegraph machines sitting on the different desks. The mist shifted around them with each step as if creating a path for them to walk. As she strode forward, Sister Jey Ma ran her finger over the dust, then approached another dilapidated door at the far end of the hall. She removed a key from around her neck and unlocked the door.

Christof stumbled backward as mist fumed out of the doorway. It wrapped around them, causing Christof's head to spin.

Sister Jey Ma walked into it without hesitation. Once it settled, Christof caught a glimpse of the interior.

Elder An Drew stood at a table with a narrow-faced woman beside him. A basin of silver liquid sat on the table before them.

Beside it lay a jagged knife.

And across the room, sitting in a chair, sat the little boy—the one with the strange red eyes and the vacant stare. Lieutenant Drayton had asked him about the boy, and so did those two strange Magii in the tavern. Now, he was right in front of the child.

Could Christof save him?

What were they going to do to him?

What are they going to do to that child?

Sister Jey Ma approached the two by the table. "I have it."

"Then so it must be," Elder An Drew replied.

The narrow-faced woman raised the knife and doused it in the silver liquid. Mist spun around her fingertips as the silver liquid traveled up the blade. Christof couldn't be sure what was happening, but at the heart of it, magic ruled.

"What the hell is happening?" Christof hissed.

"What we've been working on for months. We have finally perfected it." Elder An Drew said, "We just were missing one last piece. Sister?"

Sister Jey Ma reached into her pocket and removed what appeared to be a twig. "Straight from the source."

"A... stick?" Christof gawked.

"Not just any stick... one that belongs to life itself." Elder An Drew broke the stick in half.

"What does that mean?"

Sister Jey Ma rolled her eyes. "It's a twig from Bria."

"So what?"

"It has very strong magic. It is the last piece that we need," Sister Jey Ma remarked.

Christof glanced at the child again. "What is going to happen to that child?"

"Christof—"

"Answer me!"

Sister Jey Ma glanced at Elder An Drew, then back at Christof. "He will help mend the Effluvium. With that basin of silver, a gust of mist, and Bria's magic...it will create the perfect reaction to erase the damage done to the Effluvium."

"What rift? You ain't told me none of this!"

"Why do you think magic has gotten stronger? Why are monsters roaming? Why can people see it? The Effluvium has weakened and shattered. It is what we vowed to protect. The child is the key."

Christof glanced one last time at the child fidgeting in the chair. "Does he know?"

"We have explained it to him." The narrow-faced woman said as she scattered the pieces of stick over the silver basin. With another spin of mist on her fingertips, she took the blade and dipped it into the liquid three more times. "It is ready."

She handed Elder An Drew the blade. He took the blade and cut open his own hand. Blood dripped to the ground.

Christof held his breath as the Elder approached the child. The man took the child's face in his hand. Two giant red eyes stared, tears filling the corners of them. He whimpered and squirmed.

If Christof had been a better man, he might have reacted. But instead, he stood there as the Elder raised the blade.

He turned away as the child let out a shriek.

Then silence.

"Very good." Elder An Drew said. His voice sounded distant, as if fading away.

Christof closed his eyes. What would he tell Lieutenant Drayton?

No one ever told him the *why*.

"Christof, it's over. It's okay." Sister Jey Ma patted his arm.

He opened his eyes, wincing. For a few seconds, a headache danced across his forehead, before vanishing.

The child lay on the floor, alive, but with blood dripping from his face.

No, not from his face.

From two large gaps where his eyes once resided.

Christof spun back to face Elder An Drew and the narrow-faced woman, "How could—"

They no longer stood in the room, leaving behind but a subtle trail of burgundy mist.

"Where the hell did they go?" Christof turned back to Sister Jey Ma. "There's a dying child on the floor!"

"Then you best go take the child to the infirmary." Sister Jey Ma turned away from the scene, hands behind her back as she strode to the door.

"But where the hell did they go? You didn't answer me!"

"The Effluvium is healed, and they are where they must be." Sister Jey Ma said again, voice level. "Now, if you want to save that child, get him out of here. I would hate to see any more lives lost today. But return to the Senate Chambers by sunrise. We have things to do."

Before Christof could respond, she left the room, leaving him alone with the child coated in vermillion.

CHAPTER FIFTY-ONE

THE ERASURE

Morning came with a breakfast of ham omelets... Yaz's new favorite.

Anandi prepared them with Mitzi in the kitchen, while Yaz and Chander sat in the tavern with Preston and Timothée. Micca did not come down from the room; although Yaz knew better than to ask Timothée why.

They sat together as Anandi placed the omelets before them. Every one of them, except for Preston, who played with his crayons, devoured the meal. *Do ghosts even eat?* Yaz wondered as she ate the last bite of food. It didn't seem all that fun being a ghost.

Yaz finished her meal around the time Brent came downstairs, leaning on his cane as he stumbled down the stairs. He smiled at her as he entered, then took a seat by the window. Yaz contained her excitement; she didn't want to invade his Mist Keeper business.

So she continued to watch from the corner of her eye as she helped Preston with his crayons. Chander watched as they drew, his own attention unwavering. Yaz wished she could be like him; hide her interest, stay calm and collected. But she wasn't Chander. She wasn't even Anandi.

She was just Yaz.

And from the corner of her eye, she kept watch as Caroline joined Brent at the table. A few minutes later, Malaika entered the tavern and plopped herself down at the table as well.

"What do you think they're talking about?" Chander asked after Timothée left the table to go check on Micca.

"Mist Keeper stuff?"

"Well, yeah... but what else?"

Yaz shrugged.

Preston fidgeted with a few crayons beside them. He'd been quiet for the most part, but as soon as Timothée left, he immediately perked up in his spot. His red eyes widened, and he brought both of his hands to his lips.

"Pres? What's wrong?" Chander asked.

The child spoke, hoarse, in a whisper. "Red."

"You want your red crayon?"

"Garr. Red."

"Huh?"

"Garr."

"Garr?" Chander glanced at Yaz. She shrugged.

Preston continued to mumble the nonsensical word under his breath, his gaze unfocused.

"Do you think Brent knows?"

"I can ask," Yaz bounced to her feet. At least she had a reason to interrupt now.

But before she raced over, Jewel emerged from the stairwell, dressed in a long golden robe. Tomás followed close behind her with the giant she'd seen around the tavern.

Jewel scanned the room. She didn't move, eyes glazing as she seemed to analyze each person. Her gaze rested on Preston. "The child is breaking…"

"He's upset. He's not breaking." Chander muttered.

"No… he's breaking…" Her voice trailed, face paling at the sight, like a lost girl.

"Jewel!" Tomás raced to her side. "What is it?"

Jewel glanced at her subordinate. "Oh. Hello."

"What is bothering you? You seem… perplexed."

Jewel's face hardened at once. "I am fine, Tommy. Please get me my morning cup of coffee. Milk, sugar, and a dash of cocoa."

"Oh, yes, of course." Tomás rushed to the kitchen with the giant behind him. Jewel did not seem to recall anything about Preston and traveled to the far end of the tavern where her booth waited. No one dared sit next to her; this was her domain, after all.

With Jewel out of the way, Yaz once again rose to speak with Brent. The man sat engaged in his conversation with Malaika and Caroline, but when he caught sight of Yaz, a smile crossed his face.

"Good morning Yaz."

"Hi Brent..." Yaz fiddled with her sleeve. "I was wondering if you could look at Preston. He's acting strange."

"Oh, um, a'ight. Let's check it out."

As Brent climbed out of his seat, Preston squealed across the room, catching the attention of Jewel. She raised her brow.

But Preston didn't care. In a fit, he rubbed his eyes, shaking his head back and forth in pain.

"What's wrong with him?" Chander asked Brent as they approached.

Brent knelt before the little boy. "What's wrong, Preston? Do your eyes hurt?"

Preston shook his head.

"Can you tell me what it is, then? That way I can help?"

"See..." Preston mumbled. "Garr... see... see..."

"Garr? Your brother?"

Preston nodded, then winced again, "And... and... red."

"Like the color?"

"Blood..." Preston murmured. "He bleeds...."

"What?"

"The eyes...red...they...red...."

Yaz glanced at Brent. He continued to watch Preston.

"What is happening to Garrett? Tell me, Preston." Brent begged.

The child shook his head.

"It's okay. Think of something less scary, a'ight? Then we'll figure it out."

"Yeah! Do that!" Yaz chimed in beside Brent. "Think of something that makes you happy. You can do that, right?"

"Garr..." The child sobbed again and covered his eyes with his hands. "Garr!"

"What's wrong with him!?" Chander asked.

Yaz stepped a few paces away from Preston. Malaika and Caroline had inched across the room to join them. From the kitchen, Tomás watched through the window, with the giant peeking out over his shoulder. Even Jewel kept staring in awe.

"Preston, look at me. You're safe here, a'ight?" Brent reached for Preston's hands.

The boy refused to pull them away from his eyes.

"Preston, please look at me." This time, Brent slowly removed one of the boy's hands from his eyes.

He froze.

And Yaz nearly screamed.

Blood dripped like tears from the little boy's bloodshot eyes.

"What the hell is happening?" Chander barked, face pale.

"I... I don't know..." Brent wiped the boy's eyes. The blood grew thicker.

Preston didn't stop screaming. The Mist Keepers surrounded him, each taking a different role. Tomás had returned from the kitchen to take Brent's place before the boy. All the while Caroline inched back towards Jewel, and Malaika joined Brent's side. Everyone moved like a clock, finding a place, trying their best to quell the screams. Even the giant took a solemn stance in the back of the room, without an inflection of emotion on his face.

What would people who couldn't see Preston think? Would they just think a bunch of people had gathered, for no real reason? Or something else entirely?

To Yaz, it was like a nightmare. To anyone else, it was a performance.

Yaz didn't want to watch, but she couldn't turn away, gripping Chander's arm in fear. The boy held her hand tight, his gaze directly on the child.

"What's happening to him?" Yaz whispered.

"Why would I know?"

"I dunno!" Yaz sniffled, "But he's screaming and in pain!

The scene continued to unfold before her like a picture show. Tomás kept trying to get the child to calm, placing his hands on the child's forehead and mumbling something in a foreign language. For a moment, Preston's tearful eyes focused, only to roll back into his head. Drool gathered on his lips.

Followed by another shriek.

Yaz screamed as well.

The child's eyes had vanished. Two dark holes sat in their place.

Bleeding.

Empty.

Vacant.

"What just happened?" Yaz squeaked.

Before anyone could answer, a red glow pulsated from the window. It blanketed over everyone. Some of the tavern patrons at another table rubbed their eyes, then resumed their conversations as if nothing had happened. A few winced in pain. But no one screamed like Preston.

Yaz knew for sure that this wasn't a Diabolo. It was something else.

Something worse.

"I never thought something like this was possible... but of course Ningursu figured it out..." Tomás whispered as he stepped back from the child.

"Figured what out?" Brent asked from behind Tomás.

"The Erasure of sight..." Tomás whispered. "Everything had to come together exactly right for this to work. He must have played the game right. Only those of the Mist can see now."

"Elimination of sight. Kek mentioned something about this."

"Ningursu found a way to infiltrate the connection between seers...by using Garrett and his brother, by the looks of it," Tomas muttered.

"So no one can see us anymore?" Brent continued to ask.

"We're nothing more than ghosts."

"No...there has to be a way..." Brent pivoted to Malaika. "Where's Bria?"

"What? That's where your mind went?" Malaika asked. "Just tell me!"

"Brent, you won't be able to communicate with her. We told you that you exist in our realm now," Tomas interjected.

"Even ghosts can interact with the living world. So there has to be a way."

Yaz tried to keep up with the conversation, but her head spun as each person shouted something different. Why couldn't they take turns speaking? She couldn't keep track of each person; she only understood that something terrible had happened.

"Why can we still see you?" Chander interjected into the conversation from beside Yaz.

Tomas eyed Chander. "Because you are between life and death, potential Mist Keepers who have not yet chosen their path."

"So that's why I don't feel any different?" Yaz asked.

"Yes. Now more than anything, you all will be very important. We'll need to work with Kek and others to decide our next course of action. Varden, do you think you can facilitate—Tomás turned towards the giant, "Vardy!?"

Yaz followed Tomás's gaze.

"Vardy! Can you hear me? Can you see me? VARDEN!"

The giant's eyes dripped with blood.

CHAPTER FIFTY-TWO

WHERE SHE BELONGS

The tunnels waited before Bria, untouched, like she had never left them. As if they'd been waiting, the vines and roots seemed to recede to the side, clearing the path for her away from the chaos. They were back; her tunnels had returned to her after nearly a year. She had never been apart from them for so long; even in Mert, the locked doors were her own doing. The tunnels were where she learned, where she thrived, and where the truth came alive.

But most of all, now, she hoped they would take her back to Brent.

She pressed her fingers to the vines on the wall like in a prayer. These vines had been like her best friends in childhood. Seeing them again left a strange warmth in her chest; she was home.

But she didn't have time to relish their familiar touch. The weight of the events in the Senate Chamber rushed back to her; the heartbreak of Lana's death held her happiness down by an anchor. She was safe. She was where she belonged.

But in a matter of minutes, her world had crumbled.

Now, she only focused on one thing, pushing Lana and the Senate to the back of her mind. She had to focus. She had to find him.

I'm coming, Brent. She clenched her fists. With the determination of Rhodana the Forest Queen, she marched ahead.

She kept Brent's name on her lips and in her heart as she walked. If she focused on that, then the world didn't seem so heavy. Every thought went back to him; what state would he be in when she threw open the doors? Would she be able to handle Ningursu alone? If a link existed between him and Jemma, then he must already know she was coming.

No, she probably couldn't take him alone. But she didn't care. If she moved like the bark of the tree, blended into the Library's walls, she might find Brent and set him free. They would stand together against all the evil in the world. At night, they would talk and giggle, telling stories and smiling.

But the dream vanished as she entered the junction.

The door to the Library hung on its hinges, opened wide and broken. A few pulses of mist poured from its opening, while a dim light captured the junction in a haze.

She slowed her pace as she approached the doors. Inside, the Library was nothing more than the hollowed-out insides of a tree. Mud and brambles lay across the floor, while murky water gathered in puddles, a remnant from her own battle with the Council. The rest had nothing to do with her attack. No longer did the glass ceilings stand, dissolved into a misty rainbow, and the bookshelves lay scattered on the ground, with books strewn in every corner.

Bria's stomach flipped as she stepped into the hollow tree. Whatever world once existed had vanished, as if torn apart like paper and cast aside to dust. Even the rooms that once gathered throughout the Library had turned into broken monuments. Offices stood only with door frames and crooked desks, the galley harbored rotting food, and the endless rooms of magic had long drifted to sleep.

As Bria walked along the perimeter, she paused at the entrance to the Pool, where she and Brent had met Nedo and subsequently helped end his life. This pool that once shimmered with silver, now only sat as a dried-up bed of peonies.

She picked one peony off the ground and held it in her good hand. The petals crumbled to dusty, leaving a trail of red on her fingertips.

"Brent... where are you?" She whispered as she backed away from the dead pool.

Bria didn't loiter long in that room, trailing along the back wall, counting each bookshelf, and taking stock in the number of lights. Could this all be a trick to lure her here? Surely Alojzy wouldn't have let his Library fall.

But everything was vacant. She felt nothing but the tree breathing around her. Even the mist had died out, leaving a void in the once grand library.

I wish I saw the stories... then I'd know where he is... Bria hopped over a puddle. Just beyond the layers of fallen bookshelves, the crooked gates to the crypt waited. Unlike when she last stood before it, the crypt looked more like a rickety old gate than a terrifying enclosure. She still slowed as she approached it, her stomach churning. Memories of her own time in the crypt, those few days that left her pained and weak, flooded back over her. The walls had shifted, the voices haunted her, and she had temporarily fallen victim to Ningursu's own attack.

He hadn't let go of her. If she saw him again, would he take control of her magic with a single smirk?

Or was the outcome of the Senate Chambers his new game?

She swallowed her fear and stepped forward, letting the darkness of the crypt wash over her. With each step, she let her eyes adjust deeper into the prison.

But the endless prison no longer existed.

Rather, just rows of cells greeted her. They didn't twist and turn like she'd experienced, but sat there, empty and lifeless.

No one existed in these jail cells.

It was only a museum of their pain.

She peered into each cell as she walked along, praying that Brent might be sleeping against a wall.

But every door hung ajar, reeking of old food and feces, but none of human flesh.

She pulled her cowl up to her nose and winced as another whiff of human excrement raced past her. But for quick glances, she hurried along past each cell. She only imagined the pain that the prisoners had experienced. Where were they now, though? Did Ningursu take them away for a greater cause? Or did they escape?

And where was Brent?

At the end of the cell block, Bria stopped at a silver coated basin. Once holding a murky pool, now it sat empty. Not even a peony waited for her.

No one did.

She shrank against the wall in defeat, staring at the cell on the opposite side of the hall. *Of course, they took*

Brent away. It's not like they would keep him here. That would be ridiculous. She sucked in her lips to stop the tears. It had been wishful thinking to find Brent... or anything, really that might give her a clue he was himself.

What did she expect, after all? In a blink, she lost everything. Would she even be able to return to Rosada? They had a *reason*, even if fake, to hunt her now. Jemma would blame her for the downfall of the Senate.

And in its place, who knew what might rise from the ashes?

The torchlight flickered above her, catching her shadow against the fall wall. When the light hit it just right, visible scribbles coated the stonework.

Bria approached the far wall, squinting at the words. Fresh handwriting lay on the wall, in a familiar chicken-scratch that she memorized.

"Brent..." she traced the handwriting. It layered the cell, shifting between different languages as granted by the mist. She recognized the different names of the Mist Keepers, and occasional paragraphs in Rosadian that echoed stories, both familiar and new.

He was telling stories to himself to stay sane... She stopped her fingers over a repeated phrase that covered a corner of the old cell.

My name is Brent Harley.
And I am fighting for—

My family.

My home.

My beliefs.

And Bria.

Constantly Bria.

The phrase repeated, growing sloppier with each scribble.

But without a doubt, it belonged to Brent.

"What happened here, Brent?" She asked. "Where are you now?"

She didn't expect a response.

After all, the Library sat vacant.

Empty.

Alone.

With only weeds as friends.

CHAPTER FIFTY-THREE

A Message from an Invisible Man

Red.

This time it was red.

It flooded the sky, surrounding Brent as he raced from the tavern.

He left the tavern as soon as Varden's eyes began bleeding. Sight stolen with a mere blink. He remembered now what Kek had told him; the seers were a network. If one had been harmed, then it meant all would be harmed. That's what had happened, wasn't it? Ningursu had done *something*. What, Brent didn't know. But it had stolen sight, destroyed the network, and left all the seers bleeding and blind.

Would it affect Bria? She wasn't a seer, but Brent's worst fears settled in his stomach.

Grumbling, Malaika had found her on the map. But her location surprised them both.

She's in the Library. Brent kept reciting to himself as he hurried along the path, his knees threatening to buckle. He had to find an entrance. Where? There had to be a way inside the tunnels.

By the looks of it, she was alone. No other Mist Keepers loitered, although that meant nothing.

He had to get there.

With his thoughts nonstop, he checked alleyways for entrances as well as random crevasses in the wall. None of the trees budged at his touch.

Until he reached the river, where a few trees waited, bowing against the red smoke and wind. It felt like when he first became a Mist Keeper. He tested each tree's roots until one budged.

And beneath the root, the ground parted, revealing a muddied stairwell. Brent laughed. *I'm coming Bria.*

The tunnels had always fascinated him. With Alojzy's story a part of him now, the tunnels' past unfolded. The man had built them with a wave of mist.

But they remained now a possession of someone far more powerful.

The tunnels had changed. They didn't pulse with mist anymore, other than the strange red smoke lingering in the air, but with vines and roots. Some pathways had collapsed on themselves, leaving Brent with no other option but continued forward to the junction.

There, the stories collided. He saw his past collide with his present; moments of time held by the mist. But the newest story of them all belonged to Bria as she approached the Library door. His heart raced. She was here! She came on her own free will!

He nearly dropped his cane as he followed her tale into the Library.

Only then to freeze with her story at the sight.

The Library lay in shambles. He remembered it collapsing as he fought Ningursu, but now it stood before him like nothing more than a relic, overtaken by weeds. *They didn't rebuild or return. Where are they now then?* He trailed behind Bria's story, taking in the collapsed shelves. A book lay on the floor before him, its font faded and pages water stained.

"I'm sorry. I... didn't mean to hurt you..." He whispered to the book as he placed it in his coat pocket.

Again, the stories followed him as he walked. He kept focused on Bria's tale but found himself distracted by another. Just near the crypts, he watched as Caroline's story threw Ningursu's head across the room. The skull toppled through the air, then hit the far wall, cracking at the top of the skull.

Aelia had rushed over to him.

And Ningursu whispered, smoke pulsing from his lips, "Let it fall, Aelia. The next steps must be planned accordingly."

"You mean the Erasure?"

"Yes. If the Library falls, then we must prepare to complete the Erasure. That's what the seer said."

Then, the story faded with the black smoke.

So they prepared for this. This must have been why Ningursu interrogated Kek back when we were imprisoned. They mentioned something about sight. But...someone helped Ningursu. It sounded as if a seer told them the future, so they could prepare for every move. But who would betray Kek?

He shook the thoughts into the back of his head for later. For now, he had to find Bria.

And the story returned, leading him deep into the crypt.

But the crypt no longer twisted. Only cells greeted him, like a common prison.

The story took him far into their embrace. He focused on Bria and Bria alone. The stories of the different prisoners might have reached for him, but he didn't have the time. He would focus on them later, to help build his school.

Later. It had to be later.

His entire body froze when he saw her, kneeling in a cell, reading notes on the wall. She looked as beautiful as ever, despite her clear exhaustion. Dry blood dripped from her head, her little branch reaching over the actual cut to cover it. Meanwhile, her branched hand moved with ease, her magic wrapping around her like a constant beat.

"Bria…" He whispered.

She did not turn.

"Bri?"

He approached her side. She didn't flinch, focused on his old handwriting on the wall.

"Bria!?" Brent yelled, just a few paces from her now.

Nothing.

"Fuck!" He cursed, slamming his cane against the wall. A single stone fell. *She lost her sight. Shite.*

Bria jumped as the rock hit the ground. "Who's there?"

Brent tried again, a spark of hope in his heart. "Bri… it's me…"

"Show yourself!" Bria laced her fingers into the wall.

She heard the rock but can't see me… He tapped his cane on the ground, thinking.

Bria continued to scan the room. "I hear you. Where are you?"

He continued tapping the cane, whispering under his breath, "I'm right here…"

"Marisol!? Is that you? I know that's tap-code!" Bria continued to grip the wall, fingers clawing at the stone.

Tap-code? Brent had never learned tap-code. Well, perhaps not directly. He'd released enough souls, seen enough stories, that perhaps… someone did.

"It's me… it's Brent…" he said, still tapping his cane. Naturally, the rhythm followed.

Bria tapped the words with him on the stone, slower than before, fingers shaking with each word. "B… r… e… n… t… Brent?"

He tapped again. "I'm right here…"

"I can't… no… I must be imagining things… I…"

What can I do to help her? He glanced at the wall where his chicken-scratch covered the wall. The piece of stone he had used to scratch into the wall still sat on the floor.

He picked it up and wrote quickly on the wall.

Bria. I'm here. Right here in the crypt with you. I promise it's me.

She turned to the scratching noise, "Prove it's you."

How?

"Write something only Brent Harley knows."

Brent pondered. There were so many private moments between him and Bria. Which one to choose?

We used to drink and smoke by the cows when we lived in Newbird's Arm. One time, you named a cow Pig.

"That's common knowledge," Bria scoffed.

What?

"Give me another."

Brent tapped the stone on the wall, then wrote, *I named the mole on your back Kevin.*

"That's private..." Bria whispered, then stared at the wall. "It is you. Where... where are you?"

Brent held back his own tears, scribbling the next few sentences.

I'm here. Right next to you. Sight is gone from the world. I don't know how, but Ningursu did it. I think he used the twins— Garrett and Preston. The ghost boy is with me in Mert, and he started reacting before Varden did. Brent paused, a realization coming to him at once. *Yaz and Chander could still see. They're alive with mist inclination...so I guess that's why.*

"Wait—if they're alive...does that mean you're dead?" Bria's voice cracked.

In a sense. I've transformed into a true Mist Keeper, as they call it, I guess.

"But...no...you can't be one of the invisible people..." Bria whispered, pulling Brent back to the memory of when he first learned of the world of the Mist Keepers.

Even then, she'd been so distraught, unable to see what he saw in the tunnels.

It's not the same. It'll never be the same.

"But I still can't see you!"

I know. But I can communicate.

"You can..." Bria touched one of the words and frowned. "But how?"

*From what I gather it's like...*Brent paused, pondering how to word the next sentence, *I guess the best way for me to describe it is with a story.*

Bria didn't say anything.

Brent slowly wove a story, writing one word at a time. If it were true, he couldn't be certain. So many tales wove together after all this time. But as he wrote the story, everything came into view. He understood the truth...and he hoped Bria would understand as well.

The story goes a little like this: There once was a woman who lived in the wall of a big house. She didn't come out much, and most people didn't even know she was there. Except for a little girl with a big imagination. At night, she left cookies out for the woman, and in the morning, the cookies would be gone. She never saw the woman, but the evidence was clear.

The little girl tried to speak to the woman through the wall, but the woman never responded. She sometimes tapped on the stone, or left a note by the door, but she never spoke.

So the little girl grew into a young woman. Sometimes she forgot about the woman, but every once in a while, a note or a noise would prove a reminder.

The woman never left. But the once-little girl remained. Even after her parents died, she remained in the house. She never planned to leave...but the unexpected occurred. A storm blew through town one day, and a tree crashed into the wall, opening it up for all to see. With the walls erased, finally, the once-little girl could meet the woman.

And that woman was a racoon.

"A racoon?" Bria almost seemed to laugh.

Why not?

"The racoon could write?"

Let me have my fun.

Bria smirked, then her eyes fell. "It's a silly story."

But it explains what's happening here, doesn't it?

Bria nodded, her eyes locked on the writing. "So...with sight stolen...it's like a wall has formed. We're not...separated. Just...blocked."

And I can communicate through the wall, but only by certain means.

"By means that impact the physical world..."

I guess so.

"But...if sight is gone...how come I can access the Library? The tunnels have always been mine, but the Library was off limits prior to you."

Because the Library belongs to you now. It's more part of the earth than part of the mist.

"I... but..." She sat back on the floor, tearful and scared.

Brent stayed beside her. What could he do? It felt wrong to hold her, not when she couldn't see him. So much had happened. He could feel it pulsing from her stories.

But he promised her long ago not to look; these were her stories, and he respected her too much not to invade them.

"Bri..." he placed his hand on top of her branched hand.

She didn't flinch.

But her branched hand did.

A few twigs and pieces of bark rose from the hand itself and wrapped around his fingertips and down towards his wrist. It wasn't a full hand. More like a temporary placement of roots. Even as he removed his hand from Bria, the roots stayed.

He tapped with his cane, *Bri. Look.*

Her eyes widened. At once, she took his hand, staring at the roots.

At least you have a way to find out where I am. Brent wrote into the ground.

"Yes..." she whispered.

Then she pulled his hand close, hugging it while tears filled her eyes.

I'll tell you everything, Bria. But it's a'ight, we're together now.

Even through the mist.

CHAPTER FIFTY-FOUR

A CASTLE OF CYPRESS

Bria sat with Brent in the heart of the Library all through the night. She said little, leaning into the mere sensation that he was there. She couldn't see him, but with the roots, at least she knew his spot. His writing was his; the words written were his; and despite everything, at least she knew he was there.

He wrote with fury in a water stained book everything that had happened to him over the last few months. Bria hung onto every letter, gripping tight to the skeletal twigs of Brent's hand. The mere presence comforted her. Despite everything, he remained.

Constantly.

Brent finished writing, recalling his time imprisoned in the Library, his adopted pineapple friend, and the nature of his mist. His writing pace slowed when he spoke of a strange black stain on his stomach, causing weakness throughout his body. They let the reality hang in the air for a bit, before Brent turned to his tale. His exuberance returned as he discussed the idea for a school. Despite everything, even his writing conveyed the truth: he was Brent Harley, and even prison didn't change that.

Once he finished writing, they sank into silence. Bria wrestled with his words. He'd learned so much about Caroline, Alojzy, and even Julietta... but so little at the same time. She knew the words on the page didn't translate everything he learned.

How much did this Library hold for him now? How much more would he uncover?

Well, really, it wasn't really a library anymore, except in information alone. It was a swamp, with remnants of death loitering in the shadows. She found the remnants everywhere; in the books on the shelf, the broken glass, and the dead Pool coated in wilted peonies.

Despite the nature of the ruins, there was something remarkable about them. Nature had reclaimed the Library. She easily controlled the walls, shaping them into stairs so she could climb, or commanding flowers and branches to grow.

The Library had returned... in the shape of a tree.

Brent must have followed her gaze, as he scribbled on the page.

You said it before. The Library is a tree. The way I see it, this place is abandoned. So it is yours for the taking.

"Didn't I try that before? When we locked the Mist Keepers out the first time?"

I don't think they're coming back. And you're stronger now. This can be your palace.

Bria eyed the ceiling. If she claimed this as her home, she might transform it into everything Ningursu never wanted: a haven for those fleeing the Effluvium's wicked embrace.

"Don't you want to use it for your school?"

This would be the obvious place... and the first place that Ningursu will look.

Bria squinted at the ceiling. It moved upwards, like the trunk of a tree, with remnants of broke pathways and doors crisscrossing through the roots. How could she make this palace?

And where would it rule?

"I want to check something," Bria said.

Where are you going?

"Up. Come on."

Bria placed a hand against the nearby wall. The bark of the tree turned over, slowly forming a staircase. It was so easy, wasn't it? Controlling the plants came as easily as breathing.

Bria ascended the stairwell. Steep, she forced her way through the aches in her calves as she reached the top. There, a thick mist greeted her. It started light, like a gentle drizzle, then thickened with each step. Soon, it blanketed her, no longer able to see in front of her as she climbed from the last step and onto the muddy ground.

Bria squinted. The white blanketed before her. But the way it breathed, she knew it wasn't the Effluvium's mist, but just a thick fog, natural for the area. She wracked her mind over the Rules of the Apothecary. *Water is made of two elements: hydrogen and oxygen. Oxygen is your inhale.* She opened her mouth and took a deep breath, focusing on the air going into her lungs. She absorbed the element, imagining the way the oxygen coursed through her body, giving her light.

With each attentive inhale, the mist lightened, falling away from their surroundings. After going through these motions for a couple minutes, finally she saw beyond her fingertips, and into the swamp that lay before them.

She recognized the cypress knees at once. They poked in her direction, like sculptures and monuments to the dead. A few wrinkle-faced wood storks loitered in the murky water. Nix barked and chased after one. The birds flew at once, leaving the dog jumping in the air.

"We're in Volfium... I've only ever seen wood storks here..." She smiled to herself, recalling when she took

Brent to a café just south of the Rosadian border. She said he reminded her of the birds.

That had been soon after he realized she was Rho.

Soon after, she thought he would hate her.

And soon after all the truths came out in the open.

It felt like a lifetime ago.

But now, without a doubt, she was back in those swamps. With Brent loitering behind her, the skeletal branches floating a few steps behind her in the stairwell.

It was obvious now, as she stood amongst the swamp. The Library existed as an endless sinkhole, still masked in a gentle mist, but with a gathering of cypress trees acting as a wall. She'd never seen cypress trees so tall; they towered as high as the baobab trees she explored in the land of Yilk.

Their height wasn't the only thing that caught her attention. Rather than the standard brown bark and green leaves, vermillion coated every part of the trees. From its bark to the leaves, these trees bled.

Bria approached one and placed her hand against it. She felt its weak heartbeat, begging for a purpose.

"Even the swamps are suffering," Bria whispered. When she first discovered the tunnels, she always loved venturing to the swamps: in Grover's Marsh, in Volfium, and elsewhere across the world. They always burst with life.

But now, they were rotting away, bleeding out.

Red would turn to black.

Everyone would suffer.

"I brought back the Necrowood… I can bring this back too…"

Tapping followed. Bria turned to where Brent had placed his notebook on a nearby stump.

Bria. Be careful. Micca told me what happened in the Necrowood.

Bria frowned. Brent was right, of course. If healing the Necrowood put her to sleep for weeks, what would the entire swamp do?

She wasn't strong enough.

And even if she was… she couldn't do it alone.

"I might not be able to heal it now… but I will some-day…" Bria said. "Especially now that I have a castle beneath it."

So you're claiming the Library?

"Yes."

I knew you would.

"I just have to make sure no one can reach it." Bria ran her fingers over the trees again. A lot would have to change; the Library would need to be reformed.

But first, she needed to protect the sinkhole from above ground.

She focused her energy back on the surrounding vermillion cypress trees. Their cones slept in the mud around her feet. They called to her, wishing to change, yearning to grow.

This would be her palace. Not just for her—but for any Magii afraid to act, or any Magii with their powers stolen. What would have become of Lana if she had a place to hide? Would she still be alive?

"This is for you, Mom. For everything our family should have been."

With one inhale, she instructed the seeds to grow, drenched in vermillion blood. They wove together around them, mingling with the tower cypress trees. Like a sculpture, Bria delicately wove her fingers through the branches, not only growing trees, but lattices and walls. They bowed to form archways, knitted together to form doors, and grasped branches to form a domelike ceiling above them.

And in their last breath, the cypress trees shed their vermillion coat, to sigh in a deep wave of green.

Bria gasped and stepped back, catching her breath before glancing around her creation. She stood in a long entry-hall style room, barebones but the clear beginning of something that said one thing:

The Library of the Council stood no more.

It belonged to the Forest Queen.

CHAPTER FIFTY-FIVE

THE VESSEL

Christof carried the limp child in his arms back into the tunnels that linked to the Senate Chamber. The child hardly breathed, but he lived. Christof's entire body trembled with anxiety, playing back the events in his mind. None of this made sense. But for now, he would wait and see—if he fled, it would be with the badge of a traitor. No one would believe a defector guard.

The trek through the tunnel trailed on, the blood continuing to stain Christof's chest. He'd done his best to wrap the boy's eyes, but stains already covered the wrapping.

"Who's there!?" someone shouted from down the tunnel.

Christof rounded the bend. The guards he'd found in the tunnels earlier all sat against the wall, with Lieutenant Drayton taking stock of the squadron. The lieutenant's face snapped upon seeing his son.

"What the hell happened?" Lieutenant Dray asked.

"I honestly don't know." Christof said. "They said it was for the Effluvium."

"He's a five-year-old child!"

"I know."

"He's blind!"

"I'm sorry," Christof said again.

Lieutenant Drayton cursed and pulled his son out of Christof's arms. His entire body shook with rage.

"I'm sorry sir. Really." Christof had nothing else to say.

The lieutenant didn't meet Christof's gaze. "Just get out of here, Cadet."

"Lieutenant—"

"You are dismissed, cadet."

He debated telling the lieutenant about what happened but decided against it. In all reality, he couldn't even explain it. They cut out the child's eyes. What more could he say? That he tried to stop it? He didn't. He couldn't.

The lieutenant wanted nothing to do with him. As far as Christof could tell, the lieutenant blamed him just as much as anyone.

So, reluctantly, he left the child with the lieutenant. Anything would be better than staying in the Capitol.

Christof turned back down the tunnels. Part of him wanted to keep running—but where? The tavern was off limits, Magii roamed the streets, and he had killed someone. Who he killed, it didn't matter, but it happened.

Like every death, it would be a permanent staple in his heart.

Where would he go? What could he do? He had nothing.

No one.

Except Sister Jey Ma.

It was as if she beckoned him back, luring him with a tether. He had no choice. This was his role. His duty.

Whether he liked it or not. She had made sure that no one else would welcome him.

With the weight of that revelation, Christof arrived back in the Senate Chambers. The bodies of the Senators no longer sat at the table, leaving only the blood to stain the floor, and the room twisting with red smoke.

Was this the purity of the Effluvium?

Sister Jey Ma waited for him at the head of the table, draped in a new red robe. Her hair fell to her shoulder. A silver year glass hung around her neck.

"So you have come back to me?" Sister Jey Ma asked.

"Did I have a choice?" Christof snapped.

"You always have a choice. I did not think that the recent events would compel you back to my chambers."

"I am a guard. Everything I do is for the Effluvium." The words fell from his mouth without emotion.

"I see." Sister Jey Ma leaned back in her chair. "It's been difficult these last few months, haven't they, Christof? But I think it has all been for the greater good. The Effluvium will thrive now; magic can't survive when the Effluvium pulses with life. I see it all now, Christof. And I want you here, by my side, through all of it. You have been my rock."

"Even though I left you?" The words slipped out of Christof's mouth.

"But you came back. You always come back to the Effluvium. So I do not want you to leave. You are a perfect specimen of loyalty. And that is what I have needed."

"A perfect specimen..." Christof repeated.

"And that is a compliment." She smiled. The smile didn't belong to her. It belonged to the magic that had woven its way into her heart.

This was not Sister Jey Ma.

Or was it? Had she been Sister Jey Ma all this time—leaving behind the kind Sister of the Order Christof had known?

When was she last... Jemma?

"Ah! There you are!" Sister Jey Ma rose from her spot.

He turned.

A goblet floated from across the room. Red mist gathered around it, as if something carried it forward. A murky gray liquid sifted inside of it.

"What the hell is that?"

Sister Jey Ma did not respond as the goblet floated over to her. She held her hand out, and the goblet stopped moving. "Thank you."

"Who the fuck are you talking to?" Christof barked.

"It doesn't matter." Sister Jey Ma raised her head. "I thought I told you not to curse."

"Dammit, Sister Jey Ma!" Christof finally exclaimed, "This has been ridiculous! Now there's a floating skull! Tell me what the hell is going on!"

"As I said, Christof, you are the perfect specimen. Loyal, not too bright, but loyal." Sister Jey Ma approached Christof as she spoke. Gasps of yellow, red, and black smoke trickled from her lips. Once she reached him, she took his hand.

Christof grunted.

"I want you here, Christof. Because you are perfect." Sister Jey Ma cupped his cheek. "We will protect the Effluvium together."

"Sister Jey Ma—"

Before Christof could finish his sentence, Sister Jey Ma kissed him. Hard, with her hands pressed to his body, she would not slacken. Christof's body froze, taking in the kiss.

But then he began to choke.

As Sister Jey Ma pulled back, a trail of black smoke poured out of her mouth. Christof stumbled back, clenching his chest and coughing.

"What did you—" He hacked.

Sister Jey Ma returned to the goblet and lifted it from the mist. "What had to be done for the good of the Effluvium. You will be its vessel now—until a better one comes along."

"Jem—" Christof coughed again. It felt as though something wrapped around his heart, squeezing the organ and scratching into his lungs. He could no longer breathe and he fell to the floor.

Sister Jey Ma walked over to him. She knelt before him and brushed his cheek with the back of her hand.

"Now drink. Cleanse your pallet and your mind. For the Effluvium." Sister Jey Ma recited.

As spots filled Christof's vision, Sister Jey Ma lowered the goblet to his lips and forced him to drink.

THE STORY COLLECTOR'S ALMANAC

Also by E.S. Barrison...

Tales from the Effluvium
Speak Easy
These Sanguine Tides

The Unsought Fairytale Collection

AUTHOR'S NOTE

Thank you so much for taking the time to read *The Seeds of Vermillion.*

If you enjoyed this book, I would appreciate it if you could:

Review this book. Reviews are a great help to an author. If you enjoyed this book, please consider leaving a review.

Tell Others. When you share this book with others on social media, you're allowing others to discover this story. Word-of-mouth is one of the best sources of marketing for an author.

Connect with me. If you want to find out about my upcoming releases, stop by my website at www.esbarrison-author.com or connect with me on social media.

Thank you!

E.S. Barrison

ACKNOWLEDGMENTS

To all the following, my thanks, for your support, friendship, and kindness throughout this process:

To my parents, for accepting that their daughter might have a problem with her imaginary friends.

To Moira, my cover artist, for all your hard work on this amazing cover.

To Charlie, my editor, for helping me uncover glaring plot holes and their solutions.

To Matthew, for putting up with my antics, and actually reading the story despite the lack of a *certain scene* that will never be added.

And finally, to my readers, Thank you for continuing Brent and Bria's story. I hope you pick up the next one.

Without all of your support, this story would not have been possible.